The
Far Corner
of the
Greenhouse

K.V. CASE

Published in the United States of America

Scripture taken from the New King James Version ®. Copyright © 1982 by Thomas Nelson, Inc. Used by permission. All rights reserved.

Cover Design by Lynnette Bonner of Indie Cover Design – www.indiecoverdesign.com
Images Copyright:
www.bigstock.com - #49165466_XL
www.peopleimages.com - #21118 and #421207
http://www.photos-public-domain.com/2012/04/23/grape-hyacinth/
http://www.photos-public-domain.com/2011/04/04/pastel-green canvas-fabric-texture/

Book Layout ©2013 BookDesignTemplates.com

The Far Corner of the Greenhouse/ K.V. Case.
ISBN 978-1-4936737-6-6

DEDICATION

To survivors everywhere
and the people who love them back to shore.
To everyone who prayed for my safe return to me;
to Flo, who helped paddle my lifeboat,
and to my rescuer, healer and the reason I live and am sane,
my Lord Jesus Christ.

For your Maker is your husband,
The Lord of hosts is His name;
And your Redeemer is the Holy One of Israel…
—ISAIAH 54:5

ACKNOWLEDGEMENTS

There are many whose lives touched mine on my journey to and from the far corner of God's greenhouse. They are the individual blooms that have grown in the garden of my life, some fragrant, some thorny, all contributing to the variegated thing of beauty that God is making of all our lives. To name them all would not be practical or wise, but I would like to acknowledge a few who helped to make *this* book, a small spray within a much larger bouquet, possible.

My heartfelt thanks to Dr. Robert Morgan and the Heroes Program of the Mailman Center in Miami, to the Living Water counseling ministry of First Church West in Plantation and to Calvary Chapel Fort Lauderdale, the home where I did my real growing up. To Lorna and Mabel, Earl and Del, Theresa, Gloria and Pam.

To Lynnette Bonner at Indie Cover Design, for invaluable help that saved me many missed steps on my publishing journey, and for an awesome job preparing this book to be judged by its cover.

To my family, whom I would not trade for all the treasures in wherever:

To my parents, whose legacy lives on long after them, who taught me to appreciate the beauty and the power of words, and whose lives and faith left me no choice but to believe.

To Patty, Chris and Karl, my "last-four" compadres and my very first critics, who laughed, griped and demanded more. To Mike and Bev, for stopping by the far corner on their way through the valley. To Judith, child of my heart.

To Flo, sister, friend, and surrogate grandma.

To everyone who has ever prayed, listened, given, babysat, folded laundry, done repairs, or helped solve my computer woes.

To Michael, Symphony and Jewel, my reward and my heritage, for liking their salmon straight from the can, and for believing all things.

And to the God who blessed me with all these and so much more.

I am the true vine, and My Father is the vinedresser…every
branch that bears fruit He prunes, that it may bear more
fruit…
I am the vine, you are the branches. He who abides in Me, and
I in him, bears much fruit…

–JOHN 15:1-5

Prologue

…for without Me you can do nothing.

–JOHN 15:5b

Leo Ramsey reminded Stone Patrick of someone he'd spent over half his thirty-eight years trying to forget. A sinewy runt of a man, he was bleached and bronzed and leathery from twelve-hour days sweating a living under Miami's blistering sun...and in need of the kind of behavior modification that a Christian counselor ought not to be contemplating.

"She always pushing me, man," he told Stone at his intake interview, one knee swinging in a jerky rhythm that rattled the desk between them like his blustering was beginning to rattle Stone's nerves. "Like she asking for it or something. I mean, I swear sometimes there's no getting through to her except I...unless I..."

His restless amber gaze collided with Stone's, and he swallowed the rest. "I ain't saying it's right or nothing, but you'd a think she'd know better by now. I mean..."

Lord, I really don't want to work with this jerk.

Not because he didn't know that but for God's grace he'd have ended up in Leo's shoes, but because he'd signed on with Oasis Ministry to help the guys who at least knew they needed help.

After a decade working the kind of programs where most of the marriages were already dead, buried and rotting, it was worth the pay cut just to have the freedom to offer God's hope to those who dared to want it. Playing at impartiality with the likes of Leo didn't figure anywhere in there. That road likely led only to helplessness and frustration, and he didn't do helpless and frustrated too well.

No, P.J., stop! Leave her alone, you—

Whyn't you come over here and make me?

"...but she come out of it smelling like roses, see, and me...I'm the one who—"

"What'd you come here for, Leo? Score points with the judge?"

Leo's jaw dropped for a second before his eyes slowly hardened. "I already done what the judge ordered. This don't count for nothing. Was just that Beth told m...I heard Beth had joined up, and it says here on the brochure that your program—"

"Forget the brochure. What do *you* want?"

"My wife back. Thought that's what you people was supposed to be helping me with."

"Gimme one good reason why we should."

"'Cause I...What the heck is your problem, anyway?"

Your beer breath, the way you strut and crack your knuckles and flex your fists. Your stinking attitude, your...

Stone reined in his thoughts and pulled his intake logbook toward him. "Look, Oasis isn't gonna work for you. You're not ready." He opened the book to January 19th and started writing.

Leo's eyes darted from the page to Stone's face. "What's that mean? What you saying?"

"That Beth'd be better off leaving things the way they are. And that we'll do what we can to help her make sure you stay on your side of the 500 feet."

Something like panic disrupted Leo's cocksure expression. "She's my wife, man," he protested, his voice cracking.

Scared of losing her, was what he was. Out-of-his-mind scared.

Yeah, P.J. too. Much good that had done anybody.

"Hey, I love her, all right?"

Your P.J. loves you, Ginny, you know that...here, let's take a look at that lip...

"You think I *want* to keep doing that junk?"

Aw, babe, why'd you go and make me do this to you?

"I'm trying to do the right thing here. I just need some help, is all. Whatever it takes, I'll do it. Serious."

Desperation. It was a start. Stone drew a steadying breath and laid down his pen. He'd worked with guys who had a lot less going for them, just never with anyone who stirred up feelings in him he hadn't known were still there.

He tried to shake them now, closing his mind on the intrusion of his own memories. He leaned forward, forearms on his desk, and held Leo's gaze. "Two things you've got to keep in mind here, Leo. First, you helped make her what she is. Second, it took her three years to get there. It's gonna be a long bumpy ride back to who she is."

Leo stared blankly at him, cracking his knuckles. "I don't get you." He leaned forward, his expression pained in its earnestness, his breath fermenting beer.

Stone disciplined himself not to draw back. He offered the untouched dish of assorted candy that he'd got from the office grab bag Christmas and, while Leo busied his hands with, it reached for another analogy.

"All right. You wake up from a snooze one lunchtime to find your buddies have roped you to some steel uprights and disappeared. And you've got a lightning storm coming straight at you. What do you do?"

Leo laughed, releasing a puff of peppermint and beer. "I'd make like Samson, man. Put everything I got into it."

"What d'you suppose would happen to anybody fool enough to be standing too close to you when that rope snaps?"

"Ouch." Leo grinned, flexing his elbows. "Smack in the ribs."

"'Cause you've got this momentum building, right? Takes a second or two to break it, even after you're free."

Leo nodded sagely, fingering his goatee. "I get you."

"Good. 'Cause that rope you had Beth bound with these

past three years just snapped. Only she's trapped inside that split second of time before her momentum breaks. Oasis is a safe zone for her to catch up with the fact she's free. Learn from other women who've been through the same thing—"

Leo's eyebrows peaked. "Who, Dr. Lester's daughter?"

Stone schooled his expression to remain impassive. "What about Dr. Lester's daughter?"

"Been through that kind of thing?"

"Didn't ask." Well, he hadn't. "But she...has a special thing for women who have." One presumed. "So she's there to learn from Kayla. She'd take over the women's group if and when Kayla leaves." *In her dreams.*

"Anyways..." Stone shook his head and stared at Leo, his previous train of thought absconded.

"Beth," Leo prompted. "She's got this momentum thing going." He grimaced, slipped Stone a rueful glance. "Needs some elbow room."

"Bingo. Welcome to Oasis." Stone pushed a registration form across the desk at him. "Bring this with you on Thursday. And leave the beer for after."

Five days later, came the frantic late night phone call from one of Beth and Leo's neighbors.

A dry sob raked Abigail's throat as she ripped northward on the Florida turnpike ramp. One hand steadying the wheel, she swiped impatiently at her eyes with the other, hot tears threatening to blind her as rage gave way to guilt and horror.

God, I didn't do it on purpose. I didn't expect him to come after me. I really didn't.

But he had, the second she slammed out of his house, had to be. She'd heard the sickening thud of metal against flesh as she stormed down the porch steps. Heard Stone howl and curse a blue streak. And had been too much of a coward, even when she realized he was no longer following her, to so much as turn and fling him a hasty apology.

Lord, I don't know what's the matter with me, but I feel so ugly. On top of ashamed, confused and frightened.

She was not in the habit of losing her temper like that. And she'd had cause, God knew, more cause than Stone Patrick had given her in the few months she'd known him. There'd been times in her life she wished she'd gone ahead and blown a fuse or two. Times when she'd supped and swallowed and continued being her usual even tempered self. Her inability now to maintain her composure around this one man frightened her more than just a little.

Something just seemed to happen to her when she got around Stone Patrick. She felt at times like she was outside herself, looking on in horror at her behavior and helpless to do anything about it.

Stone had had that effect on her almost from day one.

Today's confrontation hadn't begun with his summoning of her to his office this morning. It had been five months in the making...

Try to work with him, Abigail. He comes off a little rough, I know, but...hey, it's part of the package.

He *was* rough, and not just a little. And half the time just for her benefit, just like his jeans and rolled up sleeves were probably for her benefit. No grown man of his sensibilities could care so little about his appearance.

You ever take a good look at some of those men he works with?

Wasn't by God's Spirit anymore, but by Stone Patrick's might and bluster.

Not exactly, but they have their uses too.

So did she. Moreover, *she* had been married. He, at age thirty-eight, was still brushing off the matchmakers with his lame married-to-the-gospel act and dodging all the single sisters who were openly "looking."

Sure her father had mentored him himself, taken him through a crash course of sorts. But where did he get off, telling everybody what to do? Vetting her before she could come on board. Insisting she start out on probation, to prove who knew what point. She who'd been working in her father's ministry from the time she'd had to climb on a chair to reach the top drawer of the filing cabinet.

Yes, but he's been here for most of the five years you've been gone.

Gone. She hadn't been *gone.* She'd been doing what the whole world had been waiting with bated breath for her to do, leaving and cleaving like all normal Christian girls within her father's sphere of influence did sooner rather than later.

Well, she was back. And her father was glad to have her, shaken as he was over her loss. And if her father hadn't obviously recognized that Oasis needed a balancing act, he wouldn't have encouraged her as he had to get involved with it. So if Stone Patrick couldn't handle her daring to have an opinion, tough.

What did he think he was, anyway—indispensable? And with exactly what kind of qualification?

The right kind, her father claimed.

So he came from a rough background, or whatever. Had probably been through things she'd only read about in her father's *Dear Dr. Lester* column. But he'd been saved…what? Three years and some months. No seminary or formal training of any kind. Just his sociology degree and his attitude. And now there he was, ministering to people who'd been Christians from they were so high.

Can't always measure spirituality in years, Abigail.

Maybe not, but she could certainly recognize its fruit. Patience, longsuffering, and all the rest. None of which had ever been found in Stone Patrick's possession.

He's come a long way, trust me.

Not far enough.

Tell Reverend what's-his-face to go take a flying leap.

In response to which her father could only chuckle.

He sings to the tune of a slightly different hymnal, but his heart's in the right place.

And so she'd tried to sit on her objections when he bucked the rules and when he flailed her for doing the same. Tried not to take it personally when initiative after initiative of hers had been slapped down, and swallowed the criticisms he dished out in the name of training.

He was never out of them. Last week, it had been her schedule. This week, it was Beth. But it could just as easily have been the new brand of coffee she introduced to the staff lounge, or the shape of her nose. If her blunder with Beth hadn't triggered their blow-up, something else would have, sooner or later.

By the time she received the summons to his office this morning, the fuse had already been lit…

The anti-Eric, she thought as their gazes collided across the width of his cluttered desk. From the unruly tobacco-brown locks hanging past his collar to the scuffed tips of his brown leather boots, Stone Patrick's raw brand of masculinity jarred and jolted after the polish and discipline of her late husband.

He looked more of a menace to womankind, if anyone asked her, than any of the wife abusers he was supposed to be helping rehabilitate, and he was about as angry as the most dangerous of them.

Angrier, his near-black eyes stormy beneath heavy brows that seemed carved into a permanent scowl, his husky rasp of a voice deceptively low as he asked, "You told Beth to *what?*"

Abigail held his gaze unflinchingly. Whatever was eating him hadn't a thing to do with Beth Ramsey. More like which side of the bed he'd rolled out of that morning. Okay, so she'd probably said a little too much to Beth, but he wasn't to know that, since he hadn't even heard the half of it.

She began patiently, "She's got a lot of pent up anger—"

"Oh, does she?"

"She does so. Believe it or not, husbands don't have a monopoly on—"

The harsh scrape of metal on tile jarred the rest of that thought out of her head. That fast, Stone was on his feet and skirting the desk round to her side.

Abigail blinked and backed up a half step, if only to avoid having to crane her neck looking up at him.

His eyes flickered, his footsteps faltering. The next second, he had put the width of the desk between them again. With a jerk of his chin he indicated the only chair besides his not laden with stacks of files or reading material and growled, "Sit down."

"I hear perfectly well on my feet, thank you." She could at least pretend to be in control. And she didn't need him towering over her any more than he already was.

"On second thought..." He dropped down into the swivel chair behind his desk and kicked back, propping his boot heels on the edge of his cluttered desk. "Stand right there."

Sitting or standing, his size alone was enough to give her

pause. Probably just shy of six feet but a giant to a petite size four who nearly hadn't made it past five feet. Solidly built, his shoulder's bulk testing the strength of his double seams and his forearms straining against the rolled up sleeves of the plaid shirt hanging loose over his t-shirt and worn jeans.

Behind his desk or inches from her face, he was just as imposing, that hard *I'm-waiting* stare he was pinning her with enough all by itself to make her squirm.

Like some child hauled before the principal for a scolding. Abigail ground her teeth and sank into the empty chair facing his.

He lowered his feet immediately, eyes not leaving her face. She met his gaze squarely, chin inching higher, then lower again at what she saw in his eyes.

Those eyes looking back at her suddenly, strangely, didn't seem to belong to the same man who for five months had ignored and derided and seemed barely to tolerate her.

Her eyes dropped discreetly to his hands, her gaze drawn as it so often was by the expressiveness of those hands, now clenched, white-knuckled, on the desk in front of him, and saw what she never had before in five months of resenting and resisting him.

He had a temper. A serious temper. She registered the startling discovery. And felt the tension ooze out of her, even as it seemed to mount on Stone's side of the desk.

The atmosphere was charged, a lingering air of suppressed violence evident in the very self-control he exerted, from the abruptness with which he'd confined himself behind his desk to the fine tension in his hand as he rolled a pen back and forth between forefinger and thumb.

He not only had a temper but was right that moment acutely conscious of it. As if he was suddenly sensitive about the image he was projecting. Very sensitive. She'd seen it in his eyes just moments ago when she retreated from him on reflex, and it was there now in his posture that had gone from aggressive to curiously defensive. Interesting.

She took a moment to regroup, the suggestion of a hidden vulnerability behind that thorny exterior disarming her as effectively as if he'd suddenly shrank a couple of feet. Temper she could handle. There was enough psychology and self-defense and old-fashioned smarts dispensed through ministries like Oasis to equip a woman to deal with the threat of that kind of violence...the kind that left scars and bruises, anyway...

Abigail released a pent up breath. "Beth has trouble confronting," she expounded, emboldened by her reading of him. "Leo in particular."

"And you figured a confrontation was all she needed."

His pen stabbed at the desktop, adding a few more indentations to the wood's already sizeable collection.

"As in talking things out, yes. For starters...if she's ever going to be able to move on, anyw—"

The pen went flying. "It's not your job to get her to move on. Our ultimate goal, *as per the mission statement approved by your father,* is to help restore the marriage if at all possible—"

"Yes, well if there's any chance of them patching things up—"

"As of now they're about slim to none."

"Oh really? Because she dared show some backbone and stood up to him?"

"Because she's in the hospital nursing a concussion and two broken ribs...on top of facing contempt charges—"

"Contempt ch—"

"—and because he's now looking at jail time for assault *and* for violating a restraining order. And because even if their love manages to survive that kind of mess, the judge just might exercise her authority to make the injunction permanent, regardless of what either of them wants."

Abigail swallowed. "Restraining...b-but she never..."

His eyes narrowed. "Did you bother to ask?"

"Why would I?" she flared, taking refuge in anger. "It's not a community outreach we're running; it's a ministry to our members, who happen to be Christians. Forgive me if I wasn't looking for the makeup of the group to resemble some battered women's shelter on Heathen Ally."

He took a deep breath and seemed to be struggling to hold on to his temper. "Are you aware that down on *Heathen Ally* social workers are red-flagging Christians as high risk for domestic abuse?"

"Sure they are! Cause we discipline our kids, and live our lives according to that antiquated thing called the Bible. That's reason enough right there for them to raise all kinds of flags."

"I'm not talking high risk for spanking and a belief in the death penalty, so you can get off your soap box. I'm talking domestic violence—battery, rape, murder. Think maybe there might be a reason? Not that I'd expect Eric Carmichael's widow to know anything about that."

Abigail bit down on the retort that sprang to her lips. "I know what domestic violence is. You don't need a sociology degree to figure it out. And I realize a man with an unimpeachable Christian witness must have posed all kinds of threats to someone like you, but kindly leave my husband out of it."

"You got a problem with my sociology degree?"

"I have a problem with you thinking it gives you the authority to override the manual, and as I recall, the manual says—"

"The manual. *The manual.*" He spat the word like he would an obscenity, and then his voice hit the ceiling. "How about the part that says you're not to have any unauthorized one-on-ones with any of the participants?"

"I didn't."

His eyebrows shot up. "No? So who was the third party? Cause they need to be in here too."

She swallowed. "There wasn't. She...Beth and I met up in the passageway. Wasn't anything planned. She said hi. What was I supposed to do?"

"In your case, try *Hi...how are you...see you next week* and keep going. I'm pretty darn sure she didn't ask you for any advice."

She hesitated only briefly before drawing in a deep breath, chin tilted and shoulders squared. "As a matter of fact—"

"Save it!" He flung back his chair and was towering over her, glaring, his jaw working. "I'm finished arguing with you. That's *it*. I don't want you anywhere near this ministry till you start showing some regard for—"

"Ex*cuse* me?" She drew herself up to her full five feet one and a quarter inches. "In case you think it's your place to order me around—"

"I just did!"

"—I have equal say with you on these matters. That was my understanding from the beginning. A-and kindly do not raise your voice at me."

He lowered his voice a fraction, his jaw tightening with the effort. "Your father put me in charge of this ministry from ever since it was nothing more than a glorified slugfest. Bunch of rebellious women in one corner planning insurrections against their husbands and a bunch of angry men in another, venting and blustering and waiting to get even. You can't live with the way I do things, we've got a front, a back and a side exit." He tossed a half-size booklet at her. "Here, take this home with you and read it."

Real Answers for Real Problems: Oasis Ministry at Grace Community Church.

"I've already read it——"

"Read it again—"

"——and have my own opinion about how it was put together, I might add."

"—and then read it some more, until you understand our ministry objectives and strategies. And then you either get on board or you get yourself a flannel graph and go back to teaching Sunday school."

Abigail gritted her teeth. "If I'd wanted to teach Sunday school, that's what I'd be doing. I chose to work with Oasis because I have as much to offer as you do, if not more."

"I couldn't care less if you'd discovered the secret formula to happy ever after. I will not work with you constantly pulling against me. *Dismissed*."

She tried. Opened her mouth more than once to tell him where he got off, but couldn't trust her voice to remain steady. Couldn't put two words together sufficiently cutting to put him squarely in his place.

She did eventually, of course. Minutes later, after she'd spun out of his office and was storming down the corridor toward the exit. She wasn't about to crick her neck trying to stare him down.

She'd lost enough arguments before the advent of Stone Patrick to know when her speech center was about to be short-circuited by hurt and rage. She never failed to come up with the most brilliant comebacks...hours later when she was in a corner licking her wounds and fighting tears.

Not this time around. Not ever again. Different fight, same enemy. Only she wasn't outnumbered and defenseless anymore. She wasn't some gullible fool hoodwinked by fear and superstition. And Stone Patrick wasn't some sacred talisman standing between her and God's wrath.

And last time she checked, she was still Richard Lester's only child.

So she reminded herself as she hesitated outside the heavy oak door at the end of Grace's east-wing corridor, her courage momentarily failing her. Her temper having had a chance to cool on the long march from Stone's office in the west wing, she couldn't help a niggling of guilt at what she was contemplating.

It wasn't her way. Or that of the man who occupied the office suite on the other side of the door. Otherwise, she couldn't have enjoyed the open and harmonious relationship that she always had with the rest of the staff. The rest of the staff excluding Stone Patrick, that was. There was nothing open or harmonious about the constant tug-of-war between them, only it wasn't because of any supposed advantage that being the boss's daughter gave her. For if there was anyone being discriminated against, it was her.

Maybe it was time for her to balance the scales. She was, after all, the only employee at Grace who could take a complaint straight to the top and expect an audience at a moment's notice. The only one, for that matter, who was able to sidestep protocol and the chain of command by simply showing up for dinner.

As things stood, the only thing standing between her and the cure to Stone Patrick was the closed door in front of her. That and her own scruples.

Her scruples she couldn't easily rid herself of, of course; she could at best manage to sit on them for a bit. The door, on the other hand...

She drew a deep, fortifying breath and knocked.

2

Stone slammed his screen door shut and kicked it for good measure, wishing it was sturdy enough to take the full force of his frustration. Glad for the sake of his aching cheekbone that it wasn't.

Would have served him right, anyhow, if it was barbed wire and steel he'd got whacked with instead of aluminum and mesh. He'd blown it with Abigail. *Again.*

Only this time he'd managed to hurt as well as offend her. And still wasn't sure why. He'd been careful. He'd been gentle. He'd chosen his words. After the giant leap their relationship had taken that afternoon, he'd have thought he was past having to walk on eggshells around her. Never mind the fact he made a living walking on eggshells.

Yet here he was, for the second time that day, staring at the empty space she'd just filled and wondering what the deuce had gone wrong. This time, though, she hadn't stalked out so much as she'd bolted. And left him with his emotions in the same tangled mess she'd left them in earlier at work.

A worse tangle. Their relationship hadn't been this complicated this morning.

They hadn't *had* any relationship to speak of this morning. None of the frustration and sympathy that was warring now in his chest and conspiring with the lingering traces of Abigail's scent to undermine a lifetime worth of resolutions and take him places he had no business being. This morning, he'd simply said to France with her after she stormed out and had gone to his locker for aspirin. Got into a fight with yet another door and won it too.

Then again, in all honesty, that locker door was the least of what he'd found himself fighting outside the staff lounge this morning...

He yanked open the locker door a second time to free his snagged shirttail, kicked it shut again, almost slamming his hand inside, dropped the bottle of aspirin he'd just retrieved, and cursed the hormones God had saddled him with.

He didn't know who was the bigger fool, himself or that ostrich-headed termagant he'd just tangled with.

There she'd stood on the other side of his desk, looking down her cute little peanut nose at him and twisting her sainted dead husband's ring on her finger while she lectured him about what the manual did and didn't say. And hadn't the sense enough to know she was heartbeats away from being hauled across his desk and kissed speechless.

And here he was minutes later, madder than any woman had ever had the power to make him in his life, and still racking his brain trying to identify the tantalizing scent he'd come to recognize as peculiarly hers.

Her *scent*. He was obsessing over her scent, for heaven's sake, when it was that unruly evil in her mouth called a tongue that he needed to be worrying about.

So what if the air around her was always delicately scented with something soft and floral and hauntingly familiar and the memory it evoked was achingly sweet and barely beyond the reach of his consciousness?

And so what if her silky red-brown hair invited him with every move of her head to see if it felt as soft as it looked? And what if one direct look from her strange peat-brown cat eyes had the power to make him trip over his own thoughts and forget mid-sentence what it was he was ranting at her about? What good did any of that do him when she was blind and deaf and clueless and exactly the kind of female it was his life's mission to avoid becoming entangled with?

Charm is deceitful and beauty is passing, but a woman who fears the Lord, she shall be praised.

Didn't he know it.

"Acquire a taste for I-Peter-3 beauty," Doctor Lester had counseled him when he gave him his Christian boy-meets-girl talk. Translated, go for the girl with the "meek and gentle spirit." Like the Bible Sarah, who'd called her husband Lord. He had yet to come across one of those anomalies, but he'd seen a few couples who came close. Amazing that poor Doc had managed to raise the anti-Sarah.

Around Stone Patrick she was, anyway. She'd been the model of wifely virtue toward her husband, from all accounts, the reason her father had been so eager to have her involved with Oasis. And to think he'd been leery of her coming on board because he'd been expecting some mindless doormat brainwashed by that authoritarian ex-pastor of hers. Hah! She'd probably argued the poor man up a gum tree and off a cliff, was more like it—

And now he was smelling things. Smelling her. That hint of something warm and fragrant and rare...

Far above rubies.

What? That scent? He could believe that. Something exclusive. His nose didn't remember having come across it before, and his sense of smell was keen.

But not *that* keen.

Lord, she's gotten not just under my skin but into my head, cause I'm smelling her for sure. Somewhere behind him, in the vicinity of the locker stamped with the Tweety Bird sticker that was her trademark.

Her worth is far above rubies.

Ah yes, the Proverbs 31 woman. That rare creature. *Really though, Lord.* He didn't doubt whose voice it was whispering through his spirit. He'd felt that gentle breath often enough before.

The heart of her husband safely trusts in her.

No doubt. Too bad she hadn't made the leap from the pages of scripture into the real world.

A locker door behind him rattled. Abigail *was* there. In his scuffle with his own locker he'd missed the muted patter of the soft-soled shoes she wore around the office.

"Come to get your stuff?" he murmured without turning.

"As a matter of fact, yes. Congratulations."

It wasn't the words so much as the unfamiliar huskiness in Abigail's soft voice that caught Stone's attention.

He turned around, sorry he'd taunted her. "Hey. What's going on?"

She dragged her key out of the lock, reinserted it and rattled the door furiously.

He crossed the narrow corridor to her side. "You quitting on me?"

She gave him her back.

He circled her. "Come, talk to me." He waited. "Yell, then. Throw something at me."

She sniffed. "Don't stress yourself out trying to be nice to me. Just go right ahead and be your usual ornery self."

"Can't. I'm wired to react this way to women in distress."

"Yes, well, don't worry...you won't have me to squander your sympathy on much longer." She banged the door with the heel of her hand, winced and shook her hand.

"Watch it." He nudged her aside, carefully maneuvering the stuck key out of the lock and inspecting it. Selected a different key from the ring and slipped it in. A second later the door swung effortlessly open.

She avoided looking at him as he handed the keys back to her. "Excuse me."

He stepped aside, and she yanked an oversized Tweety Bird tote from the bottom of the locker and started stuffing the contents of her locker into it.

"You're welcome."

"Thank you." She had the grace to look ashamed. Like he'd expected she would. She wasn't normally ill-mannered.

Or angry, spiteful and uncooperative, for that matter. Only with him.

He kept his voice neutral as he asked, "So what happened?"

Something had. She was not herself. She darted him a wary glance, and something he saw in her eyes grabbed him in the gut. A wounded, almost defeated look.

"Come, let's go talk in your office," he urged. Hers was the closest to the locker room.

She hesitated and seemed to lower her guard. Probably weighing the urge to tell him to get lost against the lure of the sympathy he was offering. She looked sorely in need of some sympathy, even from him, and it just about banished the last of his ire.

He made the decision for her, placing a hand lightly in the small of her back and steering her away from the locker. His hand nearly spanned the back of her narrow waist, and the shocking evidence of how little of her there was underneath her burnt-orange silk suit cut through him like a bolt of electricity.

He dropped his hand, a familiar queasiness growing in his stomach.

Inside her office, he hooked a chair forward with one foot, gingerly removed the two-foot-high Tweety Bird occupying it and placed it on the shelf amidst her collection of other Tweety paraphernalia. Then he sat and waited patiently while she sat hugging a Tweety Bird cushion to her chest.

She sniffed. "He...I've decided to take a break from Oasis."

Much good it had done her, being Richard Lester's only child. She might as well have been some orphan the ministry supported in Biafra, for all the good it had done her this morning in her father's office.

A familiar ache blossomed in Abigail's chest as she

turned onto the back road of Southwest Ranches. Picket-fenced acreage and the smell of horse led the way to the heart of one of only a few pieces of suburbia that had managed to resist the rabid over-development that had redefined much of South Florida.

Among the solitude-loving few who called the subdivision home were a congressman, a football player, and what's-his-face from the renowned Grace Community Church in North Miami.

At the corner of Pembroke and Paisley, adjacent to what had to be the most pampered acre of green in Broward County, Abigail crawled to a stop in a line three cars long. Traffic jam, for these parts, even at four in the afternoon.

Peak hour traffic, sparse as it was in this corner of the county, invariably slowed at this particular junction. Cars lingered a little longer at the stop sign while gazes filled with anything from awe to envy drank their fill of the aesthetic feast laid out on the oversized southeast corner lot.

Against the crisp blue brilliance of the Florida January day, the garden at the corner of Pembroke and Paisley was breathtaking in its beauty. A skillfully manipulated riot of colors that bore testament to its owner's green thumb, 500 Pembroke Circle had become a landmark of sorts, and not because of who lived there.

Abigail turned a jaundiced eye on it as she waited on the cream Lexus that had stopped in front of her. It was an eyeful, she supposed. Under normal circumstances, she'd have been in awe of it herself. Under normal circumstances.

If she wasn't less appreciative than most of the kind of sacrifices the owner had made on the way to being crowned "the conscience of the American family." If she could overlook the fact that that garden had better luck capturing the man's attention than his own child ever had.

You more than captured it this morning. You held it.

Sure. For all of five minutes or so. That was how long it had taken for open and attentive to turn into something else.

Abigail swallowed the bitterness that surged up with the memory and eased off the brake as the Lexus in front of her finally moved on. Ahead of her, the empty road seemed to beckon as it wound its way through acres of green.

She was halfway across the intersection before she caught herself. For a split second, she found herself poised between the right turn that led to home and the unfamiliar stretch of road ahead. And then she was making a hard right, followed by another, and slowing in front of the security kiosk.

Mechanically, she punched in the code that opened the black iron gates and with a heavy heart passed between the massive coral pillars.

She held her breath a few minutes later as she aimed the garage door opener, and released it on a soft whoosh as the door slid upward. No tan Buick occupied the space beside hers. The keynote address he'd been preparing for an upcoming leadership conference when she barged in with her ultimatum must have taken till now to complete.

She'd almost changed her mind about disturbing him once outside his door, the constraints of a lifetime hard to ignore.

Daddy's talking to God. We don't want to interrupt.

Except she was no longer a five-year-old struck dumb at the thought of Daddy engulfed in God like Moses on the mountain, unwilling to brave either God's glory or her father's disapproval. She was his partner in ministry. A valued one, she'd been assured more than once.

She drew a deep breath and knocked.

"Come." The quiet, well modulated baritone that for millions had become synonymous with faith and family values still sparked a certain gladness in her heart.

As did the warmth that crept into the pale blue eyes when they settled on her. He didn't look surprised to see her less than an hour after she'd brought him his coffee and bid him good day. They often didn't see each other after that till over dinner at home in the evening.

Not much ever caught him off balance, though. As a

child, she'd been convinced he had an inside track to her naughtiness. She'd felt compelled to confess her sins to him the minute he landed from one of his speaking tours. The fact that it had earned her nothing more than a squeeze and a grave reminder to "Tell Mommy sorry and then go talk to Jesus about it," had only encouraged the habit.

The memory of that acceptance returned to reassure her now, and she felt the leftover tension from her fight with Stone ease away.

"Hi, Daddy. Can you spare a minute?"

He didn't hesitate. "Yes, precious girl. Anytime."

He clicked his pen shut and laid it down. Rolled it toward the horizontal groove at the top of his desk and settled it there before giving her his full attention.

The years peeled back and with it a few of the layers that had crusted over their relationship. For a moment, the impulse to launch herself at him, bury her face in the breeze-fresh crispness of his powder-blue shirt, breathe in the lemony tang of his aftershave and startle an indulgent chuckle out of him was almost as strong as it had been in the days before she learned to be mindful of his clothes and the "important appointment" he had that day.

He didn't have any scheduled for today, but she swallowed the wayward urge nevertheless. She sank instead into the chair beside his desk and let herself be enveloped in the calm that always seemed to surround him. He created order wherever he went, his office Spartan and down to the last pencil as methodically arranged as the rest of his life. It was the perfect backdrop for him.

But for impossibly shaggy eyebrows that angled upward at the outer edges despite his best efforts, he was the neatest man she had ever known, barring one. Clean shaven, starched and ironed and polished, with an erectness that added inches to his slightly below average height and a military precision to his movements that made the gentleness of his disposition totally unexpected.

Every woman's dream, her mother had declared, with that secret smile that always lit her face when she talked about him. And it was a lot of the same qualities in Eric that had first caught Abigail's attention.

And the glaring absence of said attributes in Stone Patrick that so underscored his drastic departure from everything she had come to associate with male authority. Stone Patrick might issue orders like he was some kind of commando, but there was nothing either mild or orderly about him.

"Stone, eh?"

She met her father's knowing gaze and nodded cautiously, gauging his reaction. His expression had grown weary, almost strained, she saw with a pang. Almost as if he knew what was coming.

Abigail closed her mind now on the memory of what had followed. She couldn't undo any of it, and wasn't sure she wanted to. She shoved the temptation to the back of her mind, along with all the other do-overs that could never be, let herself quietly in through the kitchen and trekked wearily up to her room.

Furlough. Stone rubbed the back of his neck and stared out at his empty carport like he'd stared back at Abigail when she dropped her bombshell.

Abigail's stricken features, small and delicate next to Tweety's humongous head, stared back at him. He felt it again as he had sitting across from her in his office, the tightening in his gut...

"Why now? What happened all of a sudden?"

She lifted a shoulder. "What does it matter? You got what you wanted."

"I never said—"

"Yes you did—"

"I didn't mean it, and you know it. I don't have the authority to send you anywhere."

"But it's what you wanted. Well, now you have Da—my father's backing."

Stone stilled. "What?"

"You heard me." She got to her feet.

"Sit down."

The gruff order startled her into obeying, but the second she did she glared at him.

He sighed. "Why don't you tell me what really happened?"

"I just did. If you don't believe me—"

"The parts you left out, then."

She pressed Tweety closer. "He—" She swallowed. "He suggested I go on furlough. While I consider the possibility that I don't really belong here. Translated—I'm in your way."

"I don't believe that. Our disagreements are nothing new to your father. He expected them when he took you on board. Welcomed them, probably. Checks and balances sort of a deal. He knew I was green and needed somebody more grounded in the faith to give me balance."

"Yes, well, that was before I told him it was either me or you."

"I see." That was a shock. Not that she'd tried to get rid of him, but that her father had responded the way she claimed he had. He knew Doc liked him, valued his contribution to the counseling ministry at Grace Community Church, but no way would Stone have expected to win a contest with his beloved only child.

It was no victory at all. Aggravate him as she did, he didn't enjoy seeing the fight knocked out of her the way it evidently had been. She was doing her best to appear flippant, but whatever her father had said to her had hurt her. And if it made him as uncomfortable as it did, he could just imagine how she must feel.

He got to his feet. "Wait here. I'll talk to him."

Her mouth tightened. "Thank you, but I'd rather you didn't."

"Yeah, I know you don't need the likes of me to intercede for you with your own father. It's not what I propose to do. I need to let him know what part I've had in all this."

"He knows, and he's already decided you're right—"

"It's not about who is—"

"—and it really doesn't matter anyway, cause I don't know if I want to be part of Oasis anymore."

He stilled. "You're just saying that because you're mad and hurt."

"Maybe. Or maybe it's been five months coming and I've been fighting it and that's the real source of the conflict between us. I'd like to take the time off to figure out which."

Stone dropped back down into his seat, pressing two fingers briefly to his temple. "Can we talk?"

Abigail regarded him suspiciously, as if it were a switch and not an olive branch he was holding out. "What about?"

He sighed. "Whatever you think we should talk about, okay?"

"I didn't say I want to talk."

He exhaled forcefully. "Fine. We'll talk about what I want to talk about. We should have long ago. It's a disgrace what we've been doing, fighting and pulling against each other and expecting at the same time that God is going to use us to unite the very people we're fighting over."

"Well then, you can start by telling me exactly what it is that you have against me. You've been set against me from the day I came back to Grace."

He gave her a thoughtful look. "You want to know exactly what my problem is with you? 'Cause I—"

"On second thought, I don't." She shot to her feet. "I don't have to listen to it. A-and I'm not going to, so you can send it right back to whatever pit you dredged it up from!"

She was fists-drawn, teeth-bared defensive. And scared. He saw it in her eyes, and it stopped him dead in his tracks. He hadn't managed to scare her when he towered head and shoulders over her in a rage, voice hitting the ceiling, but he was scaring the daylights out of her now that he had his temper under control. She was in a positive panic. Because he'd offered to tell her a few stiff truths?

"Sit down." He said it softly, almost placating.

She blinked once, twice, and sank back down into the chair.

He massaged his temple again and started over. "That came out wrong. I'd like to...discuss my...concerns. And hear yours." She inclined her head to indicate she was listening, and he began carefully, "The women who come to Oasis are not your average women's fellowship crowd. These women have serious issues. Five easy steps to wedded bliss isn't gonna do it for them. They're trapped in a real-life nightmare, and they need real answers that can bring them out of it alive."

"God's truth is relevant to any situation in any age. Or social group."

"As long as it's His truth they're getting and not somebody else's watered down version of it."

"I've been teaching women's bible studies longer than you've been saved, Mr. Patrick, and I've never once been accused of handling scripture with anything but the utmost integrity."

He winced suddenly and rubbed his temple. "I wasn't challenging your integrity."

"Just my understanding of scripture."

"Your application of it. To other people's lives in particular. And I'd appreciate it if you'd lower your voice."

She stared at him in rank disbelief. "You have the nerve—I was *not* shouting."

She was perilously close to it now, and he'd have given her anything she wanted if she'd have agreed to just shut up.

If anything, her voice rose. "And what do you know about my position on anything anyway?"

He knew the church she'd been a part of for five years. Enough by itself to make her views on marriage suspect.

"You've never given me a chance to open my mouth, much less commit heresy..."

Not that she acted anything like the other woman he knew from Spirit and Truth Center.

"...and if you think—"

Silence, sudden and deafening, swallowed the rest of her protest as white hot pain ripped mercilessly through one side of his skull, wrenching a soft groan out of him. He dropped his face in his hands, shutting out the light and Abigail's suddenly anxious face, willing his stomach to stop heaving.

Hand cradling one side of his head, he sucked in a ragged breath and held it, afraid to breathe, then released it on a muttered prayer, "Jesus, help me—"

3

A lone saxophone crooned soulfully from the depths of Stone's jeans pocket, effectively stemming the flow of his memories.

Stone reached into his pocket for the cell phone he'd dropped there earlier and groaned when he saw the name and number registered on the screen.

Great. Fighting another wave of guilt and frustration, he took a moment to transition from the rocky reality of his thought life to the realm of the ought-to-be before taking the call in a voice that was as close to normal as he could manage.

"Yes, Doc."

"Stone, my boy." Richard Lester's voice was as cautiously optimistic as could be expected of one who stood in constant danger of being caught in the crosshairs of World War III. "How's the head?"

"Still on my body, sir, despite some of the urges I was having round about lunchtime today."

"Good, good. We need it there." A pause, then, with a wink in his voice, "Served its purpose, though, eh?" Another pause, while Stone scrambled to figure out just how much the other man knew about the latest encounter with his daughter. Not much, Doc's optimism would suggest, but—

"You talk any, you and Abigail? Or were you still drugged up when she left?"

No, he didn't know. Couldn't. As to whether that was a positive or a negative, that was yet to be determined. "Uh, actually..."

"No matter. It's a start. I'm glad you got a chance to see the softer side of her."

That what he called it?

"She's a good girl, our Abigail. Had a rough year, but I think she's over the worst."

He definitely would not want to see her worst.

"You busy tomorrow, or what?" Doc asked.

He should be. Tuesday being a slow day at Oasis, he typically used it for field work, starting out a couple hours earlier than usual so he could knock off by early afternoon, with enough time to make the gear shift necessary for the transition to his "day" job

On an average Tuesday. He hadn't had one of those in close to five months, as Doc knew too well. "As a matter of fact, I...thought I might drop in on you, if that's all right with you."

"Do that. I have a mind to play God for an hour or so before the day gets hot. You could give me a hand with the lifting, and we could talk some more."

"Call Abigail for what?"

"For Beth's sake, Crystal. It'd do Beth good to get together with us all. We never should have let ourselves lose touch with her for months on end. To France with Leo. What could he have done, anyway?"

"Exactly what he just did."

"Not if we'd got her to see sense and get away from him."

"Who, me? Uh-uh, sis. This girl's not going to be accused of getting between another husband and wife, clueless spinster that I am."

"Well, the court already got between them, so what's your excuse?"

"I wasn't making any. I have every intention of getting together with Beth. Just Beth. Or if you must have an entourage, there's always Kay."

"Funny."

"Might have dropped off the planet by now, huh? Or floated off it, more likely. Ah well, I guess it's just us two, then."

"It's been four years, Crystal. People change, especially after going through what Abigail has."

"That's what we thought when we heard about Eric, remember? Even when she didn't bother returning any of our calls. *Poor thing, she must have a lot dealing with. She needs time.* Well, she's had almost a year."

"Wasn't enough to get her back on her feet, though. She's back at her Dad's. Been."

"And so broken up with grief she's all up in his counseling ministry, helping to clone perfect little helpmeets just like herself. Remind me where not to go if I ever need marriage counseling."

"Well now, there's not much likelihood of that ever happening, is there?"

"Got that right. Although, you never know. You used to say the same thing about Abigail, remember?"

"Yes, but only because the guys around her couldn't get up the nerve to court Richard Lester's daughter, not because she'd doused herself in man repellant. In fact, without her Dad in the equation, she'd probably have been the first one of us to get snatched up, if you ask me. Certainly did surprise a few of us."

"Because she lucked out and snagged the only paragon left on the planet?"

"No, Crystal. Because she never had a cynical bone in her body. Because whatever her other problems, she's sweet and gracious, and because some men actually like a woman who doesn't feel she has to compete with them for her place in the world."

Bumptious, pigheaded brute. She'd show him he wasn't

boss of anybody but himself.

Chin tilted and gaze no higher than her father's collar, Abigail waited in guilty anticipation for his answer to her ultimatum. She hated doing this to him. He wasn't given to nepotism anymore than she was one to pull ranks, but she'd had no choice.

Stone Patrick had pushed her to this. He'd been pushing her from before she ever got a chance to prove whether or not she'd be any good for Oasis. Like he thought he was the one with all the answers. Like he didn't think the women who came to Oasis deserved to have someone in their corner as he no doubt was in the men's. Like he—

"Stone must either think I'm a liar or very deluded."

Her father's voice was flat.

She blinked. "Daddy—"

"I sensed he had reservations when I told him you were coming back to Grace and wanted to work with Oasis. I assured him he'd enjoy working with you, how agreeable you were and easy to get along with—"

"Must have got the shock of his life." The muttered retort slipped out even as she scrambled for words with which to defend her position.

Her father absorbed her vibes in silence for a moment, his straight-gazed psychologist's face in place, then sighed. "There was a time when you considered those admirable qualities, Abigail. What happened, hmm? Has losing Eric made you bitter against other men who didn't get called home in their prime? Or is it because Stone dares to be so unapologetically poles apart from Eric?"

"How about it's just how I see things, Eric and Stone aside? I do occasionally harbor a few thoughts of my own."

In the end, his answer to her protestations, petitions and demands had boiled down to a gentle but very firm, "I'd appreciate it if you'd accept my judgment on this, Abigail. You never had a problem doing so before."

"You never asked me to submit to the authority of someone who...who I..."

"Have a problem submitting to?" he prompted, one

bushy eyebrow cocked. He took in her closed expression in silence. "If I didn't know better, I'd say you had a problem with submission, period, Abigail."

"If I did, don't you think you'd have known it in the five years I was married?" she demanded in a choked voice.

"Not necessarily. Most reasonable Christian women don't have a problem submitting to the Eric Carmichaels among us. It's the Stone Patricks that present the real challenge. Well, guess what? It takes all kinds of people to accomplish God's purposes, Abigail, and He placed them in the church according to how they're needed. He gave us His Eric Carmichaels, and he gave us His Stone Patricks. Each of them has their role to play."

And she had yet to find hers. The weight of that realization became an ache in her chest that nudged her out of a fitful predawn sleep. Her breath came in shallow spurts, the fistful of pillow she held clutched to her cheek damp.

She rolled over, eyes automatically seeking the window and the blinds she rarely bothered to close, and stared with amazement out at the pink and gray dawn. She'd missed her nightly two a.m. appointment.

It was barely light outside when she gulped down the last of her coffee, set the mug gently in the sink so as not to make a clatter, and turned to leave the house, a whole two hours earlier than she was in the habit of doing.

"Morning," her father's voice, still husky with sleep, said behind her as she reached for the garage door knob.

She froze, braced herself and turned slowly. He was still in his pajamas and robe, unshaved, his hair finger combed. He'd been awfully anxious to catch her.

The realization comforted her some, but not enough to entice her into lingering. Her hand closed determinedly round the door knob. "Morning, Dad. I was just—"

"Rushing off so you wouldn't run into me. I know."

"Dad—"

"I won't hold you. But I did want to tell you I'm sorry if I came off a little too abrupt yesterday."

"That's all right."

"Evidently not."

No it was not all right, and abrupt was not all he'd been yesterday in his office. She couldn't remember the last time he'd used that tone with her. He'd hardly ever had to. From since forever. A wordless shake of the head that said "I'm disappointed in you," was as much as it had ever taken to bring her up short on the rare occasion she forgot herself.

After a year of unlimited free passes, his censure had been especially hard to swallow. For all that time he'd tip-toed around her feelings, cosseting and encouraging. Held her and wiped her tears without ever suspecting the real reason she cried.

There were times he'd even had to excuse her, for the four months it had taken her to finally put in an appearance at church, for her lackluster response to the effusive welcome she'd received, for her awkward silences and her occasionally unguarded words when some ill-phrased condolence touched a raw nerve. Never once had he so much as raised an eyebrow at her.

She supposed her grace period was officially over.

"Abigail, the point I was trying to make—"

"I understand, Dad, and it's all right. I...uh...we talked, Stone and I."

"You did?" He seemed greatly relieved. And expectant as he waited for her to elaborate.

The same uneasiness that had gripped her in the middle of their disagreement yesterday began gnawing at her again.

She pushed it aside. She didn't know what was with him and Stone Patrick—and it was evident there was more than just Oasis between them—but it wasn't her concern. Her father had let her know as much in no uncertain terms when she dared suggest he was afraid of Stone.

You're forgetting yourself, he'd told her in his chilliest voice.

She swallowed now. "I...think we have an understand-ing."

"I'm glad to h—"

"But I don't think I'll be going back in for now."

"Abigail—"

"Got to go, Dad. For real. Ana's got papers for me to sign." She closed the space between them to drop a swift peck on his forehead and rushed out before he could say anything else.

She wasn't about to get caught up in whatever trip he was on now. She recognized that brand of regret he was experiencing for what it was. She'd seen him go through it before. It had been there in his eyes when he gazed dumbly at the one-karat marquis she'd held out for his inspection one incredible Saturday night. In his voice when he hugged her close and gave her his blessing...

You'll always be my baby girl, no matter whose girl you become.

...And in his parting words to her on her wedding day...

Remember your namesakes. I doubt you'll ever have cause to resort to Abigail's brand of wisdom, but should you ever do, my door will always be open, no questions asked.

Five plus years later when she appeared on his doorstep, bringing nothing but the clothes on her back and the pieces of her shattered dreams, that door had still been open. Only this time when she walked through it she'd found not just the security and belonging of former times but a kind of access she didn't remember having when she was growing up.

Not just because she worked alongside him now in the ministry. Not because he was home more or sat down with her more often for meals. Not even because he'd developed a peculiar habit of leaving the door of whatever room he happened to be in slightly ajar, as if in invitation.

It had more to do with his level of awareness, of her in particular. The way he listened, giving her all of his attention without leaving a corner of his mind still engaged in whatever pursuit she'd interrupted. As if he expected that at any given moment she might have something momentous to say about whatever ministerial challenge he was facing at the moment...or some little nugget from that portion of her life that he knew almost nothing about.

Warmed as she'd been by all the attention, it didn't mean half of what it would have meant during a lonely childhood haunted by the specter of sickness and death and loss, or at the height of her motherless adolescent years. Or even later when, despite a lifetime of conditioning, she'd begun to question herself, wondering if there was a reason besides God's timing why she'd reached her mid twenties without ever having received more than covert looks from any of the marriage-minded men she knew.

It would have meant even more yesterday, the first time her newfound status had actually been put to any kind of test. Would have meant a lot too to know that her involvement in Oasis was more than just her father's latest scheme to draw her out of herself.

As a strategy it had succeeded too, more than any of the socials he'd coaxed her to, or the duty phone calls from old friends that he'd no doubt instigated. Or the sundry chores he'd talked her into assuming at church. Coming face to face with women who were so much worse off than her in every way had pulled her up short and taken her concentration off herself.

She'd begun to remember the blessedness of sharing herself with others. Not out of fear or obligation as she'd so often done in the past five years, but from a heart of compassion and of gratitude to God that she had been spared what some of these women had been through.

And then there was Beth. She couldn't put a price on what running into Beth meant to her.

What had started out as a therapeutic exercise had turned into a life mission. She couldn't remember her heart being more completely engaged in any other ministry undertaking. Her father had been delighted, of course. His efforts with her had paid off with a bonus, and he couldn't have been happier.

Till she was foolish enough to think her contribution was worth any more to him than the twenty minutes worth of filing it had taken her half a day to finish back when she was still struggling with her ABCs.

He'd been very good about indulging her then, but the screeching of the metal chair she used as a ladder back and forth across the tiled office floor hadn't done much to disrupt the running of the church office. Moreover, her little after-school "job" had kept her out of her mother's hair, and his office assistants had probably felt privileged to be babysitting Pastor's little treasure.

Taking on Stone Patrick and upsetting the Oasis apple-cart was another matter. What was more, Stone Patrick had no patience with babysitting, and her contribution to Oasis was to him tantamount to the screeching of not one but a dozen chairs, all day long instead of just after school. If she hadn't issued her father an ultimatum, Stone probably would have sooner or later. She didn't have to wonder, either, if he'd have got his way.

Her father was no respecter of persons, but he had apparently decided to make an exception of Stone. He didn't scare easily either. Had unflinchingly faced down some of the devil's toughest customers, including the deranged atheist who walked up to his pulpit and threatened to shoot him at point blank range. But he seemed unwilling or unable to wield the same kind of authority over Stone Patrick, almost as if Stone had some kind of hold over him.

She couldn't begin to figure out what that might be. They talked a lot outside of office hours. Stone had been to the house, several times. Had obviously been in the habit of doing so before she came back to live there.

She had come downstairs several times to see the two of them together in the greenhouse. Once, she'd let Stone in herself. He'd nodded at her and murmured a greeting and, rather than pretend that she had anything to do with his visit, had gone straight past her and into the greenhouse.

For all she knew, he might be on his way here right now. Today was an off-day for him at Oasis. As to whether he would tell her father about what had happened, she wasn't going to be around to find out.

Stone eyed the empty spot between the two sentry pines

at the top of Doc's driveway with mixed feelings as he eased his car through the gateway of 500 Pembroke Circle later that morning. No yellow Beetle, but that didn't mean it wasn't in the garage. Abigail parked there as often as not. Not that it mattered, anyway. Wasn't her he'd come to see.

Nevertheless, there was an odd knot of tension in his stomach as he rang the doorbell, and he wasn't sure if it was relief or disappointment he felt when the door opened to reveal who it did.

She was lanky and caramel-skinned, and she beamed a welcome at him that faltered only at the sight of his bruised face. A Papa Doc refugee, Grace pioneer and Doc's house-keeper of ten years, Odette's straight face and impeccable manners seemed always at odds with the irrepressible twinkle in her ebony eyes.

Stone ignored the question in them now, murmuring a response to her greeting, and went without invitation in search of Dr. Lester. He kept his eyes rigidly averted from the staircase as he veered toward the huge glass sliders to the right and rear of the mile-long great room. The house was as familiar to him as the offices at Grace.

A two-story, five-bedroom sprawl on an acre of green, it was more space than a small family with humble origins would ordinarily need, but just barely enough for Richard Lester's. At Christmas and Easter and a couple times in be-tween, he filled the place to overflowing with the enormous spiritual family that he nurtured as diligently as any proud father.

For someone raised in strife and near isolation as Stone had been, the relationship dynamics among the group of diverse personalities from different backgrounds was capti-vating to watch. He'd been instantly and hopelessly hooked on the fellowship, much as he had been on the God who inspired it.

Doc was where he was most likely to be found these days whenever he was home, the greenhouse off to one side of the house. He'd built it for his wife, an avid garden-er, when her illness began to make her oversensitive to the

Florida heat, but by his own confession had never set foot inside it more than a handful of times when she was alive. His current preoccupation with it was a source of bafflement to everyone except Stone.

"He just loves playing God with things that grow and bloom on schedule," Abigail had affectionately declared, Doc told him, but Stone knew differently. Abigail had it only half right. He'd spent more time with Doc in there of late than everyone else combined. The greenhouse was primarily a quiet place for Doc to cherish his wife's memory and to reflect on what treasures life still held for him.

Abigail was at the top of that list. Doc talked about her a lot as he gardened, sharing bits and pieces of her childhood with Stone in between sighing and muttering and exclaiming over the progress of his "little ones." Stone had heard so much about Abigail for so long before he met her that he'd begun to feel like he knew her.

Till he met her, anyway.

Doc's memories were almost all of her preteen years. It hadn't taken Stone long to figure out that those were the only years Doc had truly had a chance to enjoy her, before success and an ever-increasing demand for more from a devoted following had taken its toll on his family life.

Stone's heart lifted in spite of himself as he was enveloped in the cool dampness of the greenhouse. It was an enormous glass-walled affair that ran almost the length of the house, ending only where the swimming pool began. Stone had nothing to compare Doc's greenhouse with, there not being too many of them in South Florida's perennial summer. But by any green lover's standard, it had to be close to perfect.

The focal point of it all was a big, many-tiered dais visible from all the way in the living room. There, the healthiest and showiest, be it poinsettias in December or red, white and blue petunias on the Fourth of July, took their turn dazzling whoever happened through the front door.

Well, usually. There wasn't much on the dais now besides the foot-high shrub Doc claimed to have "rescued from an abusive environment." On the top shelf, no less.

"To remind her I expect great things of her," Doc had told him with a wink once when Stone cocked an eyebrow at it.

In which case it was in the right place, Stone supposed. If there was a place where any growing thing stood a chance of exceeding its potential, it would be there at the center of Doc's attention, enjoying the knowing touch of his very green thumb and the pleasant drone of his voice. The evidence of that abounded all around the greenhouse.

There was no particular order or symmetry to any of it. The place was in fact mildly chaotic, as perhaps only the site of a colossal clash between nature and artistry could be. In every direction Stone looked, fiery tropical showboats were flaunting their bold colors before pale northern beauties.

Off in one corner, glossy red anthuriums that had weathered several seasons in the shade were thumbing their long yellow noses at the fading poinsettias that had recently been demoted from center stage atop the dais.

In another corner, red, yellow, orange and pink hibiscus, big and flashy, argued riotously among themselves, while in yet another corner a half dozen orchids cradled inside coconut husks looked languidly on from an avocado tree.

Doc seemed for the moment oblivious to it all. He was in front of his potting bench at the far corner, feet braced apart and hands buried in the front pocket of his apron as he glanced with narrowed eyes from the shrub atop the dais to the empty five-gallon pot in front of him.

The potting bench was the most unsightly portion of the greenhouse, rightfully tucked away at the back and overlooking nothing but the remnants of the neighbor's once fruitful orange orchard, ravaged now by citrus canker. It was where the painful and unglamorous phases of Doc's work were carried out, the mixing and planting and pruning.

More often than not, the ground around it was littered

with plant clippings. There were big bags of this kind of soil and that kind of fertilizer, peat moss, cow dung and noxious looking formulas that promised miracles.

"Hi, Stone," Doc greeted him absently without looking up. "How's it going? You and Abigail ironed out your differences yet?"

"Not likely to happen with her off on furlough, Doc."

Doc sighed. "That's her choice."

"Does she know that?"

"Sure she does." Doc looked up. "I made it cl...what happened to your...she *hit* you?"

Stone could feel his face go hot. "Not exactly. We...had words." To put it mildly.

Doc shook his head, looking baffled. "What did you say to her?"

What *had* he said to her? Not a whole lot. Hadn't got a chance to. "Difference of opinion, sir. Over ministry matters. She doesn't take kindly to suggestions, especially mine."

Suggestion? You mean like the one that her attempts at counseling were endangering the counselee's welfare?

Doc shook his head. "Yesterday she sent word that you...when I heard you were leaving together...I thought you'd..."

"Called a truce?" Stone's lips twisted. "A ceasefire, maybe. She did what any Christian sister would have done, I suppose."

And then some...

.

M-i-g-r-a-a-i-n
Did you mean: *migraine?*

Well, duh. As in pain in the head so severe it can reduce a grown man to tears.

Not even tears at that. He'd been past that. Abigail's fingers stilled above the keyboard, a sudden stark vision of Stone's ashen features as they'd been in her office just twenty-four hours ago wiping the small sneer off her face.

He'd been no more capable of tears when the pain seized him than she had been of crowing over his sudden humiliating debility. He'd been in agony, afraid to breathe, much less utter a sound, except in prayer.

For a moment after he'd groaned that prayer, she could only stare at him, uncertainty that bordered on alarm shrinking her voice like Stone's harsh semi-plea seconds before hadn't succeeded in doing.

"St—Stone?" she whispered.

"Gimme a minute." Then, in a hoarse whisper, "Please."

When finally he raised his head, the deep bronze of his skin had gone ashen, his eyes narrowed into a pained squint. His voice when he spoke was strained. "I'm going to need a ride home. Now, if you can manage it."

"W-sure. And leave your car here, you mean?"

"Unless you plan on towing it."

She got to her feet, her head spinning from the sudden turnaround. "I'm parked out back."

He headed out the door without another word. She grabbed her bag, buzzed her father while she slipped on her heeled pumps and hurried after Stone.

She caught up with him near the exit. "Don't you want to take something for it first?"

"Left it home."

"I can get you something from my—"

"Uh-uh. Prescription."

A cool-fingered January breeze tugged playfully at their clothes as they stepped out into the dazzling midday sunshine. Stone squinted and groaned, and Abigail quickened her steps to keep up with his much longer strides.

In all her encounters with him, she'd been left feeling like a little sand fly buzzing round a giant's ear, a small annoyance one swipe away from annihilation. Just this once she felt as big as he was helpless. And too floored by the experience to enjoy it.

At her car, a canary-yellow Volkswagen Beetle, she opened the passenger door for him and waited for him to ease his length into the cramped space before gently closing the door.

She threw him a concerned look as she slid behind the wheel. "Are you—"

"Do me a favor and not talk." The pained moan that his roar had been reduced to took the bite out of his words.

She shut up. Pulled out as gently as she could from the parking lot. Looked over at him, biting her lip, and whispered ever so softly, "Sorry, but I don't know your address."

He dug into his jeans pocket and a second later tossed something into her lap. His wallet.

She opened it gingerly. His driver's license was up front, across from a picture of a beautiful, sad-eyed brunette who seemed vaguely familiar. Abigail tried not to stare at her as she took note of his address. She started to hand the wallet back to him but tucked it instead into her jacket pocket.

He lived in a small, elderly house in a sleepy, shady corner of North Miami Beach, about ten minutes north of Grace Community Church. It was one of the more stable subdivisions in Miami-Dade County, established several housing booms ago, when the average single-family lot size was much more generous than it was now.

Lined with breeze-swept sabal palms and dotted with tropical fruit trees imported by its mostly West Indian populace, his neighborhood was much like the one she'd grown up in till one of her Dad's books hit gold and they joined the exodus to neighboring up-and-coming Broward County.

It was part and parcel of why her father had latched on to Stone, she suspected, his ability to stay in touch with the "grass root brethren," as her father styled the ninety-percent portion of Grace's membership that hailed from the surrounding communities.

Meanwhile, she got to drive thirty to forty minutes to church, depending on traffic, and to feel like the foreigner in the church that had been her home since she was a baby. She was resigned to doing it for as long as she remained at Grace, too. Any chance her father might relocate the church had died when he joined forces with Stone. The needs of the community he'd once outgrown had become personal with her father then, his compassion evolving into some kind of indebtedness that Abigail didn't quite understand.

"We're here," she whispered when she pulled up in the driveway of 230 Palm Terrace and Stone didn't stir.

He sat up, groaning. At the front door, he fumbled with the key. She waited for him to single out one before taking it from him and opening the door.

Inside his house was as diminutive as the surrounding yard was spacious, not much of a match for a man Stone's size. She barely had time to register more than that before he bolted down the passageway that opened off the living room.

The sounds drifting out to her told her he was in a bathroom. And that he was losing his breakfast. She hesitated only briefly before going after him.

He was slumped in front of the toilet, hugging it. *"Out!"* he gasped, waving her off.

She ignored him, his weak voice and obvious distress banishing the last of her reserve. She grabbed the half-empty coffee mug sitting on the tank top, rinsed it and filled it with water.

"Here." She handed him the mug and pulled a towel off the rack. It was soggy, as if it had fallen into the tub, and was smeared with dried up stubble-speckled shaving cream, but it was the only one. She wrung it and handed it to him with a grimace and while he rinsed his mouth started poking into the medicine cabinet above the sink.

"Fridge top. Brown bottle."

The kitchen made the bedroom and bathroom look like something out of a home show. Except for a half-eaten bowl of cereal, there were no dirty dishes in the sink, but only because of the multitude of paper plates she could see floating over the top of the overfull garbage pail.

He was in the adjoining bedroom when she came back with the pills and a tumbler of water, stretched out on the bed in a sea of about a week's worth of discarded clothes. He eased up on one elbow and accepted the two pills she'd poured as per the instructions on the label. Tossed them to the back of his throat, ignoring the water, and eased back down against the pillow.

His hand felt around blindly in the mound beside him and tugged something out of it and over his eyes. Another towel, a used-to-be white one.

She grimaced in sympathy, looked around at the windows and realized he'd already drawn the blinds but that they weren't the light-blocking kind. She searched gingerly through the portion of the clothes pile that his body wasn't covering and selected a black t-shirt. "Here, this'll be better." Without waiting for him to look at what she was showing him, she gently replaced the towel with the t-shirt.

He seemed to relax a little deeper into the pillow. "Thanks." He heaved a shaky breath. "You c' go."

She wasn't going anywhere and leaving him like this. She wasn't even sure what was wrong with him. Her guess was he was having the mother of all migraine attacks, but she couldn't be sure.

In his living room, she stood for a moment, hands on hips, lips pursed, surveying the mess around her.

And repented. She had judged Stone wrongfully. He was a natural messy, numbered among that special breed who avoided leaving a trail of clutter behind them only by the greatest amount of effort and forethought. It was a miracle he managed to turn up every day at the office in clothes that were clean and unwrinkled, never mind their age or appropriateness.

That he hadn't always been that domestically disadvantaged was obvious. It was for sure he had not decorated the house himself. An abundance of bows and flounces and homemade cushions in country floral had made a doll house of the living room. The only thing masculine or even remotely practical in there was a big brown corduroy couch that looked as if it had been hauled in by someone more concerned with comfort than style.

The place had to have been decorated by a woman. One of his pre-conversion affairs? She was sure he'd had his share. Or had he been married? To the wistful beauty whose image he still carried in his wallet? There was so little she did know about him.

At any rate, whoever or whatever his domestic arrangements had been, they'd obviously changed when he became a Christian. For one, her father would not have tolerated that kind of compromise around any ministry of his. And for another, that polished-apple print was at least a dozen years old; Abigail remembered when it had first graced the display case of her favorite craft shop. Someone as clever with her hands as this domestic goddess of his had been would have changed it out by now.

Not to mention give the place a thorough cleaning.

He needed a woman in there, even for a few hours a week. And would probably never care enough to see about it.

Here's the number for an agency that can supply you with a cleaning woman. I never intended for you to do it yourself. Just testing you.

Abigail hesitated, her hands clenched.

What's more, there's a lot you have to learn about keeping this house the way I want it kept.

She shrugged out of her jacket and laid it over the back of Stone's big brown sofa.

You ever stop to think how it'd look if an elder or somebody dropped in and saw you barefoot and on your knees doing what I can well afford to pay somebody to do?

She slipped out of her heels and set them neatly in a corner. Rolled up the sleeves of her white pin-tucked work shirt. Heaved a fortifying breath and threw herself at the beckoning chaos like her sanity depended on it. Sweeping and vacuuming, dusting and mopping.

You want something therapeutic to do, take up a hobby. Preferably something easier on your hands than that other fixation you call a hobby.

Wash, wipe, stack, fold.

And for God's sake, do something about your nails.

One torn fingernail and a couple of calluses later, she petered to a stop and was neatening the movie collection on the bottom shelf of Stone's wall unit when he emerged from his room a couple of hours later.

5

"Because the market, it is very competitive, you see."
The thickly accented voice came from behind her.

Abigail blinked and turned toward it, surfacing with an effort from her reflections.

She stared at the dark-suited middle-aged Hispanic woman standing just beyond the archway of the computer alcove. Ana. Addressing her for heaven knew how long, while she'd been off strategizing over the mess in Stone's living room.

"Uh...what was that?"

"Things haf to be just so to get the buyers' attention, you understand. Usually, I have a list of recommendations for my clients...what to put into storage, how to arrange this, things to clean...you know—"

"Well, now that you have a key, feel free to make any changes you think—"

"Oh, but I wasn't—"

"It's not a problem with me. Really."

"I know, but—"

Abigail heaved a breath. "If you don't mind, Ana, I'd rather have as little to do with the whole process as possible. It's why I decided to go with you. Melody said you were good that way."

Ana nodded, smiled a pained little smile, and murmured, "Certainly. If that is what you wish."

"She spoke very highly of you," Abigail added, belatedly trying to soften the rebuff. "I was really glad for someone I could hand the key to and forget about...everything.

I'm...not up to much yet."

Ana nodded, her eyes softening a fraction. "But of course. You want only to sign on the dotted line, *no?*"

Something like that.

"It's no problem at all. I'll take care of whatever is necessary. Ah...excuse me. I'll just go finish up the paperwork and let you get back to your...research."

On her way out of the room, she turned, her face a polite mask with a glimmer of something like sympathy in it. "Your house is perfect, Mrs. Carmichael. There is nothing I could think of to make it show better."

But?

Abigail waited for it, for there was a definite *but* in Ana's grave voice, in those eyes that seemed so...knowing.

As if...Surely Melody wouldn't have...

No, she would not. Confidentiality was a basic tenet by which the Melodies of the world operated. If Abigail hadn't had absolute faith in that, there would have been no Melody.

It was probably just something amiss with the house. Something or other always was. Keeping up with it was a full-time occupation. Had been. More work than could be done in the time it took to sleep off a migraine attack, for sure. And not just because the great room alone could have swallowed Stone's house whole.

But before she could search Ana's face for clues, Ana was already turning away, heading back to the kitchen island littered with worksheets and contracts and percentage tables.

Just as well. Whatever the problem was, it was no longer hers.

Still, out of long habit, Abigail scanned the room, making herself see it through Ana's eyes. It was spotless. Nearly, if one overlooked the very thin film of dust that was starting to dull the gleam of polished silk and hand-carved mahogany. It would do. Compared to...well, there was no comparison. Nevertheless, she did, her eyes sweeping from gleaming wood floor to vaulted ceiling...and beyond...

To a small, chaotic living room a county away, presided over by a brown corduroy couch that had been sprawled on and curled up in at will. Beside it, a scarred coffee table stained many times over with, of all things, coffee-mug rings...and herself in the midst of it all, curiously at home, chaos and all.

From somewhere outside of herself, suspended between then and now, she watched her mind's replay of that afternoon's events. Saw herself react to the trigger, the voice that seemed to have burned itself into her psyche.

I don't care what you're accustomed to doing or why. You won't be cleaning any more houses, not even my own.

She felt it again, the compulsion, the itch of her palms...the oozing of her tension as she tackled the chaos in Stone's house...her uncertainty as she anticipated his reaction, and her confusion when she got it...

"Hey." Surprise, appreciation and, she could swear, pleasure, were all wrapped up in Stone's husky greeting when he emerged from his bedroom and discovered her still there, on her knees in front of his movie collection.

He was barefoot and bleary-eyed, but the intense relief on his face from being pain free was palpable.

Abigail sat back on her heels. "Migraine, huh?" It was a relief to be able to talk again without inflicting torture.

"Yeah. Compliments of my mom."

"How's she doing?" Abigail asked gently. Five years after having to place her in a nursing home, he wasn't quite over it, someone had told her. They must have been close.

"Good," he answered finally, sounding neither sorry nor guilty. "Adjusting."

"You—"

"Don't."

She stared, taken aback by the sudden hardness of his voice. "Don't what?"

"Don't go there. I appreciate the concern, but I don't

want to talk about it."

Talk about someone in need of counseling. "So. Anything in particular that triggers your migraine?"

"Yes, quarrelsome women." But his eyes were smiling, his voice almost caressing. There was something else along with the teasing in the eyes that met hers as he added, "Thanks. You've been an angel."

She felt herself blush. "You're welcome."

He cast an eye around. "You're not too bad a maid, either."

She lifted a shoulder. "You need one."

"I wouldn't have thought it of you, judging from those hands."

Do them yourself, or go with mother to her manicurist. Just so long as you do something about them.

"What's wrong with my hands?" She fired the challenge before she'd quite digested his words, then bit her lip and hoped he'd let it pass.

Without a word, he went down on his haunches beside her and picked up the hand nearest him. It *would* have to be her right hand. She curled it closed defensively, but not fast enough, for her fingers ended up closing around two of his. He used them as leverage while his other hand pried hers open, his eyes holding hers quizzically all the time.

She squirmed as he studied the back of her hand, petite like the rest of her, with fingers that were too short for elegance. She could only be thankful that she'd perfected a French manicure that made the best of her short nails.

"Like I remembered. Pampered and delicate."

Her breath caught for a moment before she blurted, "I have calluses," her weak voice making a confession of what she'd meant as another challenge.

His eyebrows shot up, and she wanted to kick herself as he immediately turned her hand over and smoothed his open palm gently over hers till he felt the faint ridge at the base of her fingers and at the tip of her forefinger and thumb. "So you do. I never noticed." He added something softly under his breath.

She blinked at him, not sure she had heard right.

"Proverbs 31. *She works willingly with her hands*, or something to that effect." He fingered the back of her hand, delicately, as though it were something that might break. "Let me guess...gardening."

She shook her head, fighting a peculiar ripple of pleasure at the sight of her hand swallowed up in his large one. "Too many worms and stuff."

"Not in your father's greenhouse, there isn't."

"How'd you get yours?" she asked in a rush before he could pursue it further. His palms were rough for someone who spent so much time at a desk.

His mouth twitched. "Nothing as industrious as housework." He jerked his head in the direction of the living room's sliding glass door. It opened onto a small screened patio just big enough to hold the bicycle and weightlifting paraphernalia it housed. "My remedy for the blues and a sinfully large appetite."

He let go of her hand. "I probably should tell you I feel more comfortable in the clutter, but I don't. Housekeeping just isn't very high on my list of priorities."

"Not unusual for a guy. But you can always hire somebody."

He rose and looked around him again, clearly impressed. "You've halfway convinced me to." He shot her a teasing glance. "Now all you have to do is figure out how to keep my headaches coming regularly, and you'll be able to keep me in my place."

Her jaw tightened. "I can keep you in your place without the help of your head, thank you." She got to her feet. "And for your information—"

"*Easy*. What did I say?"

Enough. "I don't manipulate people."

"I know that."

She regarded him warily. "How?"

"Because you're better at haranguing them to death." He was trying not to laugh at her. Amazingly, it made her feel like laughing at her too. She allowed a small smile to escape. And tried to keep the gratification out of her voice as she said, "Really?"

"Yes, really. The other reason I know is because I've got better discernment than whoever it is been telling you you're a manipulator."

She ignored the unspoken question in his eyes.

"On the other hand, I'd probably take manipulation over being tongue-whipped to death."

She glared. "You're not exactly sweet either, you know."

"I know."

She bit her lip. "I don't like fighting with you."

He studied her in silence for a moment, arms folded across his chest.

"Or anyone," she hastened to add.

"Hmm. So what do you want to do?"

"Go say hi to your cats."

He blinked.

She cast a wistful look out at the small porch where three bundles of fluff lay huddled in a furry tangle of orange and white and black. "I've counted three so far. They friendly?"

He laughed softly. "Go ahead. They won't scratch or anything. They just love adoring females."

"Bet she was giving as much adoration as she was getting, too," Doc commented with a chuckle.

"Oh, yes." Stone felt his insides warm, remembering. There she'd been, on her knees, wrapped in live fur and suddenly oblivious to him and all that had gone on between them.

He'd watched from the living room window for only a few seconds before going to the side door and whistling.

Enter Phantom, a fifty-pound beige mop of questionable heritage.

"Bounded in and followed his nose straight to the front porch. Took stock of things and tumbled right into the mix."

Another ripple of laughter had escaped Abby as she fought to keep her balance and get her arms around yet another admirer.

"She must have been beside herself, huh?" Doc murmured, a flicker of something like regret mingling with the laughter in his eyes.

"Just about." The sight had been priceless. And enormously instructive. His animals were good judges of character, and they tended to be a little wary of strangers. More than a little. The sight of them fawning all over this particular stranger while she melted like a Popsicle in their midst had drawn him like a magnet out to the porch...

"You never had a pet." It was a statement.

Abigail shook her head. "Couldn't. There were times we were away more than we were home. Back when we used to tour with Dad. After that...things needed to be as close to sterile as possible. The transplant drugs suppressed my mom's immune system."

"That must have been rough."

"I didn't miss having a dog. I missed not having my mom."

"I wasn't talking about your not having a dog." He bent to retrieve a cushion that had found its way out to the porch.

"Sorry," she said, brows knit. "I got distracted on the way to figuring out what to do with that one."

It was the only bold solid in his collection of pastel prints. "I'd say at attention on its tippy-toes like all the others."

She gave him a sober look. "I didn't know how you liked them."

"Soft and squishable, mostly."

Her laugh sounded oddly relieved.

He frowned. "Some nerve I'd have, finding fault with

anything you did with that mess you walked in on."

Her silence gave him his answer.

He regarded her incredulously. "Were they even on the couch when you came in?"

She broke into a grin. "A couple of them. Most were on the floor."

"I stretch out there sometimes."

Her grin widened. "One was in the fridge."

"Don't ask. It's one of those mysteries I'll wait to have solved when I get to heaven."

"And another one was lodged between the wall and the back of the TV."

"I threw it at a hypocritical congressman and missed."

She wrestled another grin. "And then there were the socks."

"I wouldn't even try explaining those away, except to say I'm deeply convinced that one of the greatest privileges that life has to offer is the freedom to walk barefoot."

She chuckled. "I'm beginning to think the place could have looked a lot worse."

"Just as well your mom never had the misfortune to set foot inside it, huh?"

She laughed, ruffling Phantom's floppy ears. "I like it."

"Oh, come off it."

"Well, not the mess, just the...I don't know. It's easy to be in, I guess."

He knew exactly what she meant. The only part of her father's house he felt completely comfortable in was the greenhouse. Being encouraged to make himself at home didn't help, either, for then he worried he might forget himself and kick off his shoes or stuff some priceless handmade cushion behind his neck.

He sank gingerly into the porch swing and steadied it. "Whyn't you get a pet once you were on your own?"

"I never was, really. I went straight from my parents' home into my husband's. He was allergic. Really allergic."

"Hmm. Well, now's your chance. Before you go and marry some guy with critter phobia or something."

"Not likely."

"That he'll have critter phobia, or that you'll marry again?"

She pretended not to hear, burying her face briefly in Cotton's soft white fur, then got reluctantly to her feet, chuckling as Pumpkin and Pepper rose with her and wound themselves lovingly round her ankles. "I have to go see Beth. If that's not a problem with you."

"We need to talk first."

Immediately she stiffened, and some of the sparkle that had captivated him the past few minutes evaporated.

"*Talk*, I said. Not throw punches."

"What about? I'm not getting into anything with her. Just a hospital visit, sister to sister."

"Could be just as dangerous."

"Sorry, I forgot it's my fault she's in there."

"Why are you so confoundedly defensive?"

"Why are you so confoundedly critical?" she shot back, her temper flaring.

"Somebody try to point out where you go wrong on something and you call that critical?"

"Or should I ask, why are you so critical of *me*?"

He stared at her, dumfounded. "I might ask you the same thing."

"You started it. From the first day I came back. You were already geared up to fight me long before I set foot back in there." She hesitated only briefly before sticking out her chin in challenge and giving vent to the suspicion that had been plaguing her for weeks. "You resent the fact I'm Richard Lester's daughter?"

"I don't have anything against you, *Richard Lester's daughter*. Why would I?"

Oh. "W...I...just..."

Stone's eyebrow arched. "I work for him, remember? Nobody made me."

You knew I was Richard Lester's daughter before you married me. Nobody made you.

Stone folded his arms across his chest and continued to

eye her quizzically. "I don't envy him his place in life, either, anymore than he envies me mine."

Now that she could believe. Stone Patrick didn't strike her as someone driven to compete with anyone but himself.

"And for the record, I happen to think a lot of your father. I admire him for his accomplishments but mostly for the heart he has for hurting people—including those from segments of society he's not terribly familiar with. We don't always see eye to eye on how best to fix those hurts, but he deserves credit for caring enough to try."

"And I don't." Her anger had fizzled some, but not her resentment.

He drew a deep breath. "The difference between you and your father is that whereas his methods sometimes border on ineffective yours can be downright dangerous."

"*Dangerous.* You think I'm dangerous?"

He saw a storm brewing in her eyes and considered his options for allaying it. "You hungry?"

"No, I'm not hungry, and you can insult me all you..." She petered out as he stalked past her and back inside, banging the screen door behind him.

He'd just finished fetching lettuce, tomatoes and deli meats from his crisper when Abigail appeared in the kitchen archway.

He ignored her for the moment and set the ingredients on the small kitchen table he rarely ever used. She'd evidently deforested it of its resident mold and mildew, and it was a relief to have a clean work surface available for a change. He'd underestimated the convenience of a clean and clutter-free environment.

Suddenly, paper plates weren't good enough. He turned away from the table to search the cupboard above the sink.

"No, I haven't eaten yet, and yes I'll have some," she huffed behind him. "Thanks so much for ask—" She petered off again, swallowing hard as he swung round to face her with two plates in his hands.

"You do it on purpose, right?"

"Do what on purpose?" She licked her lips nervously, and his eyes followed the movement and was unable to look away.

"Try to goad me."

"No, I—" She took a cautious dab at her mouth. Her fingers came away with a smear of ginger lipstick, and she stared uncomprehendingly at it.

As if she thought it was a smudge he'd been staring at. He sent up a silent plea for strength and turned back to the table. Made two sandwiches in silence. Poured her his last glass of milk and himself his last glass of store-bought lemonade.

She eyed the glasses suspiciously as he set them on the table. "Lemonade's fine, thank you very—"

He switched the glasses, then went and dug the two empty cartons out of the garbage and showed them to her. "It's all I have. *Had.* Okay? I'm not that big on grocery shopping."

"Oh. Sorry. Um...I'll have whichever one you don't want."

"Doesn't matter. I drink nearly anything. Besides alcohol." He dumped the boxes again and washed his hands. "What does matter is that I be allowed to put something in my stomach without being provoked to the point of indigestion. Or another headache."

That got to her. He could see it in the way her face dropped, like air whooshing out of a balloon.

He sighed. "Sit. Or stand. Or lie on the floor with your feet in the air, whatever you think will annoy me the most."

"I don't do it on purpose."

And now he was supposed to feel guilty. He ignored her and said grace silently, then bit determinedly into his sandwich without comment.

Three bites later, she asked him in a small voice, "Do I really give you migraine?"

He paused with the last triangular bit of sandwich at his mouth and stared at her. She looked about ready to cry.

"No, Abigail, you didn't. I've been staving it off for a

few days now." He popped the morsel of bread into his mouth. And stared at her. She was looking at him as if he'd spat on her.

 6

I wish you wouldn't call me that.

Why not? It's your name, isn't it?

Yes, except we both know you don't like it. A-and it makes me feel chastised when you do use it.

You have a problem with being chastised?

Well...no, but I'd rather it not be in association with the use of my name.

You don't deserve to be called anything else when you act like a—

"You all right, Mrs. Carmichael?"

The juxtaposition of derision and soft-voiced concern catapulted Abigail's mind out of the pit into which it had stumbled. Black-and-white text, generic and innocuous, filled her vision again as another dark memory faded into the blue-white glare of the computer screen, too abruptly for her to transition successfully out of defense mode.

"Abigail," she corrected tightly, her momentary disorientation making a rebuke out of what might easily have been an invitation. "My name's...you can call me Abigail. Just Abigail." Her gaze shifted impatiently from the computer screen to Ana's face as she hovered in the archway of the computer alcove...and checked when she saw the pink blotches marring the older woman's otherwise matt-white complexion.

Ana's hands gestured profusely in apology. "I'm sorry, Mrs...I mean Abigail...I'm so used to...I didn't realize..."

"It's no problem, Ana," Abigail hastened to assure her. "And I'm the one who's sorry. I didn't mean to snap. It's just—"

"You don't haf to explain, M...Abigail. I understand..."
No, you don't.
"I lost my husband too, you see."
"It's really not...you did?"
"Two years this August."

There was no mistaking the sorrow in the big dark eyes. Abigail met her gaze fully then and saw her as if for the first time. She bit her lip, feeling like a shrew. "I'm so sorry to hear that, Ana."

Ana smiled her sad-sweet smile. "You never truly appreciate them till they're gone. You bicker so over stupid little things...a careless word...a shoe out of place...me, it was a nickname..." She grimaced. "Thumbelina...Now, I ask you, what was that for me to make such a fuss about?" Ana smiled gently. "I bet I know what *your* hubby called you."

Abigail stared numbly back at her.

She couldn't help it that her voice quavered slightly when she told Stone, "You called me by my name."

Stone chewed and swallowed. "What else would I call you? Cotton? Or would you prefer Pumpkin?"

"You never use my name. It's always *Ma'am* or *Hey you* or something."

There was a flicker of something in his suddenly evasive look. "Eat your sandwich." So he did have a *sort of* problem with her name, just hadn't thought she'd noticed.

Abigail's no heroine. Not in my book, and probably not in God's either.

"What's wrong with my name?"

He went to work on the other half of his sandwich, watching her the whole time while he appeared to consider her question.

She folded her arms. "I happen to like my name, thank you very much...and so do most other people."

He helped himself to a half of her sandwich and continued to watch her while he ate it. "What is your middle name?"

"None of your business."

"That tells me it's either Winifred or Hortense."

"Nice try. You can go right on calling me Hey-You."

You're not an Abigail. At least, I hope not, cause I consider your Biblical namesake a woman of questionable character.

"I like Abigail," Stone said.

"And I'll just start calling you...Y-you do?"

"Mm-hmm. It suits you."

"It does?" Her eyes narrowed. "Why?"

"You've got the makings of a biblical Abigail. The right raw material, anyway, if not the circumstances."

...disloyal to her husband, talking about him behind his back to his enemy and driving him to an early grave with her ill-timed revelations. For all we know she might have wanted him dead. She certainly didn't lose any time marrying his enemy. As good as killed him herself.

"Oh yes? Well—"

"It's a compliment, Abby. C-o-m-p-l-i-m-e-n-t. It usually is when someone compares you favorably with a hero. Heroine."

She stared at him. "She is? I mean, you think she—"

"After saving her husband's sorry skin and capturing a king's heart? Yeah, I'd say she's a heroine."

She'd been any kind of heroine, she'd have known her place and tried winning her husband without a word as God intended, instead of manipulating her way into another man's affections.

Stone shrugged. "In my book she is, anyway. I'm sure if you search far and wide enough you'll find some worthy theologian somewhere who'll argue otherwise."

"Oh." Speech failed her.

"And how many years of seminary did you have again?"

As if he didn't already know. As if there weren't enough people at Grace lamenting the fact that after meeting her husband in her second year of seminary she hadn't found it necessary to finish her degree.

She treated his query as the rhetorical question it probably was and continued to regard him with a certain amount of wariness.

He cocked an eyebrow at her. "This is...uh...really important to you, huh?"

That one loosed her tongue. "Names are extremely important. Bible says so. They help shape who we are."

"Or the other way around. Maybe a little bit of both."

"You ever notice how many Bible characters live up to their name? Take Jacob, *usurper*—"

"A.k.a. Israel, *having power with God*, which God had already predetermined he would, even before he pilfered it from his big brother. And then there's Jesus—*savior*, which also derives from a root word for God. And we all know *He* already had His life mapped out for Him down to the last detail."

"Still, Judas didn't originally mean betrayer, and he didn't have to be, either. Jesus happens to have known what he was up to, but nobody made him do it. Look at Jabez. He certainly knew how to turn his destiny around."

"And then there is Abigail." He stopped, a twinkle in his eye.

She couldn't find a smile, her face tight as she tried to guess where he was headed. "What about Abigail?"

"I have no idea. What's it mean?"

She glared at him. Hesitated. Then, watching him all the time, "Literally, *source of joy*." *Father's joy*, the plaque someone had given her for her thirteenth birthday had read, but she'd never quite related to that. Her father loved her, was thankful for her, but there had not been much joy left over from his struggle to balance fatherhood with ministry commitments and an ailing wife.

"Hmm," was all Stone said as he seemed to weigh the meaning.

"Was just a Bible name my mother liked," she rushed in, compelled to ward off whatever else he was coming with. "I don't know that she even knew what it meant."

"A blind prophecy, huh?" Then, while her shocked mind was still processing the compliment, "Poor Nabal, now...who knows what his mom was thinking when she named him?" And at her blank look, he enlightened, "Fool."

"Oh." She swallowed a giggle. "Omigosh."

His eyes twinkled again. "A Stone is a solid chunk of earthy or mineral matter, whose purposes range from use as building material to weaponry. I might have killed a giant once in a former life."

She tilted her head. "Oh?"

"My Dad thought the right name would be immunization against the effects of my mother's coddling."

"And was it?"

"You tell me."

For no reason that she understood, she felt herself color.

He took note of it with a wry smile but didn't wait for an answer. "I remember making a conscious effort to live up to it, knowing how he felt."

"Hmm."

"But there's also these hormones God gave me that took care of the rest."

She gave him a dry look. "Uh-huh."

He reached for the other half of her sandwich, still untouched, and, while she waited disbelievingly for him to devour it, held it to her mouth. "Open."

She was startled into obeying and the next second was struggling to get her tongue around the biggest mouthful of food she could remember attempting to tackle since losing the peanut-butter-and-jelly race at summer camp.

He stopped her protest with a raised finger. "Uh-uh, no talking with your mouth full."

She glared at him.

He was ready for her when she got done with that mouthful. And the next, and the next...

When after her last swallow he reached for her lemonade glass, she wrested it from him with a glare. "I know how to feed myself, thank you."

He just smiled and swiped at the corner of her mouth with his thumb. "Mayo," he explained, holding up the offending smear for her inspection. "Don't make me have to get you a bib."

"So...help me out here. One minute she was eating out of your hand, literally, and the next..." Doc cocked an eyebrow at the ripening bruise over Stone's right eye and the accompanying graze on his right cheekbone.

Stone felt like an idiot. He still didn't understand how he'd blown it the way he had with Abigail. He didn't expect her father to. But he very well owed the man an explanation, if not because it was his daughter involved then because the man who'd goaded her into losing her temper was the same one he'd put in charge of his counseling ministry.

Stone cleared his throat and said in his best head-counselor's voice, "I was only trying to set up some parameters, sir. I'd just as soon have left well enough alone." For real. He'd watched her as she washed their plates at the sink. She'd been *humming*.

"But I couldn't very well ignore the fact she'd messed up with Beth."

"Well, now, you couldn't. I just can't help thinking she might have responded a little better to a more...tactful choice of words than *messed up* and *dangerous*."

Stone felt himself color. "I might not have phrased it right. My fault."

"Granted. Even so, I still haven't heard anything that would goad her into—"

"She didn't...she slammed out. I tried to follow her and caught the screen door on the rebound. The metal part of it."

"Oh. So it was just a...She apologized, then."

Stone hesitated. "I imagine she will, when she gets the chance."

Doc frowned. "You mean she..."

"She was upset, sir. Very." He could swear he'd seen the sheen of tears in her eyes before she spun away and out the door.

Doc shook his head again. "This is not like her. Not like her at all. I'm going to have to have a talk with her."

"I'd prefer if you didn't, sir. It could only make things worse, and that isn't why I came to you."

"Oh?"

"I was wondering if..." He stopped, unable to force the question past his throat. "I was...hoping you could give me some insights," he said instead.

"As to why she's acting the way she is? I don't know, Stone. She's never given me that kind of trouble. Never. Or anyone else for that matter. I don't know what's got into her."

"Her husband, maybe?"

"Oh no. She had the utmost respect for him. Can't imagine her so much as raising her voice at him, much less her hand."

"Door."

"A door even."

So much for that. "Seems I am the problem, then."

Doc gave him a helpless look. He looked so much as if he wanted to offer encouragement but was fresh out of ideas.

"I don't know what to tell you, Stone," Doc said, his attention drifting to the row of bottles and boxes on a shelf above the potting bench. "I'd like to blame it on her hot Hispanic blood, except her mother was the sweetest, gentlest soul you could ever hope to meet. But I can tell you this much: The Abigail you're dealing with is something of a stranger to me. Please believe me when I tell you the she-cat who bruised your face is not the daughter I raised."

"Tell me then about the daughter you raised. Maybe I'll manage to glean something from that."

Doc regarded him dryly. "Need I ask the reason for your intense interest?"

Stone felt his face warm again but managed to respond evenly enough, "Maybe if I understood her a little better I wouldn't keep rubbing her the wrong way."

"Hmm. Thing is, there isn't a whole lot to tell. She wasn't a difficult child. She really was not. She'd always been pretty malleable, even as a teenager. And as accommodating as the next person. More."

"Not even a little bit defensive?"

"Defensive?" Stone could see from his expression the idea was foreign to him. "No, not really. Never with me. Not with anybody else that I've observed."

Except him. "How 'bout her husband?"

"Especially not him. Like I said, she respected him too much."

Stone felt a stab in his gut. He hadn't got too much of that from her in the time he'd known her. Then again, how much of it had he shown her?

"I admit to being more than a little jealous," Doc owned, stooping and reaching for a bag of mulch under the potting bench. "After being both father and mother to her in her crucial teenage years, it was hard to watch a stranger replace me in her affections." He stood and indicated a forty-pound bag of potting soil that a delivery man had dumped in the wrong place. "Give me a hand with that, will you?"

"I'll get it." Stone hoisted it onto his shoulder and brought it over. Tore it open and half filled the five-gallon container the other man indicated.

Doc examined the label of a bottle of liquid fertilizer and set it down again. "I'd come back from a weekend trip one Monday morning and found her out of school. Doubled up with cramps at one end of the house and her mother in another kind of agony at her end. That was the beginning of the end of my itinerant teaching days."

He reached for a box of dry fertilizer, measured and poured some into the pot of soil he was preparing.

"I'm sure that's one choice you never regretted, sir."

"Yes, well unfortunately, I didn't make it early enough. She'd already stopped looking to me for whatever crumbs of attention I could offer her." He looked up. 'Do you know she is the reason I wrote *Daddy, Do You think I'm Pret-*

ty? I woke up one day and realized she wasn't little anymore and that I wasn't the only one noticing it."

He stooped in front of the planter he was preparing and stared down into it. Ran a finger round the scrolled rim. "Took me a couple of years to write that one, what with all the data gathering involved. Some of those case studies I dug up from my office practice. Had a job tracking down some of the people involved for their permission to use their stories."

"There's an awful lot of people who must be glad you took the trouble, sir."

"Hmm, yes. None of them more than me. Was some revelation. By the time I got done with it I was all fired up and ready to make up for lost time, grateful for the second chance." His mouth twisted ruefully. "That was when Abigail met her prince and went lock, stock and barrel after him."

"Isn't that what you teach that married people are supposed to do? Leave and cleave?"

"Hmm." Doc's non-answer bore little resemblance to the voice of authority that called out from the pages of his books and had struck a chord in millions of hearts over the years.

"Tough when it's your turn, huh?"

"Something like that, I guess. I hardly saw her after she got married. She was very involved with her new church. Seemed to have...come into her own, somehow. Became a lot more...I don't know...outgoing, I guess, forthright. Forceful even."

"Like she is now, you mean?" Stone murmured, tongue in cheek.

Doc chuckled. "Not quite so forceful. Somewhere in between. I figure it was the flavor of the particular fellowship she was in rubbing off on her. They were a more gregarious crowd than she'd been used to at Grace. Much more. Can't say I saw eye to eye with them on everything, but they were sincere and had the basics down right, and she seemed to have blossomed around them. Positively flourished."

Doc's mouth twisted. "Was ten times more active over there than she'd ever been at Grace. She'd always been more like her mother, reserved at heart, but cared more deeply for others than she knew how to express. I worried at one point they were too much in my shadow. Till Eric."

Ah yes, Eric. Stone suppressed a niggling of irritation, the name beginning to grate on his nerves.

You started it, remember? You wanted to know.

Because he'd thought it might be informative. And now he knew about Eric. And it was all positive, like whatever Doc was getting ready to tell him would no doubt be positive. And he suspected he was going to find it about as informative as his next migraine attack.

7

Abigail stared at the words on her computer screen and shook her head. She'd read them before, but she hadn't seen what she was seeing now. Poor Sarah. How could someone so perceptive about others' situations have been so blind to her own?

> **Sarah:** I wish you all knew him like I do. He's not stuck up at all, only comes across that way. He's actually quite vulnerable on the inside. Get this—he worries about losing me.
>
> **jojo317:** u mean like u dying?
>
> **Sarah:** No, as in me leaving him. You believe that?
>
> **Spunky:** i believe it
>
> **Sarah:** Yeah right. Me of all persons. I still haven't quite got used to the fact that of all the girls he could have had he chose me.
>
> **Duchess:** u will, its part of the process, girlfriend. but u get past the unbelief once reality sets in.
>
> **Kay:** Don't you believe it Sarah, it doesn't have to be that way at all.
>
> **Duchess:** well hello, prof, thanks 4 finally joining us with your 2 cents worth.
>
> **Kay:** Some of us have other obligations. But they wouldnt know about that would they Sarah?
>
> **Spunky:** probably never will, thank god

"Any luck?"

"Hmm, what?" Abigail blinked at Ana as she hovered

just inside the computer alcove.

"You find what you search for?"

"Oh yes." Abigail indicated the thin stack of papers still in the printer tray. Google had spat back an answer to her query that was several thousand entries long. She'd gone with a few of the more authoritative sounding sites.

"Soon we not need the doctors and their big bills, eh?" Anna shook her head in wonderment. "Well, I'm leaving now. You want that I use my key and lock the door behind me, or you almost finished?"

Abigail looked from Ana back to the screen and then out at the cream brocade walls in the formal dining room beyond. The last time she'd sat here and looked out at them, they'd been threatening to close in on her. It had taken her long enough to be able to set foot inside here again. She wasn't going to push it.

She heaved a sigh and used the mouse to select *print*. "That's all right, Ana. I'm right behind you."

"Very good, then. I will be sure to call you as soon as I have some news for you. It won't be long, I can tell you."

"Sure, Ana. Thanks." Abigail watched while the old gray memories she'd been reliving for the past few minutes emerged in black and white, then closed out her mail box along with her folder of saved incoming mail.

"...so I decided she needed room to grow," Doc concluded, getting to his feet and dusting his hands.

Stone reined in his straying thoughts and tried to refocus on their conversation. "After Eric, you mean?"

Doc sent him a wry look. "No, the fellow in Ocala I bought her from." He waited for the words to jolt Stone out of his distraction before nodding at the shrub he'd just finished transplanting into a five-gallon terracotta container.

Stone grimaced in self mockery, then cast a doubtful eye at the plant. "That the one that was left for dead at the edge of some nursery?"

"For want of a five-dollar sprinkler head replacement. Can you imagine?"

He could. A professional horticulturist such as the one Doc had got it from could be forgiven for not wanting to waste time and effort on it. He was no horticulturist himself, but he knew pretty when he saw it, and he still couldn't figure out what that plant was doing in the greenhouse, much less at the top of the dais. Its foliage was not especially eye catching, so one had to believe it had something else to offer besides greenery. The question was when.

The deep green of its leaves and its sturdy, knobby little limbs declared it to be well past the first blush of youth, but it had yet to show signs of flowering.

Doc himself didn't seem sure of what it was. It was supposed to be a vine, but it refused to stretch so much as a finger toward the narrow trellis positioned beckoningly in front of it. It was a shrub posing as a vine, was what it was. A nondescript, non-flowering shrub at that, straining under the weight of Doc's lofty expectations.

Meanwhile, the star jasmine that Doc had tried so ruthlessly to train as a shrub had burst free of all its restraints and was joyfully winding its way all over the rafters, dipping here and looping there, dropping in on the bird-of-paradise that occupied a corner by itself and annoying the standoffishness out of it while filling the air with heavy jasmine perfume.

Still, it was the little orphan shrub that had Doc captivated for some reason, and the less promise it showed, the more obsessed he seemed to become with it.

"Its time hasn't come yet," he'd keep saying. They'd been awaiting its "time" for over a year before its recent promotion to the top shelf. Meanwhile, the proud and glorious peace rose that had worked so hard at being beautiful had been relegated to the shelf below.

"She isn't here, you know," Doc said quietly.

Stone felt himself color in spite of the fact that he'd been careful the whole time Doc was talking to keep his gaze from straying as usual in the direction of the stairs on the other side of the sliding glass doors.

He kept his voice as offhand as he could as he said, "No?"

"If I remember correctly, she had to meet someone somewhere."

Who? He was just itching to ask it out loud, but there had been something so pointed about Doc's omission that he couldn't very well press without coming across as boorish. Not to mention risking another more detailed inquiry into his motives. And since he hadn't yet figured that one out for himself, he ought to leave well enough alone.

"And the answer is no," Doc said quietly.

Stone looked at him. "Answer to what?"

"The question you started to ask me earlier."

"Oh." Should he bluff it out or what?

"You're wondering if she knows, right?"

"About what happened? Yes. At least, I'd assumed she would." And had been bristling in anticipation of a reaction that had never come. There had been nothing pitying, condescending or apprehensive about the way Abigail had been handling him. "But then I wondered...but how could she not?"

Doc frowned thoughtfully. "It's entirely possible. She was out of state at the time, rooming on campus with Eric while he finished up at seminary. The dust would have cleared by the time they moved back home, and I imagine the whole thing might have been taboo. Pastor over there runs a tight ship, I can tell. And I certainly have never had occasion to discuss it with her. Nor is she one to entertain gossip."

"I'd prefer it if it stayed that way...for the time being, anyhow."

Their gazes held. Doc asked, "It ever occur to you it might smooth things between you, help her understand why it is you're so...particular and everything?"

Yeah, sure. Like she didn't despise him enough already.

"Would be a valuable lesson for her," Doc persisted.

Stone shifted. "She's got Beth right there in front of her. That's illustration enough. It is for me."

"If you say so. Well, she won't hear from me, if that's what you want. But Stone...I hope you know her enough to know she's not one to hold something like that against you. She's compassionate and fair-minded, whatever other impression she's been trying to give you, and she doesn't scare easily."

XOXO was how her mother had signed Daddy's birthday card for her before she learned to write. She remembered, for she'd saved it for years after rescuing it from the garbage pail beside his recliner.

XOX was written now across the sky outside her window, and it eased the dull ache within her that was disappointment. He wasn't going to come. Was probably tired of her, too. But God wasn't. She sighed deeply, a great peace settling in her soul. She'd always known it, even when she hadn't felt it. God loved her. He'd had his angels write her a reminder in bright neon green.

So she didn't know. She wasn't harboring some secret disdain or mistrust of him. Therefore she had to be reacting to something she saw for herself in him, small comfort as that was. On top of which, like her father said, she was simply missing her husband. *Duh.*

Over and over the rationalizations chased themselves around Stone's head as he made his way home.

The atmosphere in the greenhouse had gone strangely flat once he realized that the probability that an unsuspecting Abigail would come tripping down the stairs at any minute was zero to none. He'd left with more unanswered questions than he'd gone there with.

From all accounts, Eric Carmichael had liberated her to be who she really was. And Stone Patrick represented some kind of threat to that someone that she had become. Not because of any prejudices she'd formed against him either. More likely because of his own reaction to her.

"Could be she's experiencing a delayed reaction to her loss," her father had offered sympathetically at one point. "She tends to keep things in...except around you, that is. Maybe she's not really done grieving, even after a year. Maybe she never even started, and you triggered the process somehow."

It must have been an adjustment for her, losing her husband, moving back home, changing churches—and what a change that was—without having to adjust to him on top of it. Who knew what kind of vibes she might have been picking up from him, come to think of it. He was not exactly without a few prejudices of his own.

Maybe she just needed some space. Just as well she'd taken his dismissal to heart. *Ouch.* He'd have to apologize for that piece of rudeness. He didn't know what on earth had gotten into him. He couldn't remember ever talking that way to anyone else before, blunt though he could be.

Why did he let her get to him? Why did any of it matter so much to him, anyway?

Was in the interest of a more peaceful work environment, of course.

Right. He'd had a great working relationship with Kayla and the handful of administrative staff at the church office for years and never got that involved in the details of their personal life.

Of course, Kayla and the others didn't drive him nuts challenging him at every turn. Or have a soulful gaze that seemed to peer into his core and left him wondering what she might have seen there. Or a fragrance that vaporized his anger mid-argument and made him want to cuddle up to her in spite of everything else.

So what? He still wasn't after a relationship, other than a working one. For three plus years he'd been claiming the gift of singleness, by faith, one day at a time. And had been managing nicely enough, too, despite the efforts of the

Grace matchmakers, or maybe because of it. He was as skittish as the next guy about being lassoed and hogtied, and the hungry gazes of some of the sisters who followed his every move with eternity in their eyes had helped keep his wayward hormones in check.

Till Abigail.

Maybe that was all his problem was, come to think of it. Some inbred male contrariness akin to the thrill of the chase that made him more easily roused by a female's retreat than her advances.

Abigail hadn't so much retreated or advanced as she'd hissed and scratched, claws bared and back raised. And he was a fool to let himself be mesmerized by it.

Maybe what he needed was an antidote. Like a trip to Dade Central, see if that didn't put things back into perspective for him. He was due a visit there anyway. He'd missed a few these past months. Starting with the first week he met Abigail. He wondered now if that was entirely coincidental.

Not that he'd missed going. He hated the place. Often as he'd been there, he couldn't get used to it, the rank, medicinal smell of it, the sounds of anguish and confusion, the vacant faces...hers especially.

Wouldn't have been bad if either one of them was getting something out of his visits. As it was, he didn't kid himself that he went out of anything more than duty. What else was there? Hearing her gripe about the slop they served up in the dining room? Or drone on about a past he was doing everything he could to put behind him?

Of course, there were always those rare moments of sharing that they'd had.

I found Jesus. Thought you'd like to know.

Well, I'm glad someone did. Where was He?

Talk about an antidote. He just wasn't up to swallowing it right now.

He might not need it, anyhow. If the set of Abigail's face when she stormed out of his house yesterday was anything to go by, he was going to get all the space he needed to rid himself of the memory of her scent and whatever else it was about her that had so piqued his interest.

She was sitting on his porch step waiting for him when he got home, a paper bag of unidentified greens on the ground beside her and Phantom's head in her lap.

8

Finally got through to Beth's room," her sister's voice said breathlessly when she finally picked up the phone.

Crystal frowned. "Take your time, will you? You rush around too much."

"Habit."

"And sit down."

"Trying to." The panting gave way to a groan of effort, then a sigh of relief. "She sounded really glad to hear from one of us."

Crystal sighed. "I can well imagine. Been six months since we heard anything from her, you realize that? A girl who couldn't hold her tongue for six seconds."

"Well, *she* seems to have got your sympathy, anyhow."

"Difference between Beth and Abigail is Beth didn't *choose* to drop her friends. It was that or have the stuffing beat out of her. What's Abigail's excuse?"

"Maybe we should ask her."

"She told us already, remember? *Sorry, guys, but it's a choice I have to make.* Cause she's too spiritual to indulge in idle chatter with the likes of us. Or some such rot."

"That wasn't quite what she—"

"I know what she said, sis. Might not remember it word for word, nor do I really care to. Bottom line is, it was *her* choice to cut ties with us. She said as much."

"Yes it was, but—"

"So when do we go see Beth?"

Silence, a resigned sigh, and her sister went along with the subject change. "You're probably gonna have to go without me. I'm under orders to stay put."

"Would that be the doctor's or the jailer's?"

"My jailer *is* my doctor. Lucky me."

"Must have his hands full fending off inmate assaults in between all those house calls. Try pulling off a jailbreak and give the poor guy a break, will you?"

"Nuh-uh, how could I? He's sooooo, so sweet."

"Spare me. You're starting to sound like somebody I used to know."

"I *know* you're not talking Sarah, now. Cause there's one major difference between us. I wear prescription contacts, not rose colored lenses."

"Actually, I meant Abigail."

Silence, then, "Funny you should say that. You know, Crystal, I know how you feel towards Abigail, cause I've been there too, and with reason. But I've been doing some thinking lately, what with Beth and everything, and...well, the more I look back, the more it's coming home to me that that...*stranger* we were dealing with back then was not the real Abigail. Not the one we grew up with, anyway."

"So what is she, schizophrenic? Cause if so, there's help available right there under her own roof."

Another sigh. "Forget it."

Abigail did colors like no other woman Stone had ever seen. He'd never seen embellished yellows and oranges and lime greens carried off with such panache, all cut along classically sleek lines that fit her petite curves so perfectly they had to be custom designed. She must have cost her husband a small fortune, one he had to have loved blowing on her.

Today, the yellow linen pants suit she was wearing made something absolutely delicious of her vanilla and cinnamon coloring and tickled taste buds that Stone's past overindulgence had left jaded.

He, on the other hand, was looking his usual scruffy self

in blue jeans worn almost white and a t-shirt that hadn't been removed as promptly from the dryer as the manufacturer recommended. He couldn't remember caring two hoots about any of that before now. But suddenly he did.

Probably because of where they were. He wasn't used to seeing her here, in his home, on his front step, looking sweet enough to bite into. She was never less than tastefully put together, but at work it was always in muted colors and tailored business wear. Her church clothes were a lot more expressive, but the trappings of stained glass windows, a ten foot cross and Mrs. Pinkerton's organ playing must have conspired to insulate him from whatever effect she might otherwise have had on him. Not so now.

He dragged combing fingers through his hair, got mired halfway through in tangles, and shoved his hands into his jeans pockets instead. He focused his attention on Phantom in an effort to stop himself skidding into a state of awkwardness such as he could not remember experiencing since adolescence.

Phantom was splayed out on his back, tongue lolling, one foot jerking spasmodically and a silly look on his face as he got his tummy scratched. Stone absorbed the sight for a second and ruefully fingered the bruise on his cheek.

Abigail followed the small movement, gaped at his bruises, and became instantly distressed. She eased Phantom's head off her lap and shot to her feet. With Stone on the bottom step and her on the top, they were just about eyelevel.

She bent down and retrieved the bag of greens with uncharacteristically jerky movements and held it out to him as though it were an offering. "I got these to juice for your migraine."

He glanced down at them and tried not to look as horrified as he felt.

"It's preventative therapy," she explained. "You drink it regularly and it makes you less susceptible to future attacks."

"You an expert on migraine now?"

"As of two hours ago. I Googled it."

Courtesy rather than enthusiasm dictated he relieve her of her offering, and so he did. "I don't have a juicer," he said, remembering just in time.

"I figured. Mine's in my car."

Too bad. Thankful as he was for her offer of an olive branch, he didn't think he should have to pay for it by drinking whatever ghastly green potion she'd dug up on the internet.

His cell phone rang, and he glanced down at the name on it before silencing it. He'd need to return that one. In a minute. For now, he needed to concentrate on navigating his way past this latest twist in the road to figuring Abigail out.

He realized that she was waiting for an invitation and forced himself to say, "I have to be somewhere in a bit."

"Oh." He could swear it was disappointment he could hear in her voice. Because she'd been denied the satisfaction of presiding over her atonement offering?

"I also wanted to say sorry," she blurted. "I didn't mean...didn't know...the door—"

"I know. Apology accepted."

"A-and I wanted you to understand why I got so bent out of shape over Beth. We...she's not just somebody I counseled at Oasis. She's my friend. One of my best friends. I've known her more than half my life."

"Beth Ramsey?" He could hardly hide his shock. "Beth and you are friends?"

"Was. We...lost touch a few years back. It was kind of a shock when she walked in on group a couple weeks ago."

"I wish you'd have told me that before. I'd have understood your being so bent on going to see her. I certainly wouldn't have tried stopping you in the first place."

"I was feeling kind of guilty for losing touch with her for so long. And I was still digesting everything...her marriage and all that. It's not the kind of situation I'd have expected her to wind up in."

"That's rarely ever the case, Abigail. Nobody walks

down the aisle expecting they're going to end up in a mess a few years down the line."

"'Course not."

"And that wasn't meant as some kind of put down, either."

"I know."

There was a short, awkward silence while Stone weighed his sense of duty against his inclination to take advantage of Abigail's attack of conscience. He really needed to return that call, and he had a hunch doing so was ultimately going to involve him paying the caller a visit in person. Not enough time to do all that plus indulge Abigail's nurturing urges.

He advanced a step higher and a hand span closer and held her gaze as she stood her ground. "I've got an hour and a half or so to spare. That enough time for you to fix me up some of that ghastly green poison?"

She nodded without hesitation, her eyes alight with renewed purpose. He couldn't believe he was encouraging her, especially when it meant ignoring a phone call that he would otherwise have already returned. He was acting like a man in love.

Inside a kitchen that still bore the signs of Abby's recent bout of domestic fervor, Stone filled the sink and, while Abigail set up the juicer, gave the greens a thorough wash.

As he upended the paper bag and shook the last of the broken stems and leaves from the bottom, something else white and inedible fell into the sink along with the greens.

"Whoa...what's this?" He rescued it from the water with a quick glance at it...and then at her as she dove across the space that separated them and snatched it from his hand.

He gave her a cautious look. "Sorry, I didn't mean to get into your business. Thought it might have been a recipe or something you downloaded, or info you picked up at the health-food store." He certainly wouldn't have expected to find her private business lying at the bottom of a bag she'd brought and handed to him.

"I forgot I'd dropped it in there. It's no big deal."

Yeah, right. "I only saw a couple of screen names, that's all. I wouldn't even know which one is you." He wouldn't have figured her for the type to squander her time in a chat room.

"It's years old. I was reminiscing and decided to print it up when I—"

"Hey, you don't owe me any explanations. You weren't plotting a terrorist attack or something, were you?" She certainly was acting like it.

She turned away to stuff the paper deep into the handbag she'd draped over a chair.

He turned back to the dresser. "Come, show me what to do. Time's going."

She had him chop and hand the greens to her while she stuffed them chunk by chunk into the little electric monster's grasping mouth. Slice, pass, shove, churn, in continuous harmonious rhythm that he found oddly soothing. Not the piercing whine of the juicer or the repetitive motion of the knife endangering his inept male fingers, but the simple pleasure of working alongside her in perfect domestic bliss. He could get used to it.

But not the frothy green abomination that was the end result of their industry.

"Taste..." she offered, holding the brimming glass out to him.

"Uh-uh. You first."

She laughed and turned to the dish rack in search of a second glass.

"Here." He closed his hand over hers on the glass she already held and guided it to her lips. "Just a sip. I want to see your face, is all."

She was grinning at him over the top of the glass, before and after she took her taste. She didn't grimace, go into spasms or fall unconscious to the floor.

He cocked a skeptical eyebrow down at the glass nevertheless, said "Life insurance and other personal effects in the top drawer of my night table," and drank it all in one go.

He still preferred lemonade and just about any other drink over it any day, but it wasn't all that bad. Not bad at all. "And how often do I have to do this?" he asked, wiping his mouth with the back of his hand.

"Just once a day. At least." She reached up and removed a green moustache residue above his upper lip.

A small, uncalculating gesture, much as he'd done for her mayonnaise mouth the day before, but the delicate touch of her soft fingers was enough to almost stop his heart.

He turned away and made a production of washing the glass and the juicer.

"I'll consider getting one of these." He turned back to her, drying his hands down the side of his jeans. "If you'll come by and help me sometimes."

"Sure, why not? If it'll save me having to drive you home every time you have an attack."

He cocked an eyebrow at her. "Does that mean you're coming in tomorrow? To Grace, I mean."

"I guess." She held his gaze, hers only the tiniest bit un-certain. "If I'm still welcome."

Don't ask.

"You know you are. I know I blew a lot of steam, Abigail, but I didn't actually intend for you to pack up and go home."

She looked down at her hands. "I'd like us to be able to work together. I really don't enjoy fighting with you, what-ever other impression I might have given you."

"Me neither. But at the risk of getting my face slammed up in a door...we really do need to talk."

"I know. I—"

"Just talk. I'll try not to be so *confoundedly critical.*"

She didn't crack a smile. Seemed to be wrestling with something. Finally, she heaved a breath and asked, "What is it about me?"

He blinked. "What?"

"That you don't like."

"I don't dislike you.

"Didn't, then."

"I never *ever* disliked you."

You owe her more of an explanation than that.

He probably did, but she wasn't going to get one just yet.

"I had a knee-jerk reaction to you," Stone said abruptly just when Abigail was beginning to accept that she might have been reading him wrong after all. "And not because of any hang-ups over your father, either."

So he'd said before, and somehow she was beginning to believe him.

"Want to know why?"

Her walk, talk, looks? The fact she existed? She wasn't sure she wanted to know, brutally blunt as he could be. She braced herself before venturing, "Why?"

"Your name."

"My name? You told me—"

"It does suit you, and I do admire the other Abigail. But there was someone I knew once, before I was saved, who..." He hesitated and seemed to be feeling for words.

"Whose name was Abigail," she finished for him.

He shook his head. "*Saw* herself as one. Her husband would make Nabal look like a charm. He was brutal as well as boorish. But every time I'd talk to her about leaving, she'd spit back some drivel about waiting for her Abigail deliverance. She was praying the Abigail prayer, she said."

"What's that?" She'd never heard of that one.

"God alone knows. But it had to do with God rescuing her from her Nabal."

"She was waiting for him to die," she whispered, revolted.

He nodded. "Only she got tired of waiting."

Abigail gasped. "She—"

"Took matters into her own hands. Got free from him, all right. Exchanged the prison of her marriage for a real one, with a different kind of security."

She absorbed that in silence. There was nothing to add to it, one way or the other. After a while she asked tentatively, "This someone...she's...was someone you were close to?"

"Could have been. If we'd been living on the same planet."

"You weren't saved yet, huh?"

"No, Abby, but I am now, and I still won't tolerate that kind of delusional thinking around any ministry I'm a part of. It's beyond dangerous. It's criminal, especially when it's indulged in by those of us who're intervening in the lives of people whose judgment and self-preservation instinct is already impaired."

"I'm not delusional."

And how would you know that? You're so steeped in it you think truth is a delusion. Self-deceived people usually do. That's why they need a shrink. Or better yet, an exorcist.

"I am *not* delusional," she said again.

Stone frowned. "I never thought you were. Like I said, it was a knee-jerk reaction, my response to you." "Oh." She regarded him uncertainly.

"Didn't help either, your blindly taking the kind of stances you have in situations like Beth's. Granted you weren't encouraging her to wait it out, but you ignored the dangers. Or was ignorant of it, which is just as much of a hazard. We're not playing church here, Abby. We're dealing with people's lives. That's a responsibility I don't take lightly. Not one little bit."

She swallowed, nodded. "I understand. Thanks for sharing with me about...this other person."

"You're not the least little bit like her, either, in case that's what you're thinking." His look had gone probing, his brow slightly knit. "Is it?"

She stared dumbly back at him for just a second before shaking her head.

His frown deepened. "Hey, don't get me wrong, now. I still think there's a lot to be learned from the biblical Abigail's example. And I do believe you've got the right stuff." He reached out unexpectedly and stroked her cheek with one finger, a wry half smile tugging at his lips. "Only don't go taking up with any Nabals, hmm? Or I'm-a have to relieve you of him myself."

Her heart warmed, not so much at his words as the look in his eyes when he said them. Warm, tender and deadly serious. She'd never been on the receiving end of such protectiveness, such intensity. Not without being smothered in the bargain, anyway. It almost took her breath away.

She forced herself to shake off the fuzzy warmth stealing over her. Glanced over at the straw-colored crocheted bag slung over the back of a chair, wrestling a crazy impulse, then on a sudden decision reached for it.

Stone watched quizzically as Abigail opened up the drawstring bag that matched her mules and with a curiously determined look dug something out of it.

The papers she'd wrested from him a few minutes earlier.

He shook his head when she handed it to him, refusing to take it. "You don't have—"

"I want you to. It's not anything. Really."

He took it doubtfully. It couldn't be nothing, the way she'd grabbed it from him not even an hour ago, but she'd obviously changed her mind about him seeing it.

"It's a chat room I stumbled on some time ago, and it...just brought Beth to mind somehow. I thought it might be a starting point for our...discussions about Oasis."

"In that case..." He rolled the pages up into a loose scroll. "I'm going to save it for later, when I have more time." He stuck them in the empty napkin holder on top of the fridge. Folded his arms and regarded her steadily with his head cocked to one side. "So. How was Beth?"

She shrugged, a little irritably, it seemed. "I don't know. I haven't seen her yet. Wouldn't have wanted to have her death on my conscience."

He fought a satisfied smile. She still didn't get it about Beth, but she'd deferred to his wishes anyway. Interesting.

He consulted his watch. "Come somewhere with me?"

She regarded him warily. "Where?"

"My day job. Something I want to show you."

"Thought you worked evenings?"

"Day job being interpreted my bread-and-butter job. I love Grace, but they don't pay the bills."

"Where's your job again?"

"I move around. Tuesday nights it's the V & M Community Center."

Her mouth fell open. "Isn't that down in Overtown someplace?"

"Liberty City, actually."

"And they've got what...a handful fewer violent crimes a year than Overtown?"

"Forget it, then."

"What time?"

"In about..." He consulted his army watch. "Twenty, thirty minutes. I was just about to grab a shower and get over there."

"Make it thirty. I'll just run back home and change."

"You're fine as you are."

She'd already started toward the front door. "I'll be back before your hair dries."

Like she was going to walk into a Liberty City gathering with her white self dressed up like Easter Sunday and help him prove whatever point it was he was out to prove at her expense.

She changed into her most worn pair of jeans and a plain white T-shirt.

He was wearing loafers, khakis and crisp blue oxfords—tails in, sleeves down and buttoned up to just below his collar bone.

She bit back an acid comment. If it wasn't just like him and his contrary self. Flaunt Grace's business-attire dress code with tired jeans and rolled up sleeves and then flash his Sunday best for a bunch of battered women in an impoverished part of town.

His eyes flicked over her, but he said nothing as he let her into the passenger side of his feisty little indigo Mustang. It was fully loaded and well cared for and might as well have had a sticker on it saying, *Here I am, come carjack me.*

"Shouldn't we be taking your pick-up or something?" The black Ram had to have at least five or six years on the Mustang, complete with chips and dents and mud splashes on the fenders.

"Unless you want us to use mine." Her eyes contemplated her Beetle on the swale. The paint job was fairly new, complete with Tweety-esque eyelashes adorning the headlamps, but not enough to disguise the fact that it was an ancient relic that was barely alive.

He cast a baleful eye from the Bug to her and gave her a definite, "*No thanks.* Not the pickup either. Easier to squeeze into a parking space with this. Parking's at a premium down there, especially at this time. A lot of the garages close after hours."

He was going to stick them into the first vacant spot he could find on some dark, deserted street, was her first thought. Then, *Lord, I'm sorry I didn't check with You first.*

Not till he was holding the passenger door open for her did it occur to her that it wasn't too late to back out.

"Stone Patrick 101," Stone murmured as he turned the Mustang into the V & M's high-walled compound, "I never take a lady anyplace where I can't be reasonably assured of her safety."

Easy for him to say. He was used to traversing these parts, and looked it too. Sun-bronzed as any beach bum, that deep and abiding year-round tan, combined with those wayward locks that curled in every which direction but neat, raised interesting possibilities about his heritage. A passport of sorts into all kinds of cultural hinterlands.

By contrast, the only thing brown on her was her freckles, and she'd dare the most accomplished hairstylist to get her hair to hold a curl, or even a frizz.

He grimaced as he pulled up before a parking spot labeled *Compacts Only*. "As to whether I'll be able to get you out of here without having to lift you through the roof is another matter."

Parking was limited, all right, but given the lighting and the security guard on patrol, she could more than live with that.

Abigail watched Stone maneuver the Mustang into the sliver of space. He managed it in one well-executed attempt, the heel of his left hand on the wheel and his right arm braced along the back of her bucket seat.

He slipped the gear stick into park and threw her a wink. "I like your guts, though."

It was the closest she'd likely ever come to being called gutsy.

"Stone, my man." The uniformed bald giant greeted Stone with a hand slap and a mildly curious glance at Abigail.

"Hey, Mac," Stone returned easily without missing a step on his way to the elevator.

Abigail flashed a hasty smile in the man's direction as he tipped his hat at her and had to double up on her steps to get back in pace with Stone. "Can I get some information here?" she whispered as she hurried to keep up with him. "Like what exactly it is I'm going to?"

"Sorry, I wasn't thinking." He ushered her into the elevator and jabbed the button for the third floor. "I'm a couple minutes shy of late. The group is called Survivors. It's a court approved version of Oasis."

"The major difference being?"

"Almost all the participants were referred by the county court's domestic violence unit. A couple of them were ordered here after having their kids taken away from them."

"For abuse?"

He hesitated briefly before nodding. "Their participation

in the group is one of the conditions attached to their re-gaining custody of their kids."

❧

They sat on metal chairs in a tight semi-circle, herself and Stone and fifteen women. They were black, white, His-panic and a few things in between. And they wanted to know about Stone's bruised face.

Abigail held her breath and willed herself not to color.

Stone winked without skipping a beat and told them, "A door. For real." And then without giving them a chance to respond, he introduced Abigail and told them, "She's just here to observe and polish up her wallpaper act."

They tossed her a friendly collective greeting and seemed pretty genuine about it. A few of them looked from her to Stone with speculative gleams in their eyes. One of them had actually started to pose a question, a mischievous twin-kle in her eyes, when Stone cut her off with, "So then, that's enough about Abigail. With your consent we'll just forget she's here and be our usual boring, well-behaved selves."

That got him a few cracks of laughter, and there was a short season of nudging and winking and remembering when. It was the breathing space Abigail needed to get over the disconcerting reminder that God's grace was all that separated her from the rest of them. She took a second look at them, her vision unslanted now that she'd been knocked from her lofty little ledge and had joined them on the plains.

They were not exactly what she had expected, whatever that had been. Not to look at, anyway. A good percentage of them were dressed for the office, from soft and easy to starched and tailored, one in some kind of uniform. A cou-ple sported the kind of elaborate shiny coiffeurs favored by some of the more colorful sisters of Grace. Some wore blazers or silky knits over better looking jeans.

None of them were wearing T-shirts and Saturday-at-the-park jeans.

She could have killed him. If he'd been the one to suggest jeans and T-shirt. And if he hadn't specifically told her there was no need for her to change.

"We through exploring feelings yet, ladies?"Stone began, commanding the group's attention with his voice alone as he flipped through some pages on a clip board.

"We better," drawled one of the coiffured ladies with an expressive roll of her big eyes. "Everybody done had they say by now, and it was getting downright dangerous in here last week."

A consensual murmur echoed round the room.

"Right, then." Stone set the clipboard aside and reached under his chair for the thin stack of papers he'd collected from an office on the way in. "Today we're going to talk about moving on. Abigail..." He handed her the papers and indicated she should pass them around.

It was an anonymous poem entitled "This Heart."

> *Yesterday this heart was a flower*
> *whose home was a crack in the lifeless concrete*
> *to which it offered its fragrance,*
> *unaware it was trapped there till it*
> *was crushed*
> *beneath the feet of something that was not love.*
>
> *Today this heart is a seed*
> *yielded at the death of that flower*
> *and wind-blown into a fertile field,*
> *where it hides and awaits its season and*
> *is nourished*
> *beneath the reach of anything that is not love.*
>
> *Tomorrow this heart will again be a flower*
> *when that seed that was buried is God-kissed to*
> *life and reaches skyward, till out of the cold damp*
> *it springs and offers again its fragrance*
> *and flourishes*

beneath the sun of an eternal Love.

The reactions were varied and heartfelt and flowed spontaneously from every direction.

"Oh, I know I'm gonna love again."

"I don't know when I'll ever trust another man."

"It'll be a while, but I'll get there. Right now, it's just me and Jesus, baby."

"I got my kids to think of now. No way I'm gonna let him near them again."

"I will eventually, I guess, but my mind's just not there yet."

"He called me up and wanted to talk."

"I know what I'd tell mine if he ever had the nerve."

"He try to start that mess with me, I got my caller ID and my camera ready. Click, click, click. Here you go, Judge."

"Mara, you okay?"

"She cryin' again?"

"Look like it."

A box of tissue materialized from somewhere, and they passed it down to one end of the semicircle to the woman whose face was buried in her own lap, her shoulders shaking.

"It gets better from here, girlfriend," the woman next to her soothed, rubbing her back.

"And don't you be worrying bout them kids. It'll only be a while longer. Meantime, God ain't gonna let nothing happen to them. You gotta believe that."

Mara straightened slowly, pushing back her long dark hair and dabbing at her eyes. She was startlingly pretty underneath all the ruined make up and despite her puffy eyes. Might have been stunning before she developed those purple shadows under her eyes and lost whatever sparkle God had put in them. Her clothes definitely hadn't come out of a bargain bin, either.

She started apologizing for dropping out on them, and the others hastened to reassure her.

"You ain't got nothing to be sorry 'bout, girl. We all of us in here done did our share of crying, and some's got to cry longer than some, is all."

"Want to talk now, Mara?" Stone asked with a gentleness that sent a peculiar quiver through Abigail. He'd certainly never talked that way to her before.

Mara shook her head...and immediately began talking anyway, the words pouring out in a rush and tripping over themselves like kids let out of school.

They all listened, with varying degrees of sympathy and resignation, as she rambled in circles around issues they'd apparently already dealt with in previous sessions. Another product of a manipulative husband who had systematically destroyed her self-confidence and then tried to convince her and the court that she was mentally unstable.

Through it all, Stone's face registered attentiveness, empathy and nothing resembling impatience or censure as he carefully maintained eye contact with Mara, occasionally coaxing her in one direction or another but always listening. It was a side of him she'd rarely seen, Abigail realized with a pang. Just as well, too. She could easily become addicted to that kind of handling.

"It's just so unfair, you know," Mara said finally, winding down with a sniff. "Everybody believes him because of who he is, and even though he's the abuser, he gets to see the kids whenever he wants, and I know his visits aren't being supervised either."

Peaches snorted. "Supervised by who? His own mom? Get real."

"Do you believe they're in danger, Mara?" Stone asked evenly.

"No, but they're not with me, either, and I have to have supervised visits. When I visit, they follow the judge's orders to the letter. They don't leave me alone with them for five minutes...me, their mother. And they do it just to humiliate me."

"I know that must be hurtful. Would you rather they were in a foster home where you'd both get equal treatment?"

"W—I—no! Of course not!"

The others started twittering, then adding their two cents worth.

"Well then, girl, you better learn to live with it."

"Won't be forever, and you can get your own back once they're back with you."

"Or," Stone interjected quietly, "you could remember your pledge to put the children's welfare first. That includes not trying to alienate them from people they care about and who care about them."

"I guess," Mara conceded with a sigh. "Besides which, I refuse to be brought down to their level, them and the others, and end up being just like them." She shuddered. "God forbid."

The door opened, and a young Asian woman put her head round the door. "Excuse me, what is this place, please?"

Latrice snickered. "If you don't know, you in the wrong place, lady."

"Tell us which room it is you're trying to find," Stone suggested.

"Um…I'm not, really. I was just looking for somewhere to sit. I dropped a couple of kids off upstairs, and I—"

Josephine raised one perfectly penciled eyebrow at her. "If your kids in Survivor Junior, then this is the group you're looking for, honey. We're the Survivors, huh ladies?"

A cheer went up around the room, and the newcomer's look grew uncertain.

"What's your name?" Stone asked the young woman, consulting his roster.

"Yin, but I'm not…they not my kids or anything. I just brought them for my fiancé's Mom. They staying with her, but today she not able to bring them."

"So where they momma?" Josephine broke in. "Cause she need to be in here too."

"Yah…well, she's in a…mental facility, you know?"

A collective *Ooh*, then a mellowing.

"There but for the grace of God..."

"Y'know?"

They ended up inviting her to join them.

Stone pulled up a chair for her. "Yin, is it? Or Kay?"

She followed Stone's gaze to her visitor name tag and shook her head. "My initials. For Kei-An Yin. You can call me Kei." She accepted the seat thankfully but said little after that.

"You take walk-ins like Kei just like that?" Abigail asked Stone on the way down in the elevator. Having been the last to leave, they had the elevator to themselves.

"Not supposed to. But she needs to be in there. She's on the verge of some kind of crisis herself."

"How'd you know?"

"Her eyes. Don't ask me what. It's hard to explain. You'll learn to recognize the signs too after you've worked long enough with abused women." The elevator opened at the ground floor, and he guided her out ahead of him with a hand cupping her elbow. "I'm kind of hoping she'll come back. She stick around long enough she might see herself reflected in one or the other of the others' situation. It's happened before."

He tugged her gently back to the right as she headed left of the elevator, then slid his hand up her arm and across her shoulder to keep her in step with him. "Kinda what happened with Mara."

"Mara was a walk-in?" she asked, trying to concentrate on his words and not the musky warmth of him.

"Acted like it at first. Sat through the first couple of sessions with her chin up and her mouth zipped. Didn't see why she had to be there. Denial. Till she heard Peaches' story. She's been crying ever since."

He waved at the security guard, held the door open for her, and matched his steps to hers again as they stepped out into the balmy night air.

"Who's the *them* she was talking about? Not her in-laws. The *others*, she called them."

"Her church people."

"Her *church*? But...well, is she telling the truth about him or not?"

"I'm not there to form opinions, but I think she is, yes. So did the judge, obviously. He did grant a restraining order."

"Then why'd her church people not—"

"Cause it's their pastor she's giving against."

"Their *what*?" She sank into the passenger seat as he held the door open for her. "The husband who beat her? A pastor? Of *what* kind of church?"

"One much like ours. And a fairly popular one, I might add. You'd probably recognize the name if I told it to you, but I won't."

She digested that in stunned silence while he made his way round to the driver's side, feeling slightly sick to her stomach as she revisited Mara's story in the light of what she now knew.

"Like I've said before," he said as he slid in beside her. "Abusers come in all shapes, sizes and colors, from all walks of life and all faiths, even ours."

She looked at him. "Know what? She might not be the only Christian in there, either. The way some of them talk, you'd almost think they were."

"Ten of the fifteen of them are. We don't keep those kinds of records, you understand, but I do my own mental tallies, for my own purposes. Some of them share their faith openly in the group, as you saw for yourself."

More openly than some of the most ardent church goers she knew.

"Couple of them will say things to me outside the group—in the elevator, parking lot, what not. I've counted ten so far. Half of those have Christian husbands, two of them ministers."

She felt her jaw go slack. "I worse can't see them abusing their kids. I mean——"

"They didn't, as far as anybody knows."

"So why—"

"Because they failed to protect their children from the trauma of having to witness their own mother's abuse. In Florida, that's child abuse and grounds for your kids being taken from you."

Abigail swallowed. "Corey...Beth's little boy..."

"I know, I've met him." He buckled his seatbelt and paused with his hand on the ignition switch to send her an unsmiling look. "Think we can talk now about Beth?"

10

Abigail cast an uneasy glance around them as they sped past the I-95 turnoff. Just as they'd approached it, Stone had glanced at his watch, switched lanes suddenly and kept going. She definitely didn't remember them traveling this far on 441 on the way down.

What was more, it was a different 441 from the segment she was used to in Broward County. It was dark and deserted, and it was the home of the smash-and-grab epidemic that had terrorized tourists a decade before. Her and Stone not being tourists didn't comfort her any. Any strange face that looked as wary and out of place as hers probably did was an immediate target.

"Where's this?" she asked, trying not to sound as nervous as she felt.

"Gimme a sec." He'd punched a number on his cell phone and had it to his ear.

"Hey, I got your message, but I...uh...was tied up, and then I had work...Now too late?...He is?...See you in five, then...more like three. I'm right near Sixty-second and Seventh."

"Where are we going?" Abigail asked as he slipped the phone back into his breast pocket. She wasn't sure she wanted to be disembarking anywhere that was within three minutes of the deserted commercial district they were passing through now.

For answer, he turned east on Martin Luther King Jr. Boulevard. Two quick turns later and they found themselves in a residential district. It was an old neighborhood and one with more concrete than she was used to seeing in residential South Florida, but with a sad, determined kind of dignity about its whitewashed doll-sized houses and swept yards.

One house stood out from the rest, with mildewed walls and scraggly weeds growing up out of cracks in the concrete. The house that Stone pulled up directly across from. He jerked his chin in its direction as he thrust the gear stick into park.

"That's Beth and Leo's place there."

Abigail stared at it in shock, unable to picture Beth living there. Beth had come from a family of modest means, but they'd always made the best of what they had. Her mother had to have been heartbroken to know what her daughter's living standard had been reduced to...assuming her mother had ever been allowed to come there, or even knew where her daughter lived. Who knows what part heartbreak had paid in her sudden death less than a year into Beth's marriage.

Stone nodded in the direction of the house they were parked in front of. "Couple over here's been keeping Corey since Beth went to hospital. They're the ones who called me when it happened—the wife, anyway. She called earlier wanting to see me." He sent her a small smile. "But the lure of that green juice was too strong for me to resist."

"Yeah right. That her?"

A young woman had opened the front door a crack and was peering out at them. Stone raised a hand in greeting, and she came out onto the tiny porch.

She was a pretty Latino with waist-length hair and wouldn't have had any problem competing with Abigail's green juice if she hadn't been so obviously spoken for. She was very pregnant, as many as eight or nine months, was Abigail's guess, with a sleepy toddler balanced on her almost non-existent hip.

"Hal*lo*, Abi*gail*," she lilted with a flash of even white teeth when Stone introduced them.

Her cheerfulness was infectious. A smile tugged at Abigail's mouth. "Hi, Ileana,"

"Sorry I can't ask you both in, but my husband—"

"No problem," Stone assured her. "I've got to get this young lady home before too long anyway. What's up?"

Ileana hitched her drowsy burden higher up on her hip and drew a deep breath. "First thing I wanted to tell you is—" She cast a look behind her into the open doorway before continuing, "—that little boy needs help. I'm no specialist, but I have three kids, and I'm telling you, he's a ways behind normal."

Stone frowned. "How so?"

"He doesn't respond at all or show any sign he even understands. I think maybe he's autistic or something. My husband thinks it's emotional, and he is not happy one little bit. He's already got his own issues with the police, see, and he don't want nobody saying little from this he had anything to do with whatever's wrong with someone else's kid. Me neither, cause whatever else he is, he is not a child abuser."

Stone nodded. "I hear you."

"Which brings me to the second thing I want to tell you: I really want to help little Corey. My heart goes out to him, you know? But I don't know how much longer I can keep him." She rubbed her belly ruefully. "Another three weeks or so and I really won't have the room."

"I understand, Ileana, and I haven't forgotten about you or Corey. I just don't want the authorities involved if I can help it. Give me a few more days, and if I don't come up with something by then, I'll make other arrangements, I promise. If I even have to take him myself."

"He can stay by me till Beth comes out," Abigail offered immediately. "It wouldn't be a problem." She'd likely have been the person Beth would turn to at a time like this if the last four years of separation hadn't happened.

They both seemed to hesitate, Ileana giving Stone an odd look.

"Really," Abigail insisted, warming to the idea. There was space enough at her father's house, and how much trouble could one lost little four-year-old boy be? "I could take him to work with me, and—"

"I'll take you up on that if nothing else works out," Stone interrupted smoothly. "But we don't want to move him around more than we have to."

"Well, how long is Beth going to be in there, come to think of it? And why would the authorities have to be involved, anyway?"

Stone leveled a closed look at her. "We'll talk later."

Abigail felt a stab of anxiety. "She *is* just in there for observation, isn't she?"

"*Later*, I said." His eyes held hers with a flash of impatience that whispered *shut up*.

She looked over at Ileana, whose expression had gone stoic, and clamped down on her questions.

Ileana raised a shoulder, looking apologetic. "I wish I could help out some more, Stone, but I really can't keep h—"

"Hey, Spidey, what's up?" Stone cut in, the volume of his voice pointedly drowning out Ileana's, and they followed his gaze to the open doorway where a little boy in Spiderman pajamas had just shuffled up.

He was beautiful, with big dark eyes and glossy dark hair that didn't immediately put Abigail in mind of either Leo or Beth.

He looked sorely in need of a good hug.

"Hey, buddy. Remember me?" Stone held his arms out to him and waited for him to choose whether to use them or not.

Corey remained where he was, his expression cautious.

Ileana cleared her throat. "I think maybe what he's trying to tell you is that girls hug, boys shake hands." She gave Corey's back a gentle rub. "And you most definitely are a little boy, eh *papito*?"

Corey didn't so much as nod, his body stiff as a board beneath the touch of her hand. Ileana sent Stone a look that said, *See?* Stone ignored it.

"Oh yeah? Well, watch this." The next second, Stone

had swallowed Corey up in a hug that swept him clear off his feet. "You gonna call me a girl now, huh?" he growled, his fingers playing delicately up and down Corey's rib cage. "Huh? *Huh?*"

Corey froze at first, his expression almost comical with shock. Abigail held her breath. Stone adjusted his aim lower, then higher. Corey gasped, wriggled and dissolved helplessly into giggles.

Abigail released her breath.

Over the top of Corey's head, Stone mouthed, *"Autistic my foot."*

"He's selectively mute, would be my guess," Stone told her as they buckled themselves back into their seats. "Won't know for sure till he's properly evaluated, but I'd say what's going on with him is almost all his mommy and daddy's doing."

"When I saw him at Oasis I just assumed he was...you know...slow, him being a preemie and all that."

"He's had three years to catch up. They're usually three-quarter way there by then."

Abigail shook her head. "I just never imagined..."

"We usually don't. Especially not in the church. We'd sooner believe the devil's in the kitchen corner hatching some elaborate scheme against our kids than accept we're doing a more than adequate job of messing them up ourselves. Fortunately for Corey, he's still young. Young enough to possibly escape any lasting effects."

"He seems pretty smart too. I'm not sure how I know, but I feel so."

"His eyes. I'd say above average intelligence. He just needs a stable environment to thrive in and time to heal." He checked his rearview mirror and eased out into the road. "I'm going to see to it he gets it, too," he muttered grimly as they drove off. "Even if I have to comb the entire United States to do it and interview every single person with the name Ramsey or Reid. Starting with Beth."

Abigail frowned. She knew Beth had been Reid before she married Leo, but that didn't explain what he'd just said, or why he and Ileana were acting as if Corey was homeless.

Didn't explain either why, in addition to being issued a gag order concerning her own friend, she'd had her offer to help out with that friend's child rebuffed without the slightest consideration. And who was this Ileana, anyway, that made her so much more trustworthy than she was?

"I'd appreciate it if you'd go with me to see Beth sometime soon," she said stiffly. "Or tell me whatever it is I need to know before I can go by myself."

She didn't see what there was for them to talk about, anyway. He had to know by now she had no intention of going to visit Beth without his say so. Even when she'd slammed out of his house yesterday, she'd been driven more by hurt and frustration than by defiance. She was even less likely to flout his wishes now that he'd given her a glimpse into the lives of women in situations similar to Beth's, women who undoubtedly were benefiting from his guidance.

"I'd have taken you tonight," he surprised her by saying, his voice even. "But we'd have caught maybe five, ten minutes max of visiting hours. It's not going to be enough."

Enough for what? Interviewing Beth along with all of her and Leo's family? What for? "So...what exactly do you plan on saying to her?"

"That we love her and will be there for her every step of the way. And that I'm giving her an ultimatum. Either she turns Corey over to a friend or relative who can care for him till she's got her act together—"

"B-but she's not the one—"

"Abby."

"I'm not arguing. I'm just—"

"The court won't make that kind of distinction once they've determined there's been abuse. Did you learn anything at all from tonight?"

Of course she had. But this was Beth they were talking about, her friend, her sister, however estranged. Not some case study among a trillion others like hers.

"So...she turns Corey over or else what?" she asked tightly.

"Or else I'll personally see to it she winds up in a mandatory program like Survivors. And that time she'll have zero control over where Corey goes." His voice was as cold as it had been warm only seconds ago.

"You mean it."

"I don't make idle threats. There are three sides to this particular story, Abby, and too often we only consider two of them. Kids don't deserve to be hurt by circumstances they aren't responsible for and have no control over."

He changed gears just then, and there was a controlled violence in the movement that caught her attention. Her gaze traveled down the length of his arm to the hand on the gear stick and fastened there.

She knew those hands pretty well, long and shapely and the same warm brown as the rest of him. They drew attention to themselves because they fidgeted when he was agitated, as he often was in his dealings with her, twirling his pen, drumming the desk, raking his hair, fingering his shirt buttons. On the drive down to the V & M, she'd been mildly fascinated by the strength that allowed him to maneuver the stick with just two fingers.

He was gripping it now with all five, hard. He was angry. Corey's situation was personal for him. He'd been through something himself as a child, she knew. Her father had hinted at it, and his explosive reaction to Beth's situation confirmed it.

But the children involved were not the only victims in situations like Beth's. A person didn't have to have gone through it personally like Stone had to realize that much.

She said softly, cautiously, "Believe it or not, women sometimes don't have much control over their circumstances, either. Or at least, they don't know that they do."

He shot a look at her. "That's why there've been support

systems put in place for them. Awareness is up, and we've come a ways in recent years. They have a choice now. I'm not saying it's an easy one, but it's got to be better than staying in the mess and subjecting your kids to all manner of—"

"But Corey's no longer exposed to that, don't you see? With the restraining order—"

"*What* restraining order? Leo's been sneaking in through her window on an almost nightly basis...*with* her help," he added at Abigail's outraged gasp.

Bolstered no doubt by *her* encouragement to confront. No wonder Stone had all but banished her from Oasis. She sent him a cautious glance. His flash of anger had given way to brooding.

"They're both treating that restraining order like a joke," he muttered. "Playing Romeo and Juliet by night and fighting World War III by day. And don't even know it half the time when Corey's cowering out on the front porch with his hands over his ears. But Ileana's seen him. Been. For months. And she swears the next time it happens she's going to call Child Protective Services."

"Would she?"

"Oh yes, she would. In fact, she says she might not wait for it to happen again. She's feeling like she'll make a phone call the first time she sees Leo sneaking in there again, which will probably be the first night Beth is home. That's why she offered to keep Corey. She figures it's the least she can do till I can work something else out for him."

"So it's already been decided...between you and her." She couldn't help a jealous pang, not only at having been left squarely out of the loop, but at knowing Stone had been more comfortable collaborating with a stranger than with her.

"What other choice do we have? Tell me that." He had obviously misread her glum silence.

Nor was she eager to set him straight. "I'm not saying that you do. But you might have tried involving me. I happen to still care about Beth. Four years of silence between us hasn't changed that."

"I don't want you involved in it," he said with grim finality.

Swallowing the hurt of that rejection, she demanded, "So what...you don't trust me not to...to..."

"I don't trust *me*. Not you, Abigail, me."

Her mouth dropped. "Don't trust you to..."

"To not rearrange Leo's face if he so much as looks at you funny once he finds out you're involved."

"Oh." Words failed her after that.

"Trust me, it's better this way. Ileana is willing, and she won't take any nonsense from Leo either, neither her nor her husband. Leo wouldn't even dare approach them, especially knowing that they know all they do. But I can see him trying to intimidate you, and believe me..."

He stopped, drew a steadying breath and changed directions. *"She* is the one who needs to be confronted. Beth. And what she needs to face up to is not all the hurts she's been through—that too—but she needs to admit her own weakness, be it only an addiction to her jerk of a husband—"

"You're advocating divorce." She couldn't believe he was the same man who had exhibited such sensitivity and objectivity while maintaining control of fifteen volatile women.

"I'm suggesting their relationship will never be healthy till they're cured of their co-dependency."

"That's a secular term that has no basis in scrip—"

"Don't!" She jumped as his open palm slammed the hub of the steering wheel, inadvertently blasting the horn and eliciting an upraised single digit from the driver ahead of them. "Don't *talk* to me about—" He bit off the rest and struggled visibly for control, while she looked on, wide eyed. This was *not* the man she'd watched in action at Survivors.

11

"Time out," Stone muttered succinctly, and Abigail nodded a hasty agreement.

If he asked her, a single timeout wasn't going to do it. There was something amiss with his game plan, and he probably needed to call the game and schedule an all-night huddle in his prayer closet.

"I'm sorry," he said suddenly two stoplights later.

"No problem."

"It *is* a problem. A big problem." He muttered it almost to himself, his expression brooding. "Look at me." She raised startled eyes to his at the abrupt command and allowed his stormy gaze to probe hers.

A long few seconds later, he asked tensely, "Did I scare you?"

She frowned. "What?"

"Just now. Back there. Did I scare you? Don't lie to me."

"I *don't* lie! Not even to avoid having my head bitten off by bull-headed counselors."

He smiled mirthlessly. "That's an oxymoron if ever I heard one." He slammed into first as the light changed, and Abigail braced a hand against the dashboard as the car shot forward.

"Ought to have put myself on furlough, is what," he muttered. "Before I started threatening you with one."

Abigail squirmed inwardly. "Well, I—"

"I'm sorry for the way I've been handling things at Oasis," he said abruptly.

"That's all r—"

"Stop *doing* that."

She blinked at him. "Doing what?"

"Stifling my apology. It's not all right. Not all right at all. Blowing my fuse over every little thing instead of trying to talk things out rationally."

"You did try a couple of times," she reminded him dryly.

"Yeah, before blowing my fuse again." He blew out a breath. "I'll make more of an effort in the future."

"And I'll try not to make it so hard for you."

He shot her an irritated look. "Why is it that whenever a person gets round to taking responsibility for their actions you start trying to justify them?"

Abigail stared at him.

Things will never be any better between us till you learn to take responsibility for your own failings, Abigail. I might not be perfect, but God knows my heart, and He knows what a stumbling block you've been.

"Abigail." Stone's prod was cautious.

Abigail shook off the stray memory. "Um...yes?"

"You're staring at me awful strange. Something wrong with what I said?"

"Uh...no. Not really." She sucked in a deep breath and fought against the urge stirring somewhere deep inside. Felt it push to the surface and finally clamped a hand over her mouth. And giggled anyway.

"I wrote Abigail."

Crystal digested her sister's tentative confession in silence for a moment, coiling and uncoiling the phone cord around her forefinger.

"I felt it was the right thing to do."

Crystal decided to keep her initial reaction to herself, her tone noncommittal as she prompted, "And?"

"I didn't send it yet. Decided to sleep on it a few days. Checked my contact list, though, at all the most likely times, to see if she was on. She wasn't."

"Well, considering it's Abigail we're talking about, you ought to try checking at a few of the most unlikely times."

"Does that mean you're softening up towards her after all?"

"It means she's an insomniac who surfs the web at night and would welcome a chat with anyone crazy enough to want one in the wee hours of the night."

"I'm not capable of that kind of depravity, especially in my condition."

Back at his place, Stone parked, saw Abigail into her car and then leaned up against it gazing down at—she could swear—her mouth.

"I'm hungry," he announced abruptly. "And not for any of that green juice, either."

She was just about to strangle on her own breath when his eyes shifted from her mouth and held hers. "Want a burger or something? You didn't have a chance to eat, either, did you?"

She shook her head. "No, but my appetite's gone to bed this late at night."

"It's nine o'clock."

"It's late for *me*, okay?" She felt the butterflies in her tummy that his warm gaze had generated begin to evaporate and an old familiar burning take their place. "I'm an early riser," she added tightly. "I'm up before dawn when you're still pushing toward REM sleep. And it's not a crime."

"*Easy*. What did I say?"

Too much. But he wasn't to have known that. She bit her lip and looked down at her lap. "Sorry, I didn't mean to be touchy."

"No prob." He straightened. "Catch you later."

She felt instantly bereft. "I...wouldn't mind following you for your burger."

"Nah, I'll grab something inside. It's the company I was

after more than anything else."

She couldn't have felt any worse. "I don't look like I'm falling asleep, do I?"

The wry twist of his mouth said he begged to differ.

"I *could* manage a milk shake." Pathetic. And now she'd gone and made herself look desperate.

He was gentleman enough to pretend not to notice, his gaze inscrutable as it lingered on her for a space. He was paying her the courtesy of appearing to reconsider, but she knew even before he straightened up that he'd already moved on and the moment was lost to her.

She swallowed her disappointment and tried to convince herself there'd be a next time and that it hardly mattered to her anyway, and started when his hand reached inside her half open window for the safety knob.

"Move over," he murmured, and opened the door.

12

I s this where you catch the Number Six?" Virginia called out to the group waiting up ahead.

They were deep in conversation. Five or six pairs of eyes glanced at her and then away, barely missing a beat.

"Where is it you want to go, ma'am?" a woman's voice asked behind her.

Virginia turned thankfully toward it. "Please, I'm trying to get to the North Miami Beach Library."

"Wrong way, hon. Library's back this way." There was something reassuring about that throat-deep voice, even if she did talk a little funny. She knew this woman. Or did she? She peered more closely at her. She was tall and bosomy and about the same shade of creamed cocoa as Mama Kay, though nowhere near as good looking. "Come on, I show you," she offered in her easy, two-toned way.

"Oh, thank you so very much." Mama Kay or not, she was a godsend. Virginia went with her in the opposite direction, just as raucous laughter erupted from the group behind them.

"Look at what you're doing," Stone said suddenly after they were seated at a stone table outside a little burger joint in North Miami Beach.

Abigail cast a hasty glance downward. She hadn't spilled anything. Her fingers swiped her chin and came away clean.

"I know. You haven't the first clue what I'm talking about. Far as you can see, you're just drinking a vanilla malt shake."

"A very large one, yes."

He smiled. "Are you, though? Technically, your mouth is sipping at it, and your throat is passing it on to your stomach. And look at your hands."

She looked. One was holding the cup, and the other guiding the straw to her lips.

"You've got your fingers in front and your thumb in back, and together they've got a good grip on the cup. Where'd you learn to do that?"

She chuckled. She had an idea where he was going now, but he was so serious, so philosophical about it. "My brain told me."

"Told *you*? Your hands, you mean. Uh-oh. Might need to have a discussion about what makes you you."

"Haven't given much thought to it." Not lately, anyway. "I get hungry, I invite myself to supper, I drink a milk shake. All of me. All of me is happy about it when all is said and done."

"Just like that, huh?"

"No books, seminars, contract."

He smiled. "Or support groups. And they manage it without competing with each other."

Something moved inside her. "Or any of them acting like they've ceased to exist."

"They're interdependent. Different from what's meant today when we talk about codependency."

"Oh."

"Understanding that is the first step back to normalcy in a relationship like Beth and Leo's. If normalcy is attainable."

He paused as if to assess her reaction to that before going on.

"I know my possibility thinking's on the minus end of the spectrum right now. But I'm dealing with reality here, Abby. And an innocent child's life. And that's why we're going to confront Beth." He held her gaze. "You and I."

She liked the sound of the last part. She liked the way he

looked at her when he said it even better. Those were not the same contemptuous near-black eyes that had bored into hers the day before when he accused her of being a danger to Beth and ordered her to keep her distance.

They finished eating in companionable silence. Or at least, he finished wolfing down his burger and fries, and she labored her way valiantly through half of the oversized shake he'd ordered her.

She watched as he scrunched up the foil wrapping for his burger and shot a three-pointer with it into the trash can across the aisle, then sat back in his seat looking a whole lot mellower. She'd keep in mind in future that he needed to be fed before being asked to tackle any of life's major issues.

She abandoned her struggle with her milk shake, accepting defeat. Propped her elbows on the stone table, chin resting on the backs of her interlaced fingers, and regarded him with her head tilted to one side. "Why aren't you married?"

He smiled, a slow, warm smile that radiated from somewhere within and creased the corners of his eyes. After a steady diet of humorless smirks, she was spellbound.

"Are you paying me a compliment, Abigail?"

She felt her insides warm and shrugged in an effort to appear offhand. "If that is how you want to take it. Why *aren't* you?"

He thought. "I never felt ready. Before I came to Christ, there was no real urgency...if you get my drift."

She felt her face warm and disciplined herself to go on meeting his eyes.

There was only serious reflection in them as he said, "The couple of times I actually thought about it I came up with a whole bunch of cons and not a lot of pros."

"And now?"

"Now? Waiting for the right woman, I guess."

Like in which century? There were close to a hundred eligible women right there where he worshipped, and that was just for starters.

"Got my eye on somebody, actually. But she's not ready."

Something stabbed Abigail low in her gut. Why she should be put out to learn he was interested in someone, she didn't know. There were enough of them interested in him. She was the only one fighting and pulling against him all the time.

She wondered what the rare paragon who'd succeeded in snagging his interest was like. Probably some nice, docile little miss who said *Yes, Stone* and *No, Stone* and who'd never do anything to upset his migraine.

She swallowed, then cleared her throat. "As in not saved, you mean?" she croaked and realized with another stab that she was hoping he'd say yes.

He gave her a dry look. "As in not up for discussion. So don't even try."

"I wasn't—" *Liar.* She fell silent.

"To be honest, I'm still a little wary. The divorce statistics in the church aren't any more encouraging than they are out of it."

She nodded. "Forty-nine percent, or thereabouts."

"Meanwhile, the Lord was showing me that there were a lot of broken marriages out there that have neither been fixed nor trashed and that there aren't too many people willing or able to minister to them."

"Not too many people they'd let minister to them."

"Precisely. The unhappily married feel like misfits among the so-called happily married...and don't know that half the smiling faces they see in church got painted on on the way to service. After a while, they start to drift from the church, and once they do they tend to lose their commitment to doing things God's way."

He reached for her milk shake. She relinquished it to him and watched while he took a sip.

He grimaced at its sweetness and set it back down in front of her. "I'd finally found my niche. In the church, anyway."

And she'd done her best to dislodge him from it.

"Your father caught on real quick. Told me there was no better person to get involved with broken marriages than someone who's suffered from the effects of one. And then he took me to the Word and made sure I understood what it takes to make or break a marriage."

"Your parents divorced?"

"Nope. I wished all the time that they would have." He said it quietly, almost flatly, but not enough to hide the fact that it was coming from somewhere deep inside.

"Fought all the time?" She held her breath, conscious that she was approaching sacred ground.

He shook his head. "Mostly he ranted and she placated. When that didn't help she started to retreat. It helped her cope, but it left me stranded in no man's land."

"She shut you out?"

"Not intentionally. She wasn't seeing him in me or any-thing like that. She just...wasn't there. Found religion and buried herself deep in the rubble of the denial-of-your-trials movement. There were times I acted up just to confound her positive-confession theories. Pretty much immunized me against God. Till your Dad succeeded in infecting me, that is."

"So...that's how you wound up in marriage counseling."

"I don't do marriage counseling. I do marriage recovery. Related but different."

"You mean divorce recovery."

"I mean marriage recovery." He regarded her bleakly. "How many of the women in Oasis are actually divorced, or even thinking about it?"

"You think they should. Like you did your parents." She stifled a yawn that surfaced from nowhere.

"I think they ought to get their act together. For their sakes and their kids'. And before they're beyond help." He got to his feet. "Come, let's go. You're falling asleep."

She opened her mouth to fire off a denial and just as quickly realized he hadn't meant it as an indictment. She went along thankfully with him and treated him to a long, measuring look as he unlocked the passenger door for her.

Back at his place, he left the engine idling for her and came round to her side to help her out. "It's late. I'll drive behind you. Wasn't thinking straight, or I'd have picked you up."

"You didn't have time. I turned up on your doorstep unannounced and ate up your time, remember? Tonight wasn't exactly planned."

"I'm glad it happened, though." His mouth twitched. "Even though I wound up scaring you half to death."

She didn't bother arguing the point. He knew very well he hadn't scared her, but it obviously fueled some internal coping mechanism of his to continue maintaining otherwise.

"I'm glad too," she whispered. For a whole lot of reasons other than Beth. Not least of which was the fact that she'd added about ten years to her understanding of him in just one night.

He cast a frowning glance over her car. "You're probably going to tell me to mind my own business, but I'm going to ask anyway. Why on *earth* are you rattling around in this contraption?"

And exactly what kind of cheapskate was your husband? was probably what he really wanted to ask.

"I like it," she told him smoothly. "It's from my college days. And it's a classic. The only reason I ever gave it up was because I didn't want to disgrace my husband. And now that's no longer an issue..."

He leveled a narrowed gaze on her but said nothing. Probably decided she was a nut case, as had all the others who didn't have the nerve like him to come right out and ask about her car.

She fought a smile as he held the door patiently while she got in. Watched him shut it and shake it to make sure it was securely locked. It was a long time since anyone had fussed that way over her. For all his rough ways, he had some quaint ideas about handling women—those he took out, anyway.

Her father had raised her with all kinds of notions of

what kind of courtesies to expect from a man, but she'd given up early on a few of the old-fashioned ones. Now here she was at the advanced age of thirty-one, wondering what it must be like to go out on a real date with a Neanderthal who opened doors for her and seated her first and walked her to her door...

Till it came time for him to haul her off by the hair to his office and give her what-for for daring to cross him.

"What's so funny?" he growled, his narrowed eyes suspicious.

She shook her head. She hadn't even realized she was laughing.

> **jojo317:** to pierce or not to pierce, that is the question
>
> **Duchess:** give it up jo, nobody cares anymore. sarah we're going to bayside l8tr, just us girls. coming?
>
> **Sarah:** To do what?
>
> **Duchess:** figure it out when we get there, girlfriend
>
> **Sarah:** So what am I supposed to tell my husband?
>
> **Spunky:** that u r going to go tour with your gfs
>
> **Sarah:** Yes, but for what?
>
> **jojo317:** mostly to break the tenth commandment (lori got some great shoes at steins) and to check out some guys while we're at it
>
> **Sarah:** Really, must we be so sophomoric?
>
> **Spunky:** well hello, thats what we r, remember?
>
> **jojo317:** u r beginning to sound just like your hubby sarah
>
> **Sarah:** Something wrong with that?
>
> **Kay:** Consider it a compliment, Sarah. Just don't expect them to know what two people becoming one is all about.
>
> **Duchess:** hey tell us, we r all ears
>
> **jojo317:** throw in a few pix, we'll pop some corn

Duchess: yeah, spare poor pastor the agony of having to take us thru premarital counseling

Kay: My short version is—just imagine you wake up one day and half of you is missing.

Duchess: lol, not the better half, let's hope

Sarah: Be serious guys.

Kay: Sarah, if you want we can continue this discussion on our own. They're not really ready for this.

Spunky: well xcuse me while half of me hop along on one leg to the mall. c ya

Duchess: who knows, maybe we'll meet us some eligible spare parts while we r out there coveting the mannequins garments. ta-ta

jojo317: l8tr

Sarah: I'm beginning to understand what pastor means about having to walk alone, Kay.

Kay: Sometimes it means separating yourselves even from other Christians. I went through the same thing years ago, a few months into my marriage. I believe I have a good ten years or so on you.

Sarah: Lately I feel like I've already begun that separation process.

Kay: Don't fight it, Sarah. Let it happen. There's a sifting that has to happen if we're going to get into that place where we can hear God's voice above the din of all the others.

Sarah: You think that is what is happening to us now, all of us?

Kay: To you, certainly, and to me. We need to flow with it. Sooner or later it'll get to the point where you're faced with a decision to cut some things loose. It might hurt, but God will give you the strength. Just look to Him for guidance. And don't expect folks to understand. God's will for our lives doesn't always make sense to others. The important thing is to make sure you're listening to His voice and not theirs.

Sarah: I will. I'm glad He gave me you, Kay. I've learned so much from you, and I don't think I could make some of the choices I'm going to have to alone.

Kay: Stay strong, and just rememb

Sarah: Remember what?

Sarah: You there?????

Sarah: Hellooooooo?

Stone put down the papers he'd been reading from and reached for the phone on the sofa table behind him, then sat for a moment with it dangling between his knees, his eyes fixed sightlessly on the tiles below.

Father, there's a piece of her heart buried in here somewhere, and she's trying to trust me with it. Help me not to trample on it.

13

Abigail answered after the third ring, triggering a peculiar flutter in Stone's chest region at the breathy sound of her voice. She'd been running, or exercising, or else just hurrying to get to the phone. Because she suspected it was him? Yeah right.

"They've got extended visiting hours on the weekend," he told her without preamble. "How soon could you make it?"

"Half hour," she answered without hesitation.

"I'll come get you."

"Why, when you're so much closer to the hospital? And we'll be back before dark, so you won't have to follow me all the way up here."

"Did you hear me complaining?"

"Thirty minutes."

She made it in fifty, in white capris and a coral sleeveless blouse and her damp hair in a French braid. And stared slack jawed at his bare feet and rumpled hair as he let her in.

"Sorry, I fell asleep. Was up earlier than I usually am on a Saturday."

The sofa still bore his imprint...along with the pages she'd given him days ago. Her eyes registered the realization that he hadn't moved from the sofa since calling her.

"Don't flip." He glanced at his watch. "We've got an hour and a half to go."

"Gee, thanks. I could have taken the time to dry my hair."

He grinned. "You didn't *tell* me you wanted time to dry your hair."

"So...why exactly am I here so early?" She didn't look that put out that she was, more like curious to know why.

"I thought we could talk about your e-chats till then. Just gimme a minute to make myself presentable."

When he came back out, she'd lost her shoes and was curled up on his couch. She seemed to have resisted the compulsion to straighten his cushions out, looking completely at home on a bed of cast off shirts, damp towels, magazines and DVD jackets. She looked...herself. And she was chuckling over a photo collage she'd taken down from his wall unit.

"These your baby pictures?"

He glanced over her shoulder to see which set had so caught her fancy. They were a series of shots taken of him at about five or six months old, being tossed, tickled, kissed and otherwise loved to death by a good-looking middle-aged black woman.

"Yeah, that's me. My granddaddy let me have them after my grandmother passed. I guess he knew he wouldn't be far behind."

She looked up at him, eyes still alight with laughter. "She must have been some trip, huh...your nanny?"

He stilled on his way round to the front of the couch. "What nanny?"

"Housekeeper, whatever. The one holding you in all the pictures." *Duh.*

He leveled a steady look on her. "You mean my grand-mother?"

"No, the...*oh.*" And her face turned red. "Sorry, I did-n't—"

"Nothing to be sorry about. She's been called worse things in her lifetime. And by members of my own so-called family."

"Oh?" Her voice was an embarrassed croak. "Father or mother's side?"

"Father's. Bunch of hicks who haven't got over losing the civil war yet. Or the fact that my granddaddy had escaped being infected with their poison. They're still living somewhere north and west of here, planning Florida's secession from the union or something. Just guessing. I don't know any of them."

"How can people be so...so..."

"Small minded?" he supplied dryly. "Given to stereotypes? Very easily."

Her face went red again. Anybody would think he had accused her outright of being numbered among the small minded. He decided to have mercy on her.

"Relax, will you? It's not that big a deal. I don't like labels any more than the next person, and I've been known to treat ethnicity questions on applications and such as optional, whether or not they were. But I'm not carrying around some outsized chip on my shoulder or anything, so please don't start walking on eggshells around me."

She relaxed for the first time since being set straight about his grandmother and stared again at the pictures with open curiosity. "No wonder your grandfather's looking at her that way. They really loved each other, huh?"

"More than. They were *in* love, seriously in love. As a kid I'd be rolling my eyes constantly when I was around them."

"How'd they meet?"

"In a GED class she was teaching."

Her eyes widened. "Having so much stacked against their relationship must have made them work harder at it, huh?"

"I guess. Didn't turn out so well for the child they had, though. My father had a hard time finding his way around the maze of labels and compartments that people of mixed races have to negotiate."

"And you?"

"Wasn't that hard for me. Different generation, different

neighborhood. Somewhat tamer hair—"

"Tamer?" she squeaked.

He grinned. "Relatively. Plus a complexion that poses as a tan."

"So it does," she murmured, eyeing him closely with what looked like open admiration. Too closely and too much admiration.

He finished skirting the couch and took a seat a safe distance from her. And tried not to stare at the bare pink toes peeking out from under her.

She immediately uncurled herself with an apologetic murmur and started feeling around with one bare foot for her discarded shoes.

He dove after them, got to them before she did and sent them sailing across the room. They landed not far from where the congressman's cushion had, and she sent him a startled glance.

"Don't." His eyes compelled hers.

"Wh-why not?"

Because your feet are gorgeous and I adore the sight of them warming the spot where my head will rest tonight.

"Because you're going to make me feel uncomfortable about my bare feet and my messy house."

She laughed. "Yeah, right." But she gave up on the shoes and drew her bare feet back up under her.

Stone's face was unreadable to Abigail as he pulled several rolled up sheets of paper from his back pocket and handed them to her. "Interesting," was all he said.

She didn't bother to look at them. She knew what they were. She waited.

"I thought we could use them as a frame of reference." She'd said that before, but she had to say something. Getting some feedback out of him was like pulling teeth. *Men.*

"Hmm. So which one is you?"

"Me? But I—"

He gave her a dry look. "Don't even try it. I already know you're one of them. I just haven't figured out which. Yet."

"Which?"

"I said I don't know yet. I'll have to sleep on it." He was teasing her.

"So what do you *think*?"

He cocked an eyebrow at her. "About what exactly?"

"*Them*. Duchess, say."

"Hard to form an opinion about Duchess. She's barely there. A cross between a snoot and a flake, maybe. JoJo, now...well, what do you say about JoJo? I hear a distinct tinkling when she talks...from the jingling of all those rings on her nose and eyelids and bellybutton and whatnot."

Abigail chuckled. "Just earrings. Lots of earrings. Five in each ear. Caused quite a stir at church back in those days. She was the youngest. How 'bout Kay?"

"Kay...is kind of creepy. I like her the least."

"*Kay*. Why Kay? She's...she sounds like the sanest one of the lot."

He shrugged. "Doesn't seem real. Reminds me of someone I knew once."

"Oh?" Another unfortunate relationship like his Abigail wannabe?

He sent her a measuring glance. "Except she'd have had to be quite a bit younger to have been running with your set."

"You've only got eight years on me, you know."

"*I* do."

But not his mystery woman, was his point. So he'd gone for older women. That would explain his ordering *her* around like she was some wayward teenager he was corralling at youth meeting.

"And anyway, she didn't have enough time left over at the end of her typical day to sort through snail mail, much less linger in a chatroom."

"What did she do?" Social work like himself, or something close to it. His work was too intrinsic a part of who he was for him not to have wound up with someone of like mind. Some capable worker bee with an active social conscience, someone who at the very least would have commanded the kind of respect that—

"Homemaking. She was seriously into homemaking."

Abigail blinked.

"Was pretty good at it, too."

The domestic goddess responsible for his decor?

As if in unconscious answer to her unspoken question, his eyes did a quick sweep of the room, the drapes, the cheery love seat across from the dour brown sofa they occupied, lingering for a moment on the perky little cushions he'd teased Abigail about arranging "at attention on their tippy toes."

"So what's in that to hate?" she said.

He looked at her. "I didn't. I gave that impression?"

"Kay," she reminded him, slightly irritated at being made to feel presumptuous. "She reminds you of Kay, who you don't like."

"Oh." He shrugged. "We had a love-hate thing going on, I guess you might say. But no, I didn't really hate her."

He stretched his legs out in front of him and contemplated his bare toes. Then, when she thought he'd said all he intended to on the subject, "Just wish I could have got inside her head and tighten a few screws, maybe even replace some worn-out parts. But to do that I'd have had to go back in time and be her dad...they didn't get along, to put it mildly, and it colored all her future relationships with men."

"You included?" she asked softly.

He shot her a look, as if the question startled him. Frowned a little as if he was only just considering the possibility of what she'd asked, and otherwise ignored the question, asking instead, "How old is she anyway? Kay, I mean."

"You know, I haven't got a clue."

"Roughly."

She lifted her shoulders. "I really can't say. I never asked her."

"How old does she look?"

She slanted him a look from under her lashes. "I never met her."

"You *never met her*. How'd she get your email address?"

"I'm...not sure. She said she'd seen me at some convention or other and heard me exchange with somebody."

"She could have been some sick freak harboring an obsession with you."

"Women don't obsess over other women. Unless they're gay."

"Uh-huh. And how'd you know she was even a woman?"

Abigail laughed. "She had a husband."

"So she claimed."

"Oh, please. If you'd read some of the stuff she wrote you'd have had to know she's for real. You just can't fake some things."

"Then why after all these years you've never been able to meet her...and her not living far from here?"

"I don't know where she lives."

"Close enough to have been attending a local convention. And that's something else strange in itself, your not knowing where she lives after all these years."

"It hasn't been all that many years. We haven't heard from her in three...four years. She was really only with us a few months."

"Oh?"

"She kind of just dropped off the map."

"Uh-huh."

"Oh stop, she's not a predator! She never did have a lot of time to spare. You might notice she dropped in mostly at the end of our chats."

"Hmm." He reached for the stapled pages on her lap, looked down at them and smiled. "Spunky's kinda cute."

Her heart tripped. She waited for more.

"Sarah sounds like a divorce waiting to happen."

She stared at him. "She was crazy about her husband."

"But not about herself. The kind of lousy self-concept likely to be latched on to by some metabolically challenged leech."

"What's a metabolically challenged leech?"

"My personal terminology for insecure men who feed on their woman's self-esteem without ever being able to build theirs up."

"You don't like her."

"There isn't enough of her in there to like or not like. Too wishy-washy."

"*Wishy-washy*. I'll have you know that of all of us she had the deepest convictions. What's more, she did her best to live up to them. You really don't know her."

"You're very defensive of her. You closer to her than the others?"

She stared pensively out through the open door at the three teenagers on one bicycle who were wobbling their way back and forth on the road. "I didn't really know her, I don't think. None of us did. I might understand her a little bit better now I've been through some things myself, but I don't quite have her figured out. But she's not wishy-washy."

"Do I know any of them, by the way? Besides you?"

"Could be. They've been to Grace a few times since I left, Dad says."

"They're not from Grace?"

"Used to be. We all married guys from other churches.

Except Duchess, who was still single last I heard. And JoJo. Got herself unequally yoked to a *really nice guy* who *respects her beliefs*, and now she can't even go to church anymore."

"I know how that goes."

"One or two of them might show up for the concert next month at Grace. Only don't expect me to point them out to you. It'd be a breach of confidence, sort of."

"I doubt they care now, anymore than you do. But I agree. Thanks for sharing it with me, though. It's been very...insightful...Spunky."

14

Beth's fine-boned face was pale and drawn against the unlikely blue-black of her recently dyed hair.

She had never had much patience with nature, or with the "hopelessly brown" hair she'd always deplored. Her decision to ignore her husband's veto against "messing with God's work" was what had sparked the crisis that had driven her to Oasis.

"I appreciate it that he likes me the way I am, Abby," Beth had complained in anguish at their first and last one-on-one encounter, "but I don't think God really cares what color my hair is, do you? I mean, it's not like I was streaking green or purple like back when."

Abigail had had to discipline herself not to point out that Leo Ramsey had never cared two hoots about God's likes and dislikes. As a counselor, she was not permitted to encourage the women's maligning of their husbands, much less add to the maligning herself.

"Hey, girl," she said softly now, dropping a gentle kiss on a pink portion of an otherwise purple and yellow face. "What's up?"

Beth smiled weakly. "Too much. I messed up, Abby—"

"No, Beth, you didn't—" Abigail swallowed the rest abruptly as hard fingers bit warningly into the side of her waist.

"Hey, you." Stone dropped his arm from around Abigail and gently chucked Beth on the unbruised portion of her chin.

He didn't even trust her to offer a little comfort. Abigail

would have been flaming mad if she wasn't so relieved. She didn't know that she had it in her to do what Stone intended.

Still, she felt like a traitor as she sat listening to him do the dirty work. He did it carefully, with a great deal of compassion, and he was gentle, and he was reassuring, and he offered so much hope, but he was firm, and he left no doubt that he was indeed issuing an ultimatum.

There were tears in Beth's eyes by the time he got done. For a split second, Abigail hated him, hated his calm and control, his cool determination even in the face of Beth's obvious distress.

She didn't care two hoots what he might think as she shot up out of her chair in the corner and headed over to the bed where he was perched. What did he know about a woman's feelings, anyway? And what did he really care?

"Thank you, Stone," Beth whispered tremulously, and Abigail froze in her tracks. "You're not telling me anything I don't already know. I just needed some help making the right decision, is all."

Abigail swallowed and backed off and spent the rest of the visit feeling irrelevant.

Meanwhile, Beth filled Stone in on details of her family history that Abigail had never once heard a whisper of. Namely that there wasn't a soul among any of her relatives that she'd feel comfortable leaving Corey with. That the family members she'd more likely trust to care for Corey she didn't have a clue how to get in touch with.

Leo's father had had his mother completely cut ties with her family in Pensacola shortly after they married and moved south. As a result, Corey had an entire branch of blood relations who were complete strangers to him and both parents.

At the end of it, Stone didn't have much more to go on than when he'd left Ileana's house the night before. Abigail sensed his frustration and the effort it cost him to hide it from Beth, and she sensed Beth sink a little deeper anyway beneath an encroaching wave of despair. Shock, fear, loss were all written in her face, along with the guilt that accompanied her growing realization that she had failed her child.

It wasn't till they were leaving, almost two hours after arriving, that the air lightened again.

Beth's eyes were following Abigail hungrily as she rose and slung her bag over her shoulder. It was as if she wanted to talk but didn't know what about. Their eyes met, and Beth's were searching, her attempt at a smile tremulous.

The years fell away, and they were seventeen and twenty-one again. A bold-faced Beth had just airily announced that she'd "gone ahead and done it" on prom night. Big sister Abigail was trying to hide her shock and disappointment, tired of being made to feel the prissy one of the bunch. Till Beth's face crumpled and she started sobbing out her pain and regret.

Looking back, Abigail had known somehow that that dropping of Beth's guard would not have happened if it had not been just the two of them sharing the moment. Not because their other friends didn't stand for the same principles Abigail did, but because it was so much easier—and safer—to maintain a facade in a group than in the company of just one other vulnerable soul.

Probably for the same reason her father never maintained eye contact with any single individual when he spoke before large groups.

That was when Abigail decided she would be back, soon and on her own, regardless of what Stone had to say about it. Girlfriend time didn't need a purpose or an explanation to happen. That much if nothing else her life experience had helped her figure out.

"You still got that overgrown Tweety Bird I gave you?" Beth asked wistfully as Abigail approached the bed.

Abigail grinned. "Oh girl, you don't know what you started."

Stone chuckled, and Beth looked curiously from him to Abigail. "What?"

Abigail felt her grin widen of its own accord. "I've got a

Tweety Bird collection like you wouldn't believe."

"For real?" Beth's nose wrinkled into her first real smile of the visit.

Abigail nodded. "For real."

Stone gave Abigail an openly curious look from his perch at the foot of the bed. "What's really the deal with you and Tweety, anyway?"

Beth waited for her answer, her interest not quite as intense as Stone's.

Abigail shrugged and said breezily, "Anybody who knew me back when would think Tweety an improvement on the kind of stuff I used to collect—keys and buttons and doorknobs and such."

"Snail shells," Beth added with a nod for Stone's benefit. "Hates the snails, but can't resist their shells." She, at least, was satisfied with Abigail's answer. Stone continued to look Abigail's way, as if still waiting for one.

Still, when it became obvious he wasn't going to get it, he didn't press. He made his way to the head of the bed and took Beth's hand.

"See you later, JoBeth."

Beth froze. "Abby, tell him he's playing with his life."

"She *hates* JoBeth. Who'd you hear call her that, anyway?"

"That notice board over there."

"Really." Abigail marched over to the dry-erase board facing the bed and promptly swiped the *Jo* from JoBeth. A person had a right to be called exactly what they jolly well pleased.

When she turned back around, Stone was giving Beth's earlobe a gentle tweak and then fingering the single silver stud it sported. "Lost yourself a couple of earrings there, didn't you?"

Beth giggled. "More than a couple," she confessed sheepishly. She touched a finger to the four empty holes that followed the outer curve of her ear. "I had all of five in each at one time."

"Okay, so you got one."

"Two. Don't forget Spunky. Three more to go."

That sobered Abigail. How could she forget Spunky?

She shouldn't have been shocked, when she really thought of it, but...did she really come across as brash and rebellious as the Spunky of years ago?

Apparently Stone thought so. No wonder he didn't want her counseling the women at Oasis.

"She missed you."

"She ask for me?"

"No, but she knows when you're due just the same."

Right.

"That you, Stone?"

"Yes, Ma'am, in the flesh."

"Where've you been? I've been waiting for you."

A deep-throated chuckle behind him teased him. "I tell you, Mr. Patrick. There's a whole lot more going on in that head of hers than anybody thinks."

He didn't doubt it for a minute. It was only drugs that they'd given her, not a lobotomy.

15

Her mother had called it her witching hour, but for Abigail it more often came closer to dawn than to midnight.

As a child, it was the time she would most often have nightmares and accidents. In recent times past, it had been the hour at which she would often wake suddenly with a sob trapped in her throat. When she'd sneak out of bed without disturbing her husband, creep into the bathroom, curl up in the bath tub with a towel stuffed in her mouth and cry herself back to sleep.

Lately, it was the time she did her clearest thinking, her hardest worrying and her most fervent praying, after having gotten in a solid six or so hours sleep. On a Sunday night like tonight, she might use the opportunity to mull over that week's Bible study notes.

Tonight, though, her notebook remained unopened inside her Bible case as she sat cross legged in the center of her bed, hugging her pillow and chewing on everything that had been happening with her and Stone since they fought over Beth days before.

She'd sighted him a couple of times at church today as she toted her craft mobile to and from the Golden Agers' class. It was his Sunday to stand guard around the grounds for the Sunday school, keeping an eye out for vandals and rounding up hooky players. Once, she had caught his eye and nearly missed her step like some star-struck teenager when he winked unexpectedly at her.

She'd felt her face warm. Of course, that was only from

the embarrassment of temporarily losing control of her cart. Like her missed step was due only to the shock of seeing something other than mockery or murder in his eyes when they rested on her.

Right.

They were nice eyes too. She hadn't noticed before how well-defined they were, with those sooty lashes that ought not to have been wasted on a man.

Before, she'd thought his eyes a tad too close together. But she knew now that was only an illusion created by his frequent scowling. She'd learned too that he scowled not only out of temper, but when he was concentrating, perplexed, or fixating for no apparent reason on her mouth.

Made her wonder what other traits, physical or otherwise, she might have missed or misunderstood about him.

She smiled when she remembered those most informative hours she'd spent with him at his home, at Survivors, at Ileana's with Corey. And sobered when she recalled his first summary assessment of her character after reading only a few pages of her idle girl chatter.

She could use a good old fashioned girlfriend chat. Except she had no girlfriends. Not the kind she could talk to the way she needed to talk to somebody, anyhow. Not anymore. Beth was too burdened down with her own sorrows; she needed a pair of ears, not an earful to add to her own.

Abigail padded over to the little white desk she'd had from high school days and turned on the laptop computer she'd bought only days ago and loaded with selected contents of the desktop computer she'd left behind at her old address.

She checked her mailbox and found it exactly as she had the last few times she checked it...empty, except for the few stray spams that had escaped her filter.

She opened a blank email screen, typed an address in the addressee field, then closed it out again. She must be losing it.

She already knew it wouldn't reach. She hadn't had a response from that address to any of her emails in over four years. The very last one had bounced back to her unopened, with an automated notice from the postmaster that the email was undeliverable. Whatever that meant.

She reached for the switch on the gooseneck desk lamp lighting the desk and paused as something caught her eye. A raised brown streak on the lamp's neck, just below the bulb. She scratched at it with a fingernail and stared at the residue, her senses recalling the taste of sweet and sticky, the smell of smoke and the sound of girlish giggles, followed by an indulgent male voice calling to them from beyond the other side of the door.

You girls be careful in there, now.

She smiled in spite of herself as she turned off the light and left the desk. She flopped back down in bed and lay staring up at the ceiling. A single tear slipped from the corner of each eye.

It was months since she had cried. She hadn't cried in the weeks following Eric's death. The tears had simply refused to come. Months later, sitting across from a kind-eyed stranger with big ears and a big fee, they had come. She had soaked tissue after tissue that was pressed into her hand, and now it seemed she'd exhausted the source of her tears, but not her pain.

There was blood everywhere. Or so it seemed when he first walked in, so stark was the contrast between crimson and royal blue. The altar was splattered with it, the not- so-innocent blood sacrificed in the name of stupidity. The air was raw with it. He couldn't breathe without tasting its rusty, salty tang.

They hadn't found anyone yet to clean up now that the police were done processing the scene, and they'd rather lock the place up and take their act to some hotel than get their hands stained with what they'd deemed was the blood of the unrighteous.

His blood. His unrighteousness. And therefore his destiny. He felt the pain rip through his heart, heard the shrill ring of the—

Alarm clock. The realization washed over Stone in a flood of relief as the familiar grating pierced the fog of his subconscious. He came awake with a groan that was part relief and part dismay. His aching body, tired from wrestling ghosts, didn't seem to know it was morning.

He slapped at the snooze button. And kept slapping it every few seconds when the ringer went off again. Finally, it penetrated that it was not the clock he was hearing but the phone. At two a.m.

Dade Central.

Not likely. They wouldn't be waking him at this ungodly hour, however grave the news they had. His hand drew back on its way to the receiver. He raised himself on his elbow and squinted at the caller ID to see who the moron was who couldn't tell night from day.

"What?" Stone's voice growled into the phone just as Abigail was about to disconnect. What on earth had she been thinking of anyway?

"Um...did I wake you?"

"No, sweetness. I only sound this way after a long night of *uninterrupted sleep*."

"Sorry."

"Uh-huh."

"I'll call you tomorrow."

"It is tomorrow. What'd you want?"

"Nothing."

"If I really thought you were waking me up at two in the morning to tell me *nothing*, I'd come over there and give you what-for. What is it?"

"It really can wait."

"Abby." The grating sound of his patience running on empty.

"You really think I'm obnoxious?"

He groaned. "When did I call you obnoxious?"

"Spunky."

"Spunky...Spunky...Oh yes, Spunky. I don't think she's obnoxious. And anyway, it's only a couple of things about her that's really like you. To be honest, none of them remind me a whole lot of you."

"But?"

He sighed. "Let's just say of the three of them she's the one who's the least unlike you. I see...shades of you in her, okay? A youthful Mrs. Carmichael."

"I guess." Her voice was down to a whisper.

"Why is that so upsetting to you?"

Abigail shrugged. "I'm not upset. I didn't know I was so...recognizable, that's all. It's always sobering to see yourself through somebody else's eyes, you know?"

"I wasn't criticizing you, for heaven's sake. Or Spunky. I like Spunky. She's got charisma. Outspoken without Duchess's cattiness or JoJo's irreverence. Classy without being stuffy like Sarah or Kay." He yawned. "Can we talk about this tomorrow?"

"All right," she whispered.

"Wait, don't hang up." A grunt and the creaking of mattress springs. "I'm-a go get myself a drink of something. Might as well. Go on, I'm listening."

Her heart swelled, and now she had his attention she didn't know what to do with it. She tracked his movements to the kitchen, imagined him padding barefoot through the darkened house, wearing only...

She gulped and fast forwarded to the kitchen, listened to him pouring, swallowing, and—

"You get up often this time of night?" he asked after a couple of minutes.

"Almost always."

"Your husband must have been a saint."

"I just felt like company tonight," she whispered.

"And you've got it, okay? Go on, talk to me. Otherwise I'm going to fall asleep on you."

She thought furiously, but her mind came up blank.

"Tell me bout your e-pals. You still talk to them sometimes? Besides JoJo, that is."

"Not...usually. I imagine we will sooner or later. To talk about Beth." As if they needed her input in order to be proper friends to Beth. For all she knew, they might all still be in regular contact with each other. Beth would not have wanted to mention it, knowing where things stood between them and Abigail.

"They been to see her?"

"Not yet. They...we could always go together." Right.

"Sounds like a good idea. Beth could use some of that right about now."

"It'd have to be without Kay," she added quickly in a lame effort to backtrack. "I...we lost touch with her."

"How come?"

"She probably got tired of listening to our inanities. JoJo and them could get really silly sometimes. Kay was a lot more mature. More spiritual."

"JoJo and which *them*? Sarah didn't seem to have a silly bone in her body. You mean JoJo and Duchess and you."

"Okay, so me. I was young. I was entitled."

"Entitled to a good spanking, is what. Conducting online relationships with people you don't know, even after they come out and admit they know you but can't reveal their identity. You ever let me catch you doing something like that again and I'll..." He swallowed the rest along with a long gulp of water.

"You'll what?"

"Don't try me, girl. "I'll get up out of this bed and get over there so fast—"

Abigail chuckled. "A fine sight you'd make, shinnying up the ficus tree."

"What ficus tree? You got a front door, don't you?"

"Uh-huh. I'd like to see Dad's face when he answers the doorbell and finds you standing there in your PJs."

"I don't wear pajamas."

Abigail swallowed hard. "Well then, I—"

"This conversation has gone far enough." But there was something else diluting the sternness in his voice.

She latched on to it. "But I'm not sleepy yet."

"Abby."

"I don't mean I want you to talk about...about anything you shouldn't. I just want to talk."

"Are you the same Abby who flew into a huff just a few days ago because she thought I was criticizing her sleep habits?"

"I'm an early riser."

"This is past early, Abby. It's insane. You have any idea what time I went to bed?"

"So you like Spunky, huh?"

"I like her." His voice lowered and grew raspy, "Believe it or not, I like *you*."

"Who...um...who'd you most likely have been...attracted to?"

"None of them, okay?"

"You have to pick one. And then I'll hang up, promise."

"Oh for—"

"Forget it."

"The one I'm already attracted to, okay?"

"You are?"

"Yes, ma'am. Want me to come over there and show you how much?"

"Um...okay."

"Abby."

"Joking."

"I think you'd better go to bed. Before you say something naughty you'll regret." He yawned, big and loud, and his voice went gravelly again. "G'night."

"Night."

Silence, and she waited for the click, but what she heard instead was his voice. It was a sleepy rumble just slightly above the volume of his deepened breathing, but she heard the words, clear as anything else he'd ever said to her.

Her breath caught in her throat. "Really?"

Silence.

She bit her lip. Had she heard wrong? "Stone?"

He didn't answer her, and a few agonizing seconds later she heard it, the soft but unmistakable sound of snoring.

16

Stone returned Abigail's tentative look over the coffee pot in the office kitchenette the following morning with a mock glower from eyes that didn't look quite fully awake.

"Well, you look nice and chipper," he groused.

Abigail ignored him, reaching for her Tweety mug while she figured out what, if anything, to say to him about his parting words the night before. She wasn't about to get all profound with him only to find out that "Love you" was nothing more to him than another in-phrase for "See you later."

"What, somebody call you at an ungodly hour and ruin your sleep or something?" he drawled.

Or something. She poured her coffee in silence, still not settled on a tactic.

"It did happen, didn't it?" He was beginning to look doubtful now. "I didn't dream it?"

"Dream what?" There, that had come out with just the right note of offhandedness.

"That you called me in the wee hours of the morning griping about why I was able to pick you out blindfolded from of a lineup of your friends."

Did I dream you said what you did to me just before you fell asleep on me? She'd forgive the falling asleep if the other part had really happened. They said that's when people were at their most truthful. And most forgetful. She slanted him a look, trying to penetrate his suddenly hooded gaze.

He returned the look with narrowed eyes. "You're looking at me funny and acting strange. What?" His gaze flicked fleetingly over himself as if to check that there was nothing amiss with his attire. He had on two of the same color boots, and everything that needed to be zipped or buttoned had been zipped and buttoned, save for his green plaid shirt. That carelessly coordinated look of his was beginning to grow on her. Casual Male.

Her gaze skittered away. "Nothing."

He sighed. "What, Abby? I snapped at you or something, hurt your feelings? I do that kind of thing that time of night."

He didn't remember.

He groaned suddenly and closed his eyes briefly, a pained look crossing his face. "Please tell me I didn't say something I shouldn't have."

He was *embarrassed*. And with the realization every last bit of the euphoria that had threatened to keep her up the rest of the night evaporated.

She added sugar and creamer to her coffee and kept her voice as airy and offhand as she could as she said, "I don't know why after five months of dealing with you I'd get upset over you acting like yourself." She flashed him a counterfeit smile, coffee mug in hand. "Excuse me while I go get my daily caffeine fix here. I'm not quite awake myself." And she squeezed past him out of the narrow enclosure and went to her office.

She half hoped he would come after her, push the issue some more and drag the truth out of her somehow, without her actually having to go through the mortifying process of telling him. He didn't.

Not at work, anyway.

She was halfway through a burger and small order of fries at her favorite sandwich shop when he appeared out of nowhere at her booth near the back and slid into the seat facing hers.

He hadn't ordered anything. Either he'd already eaten, or

he'd lost his appetite. In either case, he'd come there looking for her, not lunch.

"Abby..." he began, and now his voice was heavy. "I think I'd better explain something to..."

"You don't have to. Really, you don't."

"Yes I do. I was still half asleep. You woke me up out of a deep sleep. I barely maintain control of my bodily functions when I'm that tired, much less my words. I didn't know what the heck I was saying."

She stared dumbly back at him and tried to swallow the hurt.

He groaned again, and she saw her own regret and self-castigation reflected on his face. "Abby, you have to understand I was out in the world a long time. I've had relationships...I did that kind of thing all the time."

"All the time?" she echoed weakly.

"Well, not *all* the time...not like I was obsessed or anything...but more often than I care to recall."

"Um...oh."

"I was a sinner, for heaven's sake. Doesn't excuse my current behavior, I know. That's just plain morally bankrupt, tells me I need one of those spiritual checkups your dad talks about, and believe me, after this I'll get one, but..." He ended on a shrug and looked positively miserable.

Inexcusable? Morally bankrupt? Spiritual checkup?

"Uh...do you remember *any* of what you said?"

"Not a thing. Nothing much after all that nonsense about Spunky."

"Oh." She didn't know whether to be disappointed or elated.

"You have to understand I've been roaming the range much longer than I've been on the straight and narrow. Some things take root in a person. You yourself say you believe redemption is an ongoing process, that it...you're smiling...you little... You're pulling my leg, aren't you?"

"Uh-uh, I'm not. You did say something you probably wouldn't have if you'd been in your right mind. Just don't expect me to tell you what it is."

"'Course I don't, except...if you don't tell me, I'll proba-bly never be able to look you in the eye again or even...Abby, *please* tell me I didn't try to have phone sex with you last night."

She wished for a long time after that that she'd left well enough alone.

Once her wide eyes and flaming cheeks had given him the answer to his agonized question, he got up and went to the front counter to order, his appetite apparently back from wherever it had gone. When he returned carrying a tray with a twelve-inch sub, platter of salsa and tortilla chips, a twenty-four ounce soda and two small sundaes, her face still had not quite cooled.

He set one of the sundaes down in front of her and set about clearing his tray. She mumbled her thanks and did-dled with the sundae, while he just sat smugly across from her, clearly enjoying her discomfort.

"And you a grown married woman," he finally mur-mured, about ten inches into his sub. He shook his head as he helped himself to a couple of her cold, untouched French fries. "He must have been some saint, your hus-band."

"*Stop,*" she begged finally.

"You want out of your misery? Put me out of mine. Tell me what I said. For real."

"That you love me," she blurted. Not in so many words. His *Love you* had sounded more like an afterthought than a declaration.

"That's all?"

Now she felt like a fool. "I know people say it in parting all the time. Was just strange coming from you, that's all."

"I have never said that in parting to anyone. Except my mother, the day she...was committed."

"Oh."

"Come here."

"Your ice-cream is melting."

"Shut up and come here."

"No."

He got up and came to her, backing her up into the corner of the three-seater bench.

"Stone—"

"Shh...you'll draw a crowd," he whispered soothingly, eyeing her mouth.

"Th-there's no one in here anymore but us."

"Good."

She licked her lips nervously. "Wh-what are you doing?" She was whispering too, and she was glad she was sitting, for her legs were slowly turning to jelly.

His hands cradled her face and tilted it as he lowered his head. "Getting it right." His lips brushed the tender spot below her ear, soft as butterfly wings. "Two o'clock in the morning is no time to make a serious confession like that..."

17

By the time Stone's lips skimmed across her jaw line and slid onto hers, Abigail was sure she'd melted and would have to be shoveled up off the bench. And by the time he'd coaxed his way past her lips and started exploring her mouth, teasing and then demanding, tasting and devouring, her insides were so completely liquefied she was past knowing or caring if he'd actually said the words she now knew she was longing to hear.

He drew back an eternity later with obvious reluctance, looking as boneless and confused as she felt. Rested his forehead on hers. "Call me again at that ungodly hour of the night and I really won't be responsible for not only what I say, but what I do. You've been warned."

"So..." Her breath hitched, and she steadied it. "So what do you think could happen with half a county between us?"

"Abby, how long were you married?"

She frowned. "Five years."

"You have any idea how quickly a man with sufficient motivation can close a fifteen-mile gap?"

"No, but it would make for an interesting demonstration."

He sent her a smoldering glance. "Don't tempt me." He started leaning her way again, then straightened and put the width of the bench between them. "Then again, you wouldn't really know about any of that. Mr. Carmichael had the good fortune of never having to close any gaps bigger than a few inches to get to you."

Silence.

"Sorry. Am I trespassing?"

For answer, she slid across the seat back to him, turned her face into him and breathed in his masculine scent. "What are you wearing?"

"Deodorant soap. Aftershave. This late in the day, there's bound to be some sweat mixed up in there too."

She giggled. "Nice formula. I like it."

He kissed her nose. "Tell me again in a few years when I come in from mowing the lawn and corner you in the kitchen before I've quite made it into the shower. What are *you* wearing?"

"A custom blend I got years ago." She hesitated, eyeing him from under her lashes. "From Kay."

"Uh-huh. And what else did she—or should I say he—send you?"

"Nothing. And it's a she."

"Yeah, well suddenly I don't like your perfume so much anymore."

"You been noticing my perfume?"

"Every single day. Every time you come within ten miles of me. And right now." He leaned into her and buried his nose in the side of her neck, where her pulse was kicking up a crazy beat.

"Oh," she said weakly.

"*...does him good and not evil all the days of her life.*"

She drew back slightly. "Wh-what?"

He shook his head.

She persisted. "You were quoting scripture. Something about—"

"I love you." He was gazing deep into her eyes, and he was perfectly lucid, his near-black eyes steady and serious as they held hers.

The fragment of scripture that had teased her ears flew straight out of her head. "Y-you do?"

He nodded gravely. "I'm not sure exactly what it means, where it'll lead, but I'm willing to find out, if you are."

She managed a nod but no words.

His cell phone crooned. He eased it away from his

waistband and peered down at the screen. His face seemed to tighten, and he hesitated fractionally before silencing it.

"You need to answer that? I can wait."

He shook his head and seemed to make a visible effort to relax. "Somewhere I have to be later. It can wait." He sought her gaze again, and whatever had disturbed him seemed to fall away, his eyes growing warm again. "Spend tomorrow with me."

She'd been praying he'd ask. But then she remembered work and groaned. "Can't. Forward planning meeting, remember? If you still want me in on it, that is."

"Yeah, I want you in on it. But there's no work tomorrow."

"No? What day is it?" She checked her internal calendar but couldn't think of a holiday this late in January.

"It's Kayla's turn to take her Mom for chemo. She'd forgotten when she scheduled the meeting."

"So?" They weren't in the habit of closing down the office when Kayla had to take a day off. "I do know how to take notes, you know."

"So that makes it Go-on-a-date-with-the-boss Day. We can take our calendars along and take a stab at next quarter's schedule and have the meeting when Kayla's available."

It sounded like a plan.

"You're early."

"Heh!" a throaty voice scoffed from the doorway behind them. "Think she don't know 'bout? Call if you need me."

"What's wrong?" a higher, slightly tremulous voice asked.

He waited till the footsteps had receded up the passageway before answering. "What's wrong is I had to leave work early to come down here and see about you. Again. Don't give me that innocent look. If you know this is not my regular day to visit, you know what I'm talking about."

"That girl, she—"

"That *woman* is the reason I even know what's going on. She doesn't have to call me. You can show your appreciation for the fact that she's looking out for you by cooperating with her."

"You think it's my fault, don't you?" She was a child again, and the tortured look on her face at once pained and angered him.

"*No.*" He drew a deep breath, striving for patience, and went on more calmly. "No, I don't. But I can't come down here every time you decide you're going to act up. Keep it up and they're gonna start you back on those shots. You know you don't want that."

She swallowed. "Did you talk to P.J.?"

He counted to three and held on to his patience. "No, not recently."

"He hit you, didn't he?"

He gritted his teeth and forced himself to answer. "You know very well he didn't."

"Then what happened to your face?"

He only then remembered his still fading bruises and relaxed, shaking his head wryly. "It was a d...never mind. Come on, open up."

Stone was somewhere other than with her, Abigail finally acknowledged to herself as she brushed the last crumbs of a roast beef sandwich from her short pink denim jumpsuit. They were sharing lunch and a picnic blanket but not much else in the thirty minutes since finishing off their tour of Villa Vizcaya's botanical gardens.

Vizcaya had been Stone's choice, and she'd enjoyed every minute of their leisurely stroll through the ancient grounds. Partly because it was so breathtakingly beautiful and not very crowded, today being a weekday, but mostly because Stone had kept her snuggly anchored against his side the whole time while he played tour guide.

She'd learned something new about him. He had a serious appreciation for nature, his knowledge of the lush tropical species on display at Vizcaya surprisingly vast. Either that or her father had managed to get in some botany in between theology lessons—or whatever it was they did together in that greenhouse.

Their tour ended, he'd picked a quiet spot off the beaten track and laid out the contents of the picnic basket he'd filled at the supermarket deli. And slowly retreated into himself.

The Oasis calendars were still lying untouched on the Mustang's backseat. The knowledge would have delighted her no end, if only she had been the one reaping the attention he wasn't giving the calendar.

She watched him covertly as he opened a can of cola and drank from it, still staring reflectively out over the expanse of green ahead of them. He'd dispensed with the jeans and open shirt today and was wearing army green cargo shorts and a black t-shirt that hinted boldly at the muscular torso underneath.

He had great legs, only lightly shadowed with hair and the exact shade of bronze as the rest of him—no great surprise to her now she knew where his "tan" originated. And he smelled of soap and some subtle, woodsy aftershave that made her want to scoot closer and get a great big armful of him.

He, on the other hand, had been on his best behavior from the time she met him at his house till now and seemed disappointingly impervious to her. Disappointing not because she planned on pushing any limits, but because yesterday in the sandwich shop she'd been rather taken with the idea of him having a hard time staying out of her space.

Abigail swallowed her disappointment. She stretched out on her back and stared up through the spreading branches of the royal poinciana they were under and into an almost cloudless Miami sky.

As if distracted by her movements, he finished his soda

in a long gulp, tossed the empty can into their picnic basket and scooted closer to her half of the quilt. Her breath caught as she realized he was about to join her on her back on the ground, then released on a soundless sigh of disappointment when he positioned himself crown to crown with her, facing the opposite direction.

He was staring up at the same sun-dappled patch of blue, green and scarlet that she was, but he was for all intents and purposes several miles away.

"Tell me about your Mom," she invited in an effort to draw him back.

He took so long to answer she'd begun to wonder if he intended to when he finally spoke. "My mom has her psychiatrists just about ready to rewrite the book on senility."

"Yes?" she prompted lightly, trying not to sound too eager for the crumbs of himself that he so rarely shared.

"As an intern, I did a stint at a nursing home once, and my observation has been that senility tends to bring out whatever a person's been harboring on the inside of them all their life, secretly or otherwise. And I mean bring it out with a vengeance."

"Like how?"

"Well, your garden variety racist who grumbles in private about the black family who moved in next door will dish out the vilest insults to the black nurse trying to take care of him. And some of the most supposedly progressive thinking people show signs of a deep-seated bigotry."

"Hmn."

"The outspoken will be twice as outspoken, and the snake in the grass will rise up with fangs bared."

He brushed at a falling leaf before it could land in his face. "The sweet old ladies are usually the ones who cultivated their inner beauty while their outward beauty was still in full bloom. And the dirty old men are the ones with the demoralized wife and mile-high stack of girlie magazines."

"That makes sense."

"Sure it does, and I've seen it time and again. My Mom, now...she's a different story. Get this...she's never sat before a computer in her life. The only keyboards she knows about are the ones that make music. Tell her to hit enter and she's likely to reach up and slap the sign above the doorway. Email is mail with a typo at the beginning of it."

Abigail chuckled.

"Yet the staff tells me she's always meddling with their computers."

"Could be a curiosity she's always had."

"I doubt it. She was still lost somewhere in the seventies when the rest of us were crossing into the new millennium. I wouldn't be surprised to find out she doesn't even know what a computer looks like."

"Not likely, with TV around."

"Didn't watch it. Thought it was a tool of the devil. Which it can be, mind you, except she took it to the extreme. Not even the news you couldn't get her to watch. What's-his-name who got his start doing all those computer ads? She wouldn't know his face different from the fat guy who couldn't write a loan. Now they're having to lock their computers away from her. Were about to report her missing one morning when they finally found her in the office slumped over a keyboard, fast asleep. She'd confused the daylights out of the computer, trying to do only God alone knows what with it."

"Anybody ever tried finding out?"

"Hon, I told you—"

"Okay, but what if it's something...supernatural, like say—"

"Tu-nu-nu-nu...tu-nu-nu-nu...Welcome to the Twilight Zone..."

She plucked up a smattering of grass blades and threw them at him.

He picked one up off his chest, sniffed at the broken end of the blade, and twirled it thoughtfully before his face. She made a mental note always to smell her prettiest around him. He was as attuned to smell as Eric had been impervious to it. Chronic sinusitis had greatly diminished Eric's sense of smell, leaving him only his extreme sensitivity to the allergens that some of those smells heralded.

"Anyways, I got her one of those junior laptop things." He tossed aside the blade of grass. "You know, with the games and activities and what not. At first she was really interested. But soon as she figured out it wasn't one like the one in the office, she flung it across the room and threw a fit. Which I've never known my mother to do in her entire life. Except once."

She waited, for there was obviously something significant about that single smirch on his mother's record of temperance. But he stopped there. His reserves of shareable memories had run low.

"I'd like to meet her," Abigail offered tentatively.

"One day."

"Like when?"

"She's not herself, Abby. You'd likely be disappointed."

"So? She's your mother. I don't care what she's like."

"You'll meet her eventually."

"Why not now?"

No answer.

My mother is a woman of very...strong opinions, and very particular about some things.

"Stone?"

"Give it some time, okay?"

There are certain qualities she'd expect to see in any girl I want to marry.

"We've known each other almost six months."

He gave her a dry look. "Hardly. We've *fought* each other for nearly six months."

Just do me a favor and not let her hear you arguing back with me.

"Well, how much time do you need, anyway?"

There are one or two things we need to go over before you meet her.

"I mean, you got to meet my father before I even—"

He jackknifed into a sitting position, his back half-turned toward her. "He's not out of his mind in a—" He bit off a blue-tinged epithet and whatever else had been about to follow it and ended instead with, "I'm not ready, all right?"

His decision was final, and she knew in her bones that it

hadn't a thing to do with his mother's mental state. He couldn't have been clearer if he'd told her straight that she didn't measure up, for whatever reason.

She swallowed her hurt. "You think I care about what she's like? I want to know her because she's part of you, and I want to know all of you, good and bad. A-and if you think..." Her voice broke.

He groaned, swiveling round to face her and offering her a look that was part apology and part plea. "You will, sweetheart. You will. Hey, don't...don't cry, for the love of...come here..." He was on his knees before the first tear could fall and gathering her into his arms.

A few seconds of melding with the solid breadth and strength of him and breathing in his warm masculine scent while his lips caressed her hair, and Abigail hardly remembered what their disagreement was about.

It came out of absolutely nowhere. Big, fat raindrops that started out sparser than a lazy garden-hose sprinkler and quickly intensified into a deluge. Muttering threats at the still mostly blue sky, Stone gathered up the blanket they'd laid their fare out on and knotted the ends together, food, picnic ware and all. They made it back to the car just in time to avoid a thorough soaking.

It was only an errant cloud passing by, and the amount of blue on the horizon told them the rain should soon stop, but the ground would already have been soaked, and rather than sit around fuming at a wayward cloud, they decided to call it a day.

He didn't take her home, however, exiting the highway a good fifteen minutes shy of the I-75 turnoff and driving them to his house.

She had zero objections. One of the things she liked about being at his place was just watching him be himself. At work he tended to get all wound up. And inevitably, like an overstretched rubber band, he would snap, usually stinging her in the process.

At her father's he never seemed to be quite comfortable, except when he was pottering around with her dad in the greenhouse having heaven knew what kind of discussions about bulbs and weeds and fertilizers and what not.

She smiled now as she watched him flop down into his couch and kick off his loafers. He hadn't bothered with socks today.

He eyed her with what seemed to be extreme satisfaction. "All right, woman. Start in the kitchen and work your way down to the bedrooms and bathrooms."

His eyes narrowed at the uncertain look she gave him, but it was not *his* voice she was hearing just then.

What, your Lester pride can't deal with that?

"And if you think I mean that," Stone said, his voice dropping to a dangerously soft pitch, "then you can also go pick me a switch and come here let me teach you a lesson you won't forget."

He was angry. Close to. Because she'd almost taken his own idle jest seriously? The nerve.

But that was all it had been, an idle jest. She'd realized it a split second after she froze up in response to it. He was autocratic and forceful and like a brick wall when he stood up for anything, but Stone wouldn't demand things of the people under him just because he could.

Good girl. But I was only testing you.

She couldn't see Stone being that way even with his wife. Especially not his wife.

Not even to feed a gluttonous ego. *It's enough for me you're prepared to be obedient in the little things too. But I'm not particularly stuck on being called Lord, even if Abraham was.*

She shook her head as the memory persisted, and Stone's face shifted back into focus. She saw her own uncertainty reflected in his eyes, the unasked question she'd seen in them before that told her he wouldn't intrude without an invitation. And that was when she knew there wasn't anything she wouldn't gladly do for him if ever she became his.

Not quite ready to give as much away, she broke eye contact with him, released a pent up breath, and went toward the door he'd forgot to close behind him.

"Leave it open. Wider. There you go."

She looked at him. He'd kept it closed the other times she'd been there.

"It's got a nice view to the street," he explained. "Good insurance."

"Against?"

"The advances of amorous females, what else?"

Of course, she blushed. And of course he sat there enjoying it.

"Your husband must have had a field day with you." There was a slight question in his voice, which she chose to ignore.

There was a lull while she lingered by the wall unit studying his photo collection. There weren't many of his mother, but Abigail had already figured out which one was her. The gaunt, sad-eyed woman who was usually standing next to the brown-skinned, curly-haired man she guessed to be his father.

She was the same woman in his wallet, except she'd been much younger and less haggard looking in the passport shot, with a much stronger resemblance to Stone. There was a hint of kindness along with the sadness in her eyes. Seemed that way, anyway. Who knew if she'd get a chance to find out for sure any time soon.

She heard him stir on the couch. "Come sit down beside me and tell me what you're looking so serious about."

She complied slowly.

He patted the spot next to him and watched gravely as she took it, mindful to leave a few inches between them lest she be accused of being amorous.

"What is it, babe? I didn't feed you enough at the picnic? Or you want me to close that front door?"

She had to fight a smile, in spite of herself. But it was soon gone.

"Talk to me," he said, perfectly serious now.

She looked down at her hands, swallowed and said quietly. "I won't bother you anymore about seeing your mom, but I wish you'd just tell me..." She stopped, unable to finish.

"Tell you what?" He was determined to hear her through patiently this time, and her heart swelled with a bittersweet gratification.

"What it is about me you think she won't like. I know it's something, and I can take it. Moreover, if I know what it is, then maybe I could..."

"Shut *up*." He was livid, leaning forward now in his seat and looking like he was struggling to keep his hands to himself, but not out of any romantic urges.

"Y-you promised minutes ago to watch your l—"

His face softened instantly. He whispered, *"Shut up,"* so tenderly she felt her bones start to melt. And then he pulled her close and kissed her, slowly and thoroughly, on and on. And on...and...

"Hel*lo*?" a husky female voice sang from just outside the front door. "Stone, you in...here?" The voice had reached the living room before their reflexes could catch up.

Abigail swallowed her next breath, hers and Stone's, and started pulling away. She barely managed to put an inch or two between her and Stone before a long limbed vision in denim and lace sauntered through the open doorway with the familiarity of someone who had once lived there, or frequented it...or at the very least had a major influence in decorating it.

18

"Oh...excuse me." The stranger's husky voice had faltered, but not so the unblinking green eyes that raked over the pair of them.

With a soft groan, Stone put a few inches between himself and Abigail and regarded the auburn-haired intruder cautiously. "Hey you, what's up?"

"Sorry. I did knock. The door was open and for a moment I thought—"

"No prob. Abby, this is Shan. Shan, Abigail."

"Hello, Shan." Abigail's voice was strangled as she tried not to stare at either the chestful of provocation thrusting against the restraint of a stretch-lace tee or the sliver of bare golden skin beckoning from between the hem of Shan's blouse and the top of her low-slung jeans. She didn't know what she wanted to do most...stuff a cushion in front of Stone's eyes or her own woefully slight curves.

"Hi." Shan flashed an easy smile that was somewhat at variance with the veiled scrutiny she'd subjected Abigail to in the few seconds it had taken Stone to introduce them. It was a quick but thorough sweep of Abigail from head to toe, like one territorial creature sizing up another who'd strayed too close to its turf.

Whoever she was, there were miles of history between her and Stone. One didn't need a divine revelation to figure that one out. Was this the angel who'd once made his tiny house into a home? Not likely. She didn't exactly qualify as an older woman, was barely Stone's age, if as old. And those glossy red fingernails didn't look as if they could fit inside a thimble.

Or was she not so much a part of his past as his present...or future?

I've got my eye on someone...

Abigail felt a chill go through her.

Till she remembered the second half of his statement...*but she's not ready.*

The vise clenching her insides relaxed its grip. Of course. He hadn't grown up in church as she had. A seriously attractive man who'd lived his first thirty-plus years without the constraint of God's indwelling Spirit was bound to have been intimate with women. Shan was one of them. Past tense.

If anyone is in Christ, he is a new creation. She wasn't going to hold a man's past against him. Even if the past was tall and good looking and had the kind of curves that Abigail had only ever dreamed of. And knew it too, from the way she thrust her hips and tossed her silky auburn mane and—

"I probably should have called first—"

For real.

"—but I was in the area—"

Yeah right.

"—and I...you have five minutes?" Shan finished, with a barely perceptible flick of her eyes in Abigail's direction.

Abigail tensed and swallowed when after only the briefest of hesitations Stone responded, "Sure." He turned to Abigail. "Wait here for me?"

As if she had any choice. "Sure." To her own ears, her voice sounded tight and forced. She made herself add in more offhand tones, "I need to use the bathroom anyway."

Old things have passed away...

Shan was an old thing, Abigail reminded herself as she made her way to the bathroom down the hall. In spite of her fat hair and her pouty rear and her familiar stance and the glint of knowing in her eyes when they rested on Stone.

And the proprietary way in which she slung her arm around his hips as he led them into the kitchen.

And Stone was too mature a Christian to lose his head

over some old flame he hadn't seen in years.

"The other night after we parted ways..."

Abigail stopped in her tracks halfway down the passage-way, her insides going cold. *They'd seen each other as recently as the other night.*

So what? People ran into old friends all the time and had conversations. Stone would probably have felt an obliga-tion to share Christ with her. And she was probably sorely in need of salvation, if the thrust of her bared hips and the attitude of her clothes were anything to go by. Which meant she wasn't even close to being in the running with this particular guy, whatever other doors her curves might have opened for her in the past.

"...and I started doing a lot of thinking about what you said..."

Abigail hastened down the passageway and into the bathroom.

She looked at her watch and waited exactly five minutes, the time she figured it would take Stone to realize the woman was after him and send her packing, and then made her way slowly back up the passageway.

She tried to keep the kitchen outside the line of her vi-sion, but it was so situated that there was no way to avoid seeing it from the passageway. And there they were in full view of the open archway.

Staring into each other's eyes as if transfixed, some wordless question passing from his to hers. "You mean...?" He seemed to hold his breath till Shan nodded, a tremulous smile lighting up her suddenly radiant face.

A slow, broad grin spread across his face. It said vol-umes, if only because Abigail had never had the good for-tune to see him smile at her with such pure, undiluted joy. And the next second they were locked in a tight embrace, Shan's face buried in Stone's shoulder and his in her hair.

"Geez, Shan, that's the best news anybody's given me in a really long time," he said when he finally pulled back, and Abigail could swear she heard a tremor in his voice.

Abigail fought down a strong wave of nausea. Picked up

her pace and kept going—out through the front door and to her car.

Her Beetle was parked next to his Mustang in the carport, which ran along the side of the house and was overlooked by the open kitchen window. Abigail trod softly and crouched low as she passed under the green scalloped canopy, then froze when Shan's voice drifted out to her.

"So how's your mom? She's one of the first people I thought of once I'd made my decision. A lot of the things she used to tell us started coming back to me and made so much more sense. I bet she'd just love to hear."

Abigail waited. She just had to listen for the rebuff, small a consolation though it would be.

"Man, she'd be tickled. Might even jog her memory a bit. I'll take you next time I'm going, if you want. Once I introduce you to the staff, you won't have a problem coming and going on your own."

Abigail opened and shut the car door as quietly as she could, backed swiftly out of the driveway once the engine was started, and made a point of not using her rearview mirror as she sped away down the road.

19

I'm a man, Abigail. And God knows you don't provide a lot of insurance against temptation. I'm not saying it's right, but there's a lot worse that I could do, a lot worse that most men in my shoes wouldn't think twice about doing.

Abigail's bedroom door opened softly, and she hugged her knees a little tighter to her chest. "I'm all right, Dad," she whispered, her voice muffled in the pillow along with her face.

He didn't leave immediately. She knew she'd worried him with her mad dash up the stairs, but it had been either that or break down bawling in front of him, and he didn't handle tears all that well, for all the many passages he'd written extolling their healing virtue.

Predictably, he'd given her time to cry out the worst of them. But she still wasn't ready to talk and never would be, for she couldn't think of any sane way to tell him that the man her heart was breaking over was the same one she'd tried to get fired just a week ago.

"Really, Dad," she added with more conviction as his footsteps hesitantly approached the bed.

She felt the mattress depress beneath his weight somewhere close to her hip, and she resorted to the ultimate weapon then. "Dad, it's just cramps I'm having, that's all. I'll manage." Well, she was, a little. They'd started on the drive over, in sympathy for her wounded feelings, must be. And for all that her father was so enlightened, he'd never been completely comfortable handling some aspects of mothering.

"Turn over let me rub it better for you."

She froze. Her father had *never* once offered to do any such thing for her, and never in such an irreverent manner. He'd more likely have retreated and sent Odette up with some ibuprofen and a heating pad.

And her father's pleasant, butter-rum voice had never had that deep, grainy texture to it.

She jackknifed into a sitting position, jerking the hem of the voluminous sleep tee she'd changed into down over her knees, then grabbed the pillow she'd just been hiding in and hugged it to her middle. She forced herself to meet Stone's gaze. His dark eyes were grave and otherwise unreadable.

"H-how did you get in here?" she croaked suspiciously, sure her father hadn't let him come up here.

"I told him I wanted to apologize for being a fool and that you wouldn't let me unless I took you by surprise. He looked awfully relieved."

She straightened her spine, pushing her hair out of her eyes. "I can't imagine why you'd think you have anything to apologize f—" She backed up into the headboard to avoid the arms that reached suddenly for her. "I think you'd better leave." She didn't know what her father was thinking of, but he would never have let a guy come up to her room in the past and would have peppered her ears if she'd forgotten herself enough to allow it.

He dropped his arms but didn't budge. "Not till I've said what I came to say."

"You can say it downstairs."

"I look like some kind of doofus to you?"

"I'll come down and hear you out. Promise. *Go.*"

"You won't take the window out of here?"

"I'm scared of heights."

He smiled and got to his feet.

He was helping himself to a handful of her father's trail mix when she came down to the Florida room, clothes back on, makeup repaired and her hair in a French braid.

He started toward her, his gaze attempting to hold hers, and she put the width of an armchair between them and refused to meet his eyes.

He stopped.

Good. She wasn't going to let him past that armchair or any other barrier she could manage to shove between them till she was well and truly over him.

He drew a deep breath. "Shan and I...had a relationship once. A long time ago."

Would that be before or after the domestic diva?

"Before I got saved. Long before I knew you."

"None of my business."

"I'm making it your business, okay?"

"I don't see wh——"

"Shut up."

She almost smiled. He was sounding more like the crotchety old so-and-so she knew and less like the tender stranger who had just offered her a tummy rub. She lifted a shoulder and waited.

"Few weeks ago we ran into each other. I witnessed to her. Tried to. She wasn't the least bit receptive, but I sowed my seeds anyway like the Bible says I should. It helped ease my conscience some. I hadn't been the world's best lover to her, dumping all the baggage I didn't know I was carrying on her, and I imagine I'd left a sour taste in her mouth that made John 3:16 hard for her to swallow. She listened, barely, and that was about all. You can imagine what I must have felt when she turned up wearing that...that *glow* on her face."

She didn't need to imagine it. It had been there on his face too, plain as Shan's.

"It was pure Jesus, Abby. I was incredibly glad for her. For me too, in a way. It made me feel as if I'd found redemption for a little bit of my past. That something good had come of some of the bad after all. I haven't seen much evidence of that up till now."

She swallowed. "I'm glad," she whispered, meaning it. He deserved a chance at happiness, whatever the cost to her.

"And that's all. Period."

Her heart rate picked up.

"I don't have those kinds of feelings for her anymore."

Yeah, like she'd suddenly grown warts now that she was saved and was no longer forbidden.

"I might have at another time. Say if she'd been already saved back when I met up with her a few weeks ago. I was feeling particularly vulnerable at the time. I do have someone I normally rap with when I fall into that kind of funk—"

As in who?

"—but he was out of town and tied up. And your dad...well, it's not everything that I talk to him about. I got to thinking about some of my old friends, not having anyone at Grace I felt especially close to..."

And now?

"But then I got to talking with this girl I knew. Thought I knew."

"At church?" Her voice was a croak.

"At this place where I do counseling."

She frowned, trying to think where else he'd told her he volunteered besides Grace. "You—"

"I'm talking Oasis, Abby."

"Oh." Her voice was small. Kayla. Had to be. She was the only—

"Abby, for the love of...*come* here." He moved purposely round the chair. The next second she was in his arms, being crushed up against his chest and the breath nearly squeezed out of her.

Something just doesn't feel right between us, that's all. Like you're my sister or something.

Since always?

Maybe not the very beginning.

So what changed? Wh-what am I doing wrong?

If I have to tell you, Abigail, it doesn't even make sense.

Then how else am I going to know how to fix it?

I don't know...don't ask me!

Who else would I ask? You don't want me to talk to anybody—

You had better not! That's a violation of the sanctity of our marriage.

So then—

The truth is, Abigail, any other woman wouldn't need to have it laid out for her, and I'm tired of your cluelessness, that's all.

She was warm and soft and felt incredibly good in his arms. Too good. He groaned inwardly and drew a steadying breath, gathering the strength to let her go.

She wouldn't let him.

He succumbed for a little longer, then drew back and peered into her eyes. Tried to. Her lashes fluttered down to mask her expression before he could identify it.

"Abby?"

Hold her.

He held her. "Talk to me."

She shook her head, face buried in the front of his shirt.

"Sweetheart..."

Not now.

"Want to go for ice-cream?"

"Uh-huh."

He eased back just enough to tuck her under one arm and steered them toward the door.

She snuggled up closer to him. "Can we have it at your place?"

"Fresh out. Just as well, too. Not the best place for us to be."

"I like your place."

"You like my animals."

"I like you."

"Oh yeah?" His voice cracked and he had to clear his throat.

"*Please* can we go?" The plea seemed to escape her in a desperate rush, followed by a quickly indrawn breath, as if in anticipation of his reaction.

He sent up another prayer. "Not today."

"Why not today?" She was back in advance mode again. It was the most intriguing thing, this strange game of advance and retreat that she played, and it was playing havoc with his self-control.

"Abby, please. You're not helping me here."

She swallowed audibly, and he sensed her retreat again. He stopped abruptly and pressed her compulsively to him. "You'd drive a man to sin, you know that?" he breathed into her hair.

She stiffened, and he knew immediately he'd made some kind of colossal error. *God, please. It's your rules I'm trying to live by here. What am I doing wrong?*

20

A bigail, please, I'm trying to finish something here. Not now. Yes now. Especially now.

Why are you acting this way, Abigail? It's just not you.

She didn't want to be her. Not right now. Just for this little while she wanted to be someone else. To experience the triumph of being the last woman standing when the dust settled. Like she'd never ever truly felt, even with a ring on her finger and the bars of a gold cage securely around her.

But his arms were as hard and unyielding as the rest of him in their refusal to hold her. "I don't like being made to feel manipulated, Abigail. It makes me doubt you."

She swallowed the rejection and accepted for the first time that he did not know any more than she did what it was that made her so unacceptable.

The arms that had been trying to set her aside a moment ago tightened round her like a vise. "Whatever it is you think I meant by that, I *didn't*," Stone whispered fiercely into her hair.

"All right."

A finger slid under her chin and tilted it. Warm dark eyes held hers. "Trust me on this, okay? I'm feeling more than a little vulnerable right now, and self-denial is still fairly new to my repertoire."

Her eyes widened, and his gaze grew incredulous. "You were married, for crying out loud. Don't you know what you do to a man?"

Her gaze clung uncertainly to his in the half hope that he'd show her, and he muttered what might have been a prayer under his breath and got them out of there in a hurry.

The children. She'd forgotten the children. Walked past the cubicles where they'd been doing their homework and out through the doors, hopped the bus and rode all the way home before she remembered they were the reason she'd got a chance to go to the library in the first place.

"Virginia—"

"The children—"

"She's extremely agitated."

Of course I'm agitated. Wouldn't you be? She wanted to scream the words at them, but she couldn't get her dry, swollen tongue around them, try as she did.

"It's okay, Virginia. You're going to be fine..."

No she wasn't. They'd been telling her that for ages, but they were all lies...a bitter, hard-to-swallow thimbleful of lies, and she wasn't going to take it from them anymore.

"...found these in the bathroom. Medication cups, about a week's worth of them."

"No more. I'm not—"

"It's all right, honey...there you go...relax..."

The world receded, and she let herself fall backward into the waiting darkness with a sigh.

"Something I need to ask you," Stone began abruptly as soon as they were seated outside Dairy Queen with their sundaes. "And don't bother throwing a fit."

"What?"

"Your husband. Did he abuse you?" His voice was tight, but he could hardly help it.

Her eyes rounded. "You mean like beat me?" Her voice squeaked her shock at the very idea. "Of course not! I'd have left him the first time he laid a hand on me. That's something I'd made up my mind from the start not to put up with. No, he wasn't the least bit aggressive. Why? Do I act like somebody who's been abused?"

He shrugged. "Sometimes I just can't figure you out, is all. I feel as if I'm missing something—"

"I'm not some case study, so you can quit trying to analy—"

"No, you just happen to be somebody I'm contemplating spending the rest of my life with, and I don't want to make any more mistakes than I already have with you."

"Y-you haven't made any mistakes," she denied weakly, apparently floored by the declaration that had rolled so easily off his tongue.

"So what was it that happened just now back at the house? When you froze up on me and left me feeling like I'd manhandled you or something?"

Her eyes flew wide open. "I didn't—"

"Take it from me, you did." His voice was gentle but insistent, as were the eyes that refused to let hers go.

She went very quiet and pulled back from him, all the way back in her seat. She fingered her Tweety pendant for a bit and then let it go to clasp her hands on the table in front of her.

He leaned forward and covered them with his own. "Talk to me, baby."

"Before Eric, I didn't date," she began in a rush.

"I imagine not. Your father doesn't believe in it."

"N-not just because of that. Or what I should say is, it wasn't any great hardship, being the daughter of someone who felt that way. Boys weren't all that interested in me."

"Felt intimidated by your dad?" Not entirely a bad thing, in his book.

She shook her head. "No, they just weren't."

He didn't bother trying to hide his skepticism. "How come?"

"I was a late bloomer. Very late."

"And when you finally did bloom?"

"My petals didn't unfurl right."

He stared uneasily at her. He hadn't the first clue what she was driving at and wasn't sure he wanted to know.

"My curves forgot to come in," she explained impatiently. "For the most part."

"Which ones?" He forced his gaze to stay put and not go off on a fact-finding tour, then added dryly. "In any case, I'm sure your husband didn't notice." *He* sure as daybreak hadn't. All he knew was she was soft as silk and smelled like heaven. And that the taste of her mouth was addictive—

She pulled away as he started to lean toward her. "I'm not finished."

He groaned. "Then finish, for heaven's sake. I still don't even have a clue where it is you're going with this."

"I was saying all that to show you...to explain..." She drew a deep breath and started over. "Before we...before you consider...getting involved with me, there is something I think you should know." She licked her lips, and he stifled a groan and forced himself to stay put.

"I'm listening."

"I don't...appeal to men in...in that way."

She had got to be kidding.

"In what way?" He stared at her. She wasn't kidding. There was a suspicion of a tremor around her mouth, and she was strangling her little Tweety pendant with her bare hands.

"Which men, love? And exactly how many have you tried...*appealing* to over the years?"

"None. M-my husband."

He didn't know what to make of that. "I don't think I get you. He married you, didn't he?" His eyes pinned hers. "It *was* a real marriage, wasn't it?"

She colored. "Of course."

"Wasn't some kind of arrangement your dad cooked up with him, either?"

"No. Dad was really happy for me...I think he'd had a secret fear I'd wind up an old maid...but he didn't have anything to do with us coming together. They didn't even know each other. Dad had heard of him, but they hadn't actually met till Eric was getting ready to propose to me."

"Okay, so you were in love, then."

"Uh-huh. Or at least, *I* was."

"Why else would he marry you, Abby? From what I heard, he could have had his pick of the sisters at his church. And it wasn't because he was angling for a position in your father's ministry, since he never went after one, despite the fact your father would have loved to have him."

She didn't answer.

He asked bluntly, "So what was he...gay? Impotent?"

She shook her head emphatically. "Neither. We had normal...relations in the beginning. Or at least, I thought we did. Later I found out it wasn't all that to him. Just doing his duty, so to speak."

"He was unfaithful to you." He fought to control his voice. Her quivering voice and the dampness gathering in her eyes were doing dangerous things to him, and he wasn't going to be any help to her if he threw a fit over it.

She shook her head hastily. "No. No, he wasn't. At least...well, he wasn't, not really."

He wouldn't try figuring out that one.

"It was just that he..."

"Projected his own inadequacies onto you."

She stared helplessly back at him, as if the possibility had never occurred to her.

"Did you go for counseling?"

"With who? Get real. He was the apple of the pastor's eye, third or fourth in line to the throne. People in our position didn't go for counseling—we gave it."

"Throne, huh?" Of course. He'd forgotten which church he was dealing with. Not even a church, in his book, but a power-hungry, money-grubbing, people-wrecking excuse for a church.

"All right, who would *you* go to for counseling, huh?" she demanded, obviously misunderstanding the reason for his long, seething silence. "Especially about something so intimate. Who have you ever gone to for counseling? And don't tell me my dad, cause I know you and him don't talk anything but ministry."

Yeah, as in how to minister to you. "I never needed marriage counseling."

"You've never been married."

He'd felt that vibe before, heard that hint of a challenge in her voice, seen it in her eyes. Like *what would you know, anyway?*

Enough. He'd seen a few marriages up close. Way up close. One of them was burnt into his psyche. Still not the same as being inside one, but enough to have made him resist some of the most enticing lures.

So then, what had changed? What had happened since just days ago when they'd been at each other's throats? A couple of kisses and a few tender moments did not a future make. No more than it could change the past.

He loved her.

And Leo loved Beth. P.J. had loved his Ginny.

He didn't mean to, Stone. He loves me.

Denial upon sheer neurosis.

What was he thinking? He wasn't. Too busy feeling.

Drooling all over her, playing around with her emotions. As if...as if there could be a future for them...

Lord.

Only the erratic gallop of his wayward heart answered him.

21

Abigail watched Stone's expression go through several changes, taking him all the way from enthrallment to revulsion and a few places in between, and she choked back an acrid surge of disillusionment.

Point proven. A few minutes ago, he'd been ready to climb across the table and swallow her whole. Now he was sitting way back in his seat scowling, arms folded, and acting like he'd suddenly discovered she had the plague.

Well, better now than later, after she was wearing his ring and they were shackled together by an unbreakable vow.

"Oops, look at the time," she made herself exclaim with a look at her watch.

He frowned. "You might not have noticed, but we're in the middle of a conversation."

Yeah, like how many long, brooding silences ago? "I thought we were done."

"Abby."

"I'm sorry, okay? I really have to go." Really, before she made an even bigger fool of herself than she already had. She got to her feet and waited for him to do the same.

He continued to search her face with narrowed eyes for a moment while she kept hers trained somewhere in the region of his nose.

And then just when she thought he might reach out and haul her back down into her seat, he got up abruptly and without a word escorted her back to his car.

She didn't even remember till much later during her two-a.m. vigil that they hadn't come to any understanding about his mother...and that Shan had only had to ask once before being practically handed the key to her room.

"So, anything interesting happen while I was gone?" Kayla asked over the coffee pot at Grace on Thursday. She'd ended up taking a second day off to be with her mother, leaving Abigail enough extra work to do to make avoiding Stone that much easier.

As she spooned creamer into her coffee, Abigail cast a cautious look at the freckled olive-skinned features of the woman whose shoes she was being groomed to fill. The question was casual enough, and Kayla's steady, quiet dark gaze was its usual direct self, but that didn't mean there wasn't something more than politeness driving the question.

Kayla was a twenty-six-year-old divorcee with a sixty-two-year-old grasp of life and a lot more going on underneath her riot of corkscrew dark curls than her somewhat vague expression usually let on.

She was also loyal to Stone and respectful of his authority. In times past when Abigail had had occasion to sound off about Stone, Kayla had been never less than the diplomat, listening empathetically without ever taking sides.

"Oh, the usual," Abigail finally said. "Me and Stone had words again."

"Over Beth?"

"He told you, huh?" Why that should cause her such a pang, she didn't know.

"Actually, he didn't. But I figured he'd have had something to say about it if he ever found out. I just never thought it would lead to any of what happened happening, or I'd have said something to you. He blasted me for it."

Abigail stared at her. "He did?" She hadn't thought the efficient, conscientious Kayla could do anything to earn Stone's ire.

Kayla gave her a rueful smile. "Oh yes. You're the only one getting any free passes around here, honey. Far as he's concerned, I ought to know better. He's right too."

Abigail stared at her. *Free passes?* When? Valuing exactly how much?

Kayla smiled as if she'd spoken aloud. "You might think he's tough on you, Abigail, but he can be a lot tougher, believe me. In fact, I can't think of anyone else I've seen him being so...careful with as he is with you."

"Careful as in *how?*"

"Your feelings, I guess, and the kinds of demands he places on you. He keeps himself on a tight leash where you're concerned, believe me."

Careful of her feelings. Keeps himself on a tight leash. Abigail closed her mouth before her jaw could lock.

Kayla smiled again at her expression. "Trust me, he does. For instance...if I'd a made the same mistake you did with Beth? I'd have been out of here. Finished."

Instead of which *she* had tried to get rid of *him.*

"Oh yes. And don't make the mistake of thinking it's because of your dad that he hasn't, either. Your dad is committed to doing whatever is best for this ministry, no matter what, and Stone knows it. Something about Stone's got your dad's juices going all over again, somehow. Well, we know what that something is."

No she didn't. Stone's abusive father? It was abusive men in general that had got her father's juices going enough in the first place to prompt the founding of Oasis when Stone Patrick was just a gleam in the Holy Spirit's eye. So what was it about Stone's situation in particular that had so grabbed his gut?

She was still trying to figure out how to ask when Kayla enthused on, "Your father's never been this fired up about Oasis since he first got it going, and he really believes in Stone, as I'm sure you know."

Did she ever.

"Stone says, *it's not gonna work, Doc...*" She scowled and deepened her voice in a fair imitation of Stone. "Then guess what?" She left the rest for Abigail to fill in.

Abigail believed it. "I know," she whispered.

"But of course, Stone isn't going to this time."

Abigail scratched at a stain on the outside of her mug. "Why do you suppose?"

Kayla cocked an eyebrow at her and refrained from comment as she edged out of the kitchenette.

Abigail followed, nodding cynically in answer to her own question. "Cause when it comes down to it, he still feels weird asking his boss to get rid of his own daughter."

"Stone? Child, please. You *don't* know him."

I'm sure I don't.

"He's changed a lot since he got saved, but he's essentially the same guy at heart, and that guy is no respecter of persons, I can tell you."

"You knew him before he got saved or something?"

"Hmm. Back in college."

"Oh."

"Not in *that* way. I was already saved then. And head over heels in love with my first husband. We all went to UM on the same scholarship, is all. Took some of the same courses together. Anyway..." She took a quick sip of her coffee as they reached Abigail's door and waved a finger in goodbye. "See you in a few."

Abigail stared after her departing back. She had half a mind to run after her and see if she could get anymore out of her, but she knew Kayla enough to know she'd said about as much as she intended to. It was the longest conversation they'd ever had about Stone in the five months Abigail had been there.

"Oh, and by the way—" Kayla called out from halfway down the corridor. "In case I forget, remind me in group this evening to broach the topic of court orders. I'm sure word's already gotten round about Beth, but it needs addressing just the same." She winked. "Boss's orders."

Abigail encountered the *boss* for the first time that day at their forward planning meeting later that afternoon. She was subdued as she entered the small classroom where they were meeting, acutely conscious that it was their first day together at work since things had so drastically changed between them...and then changed again.

As she shuffled in behind Kayla, snatches of her and Kayla's conversation that morning came back to her. And as she sat across the conference table from Stone at a comfortable angle that spared her having to look directly at him the whole meeting long, she covertly searched his face for traces of the leniency he'd supposedly adopted toward her.

She saw none. No trace for that matter of the hot-eyed Romeo who had backed her into a corner of a sandwich shop cubicle and kissed her breathless. The entire meeting long, she got nothing out of him but a pretty close impression of his name.

Her first clue that he might not be as impervious to her as he was trying to make out came as they tried to settle on a start-up date for the next session of Oasis. He politely asked her if four weeks was enough of a break for her and invited her to pool her suggestions with his and Kayla's. Normally it would have been, "That a problem?" and "You're gonna have to live with it."

It was not long after that that she came to the conclusion that he was doing his best to avoid her eyes. Her heart lifted a little. If all of what had happened between them was of no consequence to him, he'd have shaken it off already and gone right back to staring her down and otherwise being his usual bad-tempered self, instead of playing at being some kind of model boss.

She felt her first flicker of doubt, however, when evening came and he still had not sought her out, throwing her a terse "See you later," as they passed each other in the corridor.

Friday through Sunday being Oasis off days, she half-hoped, half-assumed that the "later" he was talking about was sometime over the next three days. Friday was as likely a possibility as the weekend, since he was off from his other job as well.

Monday to Thursday he drove himself hard, working up to sixteen hours a day, her father had told her. Saturday night through Sunday midday, he worked just as tirelessly at Church, helping to police the disruptive elements in the youth meeting and Sunday school and helping to coordinate Grace's big-brother ministry.

Friday through early Saturday, he crashed. Last Saturday, it had been with her, and she'd developed a definite taste for it, even if it wouldn't involve anything more exciting than sitting on his couch and then visiting a friend in hospital.

By midday Saturday, she started to accept that there was not going to be any repeat of last Saturday and that maybe, just maybe, there were other ways he'd rather spend his Saturday than skidding around on thin ice with her.

Their footsteps sounded hollowly down the corridor, echoing the emptiness that the place always left him with.

"How's she been since?"

The response was cautious. "She's...calmer."

"I can see that." To his own ears, the observation sounded flat.

"I hear you, Mr. Patrick. But in here, they don't know nothing else. Long as she here, you don't have no other choice. Except prayers, of course." She looked over at him. "And I know you know how to do that."

She'd probably caught him with his head bowed over the bedrails and mistaken for faith what had mostly been frustration.

Saturday evening after getting back from Dade Central, Stone arranged a replacement for himself at youth meeting. Then he sat in his living room staring at the phone and fighting the little niggling of guilt his bailing out on them left him with. There was no sound reason for him to have canceled. He wasn't tired or sick or in the middle of an emergency.

He just lacked that extra oomph that knowing a certain five-feet-little of sweetness would be there might have given him. There was about zero chance of that. She'd never helped out at youth night in the five months she'd been back at Grace. Tonight would be the last night she'd pick to put in an appearance, after all the ice he'd heaped on her day before yesterday at the office.

The worst part was, he didn't even know why he'd done it. He wasn't really mad at her, so it wasn't about making her pay for running out on him the other night. Something had obviously upset her, and though he'd have liked to know she could trust him with whatever it was, like she'd trusted him with the other stuff about Eric, he wasn't going to hold it against her that she hadn't. Especially when he wasn't anywhere near ready to share with her half of what was bothering him.

At any rate, it wasn't her. Not her temper or her come-and-go antagonism toward him or her supposed inability to "appeal to men that way." He had a temper himself and had harbored his share of antagonism toward her, although of late it was going more often than it was coming.

As for her lack of confidence in her sex appeal, he didn't doubt he'd be able to set her straight on that one once he had the right to. If God hadn't so thoroughly revolutionized his approach to relationships with women, he'd have lost no time proving her wrong the same night she came out with her confession.

The raw truth was, she wasn't the problem. He was. He'd finally got round to figuring out that much after two days of stewing in his own company, tormented by memories of him and Abigail together last Saturday.

He'd never spent a more miserable, restless two days off than the last two. It wouldn't be the first time that his days off didn't pan out the way he liked. But usually when that happened it was because of somebody or other in crisis he'd been unable to say no to. Or some unfinished project he felt driven to finish before Monday.

This time, he hadn't even got round to doing his laundry, much less rescuing any citizens in distress. He'd barely made it through Thursday night's Survivors without losing his train of thought along with his control of the group. He'd made it to Dade Central earlier on in the day only by force of will.

He hadn't made any headway on the Corey problem, either, despite what he'd promised Ileana. Not because he didn't plan on keeping his word or because he was a procrastinator—he was anything but—but because the surplus energy with which he usually tackled community love projects like Corey seemed to have departed with Abigail when she walked away from their conversation four nights ago.

He missed her, especially the side of her he'd been seeing the past few days. Her warmth and energy infused him with a strength that made him feel like he could move mountains...or handle a thousand Leo Ramseys with grace and compassion.

What was he doing, anyway? As the man in the relationship, he ought to be taking charge of the situation, find out what it was eating her and hope that somewhere along the line he'd be able to come to terms with what was eating him.

Once he'd decided what he was going to do, he could feel his body recharge with renewed energy and purpose. He was singing moments later when he hit the shower.

He was waiting for her to make the first move.

Abigail came to the conclusion as she stood before her bedroom mirror surveying the results of her Saturday beauty fest. She'd spent the afternoon doing her hair and nails and giving herself a facial. It had become her favorite way to spend Saturday afternoon, like it had been in her single days.

She hadn't realized all those years she'd been going to her mother-in-law's beauty salon just how much she missed the lazy Saturday afternoon pampering sessions of her single days. No being held captive under a too-hot dryer, forced to listen to a dozen other women gossip and gripe. Just her and Jesus and the body he'd designed her. Hours spent wrapped in nothing but a towel with a phone wedged between shoulder and ear and nothing to worry about but how long her new nail polish would take to dry.

These days there was a bit more on her mind than nail polish, of course, but she wouldn't trade this down time for any weekend jaunt...except maybe with a certain guy whose company she'd suddenly developed a yearning for.

Not that she'd be getting anymore of those anytime soon, the way things were going. After all, she was the one who'd walked out on their conversation, and without provocation, as far as he was concerned. He hadn't actually said anything to her, hadn't got the chance. She'd come to her conclusions all on her own.

It was possible she'd read too much into his body language. It was also entirely possible that Stone was the kind of man who'd sooner cut his nose to spite his face than countenance being toyed with, or what he might have perceived as being toyed with.

She could swallow her pride and ask him straight out, or she could risk what little magic that had sparked between them fizzling out to nothing while she continued to play wait and see.

She contemplated her image a moment longer, wrinkling her nose at her hair. It was shining with health but still fine and hopelessly straight, despite the promises of the wonder shampoo the beauty store clerk had sworn by. Otherwise, she supposed she'd do. She might even have gained a pound or two, and in the right places at that. Thanks to keeping company with a man with a voracious appetite.

Satisfied with the verdict the mirror threw back at her, she headed decisively for her closet and dug up her most reprehensible looking pair of jeans.

After showering and shaving, Stone stood before the shelves in his closet, contemplating what clean clothes he had left. He needed some new clothes. The last time he could remember shopping for anything more than under-wear was a couple years ago when he'd accidentally kicked over a bottle of bleach on a pile of dark clothes he was sorting.

In this day and age, having to shop for himself needn't be an ordeal either; he didn't even have to waste his day off doing it. With all the best stores only a click away, he could buy himself an entire wardrobe in half the time it would take him to find parking at the mall. *Thank God.* He'd get round to it sometime this week. Meantime...

He rifled through his remaining stack of folded clothes and pulled out his least reprehensible looking pair of jeans.

22

There was no yellow VW in the Lesters' driveway, but Doc was crouched in front of the small pond at the top of his lawn, crooning to one of his night-blooming lilies.

He waved Stone off as he made to get out of the car. "She left already." Then, "How'd you know she was going, anyway? She thought she'd be surprising you."

Serve him right. Acting like an irresponsible, love-sick teenager. Well, no way was he going to go tearing over there now after her. All the other youth volunteers had to know by now that he was "feeling a little bit out of it" and couldn't make it tonight. Not that he cared two hoots who knew he was running after Doc Lester's daughter. He just didn't want to send the wrong kind of message to the youth.

He'd talked enough of them through their girlfriend and boyfriend troubles to know they wrestled the same kind of impulses that had kept him away tonight. Some of them did a pretty good job subjecting those impulses to priority tests too. They didn't need his example mussing the line between right and wrong.

What was he chasing after her for anyway? Yes, he missed her and no, he didn't want to lose what ground he'd gained so unexpectedly with her, but he still didn't have any answers to the doubts plaguing him since he first felt the need to put some brakes on their suddenly accelerating relationship.

He went back home, turned on the TV and sat brooding

his way through a weekend news magazine. Threw a couple of cushions at an opportunistic reverend and a lying news anchor before turning the TV back off.

He could do with some sympathetic male ears just about now. Not Doc's. Major conflict of interest brewing in those quarters.

He called Mark Scott. He contemplated dropping in on Mark but just as quickly decided against it. He'd have been more than welcome, even at a moment's notice, but he'd pass on that privilege this time. Three plus years into their marriage, Mark and Fern still acted like they were on honeymoon, stealing kisses and secret glances and generally lounging around in each other's pockets.

It hadn't bothered him before, amused him at most. But he hadn't had the kind of vulnerability he had now. The sight of those two ogling and fondling and otherwise adoring each other was likely to stir up all kinds of longings in his heart that didn't need stirring up at this particular juncture.

Mark Scott had sauntered into his life in answer to his and Doc's prayers for a "meaningful friendship" to replace the companions who'd gone from skeptical to increasingly wary of the changes Stone's conversion had brought about in him.

Up to that point, no one had materialized from among the venerable candidates at Grace. Nothing close to the friend he'd left behind half a lifetime ago and never hoped to replace. That friend had been more of a brother to him than any of the brethren he'd been told were now his "real" family.

Then had come his first Promise Keepers and a med-school intern with a sage's wisdom and a kid's sense of humor. They'd shared a room for a weekend and had shared each other's lives ever since.

Mark had been the trustworthy peer with whom a struggling new Christian could air the kind of unmentionables Stone had gradually become uncomfortable sharing with the illustrious Doctor Richard Lester. Stone, meanwhile, had been Mark's outlet from the stresses of med school.

Later on, when a more spiritually mature Stone became involved in ministry and when Mark traded the stress of med school for the vagaries of a podiatry practice, their relationship had only deepened. They'd continued to be each other's sounding board and the person they could safely get real or silly with, depending on the need of the moment.

Fern had come along after and changed the dynamics of their friendship some. No more impromptu fishing trips to the back of nowhere or camping out overnight in mile-long lines to secure playoff tickets. But Stone had come to regard her as much his friend as Mark was.

It didn't take Mark long to figure out something was bugging him. Two minutes into hearing Stone grouse about the Dolphins' dashed Super Bowl hopes, he stopped him. "All right. Is it Dr. Lester's urban outreach strategies giving you ulcers again? Or did one of those single sisters finally get to you?"

"Yeah, Richard Lester's daughter." It was a relief to finally come out with it.

He told him about Abigail, skimming over the first four months of their association and dwelling in more detail on just about all that had happened since his last migraine attack. He told him about his conversations with Doc. And he told him of the warning bells he thought he might be hearing.

Mark did what he was so good at. He listened. Didn't throw either scripture or medical jargon at him or fall over himself trying to come up with answers. He just listened, so keenly Stone could see the creases in his prominent forehead deepening and his sensitive fingers rubbing his long square chin.

Finally, when Mark did say something, it was, "You need to release her, pal."

Stone's stomach plunged. Mark was extremely sensitive spiritually. Stone wasn't sure he was ready to hear whatever new revelation he might be coming with about his and Abigail's future—or lack of one. "Release who?" he croaked.

"Who'd you think? You know who, man. Virginia Elise Rose. The other woman in your life."

23

Virginia awoke near dawn to the sound of snoring coming from the bed across the room and the feel of tears on her cheeks.

She rolled over in bed and hugged the pillow as if it would fill the hollowness in her heart. Her fingers made contact with something dry and papery, and she remembered what she'd hid under the pillow earlier when she'd heard footsteps approaching in the hallway.

It felt like a miniature beanbag, but it was only her dinner napkin and her thimbleful of forgetfulness. A moment's distraction in between her plate being cleared away and the water being handed to her was all it had taken.

The result was she was awake now with not the faintest glimmer of dawn anywhere on the horizon outside her window.

And alone for the first time that she could remember with the twin monsters that had been tearing at her insides, demanding release. Guilt accompanied by grief, both harsh and merciless, clawed their way up from the pit of her belly, filling her chest till she thought it would burst and gurgling their way past her throat.

She didn't know how long it was before the deep, wracking sobs finally died away, but when they did, it was sudden, like the turning off of a faucet, or the plugging of a hole in a dam.

She drew a final shuddering breath and stared out at the blue-white cloud passing over the half-moon and suddenly saw the triple X in the sky for what it was. When she did, she laughed. The sound of it startled her. She hadn't heard herself laugh in so long.

With that thought, her mind's door creaked open a crack and admitted another outcast memory. A name. She heard it a split second before she saw the face. Her breath caught and she gave voice to the prayer that had never been far from the edge of her consciousness, "Lord, what about Sarah?"

24

Daddy, how does God talk to you?
When I read His word, mostly.
Where in the Bible does it say He wanted you to study psylo...lo...
Psychology. He spoke to my heart, baby girl. In a still small voice.
If you listen, He'll talk to you too.

Abigail rose early, contemplated the church clothes she'd laid out after getting back from youth meeting the night before, then pulled on tennis shoes and a denim jumpsuit with custom-embroidered Tweety front pockets, left her father a note and went to the park.

There were times she couldn't hear God for all the singing and preaching that went on at church. Whether it was them or just her, or just a gray reality, she had learned long ago to recognize when it was time for a timeout.

And anyway, there'd been singing and preaching enough going on at youth meeting last night. A more jazzed up version than what went on Sunday in the sanctuary, but enough to tide her over till mid-week service.

If her father had a problem with her sporadic absences, he'd never chosen to say anything. The only One with the right to condemn her had chosen every time instead to come along with her to the park. There was no-one else close enough to her to try putting her on a guilt trip over it. Not now. Not ever again.

The sun was still yawning and stretching its way above the treetops, the dew still wet on the grass, so she left her blanket in the trunk and sat at a picnic table beneath the spreading branches of a black olive tree.

At that hour there were only a few people in the park. A small team of cyclists, a pair of joggers and one determined three-hundred-pound-plus lady steadily huffing her way around the footpath. Most sane people were still in bed.

Abigail set her Bible determinedly before her. It fell open to the page in John's Gospel that she'd marked with a church bulletin well over a week ago.

She'd left off at chapter 14. Jesus preparing his disciples for the heartache to come, promising to be closer to them when he was gone than he could ever have been if he stayed.

She hadn't been in John since the morning she'd first had it out with Stone over Beth. The day her life seemed in some indefinable way to have changed. Since then, she'd been ambling listlessly around in Psalms, grazing without much appetite, barely digesting what she read.

Chapter 15. *I am the true vine, and my Father is the vinedresser. Every branch in Me that does not bear fruit He takes away; and every branch that bears fruit, He prunes, that it may bear more fruit.*

Not that she was entirely sure she appreciated what the difference was. There had been times she didn't know if it was a fire she'd found herself in or on the wrong end of a pruning shear. It had to hurt about the same.

She sighed, scooted up on the table. Lying back with her head pillowed on her hands, she stared up at the sky and let herself sink deeper into the soft silence of the morning.

You might be bearing fruit, but they're full of worms, and God's getting ready to cut you off and throw you in the fire, fruit and all.

It wasn't anything you did, Abigail. You've got to stop blaming yourself.

He who is angry against his brother without a cause is guilty of murder, and God will judge you.

That's not God, Abigail.

Come against God's prophet and you cut off your access to God.

If it comes between you and God, it's an idol, girlfriend. Your daddy taught you that much.

Some o' y'all been raised on hogwash, corrupted by the wisdom of this world.

Love shouldn't mean having to apologize for who you are, Abigail. Richard Lester is a part of who you are, and anyone who loves you will accept that.

You been listening to the wrong voices...

They're messing with your head, girlfriend.

...led astray by the rebelliousness of your own heart.

What is your heart telling you, Abigail?

...Bible says the heart is deceitful and desperately wicked...

You keep praying about it, precious girl. You'll know it's Him when He answers.

Some o' y'all wouldn't know God's voice different from a witch with a psychology degree.

A man who is truly after God's own heart will build people up, Abigail, not tear them down.

Just don't expect to hear none o' that junk from this here pulpit. It's your faith I been called to build, not your self-esteem.

Abigail came abruptly awake, her chest squeezing. She sat up, hugging herself. She was shivering in the warm sunshine. The shaky hand she passed over her face came away damp.

She didn't even remember getting drowsy. Should have stayed in her bed. Or gone to church.

She drew a deep, cleansing breath. The voices hadn't persisted this hard since before Melody.

She needed to be up and about.

A middle-aged couple had joined the large lady on the footpath. Abigail contemplated them a moment, then got down from the table and headed back to her car.

For homework you're going to go out. Anywhere. The mall. Yes you can. Just get behind the wheel and go.

Touring the mall was not how she typically chose to unwind, especially not on a Sunday. Even before Eric, she'd considered it a pointless exercise, wandering past display after display, drooling over what she either couldn't or shouldn't have...or would rather try creating herself.

Not even when she was a teen had it been her hangout of choice. The times she'd gone along with her girlfriends, she'd done it just so they'd do the round of yard sales with her. Yard sales, she'd vigorously argued, had "a lot more character" than any mall. She certainly would never have gone off to the mall all by herself, especially when just about everyone else she knew was at church.

She went to the mall.

Stone scowled into his bathroom mirror as he inspected the tiny nick that he had just left in his jaw. His second that morning.

He swiped impatiently at the speck of red dotting the shaving cream and schooled his hand as he resumed shaving to stop keeping pace with his racing thoughts.

Other woman in my life, my foot.

Where had Mark come from with that? Stone couldn't recall once mentioning *her* in last night's conversation. Or any other recent conversation. Not that that meant much with Mark. Mark had a peculiar knack for hearing the things a person didn't say.

"Yeah, well, this time your antenna's off, pal."

He'd left that particular piece of his past behind long before he even got saved.

Mark hadn't been convinced. "You're still holding on to that li'l bit of unforgiveness that you think you're entitled to. And it's hurting you as much as it is her."

"I forgave her a long time ago. Very night I got saved." He had a healed ulcer, healthy appetite and normal sleep habits to show for it.

"You ever told her that?" Mark had challenged.

"She knows...I visit her every—"

"Yes, but have you looked her in the eye and said, 'Hey, I forgive you, we're okay'?"

"Not in so many—"

"Then do it. For your sake and hers. Abigail's too, if you love her, cause it will never work out between you two with all that junk between you."

He wasn't even sure what it was he was supposed to be forgiving at this point. Stupidity? Insanity? Those were deficiencies that needed a cure, not forgiveness. Not that she was even capable of processing an apology.

"Doesn't matter. Do it. You didn't care whether P.J. could hear you when you stood over his grave and did the same thing. Don't wait till she's six foot under to do the same for her. For yourself."

"Honest, Mark, I don't have a problem doing it. I just don't see the point."

"The point is, if she can't benefit from what you're doing, then at least you'll have found release for yourself. For your future. Cause you know what? It doesn't matter how different Abigail is from her, cause it's not about Abigail or about her. It's about you. If you don't come to grips with that, then that rage you so hate and fear will eventually become a part of you, and any relationship you have will just be a self-fulfilling prophecy."

He'd heard that before, and it made so much sense now he could smell the blood already.

"And Stone?"

"Yeah."

"After you do that, go stand before a mirror and forgive yourself out loud for being your father's son. Your biological father. You know now who your real Father is."

Stone had switched the topic on him after that, asking him about work. About the four-hundred-pound wrestler with the ingrown toenails, about the ninety-year-old amputee eager to get back on the jogging trail. The five-year-old diabetic he'd taught to play "This little piggy."

He told Mark about Corey and the dead ends he'd run

into trying to track down the estranged arm of his family. Mark reminded him of a mutual acquaintance of theirs who worked at the Bureau of Vital Statistics.

"Let me know how you make out," Mark told him. "He could always stay with us. Would be good practice."

"You serious?"

"Sure, why not? Fern'd be tickled too. You know her. And it'd take her mind off counting the minutes and seconds to her due date. Speaking of whom...Hey, babe. I was just about to come get you."

A female voice responded in the background. Fern's.

"Went to visit an old girlfriend," Mark explained to Stone. "You know how that is. *Ouch*, help...I'm being assaulted." Muted sounds of a struggle, a stifled giggle and a suspicious silence. Then, "She says go get yourself a wife and stop gossiping with me like we're a pair of women."

"Tell her I love her too."

They talked some more, chuckled a little over Fern and women in general and idly took a stab at whittling down the definition of the ideal woman to a single essential Proverbs-31 ingredient.

After a while, they petered out and Mark yawned. "I'm falling asleep on you, buddy. You going to be okay?"

"Sure, I'll let you go. You never know what time you might have to go haring off to the corner store for who knows what."

"These days it's more likely than not to be antacid, and we've got lots of that already. Talk to you tomorrow, then."

Tomorrow. What was tomorrow? Stone thought furiously.

Mark picked up on his distraction. "You not planning on wimping out, are you? Hey, I'm counting on you, man. Your time's coming one day, if I'm reading you right."

Oh *that*. He'd forgotten. "Sure. What's she want, again?"

"Don't ask me, man. I promised myself not to risk trying to figure that one out till all this is over and she's at least human again. Go ahead and surprise her."

There went his Sunday. What was left of it. Stone

groaned and slopped stubble-speckled shaving cream into his face basin. The things a guy would do for a friend.

Shopping, of all things. He could think of any number of things he'd rather have done with his Sunday afternoon after being AWOL from Grace two days in a row. Spending some quality time in the Word, for one...or trying to figure out Abigail. At any rate, the last thing he needed was a vivid reminder of what he and Abigail didn't have, and that was all an afternoon spent watching Mark and Fern adore each other was likely to accomplish.

Unless, of course...

Stone paused mid-stroke, razor angled perilously against the underside of his chin. Dropped the razor in the sink, wiped his hand on the towel slung round his hips, and with his face still half shaven went to scour his closet for the second time that weekend.

25

Abigail's cell phone rang as she parked her car and headed for the mall entrance. She glanced down at it and registered in shock that the call was from Stone's cell number.

So was the next call, and the next, minutes apart. Well. She didn't know what to make of it, so after the third call, she checked her messages, hope stirring in her chest in spite of everything.

After listening to about a minute and a half of sheer undiluted Stone, her mind went numb. His first message was curt and impatient. The second blistered her ears. The last one set a chord vibrating within her.

"Abigail, did you get my message?"

Oh yes, she had, loud and clear, exactly as her father had unwittingly delivered it the night before.

Did you see Stone at youth meeting? He came by here looking for you.

Her pride hadn't allowed her to tell her father that Stone had decided not to show up once he realized she was headed there. She'd left her father to draw his own conclusions, like he had when he found out she was planning on dropping in on youth night. He'd seemed greatly pleased at the implied improvement in her and Stone's relationship, and she hadn't had the heart to set him straight. There'd be time enough for that, after she'd set her own wayward heart straight.

Till then, she had an entire mall to get reacquainted with. She turned off her cell. She'd check for messages regularly, just in case her father needed to reach her in an emergency.

Nothing bad is going to happen, Abigail. To you or anyone you love. If God had wanted to get you He wouldn't have to wait for you to leave your house to do it.

As she stepped inside the huge air-conditioned complex, she was enveloped in light and colors and hollow acoustics, the smell of new clothes mingling with that of popcorn and roasted nuts.

She felt naughty and wayward and idle and deliciously free. And just slightly comforted by the knowledge that it was the last place she was likely to run into Stone. A man like him would have no patience with such an exercise. She could picture him tapping his watch and sighing and growling at whatever unfortunate female was misguided enough to take him shopping with her.

She ran into him in front of the baby supermarket. Besides appearing to be every bit as shocked to see her as she was to see him, he was looking harassed and out of place. And devastatingly attractive in a pale pink polo shirt and newer than usual jeans. His hair was ruthlessly restrained at his nape with a rubber band and looked as if he'd attempted to tame it with a brush and some gel of some sort. Only a man totally at ease with his own masculinity could make a ponytail and the color pink into something that was pure unadulterated male.

And only a woman could have got Stone Patrick to put that kind of effort into his appearance.

Abigail's stomach lurched as she cast a quick eye around to see who the talented female was who had bamboozled him into following her to the mall.

"You turned off your cell!" he accused, before she could fully register that he was apparently alone. "And don't bother to deny it."

Her chin went up. "I wasn't."

"Then why bother have one? How'd you know your father wouldn't have an emergency and need—"

"He doesn't. I've been checking my messages regularly."

His eyes narrowed. "Which means you got every one of

mine."

"You mean the ones that said, *Abby, answer the bleeping phone?* Actually, I didn't really consider them messages. They came across more like assaults. Or orders, and the only place I have to take orders from you is at Oasis."

He stared at her a long, heart stopping moment, his eyes slowly freezing over, before he said, very quietly, "Fine. See you then," and walked off.

Her heart plummeted to the bottom of her shoes. He didn't even think she was worth a good fight anymore.

She lost her enthusiasm for the expedition after that and before long was retracing her steps back to the parking lot.

There was an indigo Mustang parked next to her Beetle. And Stone was leaning up against it, ankles crossed and arms folded, watching her faltering approach.

Her heartbeat picked up, but she schooled her face not to register the surge of joy that coursed through her. She eyed him cautiously as she made her way to the driver-side, key in hand.

An arm snaked out and barred her way as she aimed the key at the lock. "The reason I was looking for you was not so I could assault you or order you around," he said quietly, "but to ask a favor of you."

"Oh?" Surprise made her voice uncertain.

"I have this baby shower deal I have to go to later, and—"

"Baby shower?"

"I know, I thought it was a woman thing too. I've never had the misfortune of being invited to one before. But the two love birds in question so can't stand to spend a Sunday afternoon apart that they insisted on a co-ed effort. The daddy is a good friend of mine. He made me promise him on penalty of excommunication from his Super Bowl party that I wouldn't chicken out on him, just in case the other guys did. Besides, I'm supposed to be the god-daddy."

"So...so what do you want me to do?"

"Help me pick out a gift. Please."

She hesitated only as long as she figured was necessary

to avoid giving the impression that she'd already made up her mind to say yes to whatever he asked, and then she nodded.

As it turned out, he could well have done without her help. The mother-to-be had a registry that listed all her needs from diaper pins to closed-circuit surveillance, and the assistant was only too eager to help. As Abigail watched the hyper bottle-blonde fawn all over Stone, she had to wonder how many customers who weren't attractive, ring-less and male received the kind of attention being lavished on this one.

But then soon they were out in the mall again and Stone was slinging an arm around her shoulder and matching his long strides to her shorter ones. He seemed to be making a point of signaling whoever might be interested that she was with him, and they were drawing all kinds of stares that ranged from admiring to envious.

Abigail was too busy relishing the bone deep thrill of having him at her side to be flustered by the attention.

It was a first for her. She might have toured the malls with her friends in the past, but never with a guy, not even her husband, who had been as impatient with the process as any other man. Judging from the speed with which Stone had made his selection, he was no different. But having got the dreaded task over with, he seemed to relax and to be enjoying their stroll as much as she was.

"So which one of these are you going to try to drag me into?" he teased as they passed by Macy's.

Abigail glanced disinterestedly at the display they were passing by and shrugged.

"Don't try to tell me you're not into clothes, either, cause I see the way you dress."

Silence. It sounded like a compliment, but...

You look garish and cheap...not what I expect of my wife either in public or private.

"Or aren't you quite done exhausting all the stuff your husband showered you with?"

Take one of the cards and go and get yourself a proper wardrobe.

"Abby?" Stone prodded gently, his brow knit in concern. "Sweetheart, if I'm touching you on a sore spot, just let me know. I can't know if you don't tell me."

She shook her head emphatically, the endearment and the gentleness in his voice melting away some of her tension. "I make my own clothes," she blurted.

There's no need for my wife to be playing penny ante. I'm not a pauper.

She braced for Stone's reaction, a peppery "Tough if you don't like it" waiting on the tip of her tongue, just in case.

"You serious?" His expression was incredulous, admiring, proud, anything but derisive.

She released her breath, nodding. "That's where I get my calluses. I started in junior high. Not because I had to," she rushed to add. "I just...had a taste for it, I guess..."

"You most certainly do, babe," he murmured, shaking his head slowly as his hooded gaze slid down the length of her.

She blushed her pleasure. "But anyway, I...got lazy after I got married, what with all the credit cards we had."

"Somehow I can't picture you being lazy, but..." He shook his head ruefully. "If I was married to you and you got tired of sewing, I'd probably have to get me a third job to be able to send you to the kind of places that could compete with Mademoiselle Abigail. Cause I am *seriously* stuck on the fashion trend you've got goin—*hey...*"

He stopped and returned the compulsive hug she gave him, there in the midst of multiple lanes of pedestrian traffic.

He regarded her quizzically when she finally eased away. "Was I thinking out loud again?"

"Thinking what?"

"I guess not."

"What *were* you thinking?" she prodded, eyeing him cautiously. Maybe there was a catch after all.

His eyes held hers warmly. "Something else from Proverbs 31...*Her clothing is fine linen and purple.*"

She smiled tremulously up at him, feeling the sting of

grateful tears. "I'm kind of not that big on purple, but I do like linen a lot."

"I'd buy you an ice-cream," Stone murmured as they passed the food court, "but we're going to be loaded down with so much junk already at—"

"We?"

"You're coming with me, right?"

"Well, I...you can't just bring a stranger in to a person's baby shower like that. It doesn't work that way."

"You're not a stranger. You're my...not a stranger. And why not, anyway?"

"Because."

"Yeah, sounds like a reason to me."

"Really, Stone. I can't—"

"You can and you are, or I'm not going."

"But your friend—"

"In fact, why don't I just drop the present off at the house of someone else who is going and we can go our separate ways?"

She went with him to the baby shower.

He told her the address and made her drive in front, and she could almost hear his teeth grind at the Beetle's sedate pace. But he stayed dutifully behind her and didn't honk his horn, except for the one time when the light changed from red to green while she was busy freshening up her lipstick.

The shower was at the house of the mother-to-be's sister. It was a cute pink-and-white doll house in an older segment of Pembroke Pines, and its front lawn was overrun from corner to corner with vehicles of all makes.

Stone directed her into the last available parking spot on the front swale and then wedged his Mustang into an impossibly small space between another car and a fledgling mango tree. As he joined her at the bottom of the sshaped walkway lined with pink and white begonias, Abigail passed a smoothing hand over her hair, suddenly nervous at the prospect of meeting his friends.

"You look beautiful," he told her. The look in his eyes left her no choice but to believe him. It was proud, slightly possessive and openly appreciative. If she'd ever once got such a look from Eric, she honestly couldn't recall the occasion.

With Eric, she'd simply learned to take his silent, impassive appraisals of her as a sign of his approval, knowing from experience that he didn't have a problem letting her know when her appearance wasn't up to scratch. Appearances had been everything to the people in Eric's circle, among other things. Passing muster had been of paramount importance to him. En route to the numerous functions she'd had to attend with him, he'd invariably become so tightly strung and testy that he'd neutralize what little pleasure she might otherwise have taken in the event. After a while, she'd come to dread going anywhere with him, however joyous the occasion.

A quick glance at Stone's relaxed features told her he was anything but uptight about the upcoming encounter, stranger though he was to this type of gathering. Laid back as he was socially, surely anyone as close to him as this couple was had to be of a different orientation from Eric's associates.

They weren't from Grace, she figured, or he'd have mentioned their names. Where did he know them from, anyway? His other job? Were they even Christians? He wasn't the type to automatically have cut all ties with his non-Christian friends the minute he became one—except for the Shans among them, of course.

At the same time, she didn't know him to be someone with an especially wide circle of friends. Easily as he got along with any and everybody at Grace, there weren't many that she was aware of who frequented his house or he theirs, as she suspected was the case with this couple.

So then what was it about them that made them so special to him? And what would they think of her? There was so much she had yet to learn about him. And he her.

She felt a familiar tension begin to coil itself around her insides, and she began to wish she'd never agreed to come with him.

Just then, Stone reached for her hand and pulled her close to his side. "You'll like them," he promised, drawing her arm through his as they approached the front door. "They're nauseatingly besotted with each other, but you might find it refreshing after some of the marriages you've had to referee over at Oasis."

The father-to-be, a lanky redhead with probing gray eyes, opened the door to them and immediately enfolded Stone in a grateful bear hug. "Knew I could count on you, man," he told Stone, before pulling back and subjecting Abigail to a frankly assessing stare.

"This is Abby," was all Stone said, and she was left with the distinct impression that the two had talked about her before. It left her feeling oddly gratified.

"Hey, Abby. I owe you one for dragging him over here for me. Come on, let me introduce you to everybody."

She didn't see anybody she knew. But they were a friendly bunch and either didn't know or didn't care that she was a stranger to everybody present, including the parents-to-be.

Five minutes after the introduction, the word went round that mommy-to-be was three minutes away. They started disappearing behind furniture and draperies. A few jokers ducked underneath rugs.

Crouched with Stone behind a sofa, Abigail heard her before she saw her. Her first thought was that the mother-to-be was doing a fairly decent job of pretending to be surprised. Immediately on the heels of that thought came another, like a huge stone dropping on the calm surface of the peaceful waters she'd been wading in with Stone: *Impossible...no way can that be who my ears are telling me it is...*

26

Her ears hadn't lied.

It was her. Them. A pair of mocha-skinned Jamaican-Indians who could pass for twins but who were as different from each other in temperament as greyhounds from pit bulls. Crystal and Fern. Two of her closest friends before she let her own weakness and someone else's lies separate her bit by bit from them all. Two of the friends she'd decided in her ignorance and blind conceit were a stumbling block in her marriage that needed to be removed.

She hung back as long as she decently could, unsure of what her welcome would be. She knew what she'd have said if the positions had been reversed: *Well, hello, stranger. What wind blew you this way?*

She could see it happening. See everybody's look of surprise, followed by condemnation. See them staring at her and whispering and—

"What's wrong?" Stone asked, and she realized she'd stalled in the middle of the eager push toward the Florida room where the huge cake, pastel decorations and mountain of presents had been set up.

"I...don't feel well." It was no lie. Her breathing had gone choppy, and she could hear the blood pounding furiously in her ears and feel a fine sweat breaking out on her forehead as an old familiar feeling of panic spread through her. "I'm sorry, Stone, but I can't stay. I can't."

He took one look at her face and apparently decided she wasn't faking it. "Wait, I'll take you."

"I'm okay to drive."

"Then I'll drive behind you. Just give me a minute to—"

"No, please. You're going to make me feel really bad if you desert them on account of me. I can manage, really. And I'm much closer to home than you are, remember?"

He wasn't buying it, so she told him she had to use the bathroom and while he was gone to make his excuses to the others located a side door and snuck through it. Having been among the last to arrive, she had not been backed in by any other vehicle. She was gone in half the time it would have taken her to use the bathroom.

Still, she didn't stop checking her rearview mirror till she had pulled into her father's driveway. Stone hadn't followed her. He could easily have caught up with her if he'd tried. Half of her wished he had.

Instead, he'd called her father, who was waiting for her at the front door when she arrived. He looked a little concerned and wanted to know if she was okay. He'd been asked to give Stone a call on his cell if she wasn't home within ten minutes of Stone calling.

It was a long time since Stone had been made to look like such a fool, by a woman or anyone else. No fewer than a dozen people had heard him make his excuse to Fern and Mark—something to the effect that Abigail wasn't well and might not be able to make it home on her own. There had been expressions of sympathy and messages to the effect that she should take it easy and "feel better."

Minutes later, there he was, staring grimly at the empty spot where Abigail's car had been.

"Couldn't wait, huh?" Mark, who'd followed him outside to see him off was giving him a penetrating look. "You want to go after her? Still all right by us. I'm past the worst. I figure I can manage from here."

Stone shook his head, and Mark went back in and left him. Twenty minutes later, Mark came back out with a bag of trash and found him still leaning up against his Mustang.

Mark disposed of the trash and came to stand silently next to him.

Stone looked at his watch. It was seven minutes past the time Doc was supposed to have called him in the event Abigail didn't make it home. She was okay.

He called Doc back anyway. "How is she?" he asked, his voice sounding strained to his own ears.

"Better. Gone for a nap. Panic attack, it looks like."

"Panic attack?" Stone echoed. She suffered from panic attacks? Since when?

"Hmm. Been so long since the last one I thought she was over them." Doc said it matter-of-factly, as if it were something he and Stone had talked about all the time. "Was at a shower, she said?"

"Yes. Friend of mine."

"I'm surprised she went. She's fine with crowds and church services. It's those mid-sized social events that she doesn't do so well at."

"I...see. Should I come over?"

"Perhaps not. I gave her a sedative. I'd let her sleep it off."

"Has she always suffered from panic attacks?"

Doc hesitated, as if only then realizing he might have given something away that Stone didn't already know. "Not always, no. But I'm not sure exactly when they started. Melody would be better able to tell you that."

"Melody?"

"Her therapist."

Her therapist.

Okay, so it wasn't that big a deal. Lots of people saw therapists at some point or other in their lives. Abigail had just been widowed. Reason enough for her to see one. If that was indeed why she was.

My petals didn't unfurl right.

Whatever that meant.

I don't appeal to men that way.

Or was it the other way around?

"I don't suppose you had any idea either that she and

mommy-to-be knew each other, huh?" a quiet voice asked after Stone had hung up, and Stone only then recalled Mark was still there, thoughtfully taking in his conversation with Doc.

"Not a clue." Hadn't even been aware that Fern and Crystal had spotted her among the sea of faces waiting to greet Fern.

"Well, don't feel bad. From the look on Abby's face, neither did she."

It was entirely possible. He couldn't particularly remember calling either Crystal's or Fern's name. Maybe when he first walked into the gift registry. But she'd seemed somewhat distracted then, had even acted a little standoffish the whole time the sales associate was helping him.

He forced himself to go back inside and try to recapture the spirit of the occasion. Mark was his friend and would probably remain his friend regardless of how many capricious females came and went in his life.

What seemed like an eternity later, he was at the front door behind the other departing guests, giving Fern's expanding tummy a pat and telling her, "Take care of my godson."

"Will do, Stone. You take care of you. And Abby." Her voice dropped. "Cut her some slack, will you? I've a feeling it's been a while since anybody has."

Crystal was a lot less forbearing. As she hugged him and thanked him for coming, she whispered near his ear, "Don't let Abigail's little stunt throw you, Stone."

He wasn't entirely surprised. He didn't know Crystal as well as he did Fern, but she'd always struck him as the kind of female who could be less than charitable to anyone who didn't happen to occupy her inner circle at the moment.

It was the rest of what she said that got his attention: "It's just a little habit she picked up after she got married, running out on her friends. And if she wants to know who could have told you such a thing, tell her Duchess."

Abigail allowed her sleep-weighted eyelids to flutter closed and tried to shut her mind against the memories intruding on it.

Hey there, Mrs. Carmichael. You done honeymooning yet? Cause Wednesday's the big one, girl. Doors open eight AM sharp...Really? Oh well, next time.

Missed you at prayer breakfast...Hubby needed some quality time, huh? That mean we'll be planning a shower sometime soon, or what?...Oh. Well, pardon the intrusion.

Well hello, stranger. You don't answer your phone anymore?...No kidding...Well then, how bout you call us when it's a good time, cause we don't seem to be able to figure out when that is.

So can we count on you or not? We kinda like need to know...Oh, don't give me that again...Know what? Forget it...Catch up with you later.

So they had, four years later at a party she hadn't been invited to.

It was her last conscious thought before she yielded to the dense gray mist swirling around her.

"I don't know anything about her marriage, Stone," Fern told Stone later that night. She'd been already in bed and half asleep when she overheard Mark telling him to call back the next day. She'd shrugged off the sleep and insisted on taking his call. "Nobody ever got close enough to them as a couple for that," she added, her voice grim and reflective.

"How come?"

"He was older than us and kind of serious. *She* was older than us, although we'd had miles more exposure than her. But we were still single and kind of giddy. And after she got married, it was like her serious side took over and we just didn't seem to have anything in common anymore."

"You and her? Or all her friends?" *As in Duchess, JoJo, Sarah and Kay,* he wanted to add, but he knew he couldn't if he didn't want to create more of a rift between Abigail and her friends than already existed. They weren't going to hear from him that he knew their screen names and had seen some of their e-chats. "She doesn't seem to have too many of them now," he said instead.

"She didn't ever have a wide circle of friends. She was never exactly an extrovert, in spite of her father and all. But those few friends she had she valued dearly. Used to."

"So what happened?"

"In a few words—Eric Carmichael."

"Could it have been just a case of old-fashioned jealousy? Having to adjust to the fact that she couldn't go haring off with you at the drop of a hat?"

"There could have been some of that in there, sure. Except we couldn't get her to go haring off with us if we planned it a whole year in advance. There had to be a purpose to everything. Girlfriend time didn't qualify as a reason anymore. And she simply didn't consider any of our purposes worth her time."

"You think he might have been trying to control her or something?"

"If he was, she certainly never complained about it. The opposite, in fact. She worshipped the man. Everything was Eric. Eric this, Eric that. You ask her what her favorite color is, and I guarantee you it'd come right back round to Eric. Got on our last raw nerve with it. And that's coming from someone who thinks *her* man hung the moon and the stars."

"We talking about the same Abigail here?" *The same Spunky* was what he'd almost said.

"Same Abigail, Stone. Talk to anyone who was close to her back when she was married and you'll hear the same story."

The problem was, he wasn't sure he even knew who the real Abigail was anymore. The more he heard from Fern, the harder it became for Stone to reconcile the Abigail that used to be with the Spunky of the e-chats.

And if not Spunky, who was Abigail, Crystal being Duchess and Fern obviously being Sarah? Kay? He worse couldn't see that. Abigail was too grounded in the faith, was too much of an independent thinker to have followed blindly and dumbly after some wayward preacher off on an authority trip the way Kay had.

Then again, he wouldn't have figured Fern for a Sarah, either. Love her husband though she did, there was nothing unhealthy about Fern's self-concept. Perhaps exactly the reason she was free to love her husband the way she did. Time and experience could account for the difference, he supposed, but—

"Go figure it out yourself and leave my wife to get some sleep," Mark intruded, grabbing the phone from an increasingly drowsy Fern.

Stone called him a name and otherwise took the brush-off in stride. It took a whole lot more than that for him and Mark to get offended at each other.

He didn't know Fern on quite the same level, but he knew Mark, and that he'd fallen in love with her and married her in itself told Stone a lot.

"Tell Abby I still love her," she called out groggily a split second before her husband hung up the phone.

What had made Abigail turn her back on friendship like that?

It's going to take a lot for him to trust you again, Abigail, and though he might not risk God's judgment by abandoning his covenant altogether, he's going to have a hard time staying faithful to a helpmeet he cannot trust. Problem is, he'll never be able to see you at that computer again or hear you giggling on the phone, or know you're out gallivanting with them without wondering what kind of cheap jokes or idle chatter you're entertaining about him or, worse, about a prophet of God anointed to be the spiritual covering for you both.

You've opened your marriage up to demonic attacks, Abigail. You must break that curse off you. Renounce the spirit of your namesake and keep confessing that you refuse to be the death of your own husband.

Meanwhile, you need to be working on winning back his trust. Your husband should not be put in the position of having to spy on you. You realize it had to be God Himself who overrode your password and made Eric stumble on those chats in the middle of doing PC maintenance? Why do you think that is? So you'd be forced to start thinking about what is important to you and whether you meant it when you vowed to forsake all others and cleave only to him...

Abigail pushed back her intrusive thoughts and glanced at the clock on her bedside table. Only a little after midnight, a new record for her. What did she expect, anyway, after sleeping the evening away?

She got out of bed resignedly and started pacing listlessly about the room. Paused by her desk to shut down the laptop she'd left on several days running, and stopped. The neon envelope in the top left corner of her screen was lit.

27

Hi Abigail,

> I imagine you heard about Beth even before we
> did. Thought you might be interested in me and
> Crystal tagging along when you go to see her.
> Saturday night's good for us. I know you check
> your mail regularly, so if I don't hear from you
> by then I won't bother you again.
> Fern

It had come in Thursday, when she'd been too busy
mooning over Stone to have any interest in checking to see
how many spams had escaped her filter. And they'd gone to
see Beth Saturday night and had no doubt heard that she'd
been there earlier with Stone.

It would take more pluck than she possessed at the moment to convince them he wasn't yet another man she'd
sold them out for.

When Stone strode unannounced into Doc's greenhouse
the following evening after Oasis, he didn't try leading gently up to his subject. Didn't make a pretense either of being
interested in the pain-in-the-neck shrub that Doc had finally decided to remove from its place of honor atop the dais.
Just pulled up a crate and straddled it near to the potting
bench, where Doc was mixing some fertilizer.

If there was anyone who qualified as someone who'd

known Abigail back when she was married, surely it was her own father.

"I'm going to give it a little sustenance and put it in a corner to think about its reason for being alive," Doc announced, sounding pained but determined.

"Doc, tell me about Eric Carmichael."

"What do you want to know?"

Like maybe if he had warts or crossed eyes. "I don't know. Whatever jumped out at you, I guess."

"What do you know about him?"

Apart from that he was probably a tough act to follow? "Not much."

"Well, let's see. What was the first thing that grabbed me about Eric? His voice, maybe. Resonant. But he was fairly soft-spoken. Can't imagine him yelling. Could reach the fringe of the biggest crowd without appearing to yell. A voice made for public speaking, if ever there was one."

"I get the idea." Enough already about Eric's voice. He could only imagine what his own foghorn must sound like to Abigail's ears.

"Did I mention he had leanings toward the ministry?"

"Not really. But I'd heard he was the pastor's cupbearer or some such thing."

"Armor bearer. That's church for personal assistant." He grinned at Stone's deadpan expression. "Remind me to give you a crash course some time in terminology."

"That's all right, Doc. I'm making out just fine with English. So what was he like, personality wise?"

"Quiet. But forceful at the same time, sure of himself. Very principled, dignified fellow." That seemed to unplug his memory, and he went on at length from there to paint a fairly detailed picture of an attractive, suave and brilliant people-person.

Stone felt his gut clench with the bitterness of hopelessness. No way was he going to be able to follow an act like that. No wonder Abigail couldn't stand him at first.

But she's not there now.

Wasn't where he wanted her either. And none of what

Doc was telling him was helping him understand why.

Maybe she was just a very insecure woman. He'd crossed paths with a few of those in his lifetime, and they had been incredibly draining experiences. Abby didn't come across as the type.

Then again, she might not have seemed the type when she and Eric were courting, either...not until it was too late for Eric to decide whether it was something he could live with or not. Was that what had happened with them?

"Okay, here we go..." His measuring and mixing and feeding over with, Doc lifted the plant from its shelf, jostling it a bit as he concentrated on keeping his balance on the short step ladder he had to use to reach it.

Something fell from among the hindermost branches and floated slowly downward. Stone caught the pale flash of color and moved quickly to intercept it before it could touch the ground.

It was a single creamy-yellow flower. He and Doc stared at it and then at each other. There was a triumphant gleam in Doc's blue eyes.

Stone's fingers curved reflexively round their fragile prize and did with it what he'd been in the habit of doing with loose flowers from long before he started hanging around Doc's greenhouse. He crushed one of its petals between forefinger and thumb and raised it to his nostrils, registering Doc's shocked protest only after it was too late.

"Honeysuckle?" Stone murmured, breathing in its soft but distinct fragrance.

Doc nodded, his displeasure over the flower's desecration apparently eclipsed by his pride in knowing that it had finally succeeding in wowing Stone. "Yes, but no. A hybrid. Pretty rare one. I bribed him shamelessly to get him to part with it."

"Why, if it was worth so little to him?"

"Couldn't be bothered, I guess. Doesn't sell to the general public. He's not a retailer. I just happened to spot his place from the road and pulled over on a whim. He deals primarily with a perfumer, wouldn't you know."

"So you knew all along what it was supposed to be."

"Well, of course. I'd seen the man's handiwork. Picked it out of a patch of hybrids grown to specification. I had no reason to doubt what it was."

"But you let me go on wondering what on earth it was."

"You didn't ask. You'd already decided it wouldn't flower." He smiled smugly. "I figured you'd find out soon enough when it did."

Stone raised the bruised flower slowly to his nostrils again. He smoothed one of its velvety petals between forefinger and thumb and looked closely at it. It was pink-throated with burgundy warts, little supposed imperfections that lent distinction to its otherwise understated beauty.

He'd seen more striking honeysuckle blooms, but none that smelled quite like this one.

"Honeysuckle's Breath," he said, spilling his thoughts as his memory finally coughed up the name.

It was Doc's turn to be impressed. "You do know your stuff."

"Actually, I wouldn't have known it different from any other pale yellow flowering shrub. It's the fragrance I'm familiar with."

Doc's look grew curious. "Really. I'd never figure you for a connoisseur."

"I'm not really, Doc. Just happen to know this particular one."

"Oh?"

"I've been out that way myself. I might have had dealings with a client of your horticulturist friend."

"*Hmm.*"

He knew that diplomatic *hmm* and the silence that followed it. He remembered it from their many conversations in the early days following his conversion, when an unguarded Stone had frequently tripped over dirty linen from his own past. He blushed sometimes now when he looked back at some of the stuff he'd divulged to Doc.

He'd been brand new then, anxious to get a pile of junk off his chest, and not fully cognizant of exactly who Dr.

Richard Lester was within Christian circles. Naturally Doc assumed now that some woman or other had inspired him to go hunting down rare fragrances in Central Florida's undeveloped interior. Stone left him alone with the assumption. It didn't matter one way or the other now.

"Abigail's favorite," Doc said casually. *You should know*, one sly eyebrow added.

Now he did, anyway, and maybe now he'd finally identified it he could stop obsessing over it.

"I wouldn't say this to anybody but you, Stone," Doc said, abruptly shifting back to his topic, "but I remember wondering what it was that drew Eric to Abigail. Trust me, he could have had just about any girl he wanted from among the singles, from his congregation or mine. And don't ask if they didn't throw themselves at him."

"Maybe that was the magic ingredient with Abby. The thrill of the chase."

"Oh, Abby didn't play hard to get. Didn't throw herself at him, either, if only because she'd never have expected him to be interested in her. Mind you, she was attractive in her own right, with some sterling qualities. Forgiving. An encourager. Loyal to a fault. But those aren't qualities that excite the hormones, you understand."

But underneath satin-soft skin and corn-silk hair it could be downright mesmerizing. "Maybe he wasn't ruled by his hormones."

"Obviously not."

Great. One less fault for him to pin on Eric. Stone was beginning to wish he'd left well enough alone. He might never have the nerve to make a go for her after this.

"Wasn't long before it became apparent she was the one who'd caught his eye," Doc went on. "It was quick going after that. They were married less than a year later."

"A little short of your prescribed waiting period, isn't it?"

"Yes, but who wouldn't be willing to make an exception in the face of such..."

"Perfection?"

"Nobody's perfect, not even Eric. But he came pretty close to ideal, I can tell you."

Oh joy. He'd finally found something to pin on him. He'd been guilty of perfection, or something close to it.

Words had haunted Virginia's sleep. Some words had a way of detaching themselves from their original medium and context and hanging suspended from nothing in front of the mind's eye.

Sarah's last words to her friends in particular she remembered almost word for word. She should, as often as they had played themselves back in her mind.

I'm sorry, guys, but if giving you up is what it takes to convince him my loyalty is first and foremost to him, it's a sacrifice I'm prepared to make.

Not much of a sacrifice at that, for she'd simply traded something she felt she could afford to give up, in order to hold on to what she didn't think she could have endured losing.

And before you jump to conclusions, he didn't ask me to. He wouldn't.

He wouldn't have had to. Sarah would have handed over her very soul, piece by piece, like she had her God-given, blood-bought liberty, if she'd thought he wanted it. Virginia saw that now, because she'd realized too late that that was what had doomed her own marriage. Too late to stop Sarah going down the same path.

I know what you're going to say, but before you do, ask yourself one thing: If he'd really been trying to cut me off from other people, why would he encourage me to cultivate my friendship with Kay?

Because Kay had been as blind to what him and others like him, her own husband included, were about. Because Kay had been as much of a slave as Sarah had been, both of them captives of their own fears, self-doubt and deep-seated lack of trust in God, afraid to embrace freedom because of the risks and knocks and uncertainty that went along with it.

Sarah had been so young, her ability to make the right choices hampered by her morbid fear of making the wrong ones. And she'd turned for guidance to someone who in her ignorance had helped feed the fear. Virginia saw that now as clearly as she saw the green neon triple Xs running diagonally across the night sky.

28

Y ou've gone a long way towards restoring my trust in you, Sarah. Almost makes me feel I could count on you for the same un-questioning obedience your namesake gave Abraham, even under very difficult circumstances...Could I?"

"Y-yes. Why not? It's not like you're going to pawn me off to some other man or something...are you?"

"Would you let me? No, don't answer that. Of course I wouldn't do that. It's unbiblical, to say the least, and my pride couldn't survive that kind of thing. But I might ask something of you one day that might cause you discomfort...pain, even...And now your eyes are big as saucers. Does that mean you'd refuse? Don't bother to answer. Time enough if and when the time comes. God might test you on it yet."

The pool was icy cold. Her father had decided years ago to save himself the cost of heating it in the winter months, since she just about never used it during those months. Native Floridian that Abigail was, the water's warmth had never been enough to counter the chill of the winter air, be it only a tropical winter.

With any luck, she'd catch her death of cold and...

God forgive me. What on earth am I thinking?

Just idle thoughts, was all. If life hadn't driven her to suicide yet, it wouldn't again.

She did one lap and then two and was starting to falter on the third when something snagged her hair near the shallow end. It was just a gentle tug, but a definite tug nevertheless. From a large hand, she saw as she surfaced midstroke for air. She jackknifed to her feet, coughing and sputtering as the shock of it had her taking in water along with air.

A face filled her vision as she blinked the water from her eyes and focused. Stone. Crouching at the side of the pool with her Tweety Bird beach towel slung around his neck. Bright and early on a Saturday morning.

She gulped air. "What'd you think you're—"

"Sorry. I was going to wait till you finished, but you looked like you were flagging, so..." He ended on a shrug and offered her a hand up.

She ignored it, hands on her hips, trying not to think of what a sight she must look with her hair escaping its pony-tail holder and hanging in rattails round her face. She wished now that she'd stopped to pull on a swim cap, but then again she wasn't to have known she was going to be barged in on by a...

A really good looking guy who managed to steal her breath even in rough looking khaki shorts and a misshapen olive green golf shirt. She watched him peel off his brown leather sandals, set them aside and take a seat on the edge of the pool, feet dangling in the water. He didn't plan on going anywhere anytime soon.

Ordinarily, she might have been excited at the possibility he'd come to propose they spend the day together. But not while her heart was still pounding with fright and she was still struggling to catch her breath. And not after an entire agonizing week of silence between them.

A week in which she'd gone from guilt and confusion to hope and then to pained resignation. Half-expecting him to barge his way into the center of her mini isolation and throw her lame excuse for taking a week off from Oasis— "feeling out of it," as she'd asked her father to tell him— right back at her. Hoping he'd call her up demanding an explanation for what had happened at Fern's shower, or at least just to ask how she was doing and what had caused her to freak out the way she had. Then finally accepting he'd probably grabbed the opportunity to back out of something he'd begun having second thoughts about anyway. The nerve of him.

"What do you want?" It felt like old times. Or not quite. She might be ranting, but he wasn't raving right back, his face solemn and unreadable as he patted the spot right next to him and again offered his hand.

After a brief hesitation, she let him pull her up to the side and drape the towel over her.

Self-consciously, she blotted at her hair while trying at the same time to keep the rest of her covered. His cursory glance down the length of her white swimsuit hadn't held any of the voraciousness that had been evident in them since their relationship started escalating, but she wasn't about to let down her guard, anyway. If only because she knew it would mean a swift end to any doubts he might have had about her curves not coming in.

She was immensely relieved when she sensed his eyes leave her to gaze out at the still rippling surface of the pool.

He sat silently beside her for another moment, hands hanging down between his knees, fingers trailing in the water. She fought the urge to draw nearer to the source of the heat she could feel radiating across the six or so inches that separated them.

"So you checked up on Corey recently?" she asked to distract herself.

"Did better than check up on him. I dropped him off at Mark and Fern's this morning. They don't have a deadline. Fern doesn't see him being a problem, even after the baby comes."

"Oh."

"And like you, she's got special stakes in his welfare, on account of who his mother is."

Her small "Oh" was much more subdued this time.

"Well, at least he—"

"I didn't come here to talk about Corey, Abby. And as for Fern and Crystal—or Sarah and Duchess—I'll leave that up to you to broach if and when you want to. You can tell me about it or you can not tell me about it."

I couldn't care less. He might as well have added that. He didn't even care enough to be mad at her, or at least demand an explanation. Like he'd given up on her. Like he didn't think she was worth the hassle.

All of a sudden it came back to her that she was the one who had distanced herself without any explanation and not the other way around. She was the one who owed him an explanation, if not an apology.

"I'm sorry I ran out on you like that," she blurted. "I was...I just panicked. I didn't know how they'd react, and..." She bit her lip and finished lamely, "I'm really sorry if it caused you any embarrassment."

"I don't have any problem with your panic attack, or whatever was wrong with you. Nobody can fault you for something beyond your control. But it would have meant a lot if you could have trusted me with it, allowed me at least to see you home safely. I didn't have a clue what was happening to you, and you just shut me out like...like your friends say you shut them out. I'd be lying if I told you that doesn't worry me."

"They told you what happened."

"They told me their version. Would have been nice to hear yours. Not that that's what I came here for either."

Would have been nice to hear her version. As in, he was no longer interested. What then had he come for?

I love you. I don't know what it means, where it'll lead...

Maybe he'd seen enough now to know. Maybe he'd come to tell her he didn't think it was going to work out between them after all. She could see him being enough of a pragmatist to be able to walk away from a love that promised more pain than pleasure, and from all accounts, that was what she would bring him.

And why would he bother with her anyway, especially when he had other less complicated alternatives available to him?

"What is her name?" she managed in a relatively even voice. Her gaze was trained on her lap, her hands busy with the towel in her damp hair but the rest of her tuned in to his every move.

"Who?" She felt rather than saw his sharp glance.

"The woman who spoiled you for any other relationship." She chanced a look up at him then.

He was shaking his head, his brows drawn together, and she felt emboldened to ask, "You...is it Shan?" already suspecting it wasn't. It would have been uppermost in his mind otherwise and there on his face.

"No." Emphatic, no hesitation. So was the irritated scowl that accompanied the denial.

The knot in Abigail's stomach eased. A faceless shadow from the past she could deal with, but not someone who was gorgeous and available and just down the road.

"Oh," was all she could come out with.

He looked away again, back across the sun-dappled expanse of blue, and said, his voice flat, "Virginia. Her name was Virginia, Ginny to most people."

She chanced a look at him and left off drying her hair, dropping the end of the towel she'd been using and giving him her full attention.

"She was married to a jerk named P.J. who didn't deserve her. Only she didn't think enough of herself to realize it, no matter how many times I tried to tell her."

"Like your mother, you mean?" she whispered and held her breath.

He opened his mouth as if to deny it and clamped it shut again, then muttered, "Exactly like my mother. After a while I couldn't tell you who I was riled at more, her or him."

"So what happened?"

"I walked away. Couldn't handle being a crutch for someone who kept agreeing to have her leg broken."

Still wasn't handling it.

"I'd been bent on saving her. Only she didn't want to be rescued. I eventually figured out she was never going to leave him."

"You tried to get her to?"

He lifted a shoulder. "I wasn't saved. I didn't have the

same regard I do now for the marriage bond, abuse or no abuse."

"And?" He hadn't told her the worst. She could sense there was more.

He shook his head, his expression dark. Abigail didn't need to hear anymore. Whatever had happened with Virginia had scarred him for life. On top of what his parents' marriage had done to him.

"Stone, I know how hard it must be—"

"No you don't," he cut in fiercely, his face grim.

"Well, maybe not exactly, not having gone through it with you, but I can only imagine that after what happened with your parents—"

"You don't know what happened with my parents."

"Try telling me, then!" she flashed, her temper flaring. She was trying so hard to understand, to share his burden, but he seemed bent on pushing her away and shouldering it alone.

"They didn't just argue," he began abruptly, surprising her into total stillness. "Or rather, my father didn't just rant and rave." He paused, his eyes trained on the pool's now glassy surface. "He used to beat her."

Her breath caught. "He beat you too?" It was a horrified whisper.

"Not since I was about twelve. I was bigger than him by then. He was barely bigger than my mother, and all dried out from alcohol. I take my height from my mother's side." He shot her a wry look. "And my migraine." His face tightened. "And nothing else. It made me so sick the way she supped and supped from him that I deliberately cultivated a kind of aggression in myself. As if my anger wasn't aggression enough. Everything was confrontation. At school, on the playground. Later, in my relationships."

On the job.

"By the time I realized that it created more problems than pacifism did, it was too deeply ingrained in me. I came close to hitting a woman once, and it scared the living daylights out of me. I walked away from that relationship, and that's when I decided that marriage wasn't going to work for me."

Abigail swallowed. Here it came.

"It was the best decision I could have made. It took away the pressure. I found I wasn't so angry anymore. My self-confidence grew, and after a few years of being mentored by the likes of Richard Lester, I came to believe I wasn't a werewolf waiting for my first full moon after all."

"So...when did you get saved?" His conversion didn't seem to have been a factor in any of what he'd told her.

"Like a lot of people, it took a crisis."

"Your mom, you mean?"

"Hmm."

"What happened to your dad?" She wouldn't have dared ask him these kinds of questions a week or two ago, but a lot had happened to their relationship in that time. He'd poked and prodded his way to the center of her most painful secrets and back. It was his turn now.

"He died." His expression was closed and stony.

"Alcohol?" she probed gently.

"Indirectly, I guess you might say." There was a slightly bitter twist to his lips.

"Was this before or after your mom had to go to a nursing home?"

He hesitated a second. "Before. But roughly within the same time frame." He shifted agitatedly. "Abby, I'm really not ready to—"

"Okay, okay."

"I will, eventually. I'll tell you everything you need to know. But it's still painful for me. Even after four-plus years."

"Okay, I understand. I shouldn't have pr—"

He stopped her with a finger over her lips. "There's no-one else I'd rather have prying into my life than you. Sooner or later I won't have a choice, cause if I have my way—and if it's what God wants—one day you're gonna flat out have that right."

She held her breath. "Really?"

"Really." He held her gaze, and his was quiet and serious and steady. "I love you, Abigail. So much. I ache with it. But I'm still working my way through something here, and..." He heaved a sigh. "And anyway, you know what your daddy has to say about taking baggage into a relationship, and I—"

"Not that I don't have a few of my own."

He didn't try arguing with that.

She couldn't but reach out to him then, wrapping her arms around as much of him as she could and stroking his back. He leaned slightly into the embrace, but she could feel the hum of tension in his body as he held part of himself back.

"I think I love you too, Stone," she whispered into his shoulder. "I'm not quite sure since when. It kind of snuck up on me."

"Yeah, well, mine's been stalking me openly and relentlessly since the first day you walked into my office at Grace." He eased back so her arms fell away.

"You sure had a funny way of showing it."

"Because I was fighting it like crazy."

"Why? Am I such a pain to love?"

He actually hesitated. "I'd had some...preconceptions about you."

"Besides what had to do with my name, you mean? What kind of preconceptions?"

"Doesn't matter. I was wrong."

"W—"

"And it was only partly about Oasis, anyway. See, I'd had my life mapped out, and it didn't include marriage anytime soon. Till maybe I was too wizened to be a threat to anybody and then nobody would want me anyway."

It took some creativity picturing that.

"Lord showed me how He could use my experience to help others, married or no. Especially those who weren't being reached by the Richard Lesters of the church. I shared my vision with your dad, and he got right behind me. For the first time in my life I started to see something good come of the mess of my life, and it fueled my testimony and turned food for the people I was trying to reach."

He looked at her and smiled suddenly. "And then there came this little half-pint firebrand." He turned and allowed his eyes to caress her face. "A little bit of a thing who looked like she'd snap in two if I hugged her too hard. I felt like a brute every time I got near her, and it didn't help that she seemed to know how to push my button. All the old fears came sneaking back home."

"Wh-what kind of fears?" He'd never mentioned any to her. Fearfulness was not a characteristic she'd ever associate with him.

"Of being like him."

"Oh. But you're n—"

"She brought back every one of them. Sometimes I was scared just to be around her. I'd have died rather than hurt her—"

"And you *didn't.*"

"But I didn't trust myself not to." He paused and added heavily. "Still don't."

"Oh, Stone, why? You...you've never even come close..."

"Neither did my dad, till a few months into his marriage."

"So? You're not your dad."

"I'm fifty percent him. And while we're busy declaring our baggage, alcoholism runs in families. It's in the genes. That's a fact."

"So? So does murder and madness and a bunch of other things."

If anything, his expression went even grimmer, and she realized there wasn't anything reassuring about what she'd said.

She tried again. "Stone, you have any idea how many criminals and whatnot have got saved and never went back to being what they once were? And moreover, you don't drink. You told me you didn't."

"And why do you suppose that is?"

"You avoid it like the plague."

"Now I do."

"You were an alcoholic?"

"Headed there fast by the time Jesus caught up with me. He loosed me like—" He snapped his fingers. "Overnight, literally. Haven't touched a drop since."

"Well, then—"

"Neither did my dad...for a whole year after going through AA."

"AA is no substitute for Jesus. Your dad wasn't saved." She faltered. "Was he?"

His expression darkened. "Don't remind me. I still harbor hopes that there was a split second at the end when he had time to cry out to God—like that thief on the cross, you know?"

"He died suddenly?"

"Pretty much. I really don't want to talk about that side of it, Abby."

"Okay."

"Lord knows he should have known what to do after living with my mom for thirty-something years."

"It's more than possible, Stone. God 'is not willing that any should perish,' not even those who wait for the last minute to call out to Him. And He said *whosoever* calls on Him will be saved, not whosoever does it by a certain deadline."

"Yeah, I've thought about that too." He looked at her and gave her a quick squeeze. "Thanks for not making me feel like I'm just grasping at straws."

He lowered his head, eyeing her mouth, then, a hairsbreadth away from claiming it, pulled back. Dropped his arm from around her waist and sighed.

She asked tightly, "So then, you want me to keep my distance, is that it?"

"No I don't *want* you to keep your distance. But I'm thinking maybe you should."

Her face must have shown her hurt, for his face immediately softened, and he said, "You mess with my equilibrium, Abby. You threaten my self-control, and that's putting it delicately. I'm not going to be able to think things out while I'm in the thick of a battle with my flesh. And then where does that leave me in between episodes of insanity? Still unsure of myself, of you, of us." He heaved a deep breath and said a little shakily, "Be patient with me, hmm?"

And while she was still digesting that, he pulled himself to his feet, shoved his feet into his sandals and left without a backward glance.

"I'd like a word with you if I may, Stone."

The words stopped Stone in his tracks as he exited the pool area and headed round the side of the house toward the driveway.

Doc. Tending a rose bed that was just out of sight of the pool but probably not out of earshot.

29

Stone's heart sank as he tried to recall his conversation with Abigail and figure out how much of it Doc might have heard.

"Of course."

"Let's go up a little further."

So Abby wouldn't hear. He *had* heard them.

So what? He hadn't done anything wrong. At least he thought enough of her to put the brakes on their relationship till he could be reasonably assured that he wasn't taking her down a path that was leading to nowhere.

At a wrought-iron bench overlooking an herb garden on the other side of the house, Doc stopped and sat. "Sit down, Stone. You're too big to be towering over me like that. Especially when I'm doing my best to at least appear to be in control." He smiled when he said it, but the smile didn't carry to his voice.

He waited for Stone to take a seat and then began. "You know, I've always been an advocate for children being allowed to make their own decisions and learn from the consequences. But sometimes I wonder if I wasn't so bowled over by Eric I neglected to provide Abby with even the most minimal of oversight. With the result that in spite of how well her marriage turned out and everything, I'm haunted by a feeling that I failed her somehow."

He paused, then just as Stone was beginning to suspect he was off the hook, he finished, "I don't plan on making the same mistake twice."

Stone digested that, then forced a shrug. "Can't say I

blame you, Doc."

"I'm telling you all that to say this...She's been through too much too recently to be put on an emotional roller coaster just yet. Or ever again."

"Which is to say?"

"That you need to finish working your way through whatever it is that's holding you back and make a decision one way or the other instead of having her hanging on indefinitely and falling apart in the process."

Stone fought a small stirring of resentment, reminding himself that this was the man who had proven time and again that he cared for him like a son, the same man whose counsel he'd trusted on every other issue that had come up between them.

"Fair enough," he made himself say. "But I hadn't planned on leaving her *hanging on indefinitely*." *It's hardly been two weeks*, he might have added. But he thought better of it. Abigail might only now have discovered her feelings for him, but Doc knew only too well that *his* feelings for her were a whole lot more than two weeks old. And if Doc as her father had decided that two weeks was too long, in her fragile state, to be kept riding an emotional seesaw, who was Stone Patrick to say otherwise?

"I don't enjoy living in a state of flux any more than she does," he said tightly instead.

"Yes, but you're the one controlling it. You get to say when. Because you're *choosing* to be in a state of flux."

"With good reason, Doc."

"Really. Tell me about this reason that is worth tearing two people apart over."

"I'd rather not discuss it."

"Very well, I have to respect that."

Stone rose to go.

"And Stone?

"Yes." He answered without turning back. He'd had enough of this particular heart to heart to last him a while.

"I want you to know that nothing would give me greater pleasure than one day having you call me father...should it be God's will to join our families. But I don't know that it is, and till I do, bear in mind I have a daughter to protect."

"Yes, *sir.*"

"And now I know I've offended you, cause you've gone from Doc back to sir."

"I couldn't be offended by anything you did to protect your daughter, sir. She also happens to be the woman I love."

Who was he kidding? Of course he was offended. Besides discouraged, hurt and embarrassed. He wanted instant acceptance like Eric Carmichael had got. He might not be the saint Eric had been, but he loved her just as much. More.

He sure as heaven wouldn't have left her with an outsized complex about her ability to appeal to men. What had Eric been made of, anyway, to have had trouble responding to someone like Abby? And what kind of power had he had over her that he'd managed to convince her that she was something less than achingly, delectably woman?

Even now Stone had to fight to banish the memory of her petite but undeniably feminine curves scantily covered by her swimsuit.

So she didn't look as if she'd had a surgical encounter of the silicone kind, and she didn't tease and flaunt. But she was all woman, all five-foot-whatever of her. Soft and supple and fragrant. And when she looked at him just so from underneath those gold-tipped lashes he felt like a big mindless chunk of silly putty.

Charm is deceitful, and beauty is vain...

Ah yes, Lord, but this one's got it all. The outward beauty as well as the enduring kind. He'd seen it over and over, including just now by the pool.

She opens her mouth with wisdom, and on her tongue is the law of kindness.

A single unrehearsed expression of her simple faith, and

she'd neutralized his torment over the fate of his father's soul and given his heart reason to hope.

...but a woman who fears the Lord, she shall be praised.

Worth a whole lot more than rubies, for sure, and as rare as her scent.

And he wanted to feel worthy of her. He wanted her father's blessing like Eric had got his blessing. Wanted assurance from someone other than her that he was indeed worthy of her.

I made you worthy.

I know, Lord, but being clothed in Your righteousness is no guarantee I'd make a good husband for any daughter of yours.

It must have been in some subconscious bid to convince himself of his own unworthiness that he found himself where he did later that afternoon.

I t started with a look from Phantom. *The Look*, Stone had styled it. He'd walked Phantom and was putting him back behind the fence when the dog sat back on his heels and gave him a look that said, *Go ahead, you've done your fifteen minutes duty, so now you can just lock me away again and forget I exist till tomorrow this time.* Or something close to that.

There were times when Stone would brush it off with a dry, "Don't even try it, you old manipulator you," and Phantom would good naturedly concede defeat—two licks and a woof—and trot happily away. But then there were the times when the dog would go obediently behind the gate at the first command and just sit on the inside of it with a soulful look that said, *I understand, and I'll be here when you feel like it.* Those were the ones that usually got to Stone, and today was one such occasion.

Before he knew it, they were both in his pickup, Phantom's head out the passenger side window enjoying the fondling of the breeze as they headed off to nowhere.

Or so Stone thought as he drove blindly in the general direction of north, guided only by whim and green traffic lights, his thoughts keeping time with the rhythm of his favorite instrumentalists. Till he found himself in an upscale part of northern Broward County, on a street lined with lofty grand palms and even loftier houses.

The kind he'd seen as a child from the window of a passing car on the rare Sunday afternoon his father was in a good mood and would take them driving—to see how the rest of the world lived, as he put it.

Stone's stomach clenched at the memory. It was not a happy one. For inevitably, an hour or two of undiluted envying and coveting would remind his father of all he didn't have and why. That he'd made one stupid mistake in his senior year of high school and had to pay for it by being saddled with a wife and kid when all his friends were off at college building a future and sowing wild oats.

And so he'd take them back home in a stew and make them pay all over again for the sorry turn his life had taken at age nineteen.

Stone made a turn onto a quiet dead-end street, and something else clicked in his memory. He checked the street sign. It was the street Abigail and her husband used to live on. Doc had rattled off the address once as part of an illustration of how well Eric had done for himself. He'd had no way of knowing that Stone's memory stored numbers as efficiently as any computer's.

Not that Stone had ever intended to do anything with this particular set of numbers. He wasn't sure why he found himself there now. He had no interest in seeing where Abigail had lived with her husband. He didn't need another reminder of how hopelessly short he fell of measuring up to Eric.

He'd never be able to provide for her like that, short of finding himself a gullible flock of his own and fleecing them bald. Neither social work nor Christian counseling offered the kind of perks that personal assistants to prosperity theologians apparently did.

He still didn't want to see the house. Didn't want to so much as speed past it on his way to the next intersection. Instead, he was going to avail himself of the next empty driveway, turn his pickup around, and head back the way he had come.

The house was pale yellow trimmed with white, with a deep, perfectly manicured lawn. Phantom gave an eager *woof* as they pulled up on the swale and glanced impatiently from Stone to the inviting stretch of green waiting to be trampled on.

Stone ruffled his head. "Not this one, boy. They'd have us both arrested."

A small middle-aged Hispanic looking woman who was just then letting herself out the front door came quickly down the Chattahoochee walkway. She flashed a bright white smile and greeted Stone in thickly accented English. Only then did he see the diminutive regulation-size sign stuck into the lawn at the end of the driveway.

"Is got the contract on it just sign today," the woman who'd introduced herself as Ana told him. "But I still show it to you anyway if you like. Contracts, they fall through all the time. You like, I put you on waiting list. You be first in line."

She'd kill him if she knew, and she would know sooner or later, for how could he hide something like this from her forever?

And so what if she did know? He wasn't out to steal or snoop or anything. If she'd had anything to hide, she wouldn't have put a stranger in charge of showing other strangers around her house. It wasn't even her house anyway, except legally. She'd abandoned it the day her husband died, Doc had told him once.

Ana looked doubtfully at the dog, misunderstanding Stone's hesitation. "It probably best you leave him outside."

The minute he stepped inside, he knew why.

31

The private line Abigail had reactivated only the day before got its first call as she padded her way from the patio shower, through the sliding glass doors and up the stairs to her bedroom.

Her traitorous heart skipped a beat before she recalled that she'd only just given the number to her father earlier at breakfast. Stone wasn't likely to have got a hold of it yet.

Nevertheless, she quickened her pace and dove across the bed to retrieve the phone before the voicemail could kick in. Seconds later, she banged it down again in irritation. An automated message from the telephone company, a *courtesy* call, they had the nerve to call it. Next time she'd know to check her caller ID first.

She wasn't even sure what she needed her own line for, now she thought of it. Her cell phone reception was spotty, yes, but the days of chatty girlfriends tying up her father's land line for impossible lengths of time were no more. And the only other person she saw herself committing that kind of folly with these days wasn't likely to be calling her up anytime soon.

She spent the afternoon doing her hair and nails and starting on a dress she wanted to wear to an upcoming women's conference at one of Grace's sister assemblies. Her appetite for the garage-sale spree she had planned had gone out the door with Stone. She'd lazed by the pool all morning, soaking up the sunshine as she didn't dare to at any other time of the year and meandering through a fat Beltway biography that had been gathering dust on her father's shelf.

The telephone rang again as she was painstakingly endeavoring to paint a perfect white new-moon on the tips of her right fingernails. Her left hand wobbled, and she glared from the resulting squiggle on her fingernail to the telephone, certain that her father was still the only other person in possession of her number. She didn't even pay the offending instrument the courtesy of checking its caller ID.

He was doing a tour of some home show set. The house was still fully furnished, and how. Except that real people had lived there at some time or other. So Ana said. He hadn't seen the evidence yet.

"Is being sold as is. Furniture, pictures, dirty dishes, everything included." She laughed, and he soon saw why.

There were no dirty dishes. Or anything else dirty. Or the least bit out of place.

"Is a very good buy, *no?*"

He let go a whooshing breath that had her smiling in agreement. She took him from room to room, showing him more of the same.

Closets neatly stacked, intricately folded towels primly perched on their racks as if they'd never felt the touch of a wet hand. Not a single living thing out of place.

There was something disturbing about it all. Something that wasn't right. He felt it in his gut and didn't know why.

"And wait till you see what else is included."

She showed him the garage. A three-car garage that was probably not much smaller than his entire living space. White, pristine, clutter free. Stone stared at the car parked in the center of it. A late model Volvo, from the upper end of the price scale, if his memory served him well. *That* was what she was *throwing in* with the house?

"That was hers. Is listed under contents of garage to be sold as is."

While she dragged around South Florida in an old beater

from her college days.

"The other one, her husband's, she give to his family. The memories, they too much for her, I guess." She led him back through the kitchen and reset the alarm.

"Her husband, he die suddenly of the heart attack, you know," she explained gravely as she locked the front door behind them. "She never been back to stay here since. Not even to get her clothes. The memories, they be too painful for her, you understand? The other day the first time she come inside ever."

Tell me she did some quick tidying up. Tell me she closed a drawer, washed a spoon, put even one object back in place, something.

"...And she was ten minutes, no more, at the computer and then was gone. Every other time we have to meet for some reason, is outside on the sidewalk that we do our business. And I see the pain in her eyes. Is so sad."

The pain in her eyes. A near stranger had seen it, and he, the great counselor, hadn't been able to. All he'd seen was the anger, the rebellion, and he hadn't bothered to ask why. It didn't take a whole lot of figuring out to know that she was still grieving, that, like Doc had speculated, something about having to deal with him had resurrected that grief. But no, it was much easier to believe she was insecure and confused and couldn't recognize when something was good or bad for her.

Because his own mother had been all of that and more, and because he was scared to death he would prove to be more like his father than he realized and was doomed from the womb to repeat history.

"There's someone I've been wanting to tell you about."

He'd been patiently coaxing her through her Salisbury steak and mashed potatoes and remembering the mouth-watering pot roast and baby potatoes she used to cook him not so long ago when the words erupted from him without warning and filled the hollow silence of the room.

He hadn't planned on broaching the subject of Abigail anytime soon, much less orchestrating a meeting between the two of them. Not when he was still in the middle of sorting through the tangle of his own feelings and battling stubborn doubts. That would be piling frustration on top of frustration.

But his encounter with Abigail's father must have triggered something in him. A desire to come clean, maybe. For what right had he to demand Abigail's or any woman's trust when he couldn't be open with her about something so vital to who he was and what he'd be bringing to their relationship?

She had stopped chewing and was giving him a worried look. "You sure? You know how P.J. is about people coming to the house."

Right. Wouldn't want to overlook that obstacle when it made all the others look trivial.

"It's a girl...woman," he pressed on, determined to get it said. That done, maybe he'd get up the nerve to talk to Abigail next.

The worry disappeared from her face. "That Colin certainly is nice, though."

So much for that. He sighed. "Yeah, he is. Here, you're not eating." Why did he even bother?

Her hand reached out suddenly to grip his wrist as he speared a couple of carrot slices with her fork. "Do you love her?"

His startled gaze went from the carrots to the hand curled round his wrist—a beautiful hand, long and shapely—and up into the strong-boned beauty of her face. She was searching his face intently, making eye contact. She seemed to be doing a lot more of that these days.

He stared back at her. "Yes, I believe I do love her."

The slightest of pauses, before she gave a satisfied nod, apparently relieved by his answer. "Well then, it will all come out right. Just leave it to Jesus, is all."

There were times she just plain freaked him out. She'd always been given to rare flashes of extreme lucidity, odd moments when the real her would push past the drugged chaos of her mind to the surface and startle a laugh or a hug out of him and occasionally a few tears. But those moments used to be few and far between. Lately it seemed they were happening a lot more frequently.

Or was it just that he was listening more now? What would he have seen if he'd taken the trouble more often to look into her eyes as he had just now?

Why was it so difficult for him to do that, anyway?

You need to release her, pal...

What if Mark was right?

For your sake and hers. Abby's too, if you love her...

There was absolutely no doubt in his mind that he did love Abby. His misgivings had never been about his feelings for Abigail, or hers for him, for that matter. They had more to do with the fog on the lenses through which he was viewing his life, the same fog that had made him unable to see past Abigail's rebellion to the pain she was hiding. The same fog that might also have been blocking his access to the warmth and wisdom trapped inside the brittle shell housing another woman he'd never taken the time to know.

And Mark might have had a point after all.

Not about him thinking he was entitled to some bit of unforgiveness, exactly. He didn't. He'd covered that in Christianity 101 with Doc and had accepted it. But that didn't mean he hadn't managed to hold on to a tiny bit of baggage just the same.

At any rate, it couldn't hurt to say the words again. There was nothing like the spoken word for laying that kind of ambivalence to rest. And should he find that the words simply would not pass his throat, he'd know that it was time to check himself and go ask God to grant him

more grace. Yes, why not? He'd do it. But not today.
First there was somewhere else he had to go...

32

Sunset caught Abigail under the hair dryer stifling multiple yawns and frowning over an extra-small regular dress pattern she was trying to convert into an extra-small petite. By nightfall, she was already fading and barely managed to outlast the dryer's timer.

As she turned back the bedcovers, an old habit from former times had her picking up the receiver and checking its dial tone. She had a message, its stutter told her. She checked the caller ID and only then realized her second call hadn't been from the phone company, after all.

"Hey, girl. Bet you're surprised I'm still here. So am I. Doctor wanted to run a few more tests. He'd said tomorrow, but he just came by and gave me the okay to go."

Abigail felt a twinge of guilt as she realized Beth had been almost two weeks in the hospital and received only one visit from her. She wasn't supposed to have been in there that long, of course. She'd had some lab tests that needed rechecking and in the meantime had picked up a strep infection.

Even so, Abigail had planned on going back. But her grand intentions had gone down the drain along with her resentment of Stone. In the final analysis, once Stone was back in the equation, she'd simply lost her motivation to go it alone. Sounded familiar.

Beth's voice went on, "Stone said he'd come get me anytime I'm ready...make sure I didn't have any problems with Leo and all that. But I was thinking...I was wondering...You still hate driving down here at night? Cause I was thinking..."

Abigail hit two to save the message then. She was barely processing what she was hearing, but she'd registered enough to know that whatever idea Beth had was going to depend on her going to pick her up from the hospital. Now. If she was even still there. Come to think of it, she'd probably called Stone by now. The message was hours old. Beth would have concluded by now that she was out on a Saturday jaunt, or didn't want to be bothered.

She felt a pang at the tentative, almost apologetic tone in which Beth had asked the favor, evidence of how much the years had come between them. There was a time her message would have gone something more like, "Girl, stop being such a fraidy cat and get your butt down here 'fore I hop a bus and come get you."

Abigail sighed her regret as she hung up. She couldn't drive down to Miami Regional this close to nightfall. The hospital district was teeming with life, yes, hospital staff and students coming and going at all hours of the day and night. Many of them lived in high rises renovated especially with them in mind. It was the neighboring districts that she feared, the same ones Stone had driven through to and from Survivors.

She'd be taking I-95, of course, but then she would have to exit and drive that lonely stretch of access road, with bush land on one side. And stop at the traffic lights, which were bound to be red, at the shadowy highway underpass where the homeless and destitute loitered with gaunt, dirty faces and hungry stares that could arouse pity and fear all at once.

Beth wasn't bothered by any of it, but Beth had grown up around those parts. Abigail rarely ventured down there. She'd always been sure that a potential predator would smell her fear and discomfort a mile off. And there'd be no fierce-eyed, muscle-bound protector to act as a deterrent this time.

And she was sounding as paranoid as a certain emotional cripple she remembered who'd had to be rescued from a prison of her own making.

No sooner had the thought hit her than a rush of panic threatened to engulf her. *Lord, no. I don't want to go back there.*

She breathed deeply and leafed through the mental pages of her emergency verses, narrowing them down to a couple of phrases, *The Lord is on my side; I will not* fear. *What can man do to me?*

She said it out loud, over and over till the truth of the words like molten lava burned a course to the core of her, where it solidified into faith. She felt the invisible steel bars that had been about to close in on her retreat. And opted to go to bed anyway.

Stone paused on the threshold of the vestibule of the Spirit and Truth Center the following night and felt momentarily paralyzed as a memory flashed unbidden before his mind's eye. Blood, dark red and pungent, splattered over the altar and staining the royal blue carpet below...

Why had he come?

Lord, these are your people. Help me to see them as just that, no more, no less.

What did he hope to accomplish, anyway, apart from resurrecting the putrid remains of a past it had taken him four years to bury?

O wretched man that I am! Who will deliver me from this body of death?

Only You, Jesus. And he'd been told to lay those remains on Him, not try to bury them himself.

Not so much the dead body whose spilled blood sometimes haunted his sleep and shouted, "Guilty—you're as guilty as if you pulled the trigger yourself." That kind of straightforward condemnation was easy to counteract with Scripture, and Doc had made sure he'd chewed and thoroughly digested all the appropriate verses from early on.

No, it was the more subtle torment that went with it that dragged on him as heavily as would a rotting corpse he'd been condemned to carry around with him for the rest of his days. The tyranny of his own flesh that had him continually embroiled in a fruitless struggle between his baser instincts and his God-breathed will, effectively keeping him in bondage to the very thing he was fighting. Like the self-fulfilling prophecy Mark had warned him about.

Jesus, I give it all to you. The bitterness, the anger, the pain. Forgive me for holding on to what you died to free me from.

He drew a deep breath and took one step forward into the sanctuary. *I accept that my anger will not accomplish your purposes. Deliver me from the futility of rage.*

It was a familiar prickling along the back of Brother Oswald Dean's neck that first alerted him that a disruptive spirit was about to disturb the Flow in the sanctuary. He became certain of it when he turned and saw the stranger hesitating on the threshold. It was obvious he was uncomfortable and completely out of the Flow.

"For certain men have crept in unnoticed, who long ago were marked out for this condemnation," Brother Ozzie reminded himself in a soft whisper.

A spirit of rebellion was what first suggested itself. Resistance to authority.

"They reject authority, and speak evil of dignitaries..." Apostle's deep voice admonished from the pulpit. "These are sensual persons, who cause divisions, not having the Spirit."

Confirmation. God's own words, recorded in Jude. Apostle never less than spoke God's words.

Ozzie gripped his Bible tightly in his lap and repeated the Prayer for Protection Against the Spirit of Rebellion and Mischief, just loud enough for it to count as audible but softly so as not to disrupt the Flow. For Sister Bertrand was still squirming beneath Apostle's knowing eye as he continued to rebuke and convict.

And then the stranger stepped out of the half shadows

of the vestibule and into the sanctuary, and Ozzie saw his face fully, the deep-set black eyes underneath thick, straight eyebrows, the high cheekbones and unsmiling mouth. Ozzie swallowed hard, his own breath threatening to strangle him in his throat.

It was the spirit of murder.

Stone fought the revulsion threatening to gag him and made himself continue toward the side aisle so as not to distract the preacher. He didn't strike Stone as being very distractible, his big voice sure of itself and glued to its message as it reached out like tentacles towards the far corners of the sanctuary.

Only half of the two dozen or so rows on either side were filled. Even so, Stone would have taken a seat in the rear had he not caught sight of a familiar, strong-boned ebony profile in the last of the occupied pews.

Colin Jackman. Stone headed his way with a mixture of surprise and relief and took the empty spot next to him. Colin's surprise was palpable. Something more than just surprise at that. A tension, wariness. Till Stone turned and met his gaze briefly, with the merest hint of a smile. Relief and a silent exultation flooded Colin's previously rigid face.

Colin's hand reached out across the six or so inches separating them and waited, palm up in a silent question.

Stone reached out to take it, but at the last moment Colin's closed into a fist. Surprise delayed Stone's response, but then his hand curled closed too. He watched with a strange sense of detachment as his hand, seemingly of its own accord, engaged the other man's in a convoluted ritual known only to the two of them.

Stone felt a smile tug at his mouth as twenty years of silence began to melt away, and with an unburdening such as he hadn't felt since surrendering his life to Christ, he turned and faced forward.

The speaker—presumably the pastor, from his ornate

robe—was an arresting figure. He was a big man, much like Stone, but animated and intense as Stone couldn't remember being since his teenage years. He had a resonant voice that wooed and stroked its listener and a piercing stare that would compel the most reluctant of gazes.

Abigail's ex-pastor. Z.D. Lightbourne. Man, but she must have given him nightmares.

Stone fought a smile, his interest level somewhere between amusement and curiosity, and offered an open mind and heart to the message that apparently had not long got underway.

Ten minutes later, he walked out. Before the last amen was said and he was forced to suffer their handshakes and the intrusion of their eyes and the grating of being called their brother. Ten minutes was all that was needed to answer the questions that had always haunted him. And to raise an entirely new set he wasn't even sure he wanted answered.

33

I hear you," a deep, quiet voice said behind Stone as he stepped out into the cool, fruit-scented dusk. He had not even realized Colin had followed him out.

Stone didn't acknowledge him, just kept walking till they'd reached his car on the far fringe of the parking lot, where he could make a hasty retreat if the service ended sooner than they expected.

Once there, he stood with his arms extended across the roof of his car, staring out at nothing as he tried to come to terms with what he had just learned.

He had come for answers, and all he'd ended up with were more questions.

How could Abigail have stayed in that mess for five years? How could her husband? What kind of spiritual discernment had he had anyway, to not recognize the place—he refused to call it a church—for what it was? Was Abigail even truly free of it now she was no longer there?

Of course she was. He had a still fading scar on his right cheekbone to prove it. The spitfire who had slammed his own door in his face could not have endured a minute sitting in those pews.

His mother, yes. She'd always been passive by nature, besides being sorely in need of a palliative, a prime candidate to be seduced by an authoritarian with charisma and an adeptness at manipulating truth. Isolated as she'd been, the lure of being embraced by a close-knit church family must have been hard to resist.

Grace had to work diligently to cultivate a sense of

community among its seven hundred plus members and steady stream of visitors, with prayer cells, support groups and the like. His quiet, withdrawn mother would have been lost there, but not at Spirit and Truth Center. What for him was a suffocating experience might have been for her a source of refuge and belonging.

But not Richard Lester's daughter. Not the treasured only child of the man who had taught millions of men to cherish their daughters into an understanding of how God intended for them to be loved by their husband.

Not Colin Jackman, for that matter. Not the quarterback who'd campaigned and charmed and conned his way through most of high school before making an about turn and challenging everybody's preconceptions about Christianity, including those of a religion-shy Stone.

Colin had been his best friend through junior and senior high, the one person Stone trusted with the raw truth about his shoddy home life. Colin had been a regular visitor to Stone's house, through the days of tense calm and through the days of unrestrained turbulence, unfazed by Stone's father. Stone's father seemed to have liked him, too, so much so that when Colin wanted to take "Moms" with him to church, wheedling a grudging consent out of her husband had been a breeze.

Stone remembered being intrigued enough by Colin's transformation to contemplate visiting the church himself. In the end, though, curiosity hadn't been enough to overcome his resistance to any religion his escapist mother was a part of. The more immersed she and Colin became in church life, the further he and Colin had drifted apart.

By the time Richard Lester came along and nurtured into full bloom the seed that Colin had planted, Stone and Colin had long lost touch with each other, without Colin ever suspecting the impact he'd had on Stone.

He was eyeing Stone cautiously now, as if still not quite sure what to make of him. "So...what brings you here?"

"Old ghosts that needed laying to rest."

Colin hesitated. "Your mom...is she...?"

"Still there. Keeping pretty good health. Physically, anyway."

"I pray for her all the time, man, just like always. Matter of fact, just the other—"

"What are you still doing there, CJ? How'd you ever get caught up in it to begin with, a free thinker like you?"

Silence, then, "It wasn't always like it is now."

Stone could believe that. Before Spirit and Truth Center, his mother had been a closet Christian, with a Sunday morning TV slot for a church home. But Stone's last year at home, there had been a bounce in her step and a light in her eyes as Sunday morning and Wednesday night approached. When Colin's old beater pulled up outside and honked its horn, she'd run to meet it like a girl in love.

"I'd a never have brought her here if I'd thought for a minute—"

"I know," Stone cut in, looking away from the pain and regret in Colin's eyes.

"They started out real good. On fire, sold out to God, impatient with the traditions that hide Him from us. Some ways down the road, it started being more about their passion and uniqueness than about God. Apos—Pastor being the way he is didn't hurt any, either. He sucks you in, against your every instinct. Paralyzes your will, like."

"It's called spiritual witchcraft."

"Yeah, but what did any of us know? We were backing one of God's last true prophets. When he started taking little liberties with Scripture, we didn't see it. Wouldn't let ourselves see it. When it got too bad for our conscience to ignore, we convinced ourselves we needed to stay to keep him in line. For the sake of those who didn't know better."

"Except you didn't keep him in line."

"Cause by the time the truth rose up and hit us in the face, we'd already bought into the whole authority deal and were scared to death of opposing him."

"Then don't. Just leave, and tell the others why. As it is, you're contributing to the mess."

"You have no idea—"

"No-one can gain that kind of control over another human being unless it's given to him, Colin. Enough of you start taking it back and see if the whole thing doesn't start falling apart."

"And then what?"

"What, you don't think God knows the addresses of enough healthy fellowships to place ninety-odd people? Trust Him to feed His own sheep, CJ."

Colin fell silent, and Stone gave him some time. Finally, Stone asked, "What happened to the Colin Jackman that I knew, hmm?"

Colin's handsome face that once ago had worn a semi-permanent grin was brooding now as he answered. "The consequences of taking a stand were too much for even him to handle. Condemnation. Ostracism. Doesn't sound like much, but it's unbearable for people who've let all their other relationships go to pot. Like being deprived of air, while the people you love look on and think you deserve to suffocate. And that's when you realize there's something wrong with their kind of love."

Stone shook his head. "Isn't love at all, man."

"Yeah, but just when you begin to realize that, they turn the air back on, and you're so grateful you forget everything else they put you through. Cause having their approval again is like—like breathing, only this time you're inhaling something a whole lot headier than just air. I don't know any other way to describe it except as a high."

"Starvation will do that to you too, I'm told, just before your body shuts down from an overload of toxins. Doesn't change the fact you're starving, though."

"I know, I know. But trust me, a couple rounds of that kind of discipline, and there wasn't a man or woman among us who'd have dared God's wrath by giving against His anointed. The sister under fire in there now...Bertrand...she's pretty new to the game. She's got a lot of spunk, but I've seen spunkier than her buckle under the pressure. *Way* spunkier."

Something cold gripped Stone's insides, and he made a

conscious effort to disregard the other man's unfortunate choice of an adjective.

"Was hardest on the women."

Stone swallowed, wanting to ask for specifics but not able to. It was what he'd come there for, answers, about Abigail in particular, but now he was this close to getting them, he wasn't sure if he could handle it. Not while he was still within strangling distance of the man he now suspected was responsible for turning her inside out. If the details were as bad as his guts were telling him they were, the width of a parking lot would not be nearly enough distance.

"Not your mom," Colin quickly reassured him, eyeing him warily. "I'm talking women with strong opinions and any real knowledge of scripture."

Like those who'd been brought up by the Richard Lesters of the church.

"The married women got it from two sides, Pastor and their husband."

God, I don't know if I want to hear anymore.

"Pastor'll take one look at a brother's wife and decide right off the bat where he's at spiritually and whether he's fit for any kind of leadership role in the church."

"I've done that myself on occasion."

"Yeah, well I doubt you were looking at the same things he is. Only thing that impresses him is her submission."

That S-word again.

"And I mean shut-up-and-do-as-I-say submission. And had to look like they were loving it too. He takes Paul's teaching on leadership qualifications kinda seriously."

"*Which* teaching? Cause last time I checked, ruling your household well didn't mean doing away with basic Christian virtues like kindness and gentleness and *mutual* submission."

Colin grimaced, a little sheepishly. "Well, *his* interpretation of it, then. Right or wrong, it's how he sees things, and nobody is going to argue with him, especially after the way he did his own son."

He didn't care two hoots what Lightbourne did with his

son. They were no doubt peas in a pod, sharing equally in the spoils from their plunder of other people's souls. They deserved whatever bumps and bruises they picked up along the way.

But they were also part of the inner circle that Abigail and her husband had been part of. The fact that Lightbourne's armor bearer had apparently escaped his Pastor's influence and was the best of a bad bunch didn't mean the armor bearer's wife had come out of it unscathed. Stone already had plenty of evidence that she had not.

So he gritted his teeth and made himself ask, "What happened with his son?"

"Got passed over for several leadership positions. Nobody's sure why, cause he definitely had it in him. Had more formal training than anyone else in there, for one thing, Pastor included."

"That might have been the problem right there. Could be his old man felt threatened."

Colin nodded. "Could be, come to think of it. Pastor also likes to keep people guessing. Surest way to not get something out of him is to let him know you're expecting it."

"Yeah, but his own son...come on, now."

"Well, he wasn't...technically. He was adopted, but in every way but legally. It was never finalized. Some people think that might have been the problem, Pastor wanting to keep the controls in the bloodline."

"He wouldn't be the first."

"In any case, it gave poor Junior an outsized complex. He didn't make a single move that wasn't aimed at proving his worth to his old man and everybody else."

Stone grunted. "I know a little bit about that."

"You got over it real early, though. I certainly don't see you handling your marriage like it's your last chance to win your old man's approval."

More like avoiding marriage altogether, scared to death it would bring out whatever little bit of his father was lurking in him. "That what he did?"

"Sure he did. Wasn't anybody at Spirit and Truth good enough for him, either, and that was probably his biggest mistake, marrying outside the church."

"He married an unbeliever?"

Colin shook his head. "Outside Spirit and Truth, I meant. No, Sarah was the real McCoy. Sweet girl, like a breath of fresh air, I tell you. A cut above the rest. Take a guess where he...what?"

"Sarah? Her name was Sarah?"

"Yeah, Sarah. Why, you think you might know her?"

Stone shook his head. "No, not really." Not in person, anyway. "Name rang a bell, kind of."

He cast his mind back to the handful of ladies he'd seen sitting on the front pew, trying to put a face to the name...to the emails.

Only a couple of them that he could remember could be young enough to be the Pastor's daughter-in-law. "Which one was her? Toga or Purple Hat?"

Colin chuckled. "Neither. Toga's his niece. Purple hat's married to his other son, the one who'll probably succeed him. Both of those ladies know the ropes. Sarah..." He shook his head and seemed unable or unwilling to go on.

Stone felt a stirring of unease. "Sarah what?"

"Sarah was a lot more...spirited than folks around here are accustomed to." He paused before adding, his voice flat, "Before her husband got done with her, anyway."

Stone's stomach muscles clenched, but his voice was even as he asked, "What'd he do...abuse her?"

"Uh-uh." The idea seemed to take Colin by surprise. "Well, I guess you could call it that, but I wasn't thinking physically. Pastor didn't stand for that. Your wife show up with bruises, you can kiss leadership goodbye. You can't get your wife to submit without beating her, you can't shepherd God's flock, is what he always says."

"Good for him," Stone allowed grudgingly. His opinion of Lightbourne and his disciples had improved only fractionally. Nevertheless, he was immensely relieved to have a third party back up what Abigail had so vehemently affirmed. He didn't think he could have handled learning that she might have been abused.

Colin gave him a bleak look. "She got plenty beat up on the inside, though, and to tell the truth, I don't know which one is worse. Went from a fresh-faced, starry-eyed sweetheart to a primped and painted collector's doll. Pull her little string and she'd spout all the right words. Little more realistic version of a Stepford wife."

Sounded like Sarah all right. "She...had any friends?"

"Not really."

So much for that.

"Thing is, no friendship can survive the atmosphere in there. Nobody trusts anybody else. Pastor has the lot of them convinced he can all but read their minds, see."

Or maybe their emails.

"They'll be running to him with every little nonsense, scared the Holy Spirit will rat on them and make Pastor brand them traitors."

Abigail?

"There's always a few free spirits who manage to rise above it, of course, like sister Bertrand in there. Sarah was one, and there was this other sister who left...I forget her name..."

Abigail.

"But Sarah and her weren't exactly chummy."

Except maybe by email. "Bet they could have used some friendship, though."

"Oh yes. Sarah especially. Needed some kind of an antidote to her husband." He shook his head. "If marriage is supposed to be a picture of Christ's love for His church, then that one was the anti-marriage. And the embodiment of everything that's wrong at Spirit and Truth. Poor Sarah."

"Somebody ought to have horsewhipped the jerk," was the only non-profane thought that came to Stone's mind.

"Oh, somebody did worse than that...prayed for him, that God would turn him round and use him to liberate the rest of the flock, kind of thing."

"Guess they weren't praying hard enough, huh?"

"Oh, but they were." Colin slanted him a look that was part mischief and part gravity. "The prayer had a contingency provision."

34

Virginia was praying for Sarah again and seeing her as if it were her across the room playing tic-tac-toe on the window pane. Sarah laughing and carefree and so...so *Abigail*, in tennis shoes and a cute-as-buttons Tweety Bird jumpsuit. Sarah as she had been on one of the few occasions she wasn't trying to be what she was not and as she must have been before she started listening to the wrong voices, like hers.

That was all water under the bridge now, of course. She couldn't go back and take back her bad advice or undo the harm that had resulted from Sarah taking it to heart. What mattered was that she was making amends in the only way she knew how. Like she'd made amends when the Lord first showed her where she'd gone wrong in her mentoring of Sarah and how to make reparation. She was praying.

Stone wasn't sure whether to chuckle or shudder at what Colin had just told him. "You believe that? That some undercover prayer warrior or other prayed him into his grave?"

"I'm not sure what I believe, but it's strongly rumored that that's what happened."

Part of him wanted to cheer *good for her, whoever she was,* but the other part was as sickened as he had been by the similar schemes, real or imagined, of another self-proclaimed Abigail from his past.

K.V. CASE

Spirit and Truth Center seemed to have had a special knack for turning those out. The natural outgrowth of harboring a bunch of Nabals in their midst, no doubt. For he was willing to bet Sarah's husband hadn't been the only one. It was a wonder Eric had escaped their influence. Or had he?

Well, for the most part, obviously. Abigail was no Sarah.

Stone shook his head. "If Sarah'd been like some women I know, he'd have come home and found that designer wardrobe he'd handpicked for her gone and a collection of Disney playwear in its place."

Colin regarded him with raised eyebrows and invited, "Tell me about her."

"I said *some* women."

"I heard. So what's she like?"

"Not the kind who'd ever fit in in a place like this, trust me." Not anymore, anyway. He thought of Abigail and her overdone Tweety Bird collection and tried to picture her married to a kook like the pastor's son and couldn't. He was having a hard enough time as it was picturing her at home in the church at all.

Maybe she'd never been at home there.

She had to have been at one point or another, married into the pastor's inner circle. It was what had made Stone so set against her in the beginning, so determined to kick against her addition to the Oasis team.

"She go to your church?" Colin asked, and Stone realized the other man had been watching his changing expressions intently.

Too close for comfort. He began slowly, "She—"

"Where *do* you go, anyway?"

He latched on to that one, much as he wasn't prepared to answer it fully. Colin had to have known Abigail, small as the church was and Eric such a prominent member. Had to know she was Richard Lester's daughter and that it was his church she'd gone back to after Eric died. And he didn't want to risk putting Colin on the defensive before finding out all he needed to know.

And need to know he did. There was a missing piece to the Abigail puzzle buried somewhere in it all, he was sure.

So he brushed him off with a vague, "This church in North Miami."

"But you do go regularly, right?"

Stone kept his expression offhand. "Yeah, sure." In addition to running their counseling ministry.

Colin gave him a contemplative look. Probably questioning whether he was in fellowship anywhere at all.

"So what did the big man make of his son's premature death?" Stone prodded. "Wasn't so quick to believe judgment had fallen, I bet."

Colin went along with the subject change without comment. "Oh, but he was. Got up at the funeral and made a proclamation." He leveled a look at Stone. "Ready for this?" He dropped his chin, and his voice deepened several octaves. "The *Lawd* had revealed to him that his son had missed *Gawd* by not taking a wife from among the daughters of his own people, and though it was not a sin ordinarily punishable by death, God had used him as an example to teach everyone else not to do the same. A sacrificial lamb, kind of a deal. Or some such—"

Colin's cell phone chimed, and he glanced down at it and then held up a finger to Stone while he answered it.

"Yes. Sure. I understand. I'll be right there."

His face was grim when he hung up seconds later. "My mom's hospital. She just coded. I better go."

"Oh man, CJ, I'm sorry. Want me to go with you? I'll drive if you want. We could pray on the way down."

"Thanks, Stone, but that's all right."

"You sure?" Stone searched his face for signs that he might be taking the timing of his mother's sudden turn for the worse the wrong way. They'd just been ridiculing his church's teachings on divine retribution. Old thought patterns died hard.

But he saw nothing besides acceptance and loss in Colin's face when he said, "I'm sure. You save those prayers for her other nine kids. She's got a Do-Not-Resuscitate order signed, and they're doing all the grieving stages at one go, with special emphasis on anger and denial. I'm still the only one's saved, and they've convinced themselves it's my fault she's made the choice she has. It's gonna get crazy from here on in."

"Hang in there, man. I've got your back."

"I'm glad. I've missed that. Hey, you still keep the same kind of hours?" When Stone nodded, Colin fished a business card out of his jacket pocket and handed it over. "I work nights. Here's the number. Keep in touch, eh?"

Stone glanced at it. Colin was the night supervisor for a security firm. "You know I will."

Virginia stared sleeplessly up at the triple Xs painted across the night sky. Tonight they were black as sin, and she wondered what that might be signifying. Sorrow, such as had been in her dreams.

She'd fallen asleep praying for Abigail and dreamed about Sarah. Sarah in immaculately creased white shorts and golf shirt befitting her station, red-faced from being called immature and an embarrassment in front of the whole church after she'd turned up at a picnic dressed like Abigail in a giddy Disney outfit.

Abigail's words were always with her, but it was Sarah's face that haunted her the most, the soul-deep pain in her eyes that had mirrored the pain in her own soul.

She hardly saw Sarah and Abigail as two separate people anymore, her guilt and anguish over Sarah as heavy as the burden she'd had for Abigail. For all the times she could have reached out to Sarah, if only with a hug, and hadn't because she'd been too scared to do more than play secret pals with Abigail. Too busy encouraging Abigail in her quest to be someone else, as if that was even possible. As if that would rid her of her flaws. As if there was anyone who didn't have their share of those.

Eventually, the only thing Abigail had become was lost,

like Sarah had lost her way before God came through for her. She only wished she knew what had become of Abigail, if she'd survived it all. She supposed she'd never know till she got to heaven.

She reached under her pillow and pulled out the little paper cup from where she'd stashed it earlier. They hadn't even missed the cup. She eased out the bit of paper napkin she'd stuffed down into it and contemplated its contents. It would take more than a thimbleful of forgetfulness to fix what ailed her. Still, it was all she had, and there was no denying it helped dull the pain.

She counted. She couldn't afford for even one of them to fall out and be found in her room, for they'd had no business leaving the dining room. Once she was sure nothing was missing, she rose carefully, took it into the bathroom like she'd been doing the past several days, and flushed it.

He'd found the Sarah of the e-chats. Stone knew it. The daughter-in-law of that so-called apostle fit the profile better than either Fern or Crystal.

In which case, Fern was who? Kay? Not a chance. Maybe Fern wasn't one of the four e-pals after all, as her sister was. Maybe she didn't even know anything about Crystal's e-chats. Hard to believe, close as those two were, but possible.

Maybe the ins and outs of Abigail's private girlfriend talks were none of his business.

Except that she'd made it so by bringing him into it. As if she'd been trying, consciously or otherwise, to lead him to some hidden clue to the Abigail that continued to elude his understanding.

There were other clues buried inside that tomb of a church as well, of course. But it would be a while before he could reasonably approach Colin again with anything except condolences. There was no one else with answers except Abigail, and he'd been as good as barred from seeing her.

One thing he could be certain of, with or without either Colin's or Abigail's input: Abigail being right there on spot to witness her friend's abuse—for there was no other word for what Sarah had been subjected to but abuse—could well account for Abigail's metamorphosis from the pliable model daughter who had left her father's care to the spitfire who had returned five years later. Not to mention what being a member of such a dysfunctional fellowship might have done to her, model house and husband aside.

It would also explain why she'd defended Sarah so hotly that time he'd criticized her in his ignorance. They would have been kindred spirits, both married to someone high up in the church hierarchy, both having come from another church and subject to the resentment that that must have bred among their new church sisters.

It was more than enough to have forged the kind of bond between them that would have made either of them bristle in resentment against any opinionated male who dared dismiss any of them as wishy-washy.

As to how Abigail herself had managed to survive the whole Spirit and Truth experience so relatively unscathed was another matter. Granted her husband hadn't been the jerk Sarah's was, clueless though he might have been in the sexual arena, but she hadn't existed with him in a vacuum. Five years in that church could take an enormous toll on anyone, however blissful their home life.

Maybe it had. Maybe that showcase house of hers was just one manifestation of the effect it had had on her. Maybe she hadn't escaped unscathed after all. Maybe the problems that had plagued her and Stone's relationship from day one, from her resistance to his authority to her inability to trust, were all a result of what she'd gone through. Maybe what he'd thought of as sheer contrariness was part of some coping mechanism that had helped her overcome her demons to whatever degree she had. God alone knew what kinds of wounds *his* mishandling of her might have reopened.

He had to go to her. If only to hold her and tell her he understood, that his love and God's grace would get her past the pain like he trusted it would get him past his fears. And, most important, that he'd be waiting on the other side of her healing with a future for them.

He was still in Broward County when he made his decision, a mere fifteen minutes from Southwest Ranches and the Lester home. He consulted his watch. Going on nine o'clock. Late for her. It would have to wait till tomorrow.

He'd make the time at work, find somewhere quiet they could talk, with or without Doc's approval, or take her to lunch, maybe. He didn't doubt she'd be there tomorrow. She couldn't possibly intend to fake her way through another week of "feeling out of it." And if she did, then he'd simply take a few hours off from work and find himself at her door.

35

Abigail waited for the soft click of her bedroom door closing behind her father early the next morning before reaching with trembling fingers for her phone and punching in the number of her voice mail.

No calls since Beth's Saturday night. Thirty-odd hours ago, and she hadn't found time to listen to the rest of the message, much less return the call. Too busy with Church, with wondering where Stone was the second Sunday in a row and trying not to care...

Abigail drew a steadying breath and focused on Beth's message, the part she'd already heard barely registering. Then came a soft sigh and a pause, and Beth went on with the same hesitancy with which she'd just asked for a ride.

"We could have some old fashioned girlfriend time, do some catching up. I'll let you humiliate me at scrabble, no whining, no special breaks. And I'll get back my own at checkers, if you can stand it. Or we could just lay around doing nothing."

A giggle. "Burn some more marshmallows on your desk lamp and give your dad a few more gray hairs. Or we could play it safe with some microwave popcorn, watch a movie or something...Not a word out of me if you fall asleep in the middle of it, cross my heart...I might even manage to get back up with you in the small hours...if you dare try tossing ice down my PJs again." A little sigh, then, sounding more deflated, "Either ways, I'd like to see you sometime." Her voice dropped and wasn't quite steady as she added, "I've missed you, girl."

Stomach heaving, Abigail dropped the receiver and barely made it to the bathroom on time.

"Now is probably not a good time, Stone," Doc's voice said behind Stone later that morning as Stone strode purposefully past Odette, headed for the stairs. "She's not seeing anyone just now."

Stone halted in his tracks without turning. He hadn't even expected Doc to be home this time of day. "Anyone, or just me?"

Doc sighed but didn't answer.

Stone held his breath and waited. For sounds of Doc's retreat, maybe. Didn't the man have any seedlings he had to serenade or whatever? He turned slowly.

Doc was not dressed for gardening. He was wearing midweek-service garb—blazer, no tie—and his keys were in his hands. Stone had just barely caught him. Trust his rotten luck.

Lord, I need a break here.

"Walk with me to my car, Stone. I can spare a couple minutes."

Not his idea of a break. He shook his head. "You don't understand...I just found out..."

"I know, so did I. But give her time before you—"

"She's had time. Too much. Knowing her, she probably hasn't even talked to the therapist the way she really needs—"

"Talk to what therapist?" Doc's brow knit in irritation and puzzlement. "She just heard, not quite an hour ago."

"Heard what?"

Doc's expression changed, from uptight to guarded and then weary. "You don't know?"

Stone felt a chill run down his spine. "Know what?"

"Beth." Doc heaved a deep, shuddering breath. "She died this morning."

Anyways, it's not like they're pitching me out or anything." In a few heartbeats, Beth's voice had shifted from breezy to tremulous and back to breezy, with a lightening about turn that was pure Beth. "Was my idea, really, leaving tonight. They'll let me stay if I can't arrange a ride, so don't sweat it if you can't make it. I've got Stone's cell number, and he says he can be here within half hour of me calling him, so I'll probably just buzz him, soon as I wake up in the morning. Call me at home, and we'll get together some time. Number's the same."

She rattled it off anyway and hung up in her abrupt Beth way.

As if dislodged by the jarring sound of Beth's receiver clattering to its rest, the sob trapped in Abigail's throat broke free. The numbness that had gripped her while her father broke the news about Beth eased away, and pain and guilt ripped mercilessly through her as she sank weakly down to the carpet below and allowed her dammed up tears to flow.

Blood clot on the lung. Nobody's fault. One of the risks of being confined to bed for any prolonged length of time, doubled in Beth's case because depression had kept her glued to the bed except for the times the nurse went in and routed her out of it. Till the last forty-eight hours or so, when she seemed to rebound as the time of her discharge approached.

She'd been humming as she walked around her room gathering her few things when the clot dislodged and went straight to her heart. She'd died instantly, despite aggressive attempts at resuscitation. Two hours shy of being discharged. With a smile of renewed purpose on her face and hope in her heart as she eagerly anticipated seeing the son Stone had threatened to have taken away from her.

Stone recited the facts to himself as Doc had relayed them. Over and over he rehearsed them, and found no reason, despite Doc's best efforts, to take comfort from any of what he'd heard. And every reason to despair.

"She blames me." It was a statement, not a question.

"Just give her time, Stone. She needs some room, that's all."

Not room in general, just room from him. What was more, Doc agreed. And Stone couldn't very well bulldoze his way past him. Doc was in full protective mode now, and he'd determined that Abigail needed a break away from what he'd obviously deemed to be the source of her pain.

"At least tell her I'm here...see if maybe she'll—"

"She was anticipating you'd come, and she's already asked me to tell you she's...not seeing anyone."

Not seeing *him*, was what Doc really meant. At any rate, it was a lot less painful for Stone to believe that than have to accept that he'd been relegated to the ranks of "anyone."

Doc stirred and looked at his watch. "I hate to rush you, son, but I've really got to go now. I've a funeral to plan."

And I'm not going to leave you here with her. He might as well have said it.

In the long, agonizing few seconds it took Stone to decide whether or not to accept defeat, he found himself thinking a little desperately that now would have been a good time to have Phantom with him.

Phantom had acted as bridge builder so many times when Stone hadn't wanted one. When he'd just wanted a quiet stroll with his thoughts and had had to put up with the ooh-ing and ah-ing of multiple admiring females who ogled him shamelessly while they fondled his dog. Would have been nice for Phantom to have proved his usefulness now.

And after he'd bribed his way into Abigail's presence like some love-sick teenager, then what? Bribes didn't buy trust, and she'd made it clear he didn't have hers.

He turned without another word and let himself out.

He could handle panic attacks, temper, insecurity, could swiftly dispense with her doubts about her sex appeal once he'd got her to the altar. But her lack of trust was one thing he could not see his way around. For that he'd first have to learn to trust himself.

"Uncle, Uncle! Guess what?" Corey burst out of Mark and Fern's half-open garage as Stone pulled his Mustang onto the swale within minutes of leaving the Lester home. Corey's usually serious face was animated as Stone had never seen it.

Stone's heart sank. Like he'd feared, they'd left it for him to break the news.

God, I can't handle this.

Corey stopped breathlessly in front of him and raised shining eyes to his. "Mommy went to heaven."

Stone's throat closed up. Corey knew, and he hadn't retreated behind his wall of silence. Stone hadn't expected a word out of him at this of all times. He had more than words. There was a light in his eyes and a near smile on his face.

"I heard, buddy," Stone said, fighting to keep his voice light. Poor kid, he was too young to grasp the permanence of death.

Corey frowned. "It's okay to cry, Uncle Stone. Uncle Mark does it all the time, and he's taller'n you."

That wrung a chuckle out of Stone. "Oh, does he?"

Corey nodded. "And guess what? You get to see her again in heaven, long as you got Jesus in your heart." His chest puffed out, and he patted his left breast. "Like me.

Uncle Mark helped me make sure."

"Good for you." This time the smile made it to Stone's face.

Corey sighed. "I just wish it wouldn't take so long." His chin wobbled a bit. "I miss her. And she didn't say good-bye."

Stone went down on his haunches and took his hand. "I bet she really wanted to, Corey. But the angels came unex-pectedly. They do that sometimes."

Corey nodded knowledgeably. "I know. She couldn't help it." He heaved a breath, and his face lit up again. "I told her it was okay and that I was glad Daddy couldn't hurt her anymore."

"You did?" Stone's voice was threatening to desert him again.

"I asked Jesus to tell her. Me'n Auntie Fern."

"Oh. Well now, that's some idea. Wish I'da thought of that when my daddy died."

"You can still do it. Heaven is forever." He started back-ing toward the house. "You want Uncle Mark?"

Stone straightened. "Not this time. Tell him I'll call him later. I already got what I came for."

Sort of. He'd come to comfort, and instead he'd been comforted.

At age fifteen, she'd been the last one of them to fall in love with Jesus. For her baptism she'd been invited, as per Grace custom, to choose the chorus that the congregation would sing at the moment she was raised up out of the wa-ter.

Beth had eyed Mrs. Pinkerton doubtfully and asked, "Can I give the sound guys a tape to play and you all just sing along? Cause the one I've got in mind is kinda too old for some people to know it, and it's not like we want to be giving music lessons or anything in between dunkings."

"Certainly," Mrs. Pinkerton had agreed without hesitation. She was as relieved as everyone else at Grace that Beth had finally come to Jesus and was boldly declaring it to her disbelieving friends. The wayward neighborhood kid whose parents for years had religiously packed her off to Sunday school without ever once setting foot inside a church themselves had exceeded everybody's expectations. Pinkerton was prepared to be magnanimous. "As long as it's reverent and in keeping with our worship style."

"Reverent like how?" Beth asked warily.

"Well, appropriate, then. You know—expressing some sentiment describing what your new life in Christ means to you."

Beth's nod was emphatic. "Oh, for sure. This one's like right on the money."

That Sunday evening as the strapping young deacon who was doing the baptisms set a soaking Beth back on her feet, the almost medieval atmosphere of Grace Community Church's sanctuary was invaded by a tumultous beat never before heard inside its walls, and in the space of time it took the confused sound technician to process what was happening and react, the doctrines of baptism and regeneration found expression in the lyrics of a runaway hit from the disco era.

Pinkerton was getting her own back, and with a vengeance. With the organ's plaintive notes feeding the grief-laden atmosphere in the sanctuary, Abigail fought in vain against the constriction in her throat as she watched Beth's distraught family file out behind her casket. If what Beth had once told her still held true, there weren't many believers among them, and they seemed to be struggling to hold on to the hope that her father's message had extended to them.

If she could have enfolded them in her own hope, she would have. It wasn't long ago that she had been the one sitting in the front pew, numb with shock and guilt and horror. Nursing the faint stirring of grief she felt, like she'd nursed a spark one campfire night as it struggled to become a fire amidst a pile of damp wood. But those members of Beth's family who'd known "Beth's little friend Abigail" might not even remember her, or if they did, it might just be as the so-called sister who'd spurned sisterhood as soon as she became a wife.

Leo was missing, languishing in a hospital observation ward with what most people suspected was a bad case of nerves. Most people who knew him were relieved.

Abigail couldn't care less one way or the other. The lingering sense that she had failed Beth swelled into full-blown self-condemnation, and guilt and grief threatened to overwhelm her. Dimly, she was aware that she was not reasoning soundly, that her conscience had gone temporarily amok, but knowing that didn't seem to stop her feeling the way she did.

She joined the procession, walking alone behind pair after pair of husbands and wives, brothers and sisters, best friends drawing on each other's strength, and longed for someone of her own to trade joys and sorrows with.

Her father had tried to encourage her in the hours following Beth's death, but she had *wanted* to hurt then, like she felt she deserved. Since then, he'd been busy. Busy with the grieving family, busy with the funeral, busy granting interviews to the local media, which had picked up on the story and taken advantage of a slow news cycle to focus on the problem of domestic abuse.

She wasn't even looking for words of wisdom so much as for someone who would just hold her. Behind her dark glasses, Abigail searched the sea of faces for the face of the one who had offered to be that someone.

She'd felt her heart rip four days ago as she stood just out of sight on the landing upstairs listening to her father send Stone away, wanting to call out to him, but unable to.

Halfway up the aisle, she spotted him, unfamiliar, remote and achingly dear in a dark suit, crisp as new white shirt and tie. He was standing at the end of the second-to-last pew, head down and expression between somber and unreadable, waiting his turn as the pews emptied into the center aisle from front to back.

She stared in his direction as she drew near, willing him to look her way. She wasn't sure what she'd say to him if he tried to talk to her, but she wanted with sudden urgency to experience again the thrill of having him come after her, hot-eyed and intense, his passionate dark gaze full of only her...

37

At the reception that followed at Mark and Fern's, Abigail slipped away from the other guests as a line began to form at the buffet. She made it to the powder room tucked away behind the staircase just as the tears she'd been bottling up throughout the ceremony demanded release.

She'd waited in vain for Stone to put in an appearance. The last she'd seen of him was during the recessional, when they'd been almost within touching distance but oceans apart. She'd been almost parallel to his pew when he turned abruptly to face the other direction, cutting across the pews away from the center aisle and slipping through a side exit.

She'd been sure he was on his way to Mark and Fern's. She'd so needed to see him. She'd waited on the fringe of the gathering, heartsick and lonely amid the houseful of mourners, till commonsense forced her to accept that his was one pair of shoulders that was no longer available to her.

She leaned now against the cold comfort of a tiled bathroom wall, burying her face in her hands to muffle the sobs she could barely control. The storm had been threatening since the moment she filed past Beth's coffin, maybe because of the confusion of guilt and grief that was taking her back to another funeral at which she'd felt more guilt than grief.

As she'd stared at the empty shell that had once housed her friend's vibrant, spirited soul, something about its pale, cold stillness against the casket's satin interior had brought back images of Eric's face as she'd seen it the last day of their life together. Cold and blue and still against the cream satin pillow of their marriage bed, eyes staring lifelessly into eternity, muscles still twisted by the pain that had wracked him suddenly in the small hours while she'd lain curled inside their Roman tub, too numb from his latest verbal onslaught to even cry.

She'd felt dead inside the tender inner places where his barbs usually cut the deepest, so much so that she'd begun to fancy God was granting her healing and immunity from further hurt. After all, it was the least God could do after failing to rescue her like she'd been told He would if she continued to submit faithfully to her husband no matter what.

And as for God bottling and saving every last tear she shed, as Kay had loved to tell her, He must already have harvested all of hers, leaving her no more to cry. If only so He wouldn't have to listen to her whimper and moan and ask *Why, Lord...what did I do?* one more time. It had been easier to believe that than to believe He saved them as a mark of His compassion for her suffering.

And just as easy to believe He'd saved them to use as evidence with which to convict and condemn the one who'd wrung them out of her.

God, I didn't want him to die. I never once so much as wished he would.

She'd just been seduced by her own pain into feeling like she was entitled to be free, at any cost. Entitled when freedom wasn't forthcoming to luxuriate in bitterness and doubt. What was she worth in God's economy, anyway, compared to Eric Carmichael, compared to any man?

Nothing, precisely what He'd predetermined she'd be worth when He predestined her to be a woman. Otherwise, why had he not intervened on her behalf? After all, a sovereign God was entitled to bypass mercy and execute judgment anytime He so chose. And if He chose a verdict of death to be the instrument of her freedom, who was she or anyone else to protest?

And protest she had not. An unnatural calm had taken

hold of her as she stood beside the bed staring down at the lifeless face that only hours ago had sneered its contempt at her. She'd felt no grief. Not from the instant she woodenly called 911 to the moment she watched dry eyed as they lowered Eric's coffin into the ground. Not even at his funeral when they'd passed judgment on her...

She'd felt horror, revulsion, fear, bitterness, but no grief. And when finally she'd grieved, it had been for the man she'd thought she'd married and for the trusting, giving soul who once had idolized him.

Weeks later, with the return of her feelings had come the doubt and self-condemnation. The certainty that she'd fallen beneath the reach of God's grace, a little nothing like her who had willed death on a promising servant of His.

She knew now that that kind of thinking was flawed. That she wasn't any more responsible for Eric's death than God was for Eric's abuse of her. The psychologist her father had sent her to had been a grounded Christian with no doctrinal axe to grind.

But Abigail's feelings hadn't caught up yet with her head. The feelings were so much harder to get rid of than the lies that had spawned them. Feelings had a way of fading like shadows in full light, only to loom again with the twilight.

The last time they'd come, they'd been banished by a pair of strong, gentle arms that held her close and infused her with the warmth and light of love and acceptance. Those arms were nowhere near this time.

It was just her and the God whose worship she'd foolishly stolen and squandered on one of His creatures.

"God, forgive me," she heard herself whisper, as if from somewhere outside of herself. And like bricks dislodged from the barrier damming up her emotions, her words released a flood of grief that brought with it the first tears of pure sorrow she'd ever been able to shed on Eric's account.

Corey was waiting for Stone in the parking lot of Grace

Community when Stone got outside. The night before, Mark and Fern had taken Corey briefly to the viewing and after gauging his reaction had agreed with Stone that the viewing was as much as he needed to experience of the whole burial process.

Today the scared eyes and black suit had been replaced by a keen look of anticipation and a crisp new navy and white sailor suit. And taking Fern and Mark's place was an extremely handsome, snazzily dressed couple somewhere in their sixties. A man with big dark eyes and a woman with glossy silver hair with streaks of ebony as rich as Corey's.

Tall, erect and straight-gazed, they were the sprightliest pair of great-grands Stone had ever laid eyes on.

A suspiciously silent Corey was offering Stone a handshake. Corey was looking a little uncertain and plenty stiff in his new suit, but Stone had talked with him long enough the night before to know that there was more relief and anticipation than worry behind his temporary reversion to silence. And Stone had talked long enough with the Matthews to be confident Corey would be breaking his silence before long.

Married at sixteen and parents less than a year later, they'd never been happier for their early start at child rearing than when they learned that they had a great-grandson at the other end of the state in need of a loving home. Best of all, they were Christians, with a walk that was as straight as their talk.

And it hadn't entailed him interviewing half the Ramseys and Reids in the U.S. after all, just a few well-placed phone calls to a certain employee of the Bureau of Vital Statistics and the help of a couple of internet wizards from Grace's youth group, followed by a phone call to the only Vernon and Lydia Matthews listed in Pensacola. Stone hadn't done thanking God yet on Corey's behalf.

Stone sank to his haunches now as he took the small hand Corey was offering and tugged gently till the grave-faced little boy was in his arms. Corey's sturdy little arms wrapped gratefully around his neck.

"You take care of Grandma and Grandpa, eh buddy?"

Corey's head bobbed up and down against his shoulder.

"That means lots of hugs. Great-grandmas and grandpas need lots of that to get them through each day." Stone dropped his voice to a conspiratorial whisper. "And send me a picture of that one-eyed pirate horse; otherwise I'll have to think it was all a bunch of fibs they were telling us."

Corey nodded again and eased away, still without a word.

I'm sorry, buddy. So sorry. I know how you feel, and I'd have done anything to spare you what you're going through.

"Thank you," Lydia whispered.

"For everything," Vernon added. "We'd never have had a clue if you hadn't gone to so much trouble to track us down."

Stone tried to shrug off their thanks. He hadn't done anything to deserve their thanks. If anything, he'd failed. Failed Corey, failed Corey's parents, like he'd failed his own.

But the Matthews weren't easily brushed aside. Vernon continued, "When Leo's mother left Pensacola, she never left a hint where she was going. She could just as easily have been in Alaska, and I think it was her husband's intention for us to go on guessing."

"Never wrote," his wife explained. "Left to her alone, I think she would have eventually. But her husband wouldn't have wanted her to. And that boy of theirs—"

"Glad I was able to help, ma'am," Stone cut in with a flick of his eyes in Corey's direction. *That boy* was Corey's father, for better or for worse, and they'd got Corey to agree to the move only by promising that he'd still get to see his daddy from time to time. Stone could relate to that. At that age, his father had had only to "kiss Mommy better" for all to be forgiven and Daddy to be the hero again.

"He's not going to sign anything anytime soon," Stone warned Leo's grandparents now. "Especially when it involves the branch of his family that his father's so poisoned his mind against. But with things stacked against him the way they are, you won't need it for now. Able and willing family members are always the court's first choice over foster care. Your part is to not give him any cause to complain to the court that you're poisoning his son's mind against him." He sought their gazes individually and held them.

"We hear you," Grandpa Vern said.

Stone didn't doubt they had. He nodded, chucked Corey under the chin and then stood and watched them walk away.

Only then did his triumph over finding Corey's relatives begin to fade and the crushing burden of guilt, failure and loss that had been threatening since Beth's death finally begin to settle around his heart.

They weren't exactly strong arms that made her want to lose herself inside them, and they were too slight to give the sense of security that being enfolded in a another more brawny pair of arms had given her, but they held her tightly just the same and communicated a wealth of comfort and reassurance she was sorely in need of.

It's all right. You're okay. We'll get through it. Together. We'll learn from it and be better friends to each other and others for it.

A lace-edged hanky embroidered with a flourishing F found its way into Abigail's hand. She wiped her face, drew a steadying breath and whispered, "Kay." The one word said everything that was in her heart.

Fern dropped her arms and shifted her weight on the padded bench they were sharing, rubbing her belly absently. "We tried reaching her, Abby," she said, speaking for the first time since she and Crystal had cornered Abigail in the powder room. "But there really weren't many avenues we could take without even a last name. Considering that she's well aware of that, and that our e-mail addresses haven't changed, we have to wonder if for whatever reason she just does not want to be found. Or else if she's...if she..."

Was dead.

The unsaid words hung heavily in the air between them till the silence grew morbid. Then Crystal, leaning against a nearby wall, forced a watery half-laugh and said, "Hey, three out of five ain't bad, girlfriend. We beat the divorce statistics, what say you?"

Stone let himself into his Oasis office, loosened his tie, flung it down on his desk and stared broodingly out at the lawn that his office window overlooked.

He'd never have figured himself for a coward, but he couldn't have stood there in church and pretended not to see Abigail as she passed by. Not when his thoughts had been as much with her throughout the service as with Beth's family, whom he barely knew. And he just could not have handled looking her in the eye and seeing the blame and scorn he knew would be in them.

She did blame him. Her father hadn't bothered to deny it. Blamed him for pushing Beth too hard, and she was probably right, never mind the fact that his ultimatum wasn't what had caused Beth's blood clot. There weren't three sides to every story, after all. More like four or five or six, reflecting the complexity of the choices facing the Beths and Sarahs of society, and each side warranted careful consideration.

And what did he know anyway about a woman's side of things? He who had come to manhood with no proper example of what God expected from a man. Being mentored by Doc and being able to recite Ephesians 5 backwards was all well and good, but it didn't erase those formative years he'd spent observing and absorbing his father's ill-use of his mother, or the teenage years he'd spent alternately pitying and despising his mother for putting up with the abuse, or the adult years when he'd vowed repeatedly never to place himself in a position where it was possible to descend into that kind of hell.

It was what had made him walk out on Shan when she

started showing signs of wanting a more permanent commitment from him. That was over five years ago. Five plus years later, here he was, thinking he had all the answers for the world's marital woes. Who was he kidding?

Certainly not God. Was a wonder God hadn't slapped him down right there in one of his Oasis sessions. Having the nerve to be counseling other men about the true meaning of submission when he didn't trust himself to be on the receiving end of it. Using single servanthood and dedication to the ministry as a cloak for the fact that he was just plain scared to death of the whole marriage deal.

After watching his father at work, he'd never wanted the burden of having one of God's "weaker vessels" submit to him. Not when he didn't trust himself not to take advantage of such trust. And if he couldn't trust himself, what did he really expect of the men he was counseling, men less spiritual than himself, floundering worse than him with the whole concept of leadership and submission?

He shuddered to think what he might have been imparting to them all along. Who knew why Leo had really flipped and beat up Beth? In that sense maybe her death was indeed his fault. In either case, what right had he to go on being more of a hindrance than a help to others like them?

These people are trapped in a real-life nightmare, Abigail, and they need real answers that can bring them out of it alive.

Without a doubt. Which was why there could be no doubt in his mind regarding the choice he must make.

38

It's just a few weeks, Doc. Some well needed time to sort myself out and listen to what God is saying for a change instead of assuming I already know." Stone added another book to the box he was packing. "Or been trying to say."

"Why now?" Doc stared uncomprehendingly at the carton box on the desk that Stone was methodically filling with the personal contents of his office. He'd left the house within minutes of receiving Stone's call, but Stone had already been half-way through dismantling the office when he arrived.

Stone shrugged. "What better time is there? Oasis is in between sessions, or will be, week after next. And come next week I'll be on vacation from work—"

"Your being off or not from your job never used to matter before. Of course, that was back when you regarded Oasis as more than just another job."

"It *is* more than just another job, sir. It's God's business, and that's why I have to hear from Him before I go any further. Cause if I'm not going to do it His way, I'm not going to do it at all."

"You've always felt that way. We both have. So what has changed?"

"What has changed is that right now I don't believe I have any business counseling anybody, especially not married couples. Whatever their other issues, at least they managed to get it together to the point they could actually walk down the aisle and say I do."

"We've neither one of us ever held that you have to be

married to understand what God says about marriage."

"I still don't, although I'm sure it wouldn't hurt. On the other hand, I'd definitely have something to say about a counselor who's struggling with being single and can't seem to do anything about it when there's no shortage of eligible women around."

"Struggling how? What do you mean?"

"No, sir, I haven't been messing with any of the sisters, or anyone outside the church, for that matter. But there's someone I love and who I believe loves me, and I have some questions that need answering about the reason we're not together."

Richard felt misgiving clutch at his heart, uneasily aware that he might be the one responsible for resurrecting Stone's self-doubt. What had he done? "Stone," he began heavily, "If I—"

"Hasn't a thing to do with you, sir. Not a single thing."

"You prayed any about any of this?"

"Can't say that I have."

"So...how'd you know it's even God's will?"

"I don't." Stone hoisted the box to his shoulder. "That's one of the things I'm going to find out while I'm gone."

"And what do you do then?"

Stone shrugged. "Whatever God says."

Richard stopped trying then. He wasn't going to get anything more out of him. Stone was finally coming to the end of himself, a marathon that had left him blinded by sweat and half out of his mind with exhaustion. And he would never recover from it till he took the sustenance being offered by the One who was there waiting for him to cross the finish line.

Halfway out the door, Doc turned back into the room and sank slowly into the vacant chair facing Stone's desk.

Stone stayed where he was, carton box balanced on his shoulder, one foot still propping the door open. He'd been on his way out behind Doc to make his first trip to his car, and he wasn't in any mood to revive their discussion. He'd already said all that needed to be said.

"All this time I've been listening to you sound off about...everything," Doc began, ignoring the hint. "From legalistic church by-laws to strong-headed young women who make your work at Oasis difficult. I've never once hinted at any of what's been eating at me."

Stone shifted his burden to his other shoulder and waited for Doc to get the message that now was not a good time for him to be receiving any confidences.

Then Doc added, "It concerns Abigail."

Stone let go of the door.

Doc went on. "The way she's changed—"

"She probably just grew up, sir. It happens." Was the least of what had happened to Abigail, of course, but he wasn't about to get into all that he'd found out about her former church. Was no longer any of his business, anyhow.

Doc smiled. "You sound like me counseling Mother Hen. I didn't mean that kind of change."

"What other kind is there?"

"The one that's forced and unnatural. Like the explosion that happens when you combine two chemicals that have no business being together."

Stone slowly lowered the carton box to his desk. "You're not meaning her marriage." Suddenly, every nameless suspicion he'd ever had about her marriage resurrected and started clamoring for recognition.

"I know nothing about her marriage. To my shame."

"Not that unusual, sir. You know that."

"There wasn't anything *usual* about her marriage. Deep down I've always known it, much as I've tried to ignore my suspicions all along."

"What suspicions, sir? You know something that nobody else does?" Doc definitely had his attention now.

"No, nothing specific. How could I? I barely ever talked to her, much less saw her. Busy, she kept saying. Eric wanted her to go there and Eric said she should do that, and..."

He trailed off into grim silence.

"He was controlling her."

"With all my knowledge of dysfunctional relationships, it never once occurred to me there might be something fishy about all these activities that were supposedly consuming her time. Or about why no time was ever a good time for me to go visit. Till after Eric died and she came back home."

"What happened when she came back home?" Stone had given up all pretense of leaving now, his insides strung tight as he waited for Doc's answer.

"For one thing, I found out she hadn't quite turned into the socialite I was led to believe she had. The opposite, in fact. Withdrawn, depressed, ten times the loner she had ever been. Had the worst case of social anxiety disorder I've ever encountered in my entire career. *That* is why she never wanted me to lay eyes on her."

Stone stared at him. "That what she was seeing a therapist for?"

"It's what made me send her to one. I never told you this before...was too ashamed, I guess...but the Abigail who's been giving you ulcers these past months is quite a different package from the Abigail who came back to me after Eric's funeral. She was..." He stalled, his expression pained.

"She was what?"

"An absolute mess, is the only way I can describe it. Scared of her shadow. Afraid to be alone, afraid to face people. Afraid to go out, to drive. Afraid of the sunrise, afraid of the night sky...and on and on. And about twenty pounds lighter than she is now, if you can picture that."

He could, but not without experiencing a stab of pain and having to fight down a rush of rage.

"She'd have needed more than therapy sooner or later if I hadn't intervened when I did."

"Therapist shed any light on anything?"

"Didn't offer to share her findings with me, and I didn't ask."

He hadn't wanted to know, and Stone hadn't the heart to judge him for it. Doc was judging himself harshly enough, his face about ten years older as he added, "But I'm sure there was plenty. I just went on letting myself believe it was some kind of extreme grief she was suffering from."

He snorted. "It was grief all right, but I doubt now it was over Eric's death. If I'd been paying half as much attention as I was to my fan mail, I'd have seen it for myself. Who knows what really..." His eyes narrowed as he seemed to focus in on another memory. "You know that when she got married she suddenly started hating her name?"

"I can believe that," Stone murmured wryly, remembering the etymology lesson at his kitchen table that had resulted from his calling her by name for the first time.

"Started going by the middle name she'd always hidden from her friends because she thought it was *dorky*. Then by the time Eric died, she was back to hating Sarah again."

Stone stared at him.

Doc continued looking past him to some point beyond the present as he continued. "Then next thing I know, she wanted to change *both* her names. That's about when I first contemplated sending her for an evalu—*what?* What did I say?"

"*Sarah.* Her middle name is Sarah?"

"Ye-es," Doc said cautiously. "As a matter of fact, I believe that's what her husband and his church folks used to call her. Why—the name has some special significance for you?"

39

So did he?" Crystal asked, her tight face betraying more emotion than Abigail had ever thought her capable of.

"Make me prove I was willing to endure pain in order to be obedient to him? No, not really. But he got me to agree to it, even though I knew deep down I shouldn't have to." She met Crystal's and Fern's gazes in turn, saw nothing there but understanding and felt safe to add, in a whisper, "It was like being raped."

It was the first time she'd been able to accurately describe the soul-deep sense of violation that had ripped at her over and over for almost the entire duration of her marriage.

"He did that too, didn't he?"

"Rape me?" Abigail stared at them through a shimmering veil of tears and made the admission she never had before. "Not my body. Just the rest of me. It hurt so bad, Fern, and I didn't know how to make the hurt go away. And I hated myself for letting him do it to me, but I still couldn't seem to st-stop it, y'know?."

They stared back at her, their struggle to relate as evident as the love and sympathy in their eyes. Fern's man was the antithesis of Eric, and Crystal didn't have one because she would never settle for less than what her sister had found in Mark.

Abigail cringed at the memory of her own stupidity, desperation masquerading as devotion, and reached again for the anger that had fueled her therapy sessions. An anger that had spilled over onto the first man unfortunate enough to tangle with her afterward. But the anger had deserted her. Only the shame remained.

She bowed her head and whispered the rest, "I shouldn't have been so scared of him, cause he wasn't violent by nature—"

Crystal snorted. "Violence thrives on more than just fists, girlfriend."

Abigail nodded, relieved to have something she'd always felt echoed in the words of someone who wasn't being paid an hourly fee to say it, someone, moreover, whom she'd always known to be brutally honest.

"My stomach would be...like...in knots all the time, I felt that weak and helpless around him. He had this...this will that was like an iron wall, and I just got tired of bruising myself against it. My knowing I was in the right didn't make it any easier to stand up to him. I honestly felt sometimes like it'd be easier facing God's disapproval than his." She darted a look at Fern. "That's when I finally started accepting all the things you'd said about idolatry."

She closed her eyes and absorbed the touch of Fern's hand as it worked at the knot in the back of her neck, smoothing and pinching in the same fluid motion that burned even while it soothed. Iron sharpening iron.

...So a man sharpens the countenance of his friend.

She drew a deep, cleansing breath and confessed, "After a while I just started accepting that only death could save me. Mine or his. I didn't even care which."

"Should have been horsewhipped," Doc muttered fiercely into the silence that fell when Stone finished recounting all he'd uncovered about Sarah's—*Abigail's*—life at Spirit and Truth Center.

"My response exactly when I found out, sir."

"No, *me. I* should have been horsewhipped. I failed her, Stone. My only child...there I was, off counseling the world, and hadn't a clue what was happening in my own child's..."

"You're not telling me you didn't put your own theories into practice."

Doc shook his head, his expression pained. "Would have. Only by the time I got through slaving over that book and digesting it myself, I was the last person she was looking to for that kind of affirmation."

Stone wondered if he ought not to leave that alone. He'd read all of Doc's books, that one included. He knew what was supposed to happen to girls who hadn't got enough attention from their fathers. But he found himself needing to know. "You mean she..."

"Was boy crazy? No. But she did marry the first one who showed a serious interest in her."

"Surely you're not regretting that she didn't do the dating circuit?"

Doc shook his head emphatically. "No, but don't you see? None of that means much if you're not right with you first. Dating, courtship, even an arranged marriage...you're headed for an unstable relationship, no matter what route you use to get to it."

"Did you say anything to her?"

"I didn't see it as clearly as I do now. I didn't want to see it. Maybe because I knew she wasn't going to listen to anything negative I had to say. Why would she? She'd got nothing from me but duty...second place duty at that. Here was someone showering her with attention, acting like he couldn't draw his next breath without her."

"And she was so bowled over by it all she couldn't see him for the sick little boy he was." And had a hard time now seeing genuine acceptance and admiration for what it was.

"Otherwise she wouldn't have confused his jealousy and possessiveness with love, or taken his neediness for some kind of measure of her worth. But she did, and for me to put any kind of damper on her happiness would have been to risk looking like the selfish, jealous one and losing whatever place I did have in her affections."

"So you unplugged your intuition and prayed for the

best."

"Thought for a long time that my prayers had been answered, too." Doc's mouth twisted. "How many million copies of *Daddy, Do You Think I'm Pretty?* sold, and my own little girl was having to turn to some clod for..." He shook his head, too choked to go on.

Stone gave him a grimly sympathetic look. "That book needed to be written, Doc. It just might have come along too late for this particular little girl and her dad."

"Want to take a good guess why he was so drawn to her?"

Stone gave him a wry look. "Apart from all the reasons any man with brains and eyes in his head would be drawn to her? I'd say it was because he saw something in her that he felt made her an ideal candidate for him to remold into his own image. I'd say it all has to do with why she now insists on driving that old beater around. Not because she loves old yellow VWs or hates slick new Volvos, but because it's one of her few remaining links to who she was. *Is.*"

It and Tweety Bird. He so understood now about Tweety Bird.

"Stone, you've got to go over there and talk to her."

Stone shook his head slowly, emphatically. "It's got to be her move, Doc." Ironic how *Doc* was rolling easily off his tongue now, even as he ignored the green light being flashed at him. "She's either in that place or she isn't. I'm not going to try to drag her into it."

"You won't have to, if you just talk to her. She needs a little help getting there, that's all." He waited, then asked, "Can I tell you a secret? I was never particularly enamored with that little honeysuckle plant of mine. Well, not with its looks, anyhow. Not even now it's finally proven itself. But you want to know why I strove so hard with it, and why I'm still glad I did even now I've seen how unremarkable a bloom it's put out?"

He waited to make sure he had Stone's full attention before divulging, "I knew the fragrance it was capable of producing. I knew it was rare and valuable enough for some perfumers to pay good money for it. And that it was something that gave pleasure to someone I love. The fact that its previous owner had given up on it and didn't consider it worth the cost of a sprinkler-head replacement didn't deter me any, no more than—"

"Just a doggone second...if you think I'm being influenced by what value that *idio*...that husband of hers placed on her..."

"I'm not saying that. You're missing my point."

Stone felt the fire in his chest subside some and waited grimly for Doc to make his point.

Doc considered carefully this time before he continued. "We're past having to debate her worth, you and I. You probably know it better than me. I'm talking the potential beauty of a relationship between two people who love each other, flaws, baggage and all."

Stone shifted restlessly, and Doc hurried on, "That little honeysuckle bloom didn't mean all that much to either of us till it had been crushed into yielding its fragrance. Which you did with great reverence and anticipation while I looked on, speechless with horror. Until I watched you drink in its beauty and saw a world of care fall off you in the time it took to draw a single breath. I thought to myself, *this is the purpose for which this flower has labored so long to come into being*, and the protest died in my throat."

He held Stone's eyes. "A marriage built on God's love God's way is full of such rewards, Stone. There's toil and endless waiting, discouragement and uncertainty, yes. Some bruising and pain too. Just like in nature, simply because we live in a fallen world. But mixed in with all that there's also beauty that extends itself far beyond whatever plot of earth those two people happen to be occupying...if you care to go through what's necessary to harvest it."

When Stone still said nothing, Doc gently prodded, "You want me to try talking to her?"

"I'd rather you didn't."

"Then you do it. Just—"

"I'm sorry, I can't. I won't. She's had enough of being bullied by clueless men in her lifetime. I'm not going to be one of them. Not anymore, anyway. If I believe God is in control, then I can trust Him to bring her round...if that's what He wants. Otherwise, how am I different from any of the Erics and Leos out there?"

"You couldn't be a Leo or an Eric if you went to college for it. And I mean that from the bottom of my heart."

It was the nicest thing anybody had said to him in a long while. He made a point of meeting the other man's eyes. "Thanks, Doc."

"Just let go of your anger and your fear, Stone. Grab a hold of the fact that your perfection is in Christ, and your heavenly Father is more than able to rescue you from any influence your earthly father might otherwise have had on you. And then you needn't stress anymore about blowing it with Abigail or anyone else."

"I hear you, Doc. And you're putting me in mind of something the Lord showed me the other day."

Doc's eyes grew keen with renewed hope, and Stone hastened on before he could get the wrong idea. "I was in Genesis, part where God slipped Adam a sedative and did that rib transplant deal. And you know what came to me? Up till that moment, Adam hadn't a clue what was in God's mind. Same as with everything else, he simply trusted God to know exactly what he needed and then provide it."

Doc's eager gaze had gone cautious, but he waited without comment for the rest.

"Well, guess what? Last year this time when I was going about taking care of God's business, I hadn't a clue that I was about to lose my heart to some strange creature who was half me and half alien."

He shot Doc a wry look. "From Venus, at that. Well, getting up off the operating table and trying to take charge of the procedure has left me sore, to say the least. And I'm thinking I'm gonna have to learn to do like Adam—be still and let God finish what He started—if it's in fact Him who started it. And if it isn't...well..."

He saw Doc's face sober with comprehension and pressed on, "Otherwise I might as well go pair up with a monkey or an elephant or whatever. Cause don't you know those were Adam's other options until he found out there was such a thing as a woman. Now. You ever wonder what might have happened if God hadn't put him to sleep?"

Doc's lips twitched. "I can't say that I have."

"Well, as I see it, that fruit eating debacle was just a different version of the helpmeet test. As for why he flunked it, knowing full well that Eve had been duped...I know what you told me, and I remember what the scholars have to say, but my take on it is that it was all about control."

Doc was giving him an extremely cautious look. "I get the analogy, although I have to tell you your theology is a little iffy."

"I'm just going with what makes sense to me where I'm at, Doc. See, it's the spirit of that same curse that has dogged us men down through the ages. It wears all kinds of masks and gets called by different names, but it's as old as sin. The Genesis curse abandons us to the mercy of each other's self-will. The same self-will that spawns sin. The same self-will that craves control...and tries to pass itself off as love...and leadership. In the home or in the pulpit. And Jesus dying to save us from it doesn't do us a lick of good if we still choose to operate under the rules of the curse. So—"

He picked up his box again and started once again for the door. "Until I'm sure I've got my dispensations figured out and my flesh under subjection, I'd just as soon not mess with any of God's women."

She'd exhausted the source of her tears. Again. Only this time it felt like it might be for good. Abigail looked up from splashing cold water on her face.

Crystal handed over the make-up case she'd fished out of Abigail's bag and watched, still the fashion police, while

Abigail made a few repairs.

At the door, Fern stopped and held up a hand. "Shh!" she whispered, listening. She sent them a dry look.

"Sounds like a line forming out there, girls."

Crystal grinned.

Abigail chuckled weakly. It wouldn't be the first time they'd tied up a restroom while they sorted through the major crisis of the moment.

She'd expected to dream about Beth, but that night Abigail dreamed she saw Kay. Faceless like the emails that had been their only point of contact, but recognizable somehow. Screaming silent words from behind a soundproof glass wall. Abigail screamed back, but her voice came out as barely a whisper. *Kay, where have you been? Is everything all right? If you're busy just give one of us a shout so we know you're okay.*

Kay, please. It's not working. I can't do it anymore.

Email me a phone number if that's better for you. An address or something.

It was Fern and Crystal who pulled Abigail away, not recognizing the faceless person behind the glass. Abigail fought them off. Waved to catch Kay's attention, but her arms were suddenly weighted and moved only in slow motion.

Kay, I really need to talk. And now her cries were as silent as Kay's. That was when she realized Kay could not even see her.

Then suddenly Stone was there, yelling at her for being a fool. With each angry shout, the figure she thought was Kay faded a little, till finally Abigail was calling out to nothing but empty space on the other side of the glass.

"*Now* what?" Virginia squinted and peered at the message on the screen through farsighted eyes. She'd forgot her reading glasses home again.

Not that she couldn't have done the whole thing blind-folded. She'd followed the exact same steps she always had. Same steps she'd followed yesterday without incident. What could possibly be the matter with it today? She really didn't have time for this. She hadn't started dinner yet, and she had a five-fifteen bus to catch. There was always so little time.

She sighed and looked over into the next cubicle. "You finished yet, sweetie?"

He didn't answer. He'd become so rude of late.

"Time to go, ma'am," the librarian bellowed suddenly behind her. She had to be the most loud-mouthed librarian she'd had the misfortune to meet in the years she'd been coming here.

"Excuse me, but I am not finished."

"Sorry, ma'am, but the library is closing."

"Oh—it is?"

"Five o'clock. Look for yourself. Clock's right behind you on the wall."

It was indeed one minute to five. "My, time does go quickly in here, doesn't it?"

"Not for me, ma'am, but I only work here, see." She'd never encountered a librarian with such a lousy attitude toward her job.

"Better pick it up, ma'am, unless you want to miss the five-fifteen."

"Very well. What time do you open again?"

"Nine o'clock sharp."

Nine o'clock. Way too early for her, but she'd make it with more time to spare next time.

"You're some trip, Sybil," she heard another librarian behind her say with a chuckle as she went through the door.

She wondered if they'd tricked her about the closing time after all.

No matter, she'd just keep trying, was all. It had been days now since she got that email and had to leave without answering it on account of rushing to catch the five-fifteen bus. She was going to get an answer off to Abigail if she died in the attempt.

40

Week eight. Stone's favorite Survivor session. It was graduation day. There were songs and skits, testimonials and tears and the presentation of certificates, followed by a multiethnic buffet and a lot more sweetness than anyone who'd witnessed the turbulence of week one would have thought possible in such a relatively short span.

Kei had been invited to attend, although she had never been officially enrolled. Things hadn't gone the way Stone had hoped they would with her. She'd never opened up. Just listened silently and seemed to sink deeper into some dark pool of uncertainty with every new revelation she heard. Always he had a sense she didn't want to be there but couldn't seem to stop coming back.

He'd just announced that Survivor Junior's program was running longer than expected and had taken a vote on whether or not to wait dinner for them when Kei made her move. She stood, wiggled her fingers vaguely at the group filing obliviously toward the buffet and edged toward the door.

Stone hesitated on his way to the buffet, suspecting he would likely not see her again. He hated it when anyone walked away from the group without taking something with them that would make any kind of difference to their situation.

He just didn't know what else he could do for her. He didn't even have to wrestle with the question of whether to risk his job by inviting her to church. Several of the women already had and had got vague promises from her that she'd "stop by sometime."

Before he'd made up his mind if or how to stop her leaving, someone on the other side of the door did it for him. Just as Kei backed into it, it opened and pushed against her, almost unbalancing her.

She turned to investigate. "No, no, you can't come in here," she whispered to whoever was on the other side. There was a scuffle of some sort and the sound of children's voices, several of them.

"No, honey, she not in here," Kei said. "Go back, go back." She shooed ineffectually at them.

A girl of about seven or eight pushed past Kei and into the room, yelling, "*Mommeee!*" and made a beeline for Mara.

Just then, one of the leaders of Survivors Junior came rushing up. "Sorry, everyone," she said breathlessly. "They moved so fast...Come on kids..."

"*No!* I want to see Mommy! Mommy, *Mommy...*"

Two small boys broke free and joined their sister, and pandemonium broke out for a short space, with a sobbing Mara embracing her three incoherent children while everyone else except the two people in charge looked on in a daze.

Stone consulted briefly with the other group leader before turning to Mara. "Mara, why don't you help take the kids back upstairs and see if you can calm them down a little?"

Mara went gladly with her clinging children, tossing a scornful look at the woman who had brought them there.

Kei was still in shock as she turned helplessly to the others. "Please...I didn't know...I thought she was..."

"In the crazy house?" finished one of the others. "We believe you, honey, considering who it is you gone and hooked yourself up with."

"You know my fiancé?"

"Feels like it. Been eight weeks now we've been listening to Mara cry, huh girls?"

Stone resumed his seat and slipped into observation mode while they had their say.

"Seems to me you need to sign up next time around, honey," Josephine said dryly. "Cause you ain't learned nothing in the time you been with us. Not if you still with who you with."

Kei's already pale face grew paler. "You mean...?"

"*Uh-huh*. Well now, those her kids. And her ex you with. You know, handsome preacher guy who cracked her skull? Oh, and by the way...last time I checked, the V & M ain't been changed into no *mental facility*."

"Poor girl, I thought she was going to pass out."

Mark grunted his amazement. "And all that time she hadn't a clue?"

"How could she? She saw her reflection somewhere in the picture Mara and others were painting, yes, which is why she kept coming, but as far as she knew, her fiancé's ex was under lock and key in a padded cell somewhere."

"Seems to me he needs a program of his own."

Stone snorted. "Reprogramming, more like it. He's been through one already. Except the Master Programmer isn't allowed in there."

"Thank God for Oasis, eh?"

"Yeah." It came out flatter than Stone had intended.

"Not your fault what happened, Stone. Don't let the devil beat you up over it."

Stone didn't have to wonder what he was talking about. "I know." Knew it, but couldn't help feeling like he'd failed Corey anyway. Him and Beth.

"Every other family you've helped through Oasis has been nothing but better for it. You're not going to win them all."

"I saw this one coming, though, Mark. From the first day I talked to Leo. Hadn't so much seen it as smelled it, like I smelled death on that blood-soaked carpet before I even darkened the sanctuary. I can't say why. Leo really isn't the worst of the lot."

"Just reminds you of someone who is."

"Or it could have been the Lord was trying to tell me something. In any case, now that it's happened, I feel as bad as if I killed her myself. If only because I saw it coming and still wasn't able to stop it happening."

"Well, there's still Leo. How's he doing? You talk to him since?"

Stone frowned. "To keep him up on what's happening with Corey, yes."

"I know he's got to be hurting pretty bad."

Stone shifted impatiently. "I can't deal with Leo right now, Mark. That's gonna have to wait till I've knocked the mud out of my halo and glued it back into place."

"Hmm."

Stone recognized that *hmm* and the silence that followed it for what they were and braced himself.

Mark let him squirm for a while.

"Well, pal, look on the bright side," Mark said finally. "There's always the possibility his depression will get the better of him and you won't ever have to deal with him again, not even in heaven."

The following day, Stone pulled up in front of Miami Regional's main entrance next to the scrawny denim-clad man waiting at the curb, leaned over to shove the passenger door open and waited for him to get in.

Leo avoided his eyes as he slid in and muttered a grudging, "Thanks."

Stone's eyes swept briefly over him before he pulled away from the curb. "You look like hell."

"Feel it." Leo rested his head back against the headrest and let out a weary sigh.

Stone sent him another glance as he headed down the long drive to the main road. Leo looked and sounded more like a man at the end of a particularly strenuous day than one coming home from a week-long stint resting in the hospital.

He'd lost more weight than Stone had thought he had on him to lose, but there was none of that artificial calm over his wooden features that would have suggested he'd been medicated. Knowing Leo, he'd have refused it.

He'd driven himself to the edge with a million and one thoughts of if-only and, after much contemplation and re-assurances from empathetic professionals, had managed to distill them all down to one certainty: If he hadn't sent Beth to the hospital in the first place, whatever it was that had actually taken her life would likely not have happened.

Right or wrong, it was how Leo saw it, and it was some burden to carry in addition to the heavy grief already eating away at him. It had left him a shell of his former self.

"How'd he do?" Leo asked now, his voice as subdued as the rest of him.

"Good. Took to them just fine."

"He's like his mom that way." There was warmth and sadness in his voice. Then it hardened again. "But it's just temporary. He's mine, and I'm not giving him up."

"They understand that. But you do realize that depend-ing on which way things go in court it might not be your decision to make."

Again that look of panic, like he'd used to have at the thought of losing Beth. Stone felt his first real stirring of compassion for him.

The sternness of his voice eased some as he told him, "It's not too late for you to make the right choices, Leo. Give yourself some time to get straightened out, take every course you're ordered to, and then some, and see what happens then."

Stone checked for oncoming traffic and eased out into the northbound lane. "You might even want to give you and the Matthews a chance. They're your blood, whatever else there is between you—that counts for something. I know, believe me." He squeezed into the center lane, exe-cuted a swift u-turn and took the next left turn to head east.

"Where we going?"

"Detour. They got some kind of mess tying things up back that way."

Leo stared sullenly out at the ratty scenery of the quiet side street, at the long line curling round the perimeter of the food bank mission and, further along, the bright avocado green and gold building that stood out from the drabness of the rest of the block. "What's that there?"

"The Kids' Place. Short term care foster home. For the ones who don't have a grandma and grandpa to fill the gap."

Stone slowed to a crawl as they passed it. A handful of children were playing listlessly on the gym set in the fenced yard, with bright new clothes and dull, weary faces.

Stone slanted Leo a look. "If nothing else, you can be grateful that your son's got a decent pair of relatives who'll take good care of him for you till you're able to."

"And they better not be filling his head with no lies 'bout me neither."

"Nobody wants to turn your kid against you, Leo. They better not. They've got laws against that kind of thing. You're the only one can do that." He accelerated again, swung right of the upcoming roundabout and on a sudden decision pulled over into one of the metered parking spots that lined the small triangular park in the middle of the intersection. "He's a great kid, Leo, and he deserves to be happy."

Pride flickered over Leo's features, animating it. He didn't notice or didn't care that they had stopped. "Yeah, he is, huh? Sharp as a whip, too. My boy."

"He's still crazy about you."

"Think so?"

"Know so. Weren't you crazy about your Dad at his age? I know I was."

Leo thought, smiled, but declined to answer.

"He won't be little forever, though, Leo. Or so forgiving. One day he's gonna grow up and start looking at things a little different, and he could end up a very angry young man, regardless of who ends up raising him. I know. I've been there."

Leo's knees started slapping against each other, a hunted look chasing the paternal pride from his face. "I can't bring her back. I can't go back and—"

"You don't have to, Leo. Bible says a man who's got Christ is a new creation. Old debts are cancelled and you get to start over fresh."

"Yeah, try telling that to the family court judge." His mouth tightened. "'Sides, I don't have Christ. And don't particularly want to. He ain't gonna do me no good now. What I'm-a do is find a decent paying roast and save up enough to get me a good lawyer." He looked at Stone. "You know any good ones? You should."

"I do, but—" Stone shook his head. "That's the least of your problems right now, Leo."

"Forget it, then. I'll find my own. What'd you come here for, anyway? We both know you can't stand my guts, so don't try pretending any different."

Stone decided not to. "I wanted to let you know I've got your back, regardless."

"Who, you?" Leo looked at him as if he'd grown a second head. "That the case, then you can help me get my son back."

"I can't, Leo. Only you can do that."

"Yeah, so the anger management counselors keep telling me."

"I'm not talking anger management. Anger management's not going to help you. Not by itself. Not Oasis either."

Leo gave him a wary look. "I ain't taking no more courses. I got a living to earn."

"I wasn't suggesting you take one." Stone searched around for the right words to tell him exactly what he was suggesting. Several verses suggested themselves to him, but the words wouldn't pass his throat. Leo would likely choke on any scripture he tried to feed him now, considering all the man had ever got from him until just recently was contempt and veiled threats.

Stone swallowed and set aside everything he'd had lined up to say. "And for the record, I don't hate you. Us Christians aren't allowed. I just had a hard time dealing with you. Real hard. Want to know why?"

Leo's shrug said he didn't care, but the slant of his head said he was listening just the same.

"You reminded me too much of my old man."

"Your *pop*."

"When he was your age, of course."

The look Leo gave him was wary to say the least. Stone had shared several things with the Oasis group about his father, none of them good. "That so? Well, I ain't have nothing to do with what he put you through, so don't think I'm gonna let you use me as some—"

"I already did, Leo, and I'm sorry. That's the other thing I came to tell you. As a professional, I ought to have known better."

"Oh." That seemed to disarm him some. "Well, it wasn't like you showed me no disrespect or nothing. Not that anybody coulda blamed you, with how I was treating Beth—"

"Wasn't just Beth. I took it personal, real personal. You *scared* me. I saw myself in you."

Leo stared at him, slack jawed. Stone had definitely got his attention now.

Stone pressed his advantage. "Oh yes. I'm more like you than you'd think. Was."

"You—"

Stone shook his head. "Never hit a woman in my life, thank God. But not because it wasn't in me to do it. It's all I grew up knowing. The only way I'd ever seen my father deal with problems, taking it out on somebody weaker than himself."

He turned and held Leo's now attentive gaze. "Only difference between me and him is I have someone willing and able to handle all the rage and violence I'm capable of."

"Man, she must be awful stupid."

"Not she, He."

"You mean you..." A look of revulsion crossed Leo's face, and he recoiled visibly.

Stone chuckled in spite of his somber mood. "I'm not gay, Leo. Told you already I've got it for the pastor's daughter, remember?"

"Oh yes. Then...?"

"I'm talking about the man Jesus. The only one who can honestly say He understands what every one of us goes through."

Leo's face tightened, and he looked away and said nothing.

"He's been where you are too, Leo. Might not have been married, but the Bible says He had all sorts of temptations dealing with, just like we do. Only He never gave in to them. Been there and didn't do it, I guess you'd say. It gives Him the right to plead our case to the Judge of all judges. Except He can't do it if we don't engage His services."

Leo's face was working. He looked like he was about to demand to be let out of the car.

"He's better than any lawyer, Leo. Lawyers love your money, not you. I certainly never met one who'd die for any of his clients. Or for people He knows will throw what he's offering them back in his face."

Leo turned to stare out the window, his face and his whole body rigid.

Stone shifted restlessly in his seat as he searched for the right words to say to him, afraid he was losing him and frustrated with himself for floundering at such a critical moment.

"Leo, if you could just...just..." He turned in his seat to face Leo fully...and went silent, the rest of what he'd been about to say dying on his lips.

Leo's gaze was fixed blindly on the horizon, and there were fat tears rolling down his face and dropping off the end of his chin.

Stone surveyed the crimson stained royal-blue carpet in front of him and fought down a sudden rush of bile.

There were people who made a living doing this kind of thing. Had to be. How else did other people deal with the aftermath of this kind of horror?

They'd need more than a cleaning company now. No hope now of lifting out that dried-in blood. And unrighteous or not, it was not going to lie there another day absorbing the dust from people's feet as if it was some animal that had been slaughtered there. He reached into his pocket for the carpet knife he'd brought with him and dropped down to his knees. It was his last chance to honor a man he'd always reviled...

Wake up, son. The whisper stroked soothingly through Stone's spirit, and he woke up gently, without the usual panicked jolt.

Thank you, Lord. He passed a shaky hand over his face. It was damp with sweat, like the rest of him. His body felt sore, as if he'd been wrestling something more physical than ghosts. He hauled himself out of bed and went to the kitchen for a drink of water.

Back in his room, he searched among the coins and odds and ends in the brass tray atop his chest-of-drawers for the business card he'd tossed there what seemed like months ago. It was actually just days, and he hadn't expected to be using it anytime soon. Hadn't expected a whole lot of other things to happen either.

He found the card and took it with him over to the phone on his bedside table. He'd have given anything then, including an entire night's sleep, for a two-a.m. nonsense phone call from his favorite insomniac. He'd have to settle for playing catch up with his favorite nighttime security guard and one-time best friend.

41

Five weeks after Beth's funeral, Abigail woke one Friday morning to the sound of her blinds being opened.

She didn't have to open her eyes to know who it was. She knew the instant the warm sunlight invaded the room and probed her closed eyelids. Her father had never quite caught up with the fact that she no longer needed to be routed out of bed and shooed off to catch the school bus.

"Odette tells me Mark called here at eleven o'clock last night looking for his wife," he said. "You and Crystal been ragging her round South Florida again?"

Abigail rolled over, groaning. "More like she's been ragging us, Dad, trust me. She just gives Mark that to hold so he won't suspect she's actually having fun away from him while he's home babysitting." She blinked up at him through still bleary eyes. "What's up?"

He had that look on his face that she'd been seeing so much of lately. A deeply thoughtful look, almost sad, tinged with something like regret. Except that today there were tears gathering in them.

"Dad?" she said uncertainly, struggling up on one elbow.

His answer was to drop down to his knees at the side of the bed and enfold her in a crushing embrace.

Abigail felt something cold clutch at her insides. Beth's death had left her a lot more mindful of her own mortality and that of the people she loved. She'd never again take the gift of life for granted.

"Daddy?" she faltered. "Did your checkup go all right the other day? Is there something you've been keeping from me?"

He drew a deep breath and pulled back. Shook his head, swallowed. "Only that I love you."

"Oh." She regarded him uncertainly. She already knew that, but it wasn't like him to come out and say it for no particular reason. "I love you too, Dad." *Now tell me what's wrong.*

"And I just wanted you to know that even though I wasn't there for you in the way that I should have—"

"*Dad*—"

"Just let me finish. I could have done more. A whole lot more. But I want you to know there's nothing, no book, no ministry, nothing that's more important to me than you. And that for whatever time I have you here with me, I'm going to listen more and talk less."

"Okay." Her voice had whittled down to a whisper. He had touched a nerve. "Thanks, Dad, that means a lot to me." *I just couldn't stand to see the shock and disappointment on your face if I ever got up the nerve to take you up on that offer.*

"I know your marriage wasn't what you wanted me to believe it was." He paused, while she went stock still in his arms. "Took me a while, but I finally...figured it out."

She pulled away.

His hand caught and held on to hers. "But I'm not going to press you about it. Just know that if ever you feel like talking, I'll be here."

Her throat closed up then, and she could only nod and squeeze his hand.

A few more minutes and then he was clearing his throat and setting her away from him. "And having said that..." He ruffled her hair. "When are you going to quit lazing around the house and get back to work?"

"I don't know, Dad. I guess when I'm ready." Her eyes were glued to his face, her mind clouded by a strange new sense that she might not know him as well as she thought she had, after all.

"Well, you're going to have to let me know when that will be, and if I need to start thinking of bringing someone else in. We're getting a lot of inquiries about when Oasis is starting back up, and with Stone gone, I might—"

"Gone where?" she gasped, making the sudden transition with a jolt. She'd been so careful to avoid crossing paths with Stone, volunteering in the nursery, helping out in junior chapel, playing hooky down by the pond, anything to avoid running into him. It hadn't once occurred to her he might not even have been at church. "Stone left Grace?" Something cold grabbed hold of her insides at the thought.

"Well, not yet, but I wouldn't be surprised at this point if it came to that. You might not have missed him these past few weeks—"

Yeah, right.

"But he's been visiting elsewhere. Met up with an old friend of his—"

"F-friend?" *Shan.*

"He might transfer his fellowship."

It couldn't have hurt more if someone had kicked her in the gut. "But why? Did you and him have a falling out?"

He raised one eyebrow. "Besides over you, you mean?"

Her eyes flew wide open, then narrowed. "About what?"

"Man talk," he grunted, sounding awfully like Stone. "None of your business."

"Why would he leave?" Try as she did, she couldn't stop her voice from wobbling.

"Why wouldn't he? I think it might be for the best, actually. Be easier for him to move on if he's—"

"Move on to where?"

"With his life, Abigail. Isn't that what you want?"

"Y...*no,* I never..."

Both his eyebrows went up.

She started over. "What I mean is, he shouldn't leave on my account. Why should he? He's been here all along, and...well, what about Oasis? Doesn't he care about that anymore?"

"Oh, he's not giving up on counseling. There are other ministries, you know. I wish he'd stay with mine, but unfortunately, he's convinced himself Oasis will do just as well or better without him, and I couldn't think of a good enough argument to persuade him otherwise."

"Daddy! How could you! He worked so hard. He put everything into it. He *cared*. Moreover, he knows what he's doing. He's got training, and...You should see him at work on his other job. He—"

"Really." Her father was staring at her. "Let me see...what was it you told me not two months ago? He's rough, full of might and bluster and not enough of the Spirit. Bossy and hard to get along with. And *where'd he come from all of a sudden, anyway?*" He cocked an eyebrow at her. "Did I miss anything?"

She gave him a sheepish look from under her lashes. "That was...then."

"Six...seven weeks ago."

"I didn't really know him.

"And you do now?"

She nodded vigorously. "He's got a lot of heart underneath all that bluster, Daddy. More than Eric ever had, for all his polish and everything else. And—"

"So why did you shut him out?"

"Because I was hurting."

"So was he. Even so, he wanted nothing but to reach out to you."

Guilt stabbed at her. "Oh Daddy, I didn't mean..." She drew a shaky breath. "You think it's too late for me to...if I..."

He looked at his watch. "Sit down, Abigail, let me tell you a story."

"I want to go see him."

"After we talk." He perched on the foot of her bed and patted the spot next to him.

"When is he leaving?"

"I'm...not sure. He's closing on his house today."

"*Closing on his—*"

"Mm-hmm. And guess who sold it for him?"

"Dad, I couldn't care less if he had a Martian for a real estate agent. And how can you be so...so..." She threw up her hands. "Don't you *care?*"

He grew serious then. "Yes, I care, Abigail. About you and also about him. His usefulness to Oasis is secondary to my personal regard for him, believe me, for he's become like a son to me. And that is why I'm going to risk our friendship by telling you what I'm about to."

42

"Hey there, Mr. Patrick," a voice hailed from behind Stone as he approached the main entrance of Dade Central, and he turned to see the stalwart Jamaican aide who'd been assigned to his mother the past year or so hurrying to catch up with him.

"Hey, Sybil." He liked Sybil, her big voice and open smile. Liked the fact that she looked him in the eye and still had a sense of humor. It told him a lot about the kind of care his mother might or might not be receiving when he wasn't around.

"Sticking like glue to your low carb diet, I see," he murmured when they were on their way again, cocking an eyebrow at the rice and peas and fried plantains on her tray.

"*Cho* mon, Mr. Patrick. You know them thing there's not real food. Big strapping fella like you ought to know that. But Monday morning, mark my words—"

"—you're going to give it another shot. I know." They grinned together over that.

And then his face straightened, and he asked, "So how's she been?"

"Been at it again, sir." Sybil gave him an exaggerated wink. "You know—all that research and stuff. Somebody left the office door open again, and that's where she was the other morning at five o'clock when I did rounds. Good thing they went ahead and put on the password like they should have in the first place."

For endless moments after her father finished speaking, Abigail stared at him, numb with shock.

"He told me that story," she whispered when she could finally find words, recalling in vivid detail the shocking story Stone had told her of *someone he knew once*, who he *could have been close to if she'd been living on the same planet*, and who had killed her own husband in an effort to hasten the fulfillment of some warped promise she'd wrung from between the lines of scripture.

"Only he forgot to tell me the woman was his mother."

"So you see you weren't so far off base when you suggested he was keeping secrets for me. Except the secret was my own guilt. She'd got some tapes of one of my marriage seminars and drawn all kinds of inferences from it. First one of all the tens of thousands of women who've attended over the years."

"But you felt responsible just the same."

"More than that, my heart went out to Stone, for all he'd been through. Leading him to Christ wasn't enough. I wanted to be there for him and give him some of what he'd never had from his own father. I discovered in the process that he had a remarkable grasp of relationship dynamics, especially pertaining to the woman's side of things."

"Not surprising, after all the brooding he must have done over his own mother's situation."

"Precisely. He'd carried around a ton of guilt over her, you see, felt responsible. For not intervening somehow. For leaving home as soon as he turned eighteen, even though he'd offered more than once to get her away from there and she refused."

Abigail inhaled deeply. "So where is she now? In jail?"

"Technically, no. A detention facility for the criminally insane. For all intents and purposes, a life sentence."

No wonder he'd had trouble adjusting to having her placed. No wonder...

Her head spun as all the no-wonders came clamoring for discovery all at once.

"Did he tell you what it was that caused her to snap?" her father asked.

"No."

"You would have been away at seminary with Eric at the time."

Abigail frowned. "Away from where?"

Her father regarded her in silence a moment before saying, "I had a feeling you didn't know."

"Didn't know what? Dad—"

"His mother went to Spirit and Truth too."

Abigail stared at him. "You're kidding."

He shook his head. "You might not have known each other, though. She was gone by the time you got back from seminary with Eric."

She shook her head. "No wonder Stone had it out for me. He..." She heaved a breath. "Tell me about what happened."

"His father turned up at the church one Sunday half drunk. Embarrassed his mom so badly she nearly never went back. Then had the nerve on top of it to try to stop her from going to church altogether. She flipped. Church had been the only thing holding her together, and just barely."

Found religion and buried herself deep in the rubble of the denial-of-your-trials movement. Like most members of Spirit and Truth Center.

"Church secretary called Stone's father at work one weekday to tell him to come get his wife. She'd taken up refuge in the empty sanctuary with a suitcase full of clothes, spouting all kinds of Old Testament rules about refuge and sanctuary and what not. When he went after her, she was waiting for him. Shot him right there, hanging on to the altar, with his own gun. Word got to Stone at his job. He got to the scene before they could even clean it up or...where are you going?"

"To see him." She had scrambled from the bed and was

opening and shutting drawers, pulling clothes blindly from them. "And to tell him I don't give two hoots about any of that, or—"

"You might want to wait—"

"No, I'm not going to wait."

"He's not home, Abigail. He's more than likely with her right now. He told me he was going to see her before the closing, and it's..." He consulted his watch. "...already ten minutes into visiting hours."

She stared at him from the closet entrance, undies clutched to her chest and a selection of outerwear trailing over both shoulders. "You sure?"

"Positive. I've gone along with him, several times."

"Good." She flew into the bathroom, calling over her shoulder, "Cause I'm going to meet him there. You can write down the address for me, or not write it down. I'll find it anyway."

A few houses down from Stone's, Abigail spotted a car in his carport and, heart quickening, immediately started rehearsing what she would say to him.

Oh, I'm glad I caught you. Daddy wasn't able to direct me to your Mom's place, and I—

He wasn't there. She'd already pulled into the driveway before she realized that his Mustang was missing. And that there were two other cars occupying the carport in its place.

Had the closing happened already? No sooner did she wonder that than a familiar voice, a woman's, sang out through the open kitchen window. "Shan, where'd he say he wants the cleaning stuff again?"

Fern. And *Shan?*

Then, from a little farther away, came the throaty drawl Abigail had heard only once before. "He didn't. I wouldn't bother asking him either. He's as likely as not to say pack it in with the medicine cabinet things."

A washing machine or something was going, and making

a bigger racket than Abigail's well oiled, well-tuned engine could ever hope to compete with. They obviously hadn't heard her arrive and probably wouldn't hear her leave.

She eased gently into reverse and prepared to sneak away from 230 Palm Terrace with her heart in her shoes for the second straight time.

"Abby, wait!"

Fern, hobbling as fast as she could down the front steps with her sleeping two-week-old son strapped to her middle in the slingamajig Stone had got her. Abigail groaned and closed her eyes, thinking fast.

The truth was the best she could come up with. "I had this crazy idea to go with him to visit his mom, that's all."

Fern's look grew earnest and hopeful. "So go. I'll tell you where it is."

"Nah, changed my mind." Her eyes shifted without her meaning them to, over to the silver Toyota parked behind Fern's SUV.

Comprehension dawned on Fern's face. Her eyes widened. "Abby—"

Abigail released the brake. "Gotta go."

"Abby, wait! You don't understand—"

"I think I do." *Better than you know.* "And don't you dare tell him I was here, either."

"Abby, he'd *want* to know."

"Fern Leigh Scott."

"All *right.*"

"If you tell him, I'll never speak to you again, I swear."

"No swearing; your daddy taught you better. Go on. My mouth's zipped. At least till after we've had our heart to heart."

"I wasn't aware we had one scheduled."

"We do now. Tonight."

Abigail just rolled her eyes and shifted into reverse.

So things don't turn out the way you wanted and all of a sudden you don't care for him anymore, don't want to encourage him and bring him My perspective on things.

"Lord, I've got feelings too, and—"

When was it ever about you?

She'd asked for that. "Okay, Lord, I hear you." She rolled back into the driveway.

Fern met her halfway, holding out a square of paper towel with a hastily scrawled address on it. She handed it over silently, stoically, as if she'd been tipped off. She'd probably prayed.

Abigail gave her a wry half-smile. "Thanks. Talk to you later."

"You bet. And don't you try not answering your phone, either, or I'll come over there to you. Different rules this time around, girl."

Abigail couldn't help a smile. It was good to have a nosy, won't-take-no-for-an-answer pest in her life again.

Fern stopped just inside the living room and stared at Shan. "Where you going?"

Shan stuffed her MP3 player into the fanny pack she'd just strapped on. "Out of here."

"You don't have t—"

"Yes, I do. I shouldn't have come in the first place. He warned me not to."

"He *told* you not to come here?"

"Well, asked me. Nicely. *After* he got through chewing me out for turning up without notice. Same day I came by to tell him I'd got saved. Got over his excitement real fast when he looked through the window and saw that yellow Bug tearing out of here. *That* is why he hooked me up with you. I need a mentor, he said, and it couldn't be him."

"I did tell him I was going to ask you to help, you know. He didn't seem to have a problem with it."

"Yeah, well, he was desperate. For an extra pair of hands, that is. And I'm sure he wasn't expecting her to show up." Her mouth twisted. "Neither was I. I guess when I realized she'd been missing for a while I thought... hoped..."

"I...see."

"Anyways. I do *not* want to be around when he finds out I scared his woman off a second time. Ta-ta and happy packing!"

The place reeked of body fluids and the kind of disinfectant whose vile smell was usually blamed on some innocent pine. The offensiveness of the combined odors was rivaled only by the incoherent groans and shrieks that echoed through the place from various directions.

Walking into the Dade Central Mental Health Facility, Abigail's heart constricted at the thought of Stone never being able to see his mother anywhere but in a place like this. Not even when it came time to introduce her to someone special in his life.

She didn't remember till she was signing in at the security desk that she hadn't the first idea what his mother's name was.

"I'm supposed to meet Stone Patrick here," she improvised.

"That would be Unit 3." The guard checked her ID and pointed left to where a pair of armed guards stood outside heavy double doors.

The younger looking of the two, trim and erect in stiff new uniforms, relieved Abigail of her handbag, while his counterpart, a large, mature woman with a blasé expression to match her obviously broken-in uniform, mechanically treated Abigail to a full body scan. Her bag was searched, her money, keys, cell phone and pen confiscated. "For safe keeping," she was assured. Only then did the elder nod at the younger, who punched in a code that unlocked the security doors and escorted her into the empty corridor beyond.

She stepped into the room, her eyes drawn to the single

tiny window above the bed on the far side of the room. The security bars welded onto it formed a perfect tic-tac-toe grid, and someone had been playing tic-tac-toe on it with a green neon marker.

A small smile tugging at her mouth, Abigail shifted her gaze from the empty bed across the room to the one nearest the door...and immediately stepped back out of the room.

Stone was kneeling before his mother's chair, his head in her lap, and she was stroking his hair. From the corridor, Abigail heard her say, "I forgive you too, son. I'm sure of it now, 'cause I've been flushing them down the toilet, every last one of them."

A muted chuckle from Stone, a loud smacking kiss, and then he was calling out, "It's okay, Sybil, you can come."

Abigail hesitated, then reentered tentatively as Stone was getting to his feet. It was a semi-private room, but the other occupant was for the moment away from it.

"It's me...Abigail. I...didn't mean to barge in. It was a spur of the moment de—"

"No apology needed," Stone assured her smoothly, quickly recovering from what looked like pure shock. "Come in, say hi to my mom." Still some surprise there, a considerable amount, but no censure. He held a beckoning hand out to Abigail and waited for her to draw near. If she didn't know better, she'd think he was glad to see her.

He was thinner than she remembered, his face almost gaunt, and his hair had grown a ways past fashionable and was approaching unkempt. As were the rough-looking shirt and jeans he wore, the same set she'd last seen on him weeks ago, the day they first clashed over Beth.

Before she had a chance to speculate about the reason for his altered appearance, a tremulous voice behind him was saying, "Sister? Is that you, Sister Carmichael? If you're another hallucination, please...I don't want to know."

It was a pain-filled cry from the wounded heart of a stranger, but the voice seemed somehow vaguely familiar.

Abigail stared at the woman in the chair...and then stared

some more.

The face she recognized from the pictures she'd seen— thinner and more lined but retaining a lot of its strong-boned beauty. But the voice too was vaguely familiar.

She stared some more, and suddenly the pictures she'd seen came to life for her. They were younger, happier versions of a face she'd seen time and again at Spirit and Truth Center but never had reason to carry in the forefront of her memory. Back in the euphoric days of her engagement and the first few months of her marriage before she'd gone to live on Campus with Eric at Seminary.

"Sister Virginia?" Abigail whispered.

Virginia smiled widely, and it was a rather beautiful smile that lit her eyes like Abigail had never seen it lit in the year plus that she'd encountered her at Spirit and Truth Center. "It *is* you. Oh, thank God...I've been trying to reach you."

"You have?" Abigail darted a doubtful look at Stone, who was looking on with knit brows, and then back at Virginia. She came across as a lot more lucid than Abigail had expected, much as her words didn't make sense.

It was something in her eyes, Abigail supposed. They sought and met Abigail's directly with recognition and something more—a kind of knowing.

Except they had never really known each other in anything but a casual way.

Abigail looked at Stone, hoping for some insight into her mental condition. His face was grim, but somehow she suspected it was more from shock than displeasure. When he stepped back to give her complete access to his mother, she knew she had surmised right.

She knelt in front of Virginia, much as Stone had just been doing, and put her arms where his had been, drawn inexplicably to her. Well, not inexplicably. She was Stone's mother.

And they'd once worshipped feet apart from each other. They had hardly ever exchanged more than a passing greeting, the elegantly dressed front pew occupant and the withdrawn older sister with the "problem husband."

Husband's unsaved, you know. Poor woman. It's a wonder he even lets her come to church, considering he never used to let their boy anywhere near Sunday school.

Her *son*, who'd grown up too fast, she'd heard, and who'd thought Sunday school was "sissy stuff," as per his daddy's indoctrination. *Stone.* So called because his father had had a thing about raising a sissy.

She looked over at him in a daze and then back at his mother.

"Sister Virginia...Patrick?" Abigail asked slowly, testing the sound of it. The last name didn't ring a bell. She might not even have heard it before now, except in conjunction with Stone. She had been just Sister Virginia.

Virginia gave a mischievous sounding chuckle as she placed her long, shapely hands on either side of Abigail's face. "Hello again, Abigail," she said, sounding pleased with herself. "I'm Virginia Kay." She made a face. "To the folks here, anyhow. Most everybody else calls me Ginny."

43

Nobody at Spirit and Truth Center had known her by any other name but Sarah. Except for Eric.

Just as nobody at Grace had ever known her as anything but Abigail. Except for the three girlfriends who'd succeeded in wheedling her middle name out of her.

And a fourth friend, who'd started out knowing her only as a screen name but who had gone on to learn not only her first name but all the confusion of pain and need and uncertainties that both names together had come to represent to her.

Kay.

Abigail wiped her eyes with the heels of her hands and pulled back enough to look into the face so close to hers. A stranger's face, and as dear to her as her own mother's now that she knew the voice behind it.

"Why didn't you tell me?" Abigail whispered. "For months we were sitting just feet apart from each other."

"Oh, Sister, I didn't want to impose." It was Sister Virginia of Spirit and Truth Center speaking again.

Abigail could well imagine her past dilemma. The rules governing the hierarchy of Spirit and Truth Center were unwritten and unspoken, but strictly observed. The plebs like Virginia would not have felt free to offer their friendship to the likes of the pastor's daughter-in-law.

Abigail could not even claim to have been unaware of the existence of such schisms. It was just one more evil that she'd gone along with in the name of submission, convincing herself she was not personally accountable.

She sucked in a shaky breath and forced herself to abandon the futility of lamenting the past and focus on the present, which she still had the power to influence.

Virginia-Kay, huh? That's really pretty. What's your last name? You ready to tell me yet?"

Virginia-Kay gave her an uncomprehending look and repeated, "Kay."

"Kay *is* her last name," Stone said quietly behind her.

"Oh, her maiden name."

"Her married name."

"Your last name is Kay?" she asked his mother, then looked at Stone. His eyes were glistening with moisture. "But..."

"Mine too. Was. I changed it. My birth name was Stone Patrick Kay. My father was Patrick James Kay—P.J. to most."

"Was an unbelievably arrogant thing to do, I know," Stone admitted wryly after Abigail had digested his revelation. "But I was eighteen and didn't have Jesus at the time, and it was the only way I knew to shake the ghosts that were haunting me at the time. I retained just enough of my father's identity to serve as a reminder of what I didn't want to become."

He realized even as he spoke that neither of them were listening to him, their eyes drinking in the sight of each other and their questions tripping over each other's.

"What happened to you?" Abigail was demanding, much as she might have of Fern or Crystal. "I couldn't find you. You never wrote...Well, I guess you couldn't..."

"She tried," Stone said quietly behind her.

His mother nodded. "Yes, at the library."

"On Dade Central's computer," Stone corrected in an undertone for Abigail's benefit. "Till they started locking it away."

"You mean...oh *no*."

"Before that, I guess it was at the library."

"When I took the kids," Virginia said.

"Some cousins of hers she used to baby sit," Stone explained. "Seems she had some idea what she was doing after all. Everyone except you thought she was just confused."

His mother chuckled. "Oh, I was at first, very. But I soon became quite a computer expert. The librarians were so patient, see. Back then, anyway. Nowadays they're not so helpful at all, and *so* unprofessional."

"She's always been something of a snob at heart," Stone murmured, drifting closer to them. "God alone knows what drew her to my father."

"He was crazy in love with me," Virginia sighed dreamily. She seemed to have a knack for picking what she wanted out of a conversation and ignoring the rest. "I was the only girl he ever let close to him. He didn't trust people, only me. They didn't understand him the way I did, see."

Stone saw the look on Abigail's face then, like someone about to throw up, and moved quickly to her side, helping her to her feet, rubbing her back reassuringly and murmuring, "It's okay," before saying to his mother in a louder voice, "So, Mom...what kind of mess did they serve up in the dining room today?"

Sybil waved at them as they passed the nurse's station on the way out of Unit 3 some thirty minutes later, then separated herself from the five or six coworkers assembled there with her and came toward them. Stone slowed so she could catch up with them. She was the only one of them who ever bothered to give him the time of day.

Her big eyes were openly curious as they flicked over Abigail, and Stone decided to indulge her. "This is Abigail Carmichael...a very good friend of mine. Abigail, Sybil Rhone. She's the CNA who takes such good care of my mom."

"Nice to meet you, ma'am."

Abigail murmured a response, sounding a little off kilter. Surely she wasn't thrown by his introduction. He'd made it as warm as he could without presuming. So then, what would she make of what he was going to say next?

"I've been meaning to add her to the visitor list, just didn't get round to it." Hadn't planned on it up till forty minutes ago. But five minutes of watching Abigail and his mother together, even before he realized they knew each other, and he was wondering what he'd been making all the fuss about.

"No problem," Sybil assured him easily. "I take care of it for you. Mr. Patrick, I been meaning to ask you...Who is Mama Kay?"

Stone smiled. "My grandmother, her mother-in-law."

"*Grandmother.*" Sybil looked outraged. "I remind her of your grandmother?"

Stone grinned. "It's a compliment, Sybil, trust me. She was beautiful inside and out, right up till the day she died. Not your average mother-in-law, either."

Sybil's grunt was skeptical, but she seemed somewhat mollified.

It was pure mischief that made Stone add, "Come to think of it, she was about your height and complexion too," and watched Sybil's big eyes grow bigger.

"So how did you find the place?" Stone asked as they made their way outside.

Abigail hesitated. The question seemed harmless enough, almost conversational, no hidden tension. She'd been bracing for this moment from before she walked into the building, their first moment alone, when he would drop the pretense of civility and demand to know where she got off, barging in unannounced and uninvited into his and his mother's private moment.

She could scarcely digest that it apparently was not going

to happen. There wasn't a whole lot to be gleaned from his stoic expression, but that much she could.

"I asked Daddy." Well, she had.

"Thank you." *And for coming anyway, in spite of everything.* Relief, gratitude and all that he didn't say with words were there now in his eyes. He knew that her father had given away a lot more than his mother's address. And he was okay with it. His next words seemed to confirm as much.

"I want you to know I meant it about the visitor's list. You're welcome to see her anytime you want, and I intend to let the staff know that."

"Thank you. I'd really like that." Wow, finally...Shan privileges. She hitched her handbag strap higher on her shoulder as they reached the parking lot. "Anyways, I better—"

"Abby."

Her breath caught at the sound of the pet name he'd given her on his tongue. "Yes?"

"Thanks for being there for her when you were. She never had any friends for as long as I can remember, and having to deal with my hostility on top of the loneliness and everything else couldn't have been any picnic."

"She was there for me too when I...when I needed a friend. I only wish I'd got to know her even half as well as you do."

"I don't really know her, Abby. I never did. You probably could tell me a thing or two. I didn't take the time to, back when I...when she..." He drew a steadying breath and started over. "She's a puzzle we each hold unique pieces to, I guess. Maybe one day we could...put our pieces together, see what kind of picture we come up with."

There was a question in his voice, in his eyes as they quietly held hers.

She looked away before she could trip and fall into them.

"You busy?" he asked softly.

Her heart tripped. "Now, you mean?"

"I guess. I'd say let's go somewhere later, but there's

somewhere I have to be at six."

So I heard.

"Meantime, I've got some pressing chores that refuse to be put off any longer."

Chores? Or houseguests?

He eyed her cautiously and offered quietly, "I sold the house."

"You did?" she asked, with just the right lilt of surprise in her voice.

He nodded and seemed to be waiting, as if for her to comment or ask him why. As if he actually expected her to rejoice with him or something. When she didn't, he finished, "I'm closing later this evening."

"Oh. Good for you." She adjusted her handbag strap on her shoulder. She supposed this was where she asked him where he was going and why. If she enjoyed having her insides wrung.

"I could use some help packing."

Oh no, you couldn't.

"If you have the nerve."

I really don't.

He gave her a smile that was at once wry and appealing. "You know me. I'm likely to have the socks packed in with the spoons. Would be nice to be able to put my hand on stuff once I get where I'm going."

I'm sure Shan will be only too happy to help you figure it out.

His voice became coaxing. "Take you for ice-cream when we're done. Or dinner, if you can stick around till after the closing."

And do what—help him and Shan celebrate? What did he think she was—some kind of masochist? She finally found her voice and along with it her backbone. She shook her head emphatically. "Sorry, I...I really can't." She groped around for an explanation with which to soften the refusal and couldn't find one.

While she floundered, something stole over his face that wiped the teasing half-smile from his mouth and caused the gentle, coaxing warmth in his eyes to harden into something arctic.

He was angry. And something else she couldn't quite identify, except that suddenly he was not the friend she'd come to know since nursing him through a migraine attack. He was more like the mistrustful antagonist she'd butted heads with before that. And when he said what he did next, he was suddenly, frighteningly, like someone else she had spent the last twelve months trying to forget.

44

So then, what exactly is it that blew you my way after all this time...*Abigail Sarah Lester?*" The instant Stone said it he realized what he'd done, even before he saw her recoil as if she'd been slapped, or registered the bewilderment in the gaze she turned on him. He stared back, feeling every bit the brute he'd always known he was and temporarily paralyzed by guilt, horror and frustration.

He unfroze when she started backing away with jerky movements, made a grab for her and missed as she stumbled toward her car, catching up with her only at her car door. And then stood helplessly behind her while she unlocked the door and, instead of opening it, just stood with her forehead pressed up against it, shoulders heaving as if she were struggling to catch her breath.

What did he do? Apologize? For calling her by her name? *Lord, I'm sorry I gave in to my anger. Help me fix this, and I'll let you take charge of the rest of this conversation. The rest of our lives, if it ever comes to that.*

"Abby?" She was too quiet, way too quiet.

She inhaled deeply and straightened, and he braced for something withering. Instead, she wrapped her arms round herself and began to cry.

"No, baby...no...I wasn't...come here..." He reached for her, tried to pull her into his arms, wanting to do what he'd been aching to do since hearing from Colin about Sarah— just hold her.

She wrung herself free of his hold, wrenching open her door as far as it would go with him in the way and squeezing inside. The door shut before he could stop it, and the lock clicked.

He slapped the window. "Abby, wait! Don't...don't drive when you're this upset. At least—"

The engine fired, and he barely had enough time to clear his feet out of harm's way before she shot out of the parking spot and disappeared down the lane. This time he didn't go after her. The sight of him in her rearview mirror trailing her the whole way home would likely impair her driving more than her crying would. And anyway, Someone well capable of protecting her life along with her feelings was already with her, making sure she made it home okay.

He had no idea how long he sat in the parking lot, bowed over the steering wheel, praying, agonizing over what exactly had gone wrong in between the time when they'd stood together in his mother's room with such an incredible bond between them and the moment when she bluntly rejected his overtures of reconciliation without even an attempt at an explanation.

All he knew was that in a heartbeat she'd gone from soul mate to stranger, with no thought but getting away from him. Just like that. No other explanation. And then walked away and left him sick to his stomach with hurt and disappointment.

Close on the heels of his gut-wrenching disillusionment had followed anger, quick and hot. He didn't quite understand it, except that he could feel it gushing up from somewhere deep inside, about where he'd kept the traumatized boy inside himself safely hidden away. He'd felt betrayed, exposed, raw, frustrated. But most of all he'd been desperate, to get her attention, to arrest her with the knowledge that he knew now about her pain and understood.

He'd always made a point of keeping the details of his family history from those who weren't familiar with them, because he didn't want their sympathy or their judgments and because it was none of their business anyway. With Abigail, he'd kept them hidden because, of all the people he knew, her rejection would hurt him the most.

Yet she had pushed and prodded and wept her way into the center of his mess, regardless. Because she cared, or so he'd figured as he watched her hug and cry and laugh with his mother and saw traces of the hope and healing that was blossoming within him reflected in his mother's suddenly not-so-confused eyes. Had to be she cared.

There was so much that he'd wanted to say as he watched them together. So much she seemed to want to say even as he ushered her out as soon as he decently could. But once they'd gained the relative seclusion of the court-yard, she'd gone all tense and started pulling back, her face tight as she determinedly scanned the parking lot ahead of them for her car.

He'd thought maybe she was unsure of him and had tried to meet her halfway. He hadn't intended to push. He'd told her dad he wouldn't, and he'd meant it. More important, he'd meant it when he promised God he wouldn't. But she was the one who'd sought him out, for heaven's sake. Or was it not him she'd come after, but the long lost Kay?

Had she had an inkling about Kay and come there on a fact finding mission that had nothing to do with him? Come to think of it, she hadn't acted all that terribly warm towards him, empathy aside. She'd stayed rigidly in her own space, kept her expression guarded and hadn't looked at him half as often as she had his mother. Had he assumed too much? Apparently he had. And he'd be lucky if he ever got a chance to set the record straight.

He didn't immediately realize when he turned into his driveway that neither Fern's nor Shan's car was there, but he instantly noticed the canary yellow Beetle perched on the swale.

Fern and Shan must have run out of time, for he doubted they could have finished already everything that was still in there to be done. Waiting for him in their place was Abigail.

She was on his front porch like she had been that other time they'd first called a truce. This time she hadn't bothered to let the dog out, a sure sign she did not intend to be there long. More than likely she was forcing herself by sheer strength of will to finish whatever it was she'd set out to do when she sought him out at Dade Central. She would.

Strength and honor are her clothing.

As to what exactly her purpose had been in seeking him out, he'd be better off not even trying to guess.

Lord, I give up, honest I do. I don't understand her, and I probably never will. But You do, Lord. And you understand me. Build a bridge as only You can.

Obedient to the quiet, insistent prompting that had steered her to Palm Terrace instead of home, Abigail made herself rise from the front steps as Stone approached and pass through the door he held open wordlessly for her.

He didn't once look at her, busying himself with the keys, with opening the door and holding it for her, bending to retrieve his newspaper from where it had been tossed and following her inside.

From a position near the half-open door, she watched him nudge an oversized empty carton closer to the wall unit with his foot and start filling it with the contents of the various shelves, still without a word to her.

And then she made herself respond to the news of the sale of the house the way she would have under normal circumstances, the way he'd probably *needed* for her to respond when he so tentatively broached the subject outside his mother's place.

"Why did you sell?"

He answered as smoothly as if their conversation had never been interrupted. "It's my parents' house. I moved back in after my dad died to prevent it going into foreclosure."

She absorbed the shock of that in silence while he went on.

"I couldn't afford back then to make the payments on this and pay rent elsewhere at the same time. Why didn't I sell it before this? I'd planned to, at first. Court had given me power of attorney and all that, but...I don't know. I must have been holding out some hope that one day my mom would be home and I'd get to do it right, I suppose."

"So now you've given up?"

"Not given up, no. Just decided to move on." He contemplated the ceramic angel he'd taken off the shelf—his mother's, no doubt—and looked round for the rolled up newspaper he'd tossed on the couch. She reached it first and handed it to him.

He wrapped the angel carefully and wedged it securely among the other items in the box. "Lord showed me I don't need to wallow in the ashes of the past to do right by her. I can do that right now, right where she is. If by some miracle she ever makes it out of there, I can think of any number of places she'd rather live out her days than the house where she went through such hell." A wry smile tugged at his mouth. "Lots of places my wife would rather spend the first years of her married life, more important...if she ever agrees to have me."

She endured the stab of pain that that caused her and reminded herself she deserved it. There was a time when it was her that he'd had his sights on, however briefly. Till she'd turned her back on him at a time when he'd needed comfort as much as she did. And he'd transferred his affections to someone who'd no doubt been only too willing to provide that comfort.

"In any case," he finished, "I'm ready for a change."

"Good for you." This time she really meant it. He must have heard it in her voice too, for he looked away from the

Bible reference collection he'd turned his attention to and held her eyes briefly, the expression in his unreadable.

Just as quickly, he turned back to the shelf, pulling large volumes two by two from it and stacking them in the box. "So why did you really come? Because you heard about my sorry family and felt sorry for me?"

"Because I wanted to tell you that if you ever use my name to curse me or put me down again—"

He turned. "Abby, I *wasn't*—"

"—or with anything but the utmost respect for who I am, I'll cut you out of my life so fast you'll wonder if you ever knew a girl named Abigail Sarah Lester."

He abandoned his attempts at a protest then and smiled, a slow smile of approval. "Atta girl."

She fought to steady her breathing that his sudden warmth had roughened and went on in calmer tones, "And I came because I care, and I was wrong to take my pain out on you, when you had to have your own share dealing with."

And because I'm desperate enough to hope even now that it might not be too late to undo the damage my selfishness did to us.

"No sweat. I was worried about you, is all. She was more your friend than mine, and I knew you had to be hurting. After a while, I figured you'd do all right without me."

All right, yes. No more, no less. "Thanks for caring. Not just about me, but Beth too. And all the others. I never meant...I hope I didn't leave you with the impression I think you don't care about the people you help, cause I know you do. More than I once realized."

He shrugged one shoulder but said nothing.

She watched him add his photo collection to the box, one frame at a time. She shook her head. "That's why I can't believe you'd really do this."

"Do what?"

"Quit."

His eyes flickered and shifted from hers, but he said nothing.

"What about Oasis?" she pressed, unable to leave it

alone, despite her promise to herself on the drive over that she'd set him straight about misusing her name, offer her congratulations on the sale of his house and get out of there without getting any further into his business. "Did you stop caring for them all of a sudden...all those guys who look to you for guidance?"

"Your father told you I was quitting Oasis?" He shot her a guarded look.

"He assumed you would, if you're transferring your fellowship elsewhere."

"I...see." His eyes fell from hers. "Well, I do care about them. Their wives too. Good enough reason right there for me to be going, don't you think?" His lips twisted. *"These people need real answers, Abigail,"* he said, mocking himself. "And guess what? I'm not it."

The brokenness in the words, in his voice, all but broke her too. He was not the rock that she'd repeatedly tripped over and bruised herself against up till weeks ago. Something hard inside him had crumbled into something that was as smooth and fluid as sand.

Her first woman's instinct was to reach out and enfold that naked vulnerability in tender reassurances. But even as words gushed up from her heart, something, *Someone,* touched her, and they died in her throat. And as that Someone's touch bolstered her heart, she found herself admitting the naked truth to him.

"You know, you're right. And I'm glad you finally realize it."

45

Abigail's quiet, matter-of-fact agreement got Stone's attention more effectively than any protest could have.

She held his gaze steadily as it sought hers, and she continued with all the confidence of her convictions. "You're not offering them yourself or your so-called sorry life, Stone. You're offering them Jesus and the hope He's given us all, *in spite of* all our sorry lives."

He inclined his head gravely as if to say, "True," that trace of self-mockery still in his face, but she knew he was listening.

"A-and if you think you've got some kind of monopoly on family dysfunction or that it makes you any less qualified to minister God's healing to those in need of it, then you've missed the whole point of the gospel. And if you think the ministry is some place for you to find absolution for some misplaced guilt you're harboring, then you really have no business trying to minister to anybody, not even yourself."

He cocked an eyebrow at her. "You know any ministers interested in taking on the job of ministering to me?"

Her breath caught, and she reminded herself in time not to get too crazy over the glint of warmth she thought she saw in his eyes.

"I'm sure you've already got more applicants than you can handle." She was horrified to hear the raw, bitter jealousy leak out into her voice.

She saw something like puzzlement enter his eyes. "Excuse me?"

She shook her head. "Sorry, I didn't mean to get into your business. I really didn't." She sounded pitiful to her own ears.

"Into *what* business?"

And now she couldn't help the color she could feel flooding her face, especially when she saw comprehension dawn slowly on his face.

"You stopped here first, huh?"

"I wasn't trying to gate crash or anything. I just...I was trying to find out where you...where your mother was, and..."

"I like it better the way you put it the first time. 'Bout wanting to find out where I was." He turned slowly, his gaze pinning hers.

She swallowed.

He folded his arms, head tilted to one side. "So you object to a couple of my sisters coming by to help sort out my domestic chaos, huh? Well, I'm sorry, but I had no choice. My favorite helper bailed out on me, deserted me for weeks on end. I had to settle for second and third best."

Shan, second or third best. Sister. Her heart quickened, her eyes searching his. They were warm again and full of some kind of promise.

"So. To repeat my earlier question...you know of any ministers willing to take me on as a...um...outreach project?"

She fought to control her breathing, her voice trapped in her throat. He moved as if to close the gap between them but jerked to a halt as if by an invisible leash. He seemed to swallow the impulse, his face expressionless except for a betraying tic in his cheek. And then he was turning awkwardly back to the wall unit and refocusing, with obvious difficulty, on the half emptied shelves in front of him.

One look at that rigid half-turned back and taut profile was all it took for Abigail to find her voice. Clearing her throat, she said softly, "Just one. With conditions."

"Oh?" He paused with a volume of Matthew Henry commentary in his hand, turning slightly. "And what might those be?"

"A little confidence in her ability to withstand testing, for starters. As in deal with the bullying of hot-tempered parishioners. She's developed a bit of a temper herself. It's mental and emotional cruelty that she's most wary of."

"Her, huh?" His eyes held hers.

She met his gaze squarely as she personalized the analogy. "That part of her résumé if nothing else is very impressive."

He nodded gravely. "Would you tell her for me that this particular parishioner is not wired that way? He'd sooner blow a fuse and cause a temporary blackout than burn a house down with his flickering and gashing."

She nodded, as grave as he was. "I'm sure she can handle that."

There was a moment's silence. "What other conditions would I be looking at?"

"A manse of some sort, I guess...doesn't have to be big or spotless, but there must be love, lots of it." Her voice quickly disintegrated as he abruptly abandoned all pretense of unpacking the shelf and faced her fully. "A-and k-kids."

He tossed Matthew Henry to the couch and advanced slowly once more towards her. "You plan on getting them by some means other than the usual one? Cause I haven't heard mention of a husband anywhere in there."

She held his eyes and tried to remain composed despite the rising heat in her face. Despite the hands that reached for her and closed gently on her upper arms. "I'm not in the habit of proposing to men. Especially grumpy, bull-headed ones."

He pulled her close. "Well then, let me see what I can do." He kissed her, softly, almost reverently. Then he rested his forehead on hers while he steadied his ragged breathing and whispered huskily, "Marry me, baby. Have my kids and help me keep my cushions straight. And I promise to love and cherish you like Jesus does His church. I already know I wouldn't think twice about dying for you if it came to that."

She drew a steadying breath, fighting tears. "Thanks, but I like you better alive."

"Good," he said on a soft *whoosh* of relief. "Cause I'm thinking I'd really miss carrying out all the...um...temple ministrations that go along with a live priesthood."

She lost the struggle then, casting poise to the wind and burying her hot face in his chest.

Instantly he lowered his head till she felt his lips and nose grazing the side of her throat, right where that wayward pulse had started an erratic dance, and she heard him inhaling her scent.

"Honeysuckle Breeze," he said slowly, while she struggled to keep her breathing even.

She stilled. "That's the name of my perfume. How'd you...Oh, *Kay.*"

"Guess whose blend it is."

She shook her head. "The bottle doesn't say. Doesn't even say where it was made or by whom."

He smiled, and it was a rather sad smile. "There's this field trip I went on in high school. To this organic perfumery. They make mostly spa products and a few perfumes. We all got to create a blend, name it and take a sample home." He chuckled. "It was an education. We came away with a better appreciation for why an ounce of something sweet can cost so much. Some of us came up with some pretty abominable potions. Mine was honeysuckle with just a hint of ginger, and it was a winner.

"When I gave it to my mom, she smiled and told me it was her favorite scent in all the world. I thought she was giving me a mommy line. Till I saw the tears in her eyes."

He paused, and Abigail felt around for something suitable to say. She felt awful knowing what her wearing her favorite scent must have done to him. She couldn't think of a thing to say. And how could she interrupt him anyway now that he was finally sharing a part of himself he never had before?

He went on, his eyes staring out over the top of her head to the street and back into the past. "She never did tell me why it was so special to her, but she wore it that same day, and we had one of the few mother-son moments I can recall us ever having. We sat out on the porch. She read the Bible to me and I actually listened. She read from Proverbs 31, and she admonished me as earnestly as if I was a grown man contemplating marriage. Like she knew she wasn't going to be around when that time came. It's the memory of her that I cling to the most. God knows I don't have many good ones."

"Oh, Stone, I'm sorry. I never would have taken it if I'd..."

He stopped her with a shake of his head. "I'm glad she thought of you. Otherwise it would have gone out in the trash."

Her breath caught. "What happened?"

"My father." There was no bitterness in his voice this time when he referred to his father, only sadness. "Came home in one of his ornery moods and didn't like the sight of the boy he'd named Stone cozying up around the Bible. He also decided he hated the perfume. Told her to get rid of it or he'd dump it. She must have hidden it all those years." He looked at her. "Till you came along...round about when?"

"Not long after I got married."

"I'm glad you're the one who got it, although you've been driving me crazy with it for five straight months."

"No wonder you couldn't stand me."

"Uh-uh, the opposite. Could have done a commercial for any perfumer who cared to market it, trust me."

"Maybe you could. Market it, I mean. I've gotten a lot of compliments for it. And a lot of *yeah-right* looks from women who refuse to believe it can't be bought anywhere."

"Nope. If I do anything, it will be to patent the formula and rename it. *Essence of Abigail,*" he murmured, testing the name. "I might do it yet."

There was no response she could come up with for that, except to hug him tighter and revel in the warm, musky scent that was uniquely his.

He eased back and looked down at her. "How'd you get it to last this long?"

"Eric was allergic to perfume. I just started wearing it."

"I'm glad. Not that Eric was allergic to perfume, but that—"

"I know," she whispered when he stalled uncertainly. "I'm glad it can be our special thing too."

"I have to warn you, though, that with you in the equation, Bible-story time with Mommy is the last thing on my mind."

His eyes roamed lazily over her as far as the base of her throat and then seemed to force themselves back up to her eyes. "Your...chemistry has a devastating effect on my equilibrium."

"Oh?" She nuzzled into his shoulder to hide the blush she was fighting. "You had a funny way of showing it."

"I was fighting it like crazy. But I was doomed from the get go, cause God Himself was conspiring against me. He was using a scent He created to bring Proverbs 31 back to me and show me what a treasure you are. Awesome, eh?"

She'd never been called a treasure before.

She'd been silent for so long, Stone felt a stirring of unease, and wondered how many uncharted territories there were yet to be explored on the way to loving Abigail.

Lord, tell me what to say, what to do.

Silence.

"Abby?"

Nothing. Just the bite of her nails as her fingers curled into fists. And then the dampness seeping into his shirt.

And him helpless to do anything but continue to hold her and feel inadequate..

It wasn't long before he realized it wasn't Abigail who clung to him in those moments. It was Sarah holding on to him with Sarah hurt and Sarah desperation, choking back Sarah sobs and wetting his chest through the thin cotton of his shirt with Sarah tears.

"I didn't know, baby," he groaned into her hair after what felt like an eternity of fighting back his own tears. "I didn't know." It occurred to him he wasn't being terribly coherent, but somehow he didn't think it mattered.

She seemed to understand. She whispered back, "Me neither." Then, "Did Daddy tell you? About Eric?"

"We...kind of helped each other figure things out, in between playing God in the greenhouse. With some help from an old friend of mine who is dying to be introduced to you."

He withheld the rest about Colin for now, not wanting to overwhelm her. But he just had to add, "Your father, by the way, is a very mischievous man. I never had any plans to leave either Grace or South Florida. But we'll have to see with him. He's probably just sick of hearing me drone on about you in the greenhouse." He felt her tense in surprise and confessed wryly, "Don't freak out, but I've been obsessing over you for quite some time now."

He felt a whisper of a laugh against his skin and knew she didn't object at all.

For endless moments while they continued to hold each other, those were all the words that passed between them...even after he'd nudged the front door fully open with his foot, steered them over to the couch and sank down with her into it, still with his arms wrapped around her. No other words seemed necessary for the moment, so keen was the sense of connectedness between them.

Still, he knew there would come a time for words, if the connectedness were to grow into the kind of bond that would withstand the tests that were surely ahead. After a while, he drew a deep breath and pulled back. Tried to. She wouldn't let go of him. He chuckled softly and continued to hold her.

After several more unsuccessful attempts to put her away, he offered a compromise. "If I promise not to let you go, can we talk?"

"Hmm, I like the sound of that."

"You're going to have to talk to me, precious. I know there's more I haven't heard, and I'm scared to death of making mistakes and messing up any more than I—"

His voice cracked, and he started over. "When I found out about...Sarah, I hadn't a clue how I was going to help you, or if I could. All I know is I just wanted to be with you, to be there for you, and it hurt me that I was the last person you wanted to see. I didn't have the right then to insist, but once we belong to each other I'm not going to be that easy to put off. You can't keep shutting people who love you out of your life when you hurt, love. I won't let you. I'm not Fern or Crystal. I won't stand by helpless and watch you hurting and not be able to...to..."

He drew a shuddering breath. "Or we can just call you Jane for the time being, hmm? That's okay with me too. If that's what you want."

She let go a watery chuckle against the side of his neck. A few seconds later, she whispered, "I like my name. Names. I think."

The uncertainty in her voice just about broke his heart. His arms tightened around her. "They're beautiful names, Abby, and they suit you. For all the right reasons. Is that so hard to believe?"

"Not when it's coming from you," she whispered, and his heart surged.

Thank you, God. He had to have gotten a few things right, after all. He hugged her tight. Something small and hard and sharp bit into his chest. He drew back and reached down between them. Fingered her Tweety pendant. "That Tweety is some character, huh?"

"He's a survivor," she whispered. "You have to give him that."

"Oh yes. Outwits, outruns, outmaneuvers his tormentor every time. And speaking of survivors, he'd make a great mascot for the Survivors program. Especially if there was a Tweety expert and fellow survivor around somewhere who would consider being hired to come by once every eight weeks and give a Tweety pep talk, maybe give out Tweety stickers or something."

He felt as much as heard her breath catch and went on less tentatively, "The organizers don't do God, but they wouldn't have a problem with Tweety. The ladies could learn a lot from him. I certainly did."

She looked at him through tear-spiked lashes. "You did?"

"Hmm. He's protected by the goodwill of his creator and the adoring fan club who'd scream bloody murder if Sylvester ever once got the better of him. I figure if Tweety's fan club can rely on his creator to keep his episodes on track, then I can trust mine to do the same for me. I don't fear Patrick Kay's ghost anymore, Abby, cause I know who my real Father is."

"Oh," she said softly, her gaze still glued to his.

He kissed her nose. "Know what else I like about Tweety?"

"What?"

"He never stops being his sweet, adorable self, no matter what. Never allows his tormentor to make him into something he's not. I love that about you too, Abby."

She gulped. "*Me*? But—"

"Oh, I know you've become a lot more...*spunky* than most folks were accustomed to. But I happen to know the real Abigail like few of them do. I know she's as soft and sweet and caring as she's spunky. And she's still in there, cause I've run into her time and again myself. She can go from a shriek to a whisper in a heartbeat, out of sympathy for the same bully who'd been hassling her just moments before his migraine struck. From a hooky-playing, phone-dodging mall rat to a gorgeous companion and helper that makes a man want to crow and strut like a teenager. And the God-love that shines through her soothes something inside this savage breast like no music has ever been able to."

She was crying again, but he sensed they were tears of release rather than pain. He wiped gently at them with the hem of his shirt and then enfolded her in a tender embrace, his voice as soothing as he knew how to make it as he began, "You see, Abby, it took you five long years to get to this point, and it's been a long, bumpy ride back to who you are..."

Some time later, Stone felt Abigail release a soft, shuddering breath against his shoulder before she murmured ruefully, "I'm okay with me now, Stone, but I can't help wishing sometimes I'd been more of a Spunky back then. *She* was never in any doubt about who she was, and it was probably why she ended up choosing better than any one of us did."

"Hmm. It's that spunk I think that first grabbed Mark's attention too."

She wriggled suddenly inside the arms she'd refused to leave up till then and tried to wrest herself free of him. "And not just Mark's, either!" There was a spark in her eyes that warned him they had entered dangerous turf.

It took him a few seconds to make the adjustment and a few more to dig up the right answer that wouldn't land him any deeper in hot water.

"Ouch!" he protested as her elbow jabbed his rib cage.

"You liked her!" she accused. *"Like.* You'd probably be going with her yourself if Mark hadn't beat you to it—go on and deny it."

"Going with who—Spunky?"

"Fern. As if you haven't already figured it out."

"Oh, Fern." It was a possibility. He liked Fern a lot as a sister, but he could have made the stretch to something deeper without too much difficulty if he'd had his ducks in a row when he met her, and if the timing had been right, and if...but what was the use of having his lung punctured over a mere possibility...and not that much of a possibility either, now that he'd met the love of his life?

She jerked out of his arms, replacing them with her own, and stared balefully at him. "I'll never forgive you for liking her better than me—"

"I *didn't*—"

"Or-or calling me wishy-washy—"

"She *was* wishy-washy."

"...or...or...I *what*? Oh yeah? Well—"

"Not you, her! Sarah!" And now he'd managed to confuse himself.

And offend her. She was grimly reaching for the handbag she'd dropped on the couch.

"Oh, for—*come* back here!" He hauled her back into his arms.

She let him, but he could feel her bristling in his arms. "My name *is* Sarah, and if you've got a problem with that—"

"Oh, but I do. Big problem. And one of these days I'm-a sit you down and have a serious talk with you about what it means. Set you straight on a few things."

She sniffed and eyed him suspiciously. "Like what?"

"Like, say, the fact that she was an absolute babe. Just like you." His eyes caressed her, and from the look in hers, she was having absolutely no difficulty believing him.

She melted a little more into his embrace, and he continued, "Poor old Abe, he didn't think he could compete, hatching all kinds of schemes to fend off the guys who'd be beating down his door wanting to take her from him. And in case you're getting any ideas...there'll be no gallivanting in other guys' palaces for you."

He kissed her. "No waiting any ridiculous amount of time to give me kids either. How many you want, anyway?" he murmured, eyeing her mouth as if it were kisses and not babies he was asking about.

She seemed barely able to find breath enough to whisper, "Three or four?"

He nodded. "Three or four is good. And don't bother bringing any half-brained surrogate mom ideas to me either. Not interested. We have 'em together or we adopt. Surrogate deal probably wouldn't work from the get go either. Not Abraham style, anyway." He winked. "For very practical reasons."

He savored her blush as his adoring gaze described the most obvious reason to her. "And as for the calling me Lord part..." He felt her tense slightly and tightened his arms around her. "As long as you don't ever stop looking at me the way you are now, I'll allow *honey* or *pooky* or whatever little nonsense rolls off your tongue. They're all perfectly biblical."

He eased back, the better to look into her face, eyebrows arched in challenge. "No arguments? Cause I've got chapter and verse for you, girl."

"Uh-uh, none. Just remind me to tell Dad not to let you anywhere near our Sunday School."

Epilogue

By this My Father is glorified, that you bear much fruit;
so you will be my disciples.

—JOHN 15:8

SaraGail: Hi guys. Sorry I took so long getting back to you, but things have been crazy of late, what with trying to arrange a long distance fitting for Corey, and Stone starting to get jealous of his own wedding and all. Kay's lawyer says he might be able to get her a pass to attend. She's already been cleared by the psychiatrist. Her case has been scheduled for review.

Duchess: so what really happened? was she faking it all along?

SaraGail: Not really. The psychiatrist himself doesn't quite understand it. Of course, you'll never get them to admit she was overmedicated. The way he explained it is something about her surprise encounter with me flicked the same switch that had been flicked off the day she went berserk in the sanctuary.

Spunky: i say its just pure God

Duchess: those hearing aids probably don't hurt either. since she got them I haven't heard her picking and choosing what to respond to in a conversation anymore

SaraGail: True, but whatever they want to attribute it to, she's well on the road to recovery. What's more, they're now willing to concede she's always been more "there" than anybody had realized. All those adventures of hers in their computer room weren't so insane after all. Speaking of which—I need you to dig up all the old emails you can find. The lawyer says they'll form the core of the new evidence on which he'll base his appeal. He's going to do what that court-appointed slacker should have done in the first place—present all the evidence he has that shows how she'd been systematically and relentlessly driven to the edge. He thinks there's a fifty-fifty shot they'll change the original verdict from "guilty but insane" to "not guilty by reason of temporary insanity." After that, it's just up to the psychiatrist, and we already know which way he's leaning.

Kay: And if not, I'm okay with that too. The Lord can use me just as well in here as away from here.

Spunky: kay, that really you?

Kay: You bet. All of me. Friend of mine that I recently led to Christ arranged something for me.

Duchess: you go girl

Spunky: got you some friends in high places huh?

Kay: Besides God? Not really. Just among the nursing staff. You see, there's this really nice girl named Sybil...

Dear Reader,

Thanks for stopping by the *Far Corner*. I hope that Abigail's story will turn your thoughts toward the Abigail in your life. There's likely at least one in every fellowship, school, neighborhood, or whichever corner of God's greenhouse you are currently growing in. And in case you're wondering which of Abigail's friends you are, you can find out with the *Abigail's Friends* quiz at kvcase.com.

If it so happens you're the Abigail in your particular universe, I'm so glad you're here. I pray that Abigail's story will leave you with an unshakeable certainty that you are loved, more than likely by family and friends who might be having a hard time letting you know it, and, better yet, by an awesome, loving God by whom you've been "fearfully and wonderfully made" and who loves you "with an everlasting love," bumps, bruises, scars and all. May that knowledge encourage you as you venture out of the far corner. May your blooms be sweet and their fragrance be diffused far beyond that messy potting bench where your healing began.

In His love,
KC

ABOUT THE AUTHOR

The last of eleven children born to immigrants, K.V. Case began writing as a child for her siblings' entertainment, in a household where imagination ruled and television was a last resort.

After a valiant attempt to pursue a "normal" profession, she finally succumbed to her life's calling, earning her Professional-Writing B.A degree with honors in New York. Later, she freelanced in South Florida as a writer and editor...and anything else that left her enough room to pursue her passion for writing.

Her encounter with her own share of personal challenges and decade-long struggle with writer's block has given her unique insight into the hidden wounds that can cripple as effectively as the kind that bruises and scars. She hopes that *The Far Corner of the Greenhouse* will be a pathway for readers to escape to their own secret place in God's garden and find assurance that the One who knows them best does indeed love them most.

K.V. Case now lives in rural South Carolina, where she is homeschooling her three children, listening to the trees laugh and working on her upcoming series.

Readers can connect with her at www.kvcase.com.

Made in the USA
San Bernardino, CA
15 December 2013